PSYCHE
AND
EROS

a novel

LUNA McNAMARA

WILLIAM MORROW
An Imprint of HarperCollins*Publishers*

PSYCHE AND EROS. Copyright © 2023 by Luna Mc-Namara. All rights reserved. Printed in the United States of America. No part of this book may be used or reproduced in any manner whatsoever without written permission except in the case of brief quotations embodied in critical articles and reviews. For information, address HarperCollins Publishers, 195 Broadway, New York, NY 10007.

HarperCollins books may be purchased for educational, business, or sales promotional use. For information, please email the Special Markets Department at SPsales@harpercollins.com.

A hardcover edition of this book was published in 2023 by William Morrow, an imprint of HarperCollins Publishers.

FIRST WILLIAM MORROW PAPERBACK
EDITION PUBLISHED 2024.

Leaf art courtesy of Shutterstock / NastyaTsy

Library of Congress Cataloging-in-Publication Data has been applied for.

ISBN 978-0-06-329508-7

24 25 26 27 28 LBC 5 4 3 2 1

makes or gaps she fills in, place her tale within the wider context of women's lives and place in society during the Trojan War. . . . An effective, heartfelt novelization of a famous Greek myth."

—*Kirkus*

"A captivating, feminist retelling of the classical Greek myth. . . . McNamara's prose transports you to another time and place, perfectly capturing the magic and mystery of ancient mythology. A beautifully crafted novel that will enchant fans of Greek mythology and romance alike."

—*Glamour*

"Perfect for fans of Greek mythology authors Madeline Miller and Jennifer Saint, *Psyche and Eros* retells a great ancient Greek love story."

—*Cosmopolitan*

For my father and mother

PROLOGUE

EROS

The Greeks have three words for love. The first is *philia*, the kind of love that involves liking and grows up between two people who enjoy each other's company very much. The second is *agape*, the selfless love of parents for children or between those who are like family to one another. The third is *eros*, which explains itself—connection, spark, the desire of the body to seek fulfillment in another.

Most people experience at least one of these loves in a lifetime. But it is rare to have all three at once, intertwined like a golden braid. This was what the playwright Aristophanes spoke of when he wove his tale many years after the events of this one, seeking to illuminate the origin of love in its trifold complexity. He claimed that the first human beings were born back-to-back, with two faces and four hands and four legs, each mouth chattering incessantly to its companion as they rolled like wheels over the earth. Zeus grew wary of the power of these people and split them apart with his thunderbolts. They turned into humans as we know them today, who walk around on two legs and speak with only one mouth. And so it is that love came to exist, the playwright claimed, each of us seeking our other half.

I laughed when I heard this. I had been present at the

beginning of the world, and it wasn't anything like that. It is a pretty story, though nothing could be further from the truth for Psyche and I. There is no pretending that we were two parts of some cosmic whole—she was a mortal woman and I a god when we first met, each fierce in our independence. We were not severed halves; we were complete unto ourselves. It is possible that our paths would never have crossed at all had it not been for a chance mistake.

There is something powerful in this, I think. We were not in thrall to destiny or fate, but merely the weight of our own choices. When we turned toward each other like flowers facing the sun, we were not fulfilling some prophecy or old story. We were writing our own.

PSYCHE

Despite my unusual destiny, I began life as an ordinary infant, born like any other to a rush of blood and cries of joy. Though in my case, these were followed by more than a bit of confusion.

My mother and father were the king and queen of a kingdom in rocky Greece called Mycenae. When my mother, Astydamia, learned that she was with child, my father, Alkaios, left the Mycenaean capital of Tiryns and set off across the mountains. He passed through desolate valleys and rode beneath craggy cliffsides populated by nesting griffins, until at last he came to gates that bore the words KNOW THYSELF. It wasn't his own fate he sought to learn at the Oracle of Delphi, but his unborn child's. Mine. Would I be born healthy and strong? What would I grow up to become?

When my father entered the Oracle's shadowy earthen chamber, two things struck him. The first was the smell of the place, redolent of sulfur and other scents less recognizable. The second was the sight of the woman who sat on a bronze tripod suspended over an abyss. She wore a peplos robe that swathed her body in folds of yellow fabric, and her hair was bound up in a neat braid around her head. This was the Oracle, and she stared at Alkaios with eyes out of time.

My father shivered. He was a king and used to people

trying to wheedle favors from him, but this woman wanted nothing from anyone.

A priest from the order that had sprung up around the Oracle whispered the king's question in her ear. She sat back and drank in the vapors rising up from the cracks in the earth; these were said to be sent from Apollo himself, god of prophecy, and brought true visions of the future.

A tremor ran through the Oracle. She began to speak in an unearthly voice, one that did not belong to the body of such a delicate woman. My father could not recognize the language she spoke, but the priests were already scribbling on their clay tablets, performing the complex calculations needed to interpret the messages of the Oracle. Gods do not always speak in ways that are easy for mortals to understand, but fortunately the white-bearded priests knew how to translate.

At last, they bestowed the Oracle's prophecy upon my father. *"Your child will conquer a monster feared by the gods themselves."*

My father was ecstatic. His son would be a hero! Alkaios had long mourned that he did not share the heroic gifts of his father, Perseus, but sometimes these things skip a generation. His son would be a monster killer, a hero, and people would come from all across Greece to pay homage to him.

What a pity that I was no son.

When the midwife handed me to my father on the day of my birth, he wouldn't have been more shocked if he had been given a bear cub. A girl! A girl could not grow up to slay monsters or win renown as a hero. She would spin wool in the women's quarters with her mother and aunts until she moved into her husband's house to spin wool there. She would bear children and run the household, and if she was a good woman, she would die in obscurity.

My father weighed his options. He could always abandon my infant self in some remote place and try again. Such things were more common among peasant families who struggled to feed every mouth born to them, but not unknown among royal houses. Perhaps next time the gods would see fit to grant him a son.

Then a peculiar thing happened. He looked into my eyes and fell in love.

There is no other word for it. In that moment, my father knew he loved me enough to tear down the sky itself. He loved me not for who I was, but simply *that* I was, his very own child with tiny perfect fingers and tiny perfect toes. I wish I could say that this was the natural reaction of a father meeting his daughter, but experience has shown me otherwise.

Alkaios decided that I would have the education of a prince. He knew that there would be those who questioned this decision, even his own brothers and oath men, but he held firm and called it an act of piety. Zeus's daughter Artemis, goddess of the moon and wild creatures, was given a sturdy bow for her inheritance and received worship throughout the cities of the Greeks. The Oracle said that the scion of Alkaios would conquer a monster feared by the gods themselves, and so she would.

As my father looked into my tiny, wrinkled face, he realized that he loved me more than the gods or his wife or oath men, or even his own soul. That is why he named me Psyche, which in our language means *soul*.

My mother, as far as I know, never questioned her love for me since the moment I kicked in her womb. I was her first and only child, a late-life baby. Conception had taken long enough that my father's advisors had urged him to take a second wife or even a concubine, but he respected my mother far too much for that.

She was an unusual woman, my mother, Astydamia. She grew up in the distant reaches of Arcadia where the wolf-kings still ruled their forest domains, and she might have received an education not unlike mine had she not been struck by a terrible illness in her youth. My birth taxed her further, and she spent much of her time in the dimly lit women's quarters, propped up on cushions and spinning wool surrounded by her ladies-in-waiting. My mother was as slender as a lily despite the iron in her soul, and as soon as I was old enough to think anything at all, I remember thinking that I needed to be strong enough for both of us.

Most of my care was given over to my wet nurse, a Thessalian slave named Maia. She was as broad and soft as a bed, with a booming laugh that she unleashed at the slightest provocation. She taught me simple songs and sayings and watched over my first toddling steps. In the evenings, Maia would bring me to my mother, who laid her cool hand upon my forehead and kissed me. So passed my first few years of life in the women's quarters, a place that smelled like tallow candles and milk.

When I was five years old, all of this changed.

"Your father is waiting for you, little Psyche," Maia told me one day, her wide face solemn.

My father was waiting in the hall outside the women's chambers. Alkaios was as tall as one of the statues of the gods, and today he wore the armor of a warrior king along with a serious expression. He had inherited the copper skin of his half-Ethiopian mother, Andromeda, which he had passed in turn to me. Anyone would know we were father and daughter, two of a kind, and I wanted to reach up and rub his whiskers as I often did. Instead, I took a cue from his solemnity and followed quietly alongside him, my small legs working to keep up with his long strides.

My father took me to the hero's room, which is what the servants called the small chamber in the interior of the palace. It was mostly bare, save for a sword and a shield mounted on the wall, along with an altar to send up incense to the hero's spirit. The shield was bronze and painted shades of emerald and red, though paint had been scraped in several places from what I imagined to be the claws of monsters or the swords of barbarians. At the center was the most terrifying visage I had ever seen—a snarling woman's face ringed with open-mouthed snakes. She seemed ready to leap from the wall and wrap clawed hands around my throat. I wanted to flee, but I planted my feet and stood firm.

"These belonged to your grandfather Perseus," my father told me. He lifted the bronze shield reverently and handed it to me; it clanged to the floor and took my arm with it, making me wince. The shield was so heavy that it took all my strength to prop it up against my small body.

My father told me how Zeus the Thunderer, king of the gods, had fathered Perseus, the hero who slayed the hideous monster Medusa. It was her face pictured on this shield.

"Eventually Perseus married Andromeda of the royal family of Mycenae, then became the father of Alkaios." He paused, smiling as though he held a treasure within himself. "Alkaios, who became the father of Psyche."

As he spoke my name, an upswell of pride filled me, and suddenly the shield felt lighter. I was the child of heroes and gods. I hefted the shield to a more comfortable position and basked in the glow of my father's indulgent smile.

"But you will be an even greater hero than your grandfather Perseus," my father told me. "The Oracle of Delphi spoke no prophecies about Perseus, but she had one for you. You will be the greatest hero of all."

My training began the next day. My father commissioned a child-sized bow and taught me how to draw it, painstaking in his patience. He took me on hunts, sitting me on the saddle in front of him so that I could watch as we ran down our quarry. His oath men observed this with puzzlement, unsure of what to make of a girl trained like a boy, but eventually they came to regard me as a familiar oddity. My father showed me how to heft a spear and wield a sword, and my skills blossomed.

I only went to the women's quarters in the evenings now, where Maia would cluck her tongue at the dirt caked into my clothing and my mother would ask me what I had learned that day. I told her eagerly, my words falling over one another in the way of young children, until Maia hauled me away for a bath and a change of clothes.

I spent the warmer seasons at my father's side on the practice field or the hunt, but in the winter, I went with the rest of the palace children to sit at the feet of the old blind poet as he told us stories of the gods and heroes. The poet had lost his sight early in life, and as a result he had taken up the lyre instead of the sword and shield. He was a man of no city, wandering where he willed and trading his songs for shelter and food. He brought the stories of the heroes and gods to life in the fire-lit feasting hall of Tiryns as the winter rains fell outside.

How do I explain the relationship between my people and the gods? The gods were real to us, as factual as a cup or table, but there was no love between us except for the basest kind. Gods might father children with mortal women or offer blessings to their favorites, but they might also entrap us in riddles or kill us to satisfy an immortal grudge. You could not trust the gods, though you needed to respect them.

The poet launched into the tale of the world's creation, the egg of Chaos and the immortal gods who tumbled out, beginning with Gaia the earth goddess and Ouranos the sky. I picked at a scab on my knuckle, sighing with boredom. I didn't care much for the gods, with the sole exception of Artemis, daughter of Zeus and goddess of the hunt and the moon. Sister of the sun, who ran fleet-footed along the mountains just as I did.

I liked the stories of heroes far better. The gods were immortal and had nothing to lose through their endeavors, but heroes risked everything for the chance at immortal fame. Heroes persevered against the limitations of their own mortality and became lights for other human beings to follow. Humans might even become gods by proving themselves worthy through their deeds.

I perked up when the blind poet told the story of Bellerophon, who once dwelled in this very city of Tiryns. Bellerophon was tasked with defeating the fearsome Chimera, a monster that was equal parts lion, goat, and serpent, and breathed fire in the bargain. Bellerophon was clever: He shot the Chimera with a lead-tipped arrow, which melted in its fiery breath and suffocated it. I made note of this strategy in case it came in handy when I became a hero myself. I yearned for the glory of it, my story told around campfires for generations.

How small my ideas of heroism were back then. I had not seen very much of the world, and I was certain that a few slain monsters were all that was necessary to make a hero. I knew nothing of war or death or love.

"Someday the poets will tell stories about me too," I told the other children later. They stared at me owlishly. "I'm going to be the greatest hero of them all," I added. "There was a prophecy about it and everything."

Freckle-faced Dexios, the son of the stable master, sneered. He had never taken me seriously after seeing me fall off a horse at the age of six. "You can't be a hero," he told me. "You're a girl."

I kicked him in the shins and sent him crying to his mother.

Eventually there came a limit to what my father could teach me. Alkaios was a king and not a hero, however much he might have wished otherwise. It was time to send for a teacher, but whom? Chiron was the obvious choice, but my father wasn't about to apprentice his nine-year-old daughter to a centaur. A rogue Amazon from the steppes might have done nicely, but they often died in captivity, and hiring one was out of the question since those wild women did not recognize any civilized currency.

In the end it was my mother who suggested the most promising candidate. The next day, my parents sent a letter.

A few months later, Atalanta arrived at the gates of the city.

She came alone, without an entourage or any fanfare, though word of her arrival spread like wildfire. She rode through the famous Lion's Gate of Mycenae but did not spare a glance for the stone beasts; she had killed real lions, and these did not impress her. She wore the dusty tunic and trousers of a hunter and sat atop an ill-tempered bay mare that snapped at anyone who came too close. She looked like a creature fashioned from driftwood and sinew, or perhaps a nymph from the deep forest, though the lines on her weather-beaten face and the strands of gray in her hair marked her plainly as a mortal woman. Atalanta, the hero.

Of all the tales the blind poet told, my favorites were the ones about Atalanta.

Atalanta had fought at Jason's side during his quest to retrieve the Golden Fleece, and she had been the first to draw blood from the monstrous Calydonian boar. When it came time for her to marry, she refused to be sold like a cow or sheep and vowed instead to wed only the man who could beat her in a footrace. A very long time passed before anyone could be found who was capable of this feat.

My father did not take me to the fields or forests the day that Atalanta arrived in Mycenae. Instead, I spent the morning being scrubbed and brushed like a sacrificial lamb by Maia and the servant girls. I tolerated this treatment so that I could listen to their gossip.

"Do you think it's really her?" asked the girl who had brought the hot water, leaning on a doorframe.

"It *has* to be her. There's no mistaking it," Maia said as she scrubbed my back and underarms. "There's only one woman among the cities of the Greeks who rides like that."

Dexios told me later that he was the one who took the reins of Atalanta's horse, having beaten out his two older brothers for this honor. Awestruck by her presence, he squeaked, "Is it true that you were raised by a bear?"

Atalanta gave him a vicious smile, eyes glinting. "Why don't you go ask the bear?"

The boy had hurried away holding the reins of her horse, which tried to crop a tuft of his hair with her yellowed teeth.

I went to meet Atalanta in the largest of the palace courtyards, together with my mother and father. Maia had forced me into a pure white chiton so that I looked like a temple maiden, though I didn't see the point; a hero wouldn't be impressed by fancy clothes.

Atalanta sauntered into the courtyard with the easy grace of a mountain cat. "Hail, and welcome to Mycenae," my father said, according her a deep bow. She did not return it. I felt a flicker of irritation at her impertinence; even if she was a legend, she didn't need to be rude to my father.

"There aren't many reasons I'd leave my forests and take up residence in a city," Atalanta said stiffly. "But I've read your letter, and I respect the word of the Oracle. I've never taken on a student before, though perhaps it's time. Is this the girl?"

"My name's *Psyche*," I cut in, resentful of being discussed like a dog or a horse.

"So it is. You're young, I see," Atalanta said, crouching down on her haunches so that we were eye-to-eye. "It's good to start young. I started training my son when he wasn't much older than you are now. Do you know how to ride?"

"Yes," I replied.

"Do you know how to draw a bow?"

"Yes."

"Do you accept me as your teacher?"

There was a longer pause now. Young as I was, I knew what this meant. I knew that the woman before me would shape my destiny as surely as my mother or father. Maybe even more, because where they had given me life, she would help me make sense of it.

I could have shrunk away from Atalanta, gone back to the women's quarters to live a quiet life. But I wanted to be what Atalanta was: a hero who commanded respect. Here was the woman who could lead me to the bright star of my destiny.

So I met her storm-gray eyes and said, "Yes."

"Then we begin tomorrow," Atalanta replied. And for the first time since she had set foot in the city, the hero smiled.

The next morning Atalanta took me deep into the forest, a prospect that inspired a great deal of excitement as well as a hint of trepidation. I had only ever traveled into these woods with my father and his men in boisterous procession. Now I was alone except for this near stranger. The forest was a peculiar place where anything was possible; one might encounter a herd of centaurs or a group of nymphs bathing, or even one of the gods walking alone. But no centaurs or nymphs showed themselves today—much to my disappointment—and I quickly became bored.

I began asking Atalanta questions. "Did you really sail with Jason?"

"Yes," my teacher replied, not turning to look at me. Her pace did not slow.

"Did you see the Golden Fleece? What did it look like?"

"Gold. And fleece-like."

I had been holding the last question in reserve. "Is it true that you killed the Calydonian boar?"

Atalanta's pace slowed momentarily, though she recovered quickly. "Yes. Meleager and I share the credit. Now stop asking stupid questions."

Abruptly, Atalanta sat on a fallen log and patted the space next to her. "Come. It's time for your first lesson. Tell me what you hear."

I was taken aback. I was sure that we'd come here to track wild beasts or decipher the ways of the wilderness, not to sit on a mossy log and *listen*. You could do that anywhere. But I wanted to learn, so I squeezed my eyes shut. I heard nothing, and I told Atalanta as much.

"Wrong!" my teacher snapped, so loudly that a few nearby birds took to flight. "If you are to slay monsters, you must be aware of your surroundings at all times. If you truly listened, you would realize that the wind is coming from the northeast, meaning that anything located to the south and west can catch your scent. You'd hear the songbirds chirping, which means they think they're safe and all is well. Be aware of the moment when birds fall silent—it means something has frightened them, and that 'something' might be coming for you."

I considered this. "I don't hear any nymphs or centaurs or lions," I offered.

Atalanta snorted. "That's something. Perhaps you'll make it as a hero after all."

The training my father had given me, I soon realized, had merely been play; what I did now with Atalanta was work. I didn't like it at first. For all my natural skill, I was still a pampered royal child and unaccustomed to work. Despite the pleasure I took in seeing my arrow hit its mark, I disliked being told where to aim.

From morning to night, I drilled with the bow, spear, and sword. Atalanta was a merciless teacher, and I earned more than a few bruises when I failed to deflect her swings. I hated her in those early days, and I think she began to hate me too for my stubbornness. Things might have gone badly between us had matters not come to a head one day when the chill winter rains drenched the plains of Mycenae. There was no point in ruining good bronze in the rain, so instead Atalanta sent me running laps around the city walls of Tiryns to build up my endurance.

I was miserable. My bare feet sunk into the mud with each step, and cold rain drenched me down to my undergarments. I shivered uncontrollably despite my exertion, warmed only by my incandescent rage toward the figure watching me: Atalanta, arms crossed, judgmental as a statue of one of the immortal gods.

I made it once around the walls. When I circled back to where that solitary figure stood, I halted and met her gaze. "I'm not doing this anymore," I said, stamping one foot. It sunk into the mud, and I was forced to pull it free with a sucking sound, which somewhat lessened the defiant air I had been aiming for. "I want to go inside."

Atalanta's expression darkened. For a moment, there was no sound but my ragged breath and the pelting rain. This woman who had killed monsters and enemy combatants began to stalk toward me, as slender and swift as a knife through the veils of rain.

I steeled myself. Atalanta was giving me the sort of stare that a wolf gives a rabbit, but I refused to be the rabbit. What was she going to do, hit me? I wasn't scared of that. She had already hit me dozens of times around the arms and torso with wooden swords when we sparred. I kept my spine straight and waited.

Atalanta loomed directly in front of me now. "The monsters you hunt won't go easy on you, and neither will I," she said slowly, as the downfall slicked back her dark hair. "Do you think wild creatures take a rest when it's raining? Folly. This is the best time to hunt certain quarry, especially large cats or bears, since they cannot catch your scent. I killed my first lion on a day like this."

My determination wavered, intrigue taking its place. "You did?"

The faintest trace of a smile crossed her face. "Yes. And if you run one more lap around the city walls, I will tell you about it over a cup of warm milk in the feasting hall. I'm not standing here in this awful weather because I like it, you know."

I brightened. Atalanta held her tales close to her chest, but I had managed to coax a few of them from her, and I was always hungry for more. Though her delivery was less polished than the blind poet's, I liked Atalanta's stories best because they were *true*.

I ran the rest of the course without a word of complaint.

2

EROS

My story begins before there were any stories to be told, when there was nothing but earth and sky stretching on into infinity. The sea hadn't been invented yet.

There were fewer than a dozen of us back then, the first elemental gods who emerged from the fathomless abyss of Chaos—which is, I suppose, another way to say *nothingness*. The grass of the newborn world tickled my feet as I took my first steps. I looked down. In my right hand was an elegant bow, and tied at my waist was a quiver of gold-fletched arrows. Their existence was inextricably linked to mine, as much a part of me as my fingers and toes. I thrummed my fingers along the bow's string and felt the steady hum of the power contained within.

I stretched my arms, feeling my muscles ripple beneath my skin, and took my first breaths of air. Wide-feathered wings arched over my shoulders, brushing against the belly of the sky god Ouranos. I sunk my toes into the loam, marveling at it.

The world was drawn in simple lines, unembellished, empty, and waiting. No dryads existed yet to raise forests over the earth, and the soft wind carried no scent of flowers. There was little else around—a few rocks, a bit of grass.

"What is this place?" I said aloud.

"*I believe it is called earth*," a voice around me said. "*Welcome. I am Gaia.*"

The broad ground beneath my feet quivered. I felt the attention of some vast entity focus upon me, something wider than the plains that rose to a distant line of mountains, but I was not afraid. Laughter drifted to my ears, sweet and playful.

"Gaia," I echoed, rolling the shape of the name on my tongue.

I became aware of eyes watching me, crinkling with amusement. I saw the barest outlines of a form—a proud nose, a generous mouth, hair like the rivers that were beginning to trickle through the crags in the ground.

"*A nice place, though rather lonely,*" Gaia said. Her attention drifted. "*Although not for you, it seems. Someone is coming.*"

The vast awareness faded, and I nearly staggered with its absence. When I lifted my head, sure enough, I saw a figure approaching. Unlike earth-formed Gaia, this one looked like me. She had five-fingered hands and two legs that carried her swiftly over the ground. She was my perfect mirror in female form—golden hair, bronze skin, and green eyes, though hers glinted with the cunning of a serpent.

She was Eris, the goddess of discord, disagreement, and shattered things. My cosmic twin, though I liked her no more than your right hand likes your left.

"There you are," Eris said when she approached. "I have been searching for you everywhere. We have much work to do, my dear brother. Let's go."

I looked out at the landscape that was just beginning to take shape. Jagged mountains along the horizon, and the first thin stripes of clouds in the sky. The world was empty, but it wouldn't be for long. I thought of what Gaia had said. *A nice place, though rather lonely*.

Already I could feel the straining weight of it, a new future aching to be born.

"I don't think I will," I said to Eris, who gaped at me as though

I had announced I would cram all of Ouranos's blue sky into my mouth. Dissent was new, and she was rather put out that she hadn't thought of it first.

"We're gods. We create and destroy," she urged. "This is what we must do."

"If we are gods," I replied, "we can do whatever we like."

And to suit my actions to my words, I lay down on the warm rock and closed my eyes. After some time, I heard Eris depart with a frustrated huff.

I do not know how long I slept. Sleep is not a necessity for a god, but it is a great pleasure, and we do not skimp on those. I was awoken by fingers of wind moving over my cheeks, rustling my hair. I opened my eyes and found myself looking into an angular face with eyes as blue as the cloudless sky.

"How long are you going to lie here?" the newcomer asked.

I knew him to be Zephyrus, one of the brothers who ruled the four winds. "As long as I want to," I replied. In his clear eyes, I could see a reflection of myself: golden locks, bronzed skin, eyes green as the grass beneath me. I thought myself quite attractive.

He nodded, already losing interest; I would come to learn that Zephyrus was as flighty as the winds he commanded. His gaze drifted to the bow and quiver of arrows at my side. "What do those do?" he asked.

I finally sat up, reaching out to weigh them in my hands. "Shall we find out together?" I asked, a grin creeping over my face.

I removed one of the arrows from the quiver. The wood of the shaft was polished to near-perfect smoothness, the arrowhead worked from bronze. I had the sense it was made to fly, but it remained stubbornly immobile. Then I examined the bow. One seemed to call to the other, two pieces of a whole longing to be united, so I braced the shaft of the arrow against the taut string.

The bow's purpose washed over me with unwavering certainty. A wound that knits two sides together, a weapon with the power to heal. I thought of Gaia's loneliness and knew at once what I must do.

I aimed the bronze tip of the arrow at the great blue underbelly of Ouranos, the god of the sky. Holding the bow like this created a pleasing tension, one that could only be satisfied by release. I lifted my fingers, and it flew. Zephyrus hummed in approval and summoned a light breeze to carry the arrow to its destination.

The wind was strong, and my aim was true. Ouranos's gaze fell upon Gaia, the earth, and for the first time, love entered the world.

Love of a certain sort, that is. The Greeks may have three words for love, but the gods have only one.

I was the god of desire, and it did not take me long to realize what that meant. My arrows sparked desire wherever they landed if I infused them with my will. At first, I thought this was a happy thing.

Gaia was delighted by Ouranos's advances, and soon she took him as her husband. From their union were born the divinities who ruled over the sea and memory and time, and their joy suffused the world.

I offered my arrows freely, and I drank now and then from the well of desire myself, bedding some nymph or satyr—though I made sure never to feel the sting of my own arrows, unwilling to fall too deeply. There was sweetness in sex, like climbing a tree in summer and never reaching the top. I thought this was to be my gift to the world, a delight that I could bestow upon others with their glad acceptance.

I did not know yet how cruel love could be.

I watched as the love between Ouranos and Gaia turned sour. He forbade her to have any more children, fearful that one of them would be greater than him. When she did not comply, he became vicious with her. Their son Kronos rose up in defense of his mother and succeeded in overthrowing his father, Ouranos. Then Kronos took his victory a step further: He castrated Ouranos for all to see, throwing his phallus into the ocean.

He claimed this was an act of revenge for his mother, Gaia, but the goddess of the earth was repulsed by this atrocity. Her spirit broken by her husband's cruelty and her son's savagery, she retreated from the world and fell into an endless sleep. She became the earth, and nothing else. The earth, and not herself.

My unchecked actions had brought something new and ugly into the world. I realized, then, that desire could be the cause of pain rather than joy. My arrows might fester in a wounded heart, spreading like an infection. Or perhaps love itself had been rotten from the start.

After this, I withdrew from the world of the gods. I recoiled from the lovestruck divinities who trailed after me, whispering my name with an intensity I did not understand. They smelled the desire on me, the power I ruled, and it drew them as surely as blood draws sharks. But I knew how quickly the affection in their eyes could turn to hatred, and knew I was nothing to them except a conquest. I wanted no part in it. I turned away.

Only Zephyrus remained my friend, laughing at my reclusiveness. "It will be good to visit you and get away from the rabble," he told me when I informed him of my plans.

Far away from Mount Othrys, seat of the first gods, I found a proud cliff that overlooked the sea. It was remote and desolate; the only sound was the drumming of waves against the sharp rocks. My only neighbors were the seabirds who made their nests high up on the cliffs, paying me no mind as they went about their lives. Life was spare and unchanging in this place at the edges of the earth, and nothing green grew. It might have been the world's beginning, or its end.

It was perfect. I crossed the shale beach and laid a hand on the bleached stones, which felt as warm as a living thing beneath my palm. I closed my eyes and called out to Gaia. My sister, my oldest friend.

Even in her delirium, she answered. There came a grinding high in the cliffs, and I looked up to watch as the structures of the earth shifted and rearranged themselves. With no more effort than it takes a mortal woman to trim her hair, Gaia carved a soaring home for me from the cliffside. An elegant stone staircase invited me away from the beachfront and toward the aerie, giving way to terraces laden with vibrant, sweet-smelling flowers.

Gaia had been generous. I knew that I would find everything inside suited to my taste. Meals would appear on the table when I desired them, and glasses of divine ambrosia would fill themselves in my hand. My clothing would reappear washed and mended; stains would rub themselves clean. In this place that Gaia had made for me, all of reality would bend itself to my wishes. Such were the blessings of the earth goddess upon those she favored.

I would fill this home with all sorts of beautiful things— colored glass and vibrant jewels, perhaps a pet or two. I'd always enjoyed peacocks, and cats as well. This would be a place of joy.

"Thank you," I whispered to Gaia before I spread my golden wings and flew to my new abode.

Even in this remote place, however, my solitude was not assured. I received a steady stream of messages from the other gods, some requesting the use of my arrows and others requesting favors of a much more intimate kind. I granted some of the former if the deal was good, but never any of the latter. I never forgot what happened to Ouranos and Gaia, and I would not risk being trapped in a love gone rancid.

One day, my twin sister, Eris, came to the seaside house. I found her standing in my terraced garden as she ran a hand along one of the colonnades suggestively and peered up at me from beneath her lashes. I noticed that she wore a sheer fabric draped to emphasize her figure, and that her yellow hair had been braided into a complex coronet that might have looked elegant on someone else.

What was she doing here? Normally my sister preferred the company of other gods, the better to make use of her talents. Eris spread her poison like a dandelion scatters its seeds over the earth, whispering malicious gossip into eager ears.

"You know, dearest brother," Eris said in what she may have thought were sultry tones, though they scraped like nails against my ears. "The other gods have all coupled to make children and populate the earth, but you haven't. I could help you with that."

She was my sister, but such pairings were not uncommon among the gods. Indeed, we were each other's most sensible match. Like Gaia and Ouranos, we were opposites: desire and discord, as parallel as earth and sky. Yet, I found myself seized with the uncomfortable thought that if Eris and I joined we might offset each other's powers—or give rise to something far worse.

The possibility didn't seem to bother Eris, I noticed.

"Eris, dear sister," I replied sweetly. "I would rather stab myself in the eye with one of my arrows than lie with you."

Her face went pale with rage. I did not see her again for several thousand years.

Eventually, there was a second war in the heavens. Kronos had taken to devouring his own children to prevent another uprising, but one of them escaped.

This forgotten son of Kronos came to my door one day. He was Zeus the Thunderer, only a minor god at the time. He barged into my house and sat at my great oak table, where he poured himself some of my ambrosia and slurped it down noisily.

"I need your help," Zeus said to me, violet trails dribbling into his long white beard. Despite being my junior by several centuries, he had the appearance of a stern gray-haired elder; the gods take the forms that fit them best. "My father, Kronos, is wicked, and he must be destroyed," he finished.

I laughed. "Kronos came to me saying much the same thing about his own father once. I wonder, when do you think one of your children will come knocking at my door?"

The jovial grin melted from Zeus's face and his jaw hardened. Outside, storm clouds filled the once-bright sky like growing bruises, lightning threading between them. A low rumble swept over the scene. My peacocks clucked with dread and my cats hid behind the furniture, but I sat unmoving.

Zeus pushed himself out of his chair but did not step away. He loomed over me, his expression as dark as the sky. "Very well. If you will not assist me, at least do not hinder me. But I will not forget your insolence once I take my place as king of the gods."

"Give your wife, Hera, my regards," I said sweetly.

Zeus stormed out of the seaside house in every sense of the word. Rain and lightning lashed the sky.

One day my friend Zephyrus blew into my house, wild-eyed as he shared the news that Zeus emerged victorious from his battle with Kronos. He'd exiled his father and formed a new seat of power on Mount Olympus.

Those who had served Zeus faithfully were rewarded with places as members of the Dodekatheon, the pantheon of the twelve gods. There were only five at the time, but Zeus was certain he could fill the remaining seats quite handily. The elder gods who opposed him would henceforth be known only as Titans. It was a cunning name: grand enough that none to whom it applied could complain, and yet one that set them apart from the new gods. Zeus would deal with each individual Titan differently; those who defied him would be exiled or destroyed, while others would be allowed to persist in some diminished capacity.

After his victory, Zeus went down to the deep sea, where the blood of his grandfather Ouranos had fermented for centuries. Through the alchemy of the ocean and his own divine magic, the severed parts of the primordial god became something beautiful and new. Zeus whispered instructions to the deity who took shape from that ancient crime, telling her who she was and what sort of power she would wield. She would eventually join the Dodekatheon on the peaks of Olympus, but she needed to find someone first.

She drifted with the tides for a while, startling the schools of brightly colored fish who were the only witnesses to her brief divine childhood. She watched the swaying fields of seaweed and grew out her hair until it was long enough to match. She kicked her way toward the glittering water's surface with limbs that had knitted themselves into long and shapely legs, and with her first breath of air she whispered her own name: Aphrodite, goddess of love and beauty.

Aphrodite made her way to the island of Cyprus and stepped out of the sea. It was night, and the beach glowed white beneath the light of the full moon. Undulating hills mimicked the curves of a woman's hip, and the scent of jasmine floated on the night breeze. I'm sure Aphrodite imagined that there would be attendant nymphs waiting for her with linen garments and scatters of rose petals, perhaps musicians softly strumming their instruments in the moonlight. Instead there was only me, bearing a cloth and a particularly miserable expression.

Not bothering to disguise her disappointment, Aphrodite took the cloth from me and used it to dry her damp hair, careless of her nudity. When she was done, she considered me. "You must be my new servant."

I said nothing. Like the other elder gods, I had to accept my place in Zeus's new order, however much it rankled.

Aphrodite continued. "It's Zeus's will that we share influence over the realms of desire and beauty, though I'll be taking the lion's share, of course. It seems you defied him once, so he decided to make his own love god. You *must* understand." She smiled in a way that might drive other gods wild with passion but left me feeling vaguely nauseous.

I remained silent.

Aphrodite wrapped the towel around her head and placed her hands on her hips as she considered me, moonlight gilding her naked body. She took a step toward me, then another, close enough that I could feel her breath like the hot night air. I could smell her skin, touched only by water and moonlight, begging for other caresses. I was not sure whether she would kiss me or eat me alive.

As it transpired, she did neither. Instead, Aphrodite brought her mouth close to the shell of my ear, and whispered, "Zeus believes that familial ties ensure harmony. I think he wants me to make a marriage alliance with you."

Terror sunk its claws into my heart. Aphrodite stepped back suddenly, leaving me swaying into the space she left. "But if you'll forgive me for saying so, I'd prefer a less miserable spouse." Her laughter was light and musical. "I think I'll adopt you as my son instead."

My lip curled. "I am not your son."

"Oh, but you are now," she said. "Unless, of course, you want to face the wrath of the Thunderer."

All the air had drained from my lungs, and I found myself friendless in the shadow of a tyrant. Though I was older, my strength was no match for that of Zeus. Rumors had reached me about the fate of Nereus, the old Titan sea god who had protested the claiming of his ocean realm by Zeus's brother Poseidon. Zeus's lightning bolts had scorched Nereus so thoroughly that the sea god fell into charred ashes. Lacking the strength to maintain his physical form, Nereus dissolved into the waves that had once been his home. Now he existed only in clusters of sea-foam and the flow of tides, and no longer knew his own name.

Aphrodite was new to the world but wily. She knew that the threat of Zeus's wrath might have compelled me to this beach, but it would not ensure my compliance for the rest of eternity. So she tried another strategy.

"Something new is coming, you know," she said conspiratorially. "Zeus told me about it. It's called humanity, a race of mortals to entertain and worship us. Won't that be such fun?"

I felt a flicker of curiosity. Gods love nothing more than

novelty, and being the object of worship sounded intriguing. Seeing her chance, Aphrodite added, "If you're not interested, I suppose I could ask Zeus to assign you to a different god. I'm sure Hestia would *love* having someone to help her tidy the house."

I couldn't have that. I knelt and offered fealty to Aphrodite at once. And as I did, I dreamed of small ways to revenge myself against the Olympians.

I was always careful throughout the intervening centuries. I never broke my promises, and nothing could ever be traced back to me with any degree of certainty. But I found certain ways to resist my subjugation.

For a goddess of love, Aphrodite was remarkably unlucky in matters of the heart. My so-called mother was married to the ugly blacksmith god Hephaestus—a hasty move on Zeus's part when the competition for her hand threatened to turn to bloodshed. But Aphrodite fell in love with the handsome war god Ares, and had more than a few other affairs besides. They all ended poorly.

Zeus, king of the gods, experienced similar ill fortune. His endless affairs incensed his wife, Hera, who could hardly keep track of all the nymphs and goddesses he bedded. Yet he couldn't seem to help himself. I suppose he told himself that sensual indulgences were the prerogative of a king. Zeus liked to believe that he controlled his appetites, even when all evidence suggested it was the other way around.

I gave no hint of my role in all this, and kept my arrows close. I had learned from Ouranos and Gaia what a double-edged sword love could be, and I did not hesitate to use it for my own purposes when the situation demanded.

If love was a weapon, I would wield it well.

3

PSYCHE

When I was thirteen, I traveled with my family across the hills and valleys of Greece to attend the wedding of Helen and Menelaus in Sparta.

I pushed back the curtains of the palanquin I shared with my mother to peer at the other travelers on the road. Farmers bringing their crops to market, pilgrims on the way to some temple, even whole families traveling like us. At last, my mother grew tired of this and sent me to ride with my father at the head of the convoy. He greeted me warmly and set me in front of him on his horse as he had when I was a little girl, filling my ears with tales of the city-state of Sparta. They were a warrior people, renowned for the strength of their armies. Even their daughters were trained to hunt and fight, just like me. I noted this last fact with interest.

Eventually the city came into view. It had no protective cocoon of walls, since Sparta trusted her defense to her warriors rather than stone or mortar, but an honor guard was waiting outside to bring us to the palace. They led our convoy to a courtyard where a group of men stood waiting. One of them called out a greeting and stepped forward.

He looked much like my father, but swollen. Where Alkaios was rangy and lean as a wolf, Agamemnon was a bear of a man, banded with muscle. His belly strained his tunic, which was stained with sweat at the armpits. His nose had been broken at least two or three times, giving him a lumpy, misshapen look. Even on this fine afternoon, he stank of sweat and bronze armor.

"Alkaios!" he boomed. "I didn't know you had a son."

My father shifted uncomfortably. "This is—"

"I'm Psyche," I said in a rush. I dismounted quickly and bounded toward my uncle Agamemnon. "I've heard all about you, and—"

"Oh, a daughter," Agamemnon said, the light of interest quickly fading from his eyes. He turned back to my father. "Alkaios, you're late. Menelaus and I wanted your opinion about the matter with the Argives . . ."

They turned their backs, leaving me standing in the dust of the courtyard with only my mother's covered palanquin and the servants for company. As I watched them go, my heart sank further in my chest.

My mother pled illness and was led away to the sleeping quarters; the journey had taxed her, and she needed rest. I, on the other hand, found myself being dragged down another hallway. I was hastily divested of my dusty traveling clothes by a set of servants and shoved into an old stiff chiton that smelled of must and aged cedar. I smoothed down the skirts, which were much longer than the hems of the practical riding clothes and short dresses I usually wore. Then the servants trundled me into a dark room, though I nearly tripped more than once. As soon as I was fully inside, the door slammed shut behind me.

"Who have we here?" a melodious voice asked.

It took a moment for my eyes to adjust to the gloom. This room was located in the interior of the palace, windowless, with only a few lamps for illumination. *The women's quarters*, I realized with frustration. I wondered how far I was from my father and uncles and if I could still find them.

"I'm Psyche," I replied awkwardly, looking toward the woman who had spoken to me. I wanted to show off my axe-throwing skills, not sit in the darkness with strangers. "I'm Alkaios's daughter."

"Princess of Mycenae," the woman said graciously, inclining her head. "Well met. My name is Penelope, and I am the queen of Ithaka."

Through the dimness, I could see Penelope's wide dark eyes and the mane of curly brown hair pulled back sternly from her face. She wasn't exactly beautiful, but there was a thoughtfulness to her gaze and a rare note of confidence in her voice that made her intriguing. Many years later, when I met her husband, Odysseus, I would be utterly unsurprised to learn of his connection to the goddess Athena. Penelope, with her quick hands and even quicker mind, was a mortal reflection of the goddess.

"This is Clytemnestra, wife of Agamemnon," Penelope continued, indicating a sour-looking woman, "and her daughters, Iphigenia and Elektra. Iphigenia is quite a skilled weaver, not much younger than you."

Iphigenia was indeed only a few years my junior, and she gazed at me with wide-eyed fascination. She had a sweet, open face, with cheeks like the halves of a cut peach, and the copper shade of our skin marked us as kin. Her mother, Clytemnestra, on the other hand, appeared as if she was holding a slice of lemon in her mouth. Nearby, baby Elektra slumbered in a basket.

"Where is her mother?" Clytemnestra demanded. "We can't have a respectable young girl wandering around the palace by herself."

"I wasn't wandering," I replied irritably. "My mother is resting."

Clytemnestra gave a huff of disapproval, but Penelope simply chuckled. "I bid you welcome, Psyche, and a good rest to your mother. But to finish our round of introductions," she gestured to the fourth figure in the room, "this is my sister, Helen. Our beautiful bride."

So dark was the room that I did not immediately notice the radiant gorgeousness of the woman to Penelope's left. Calling Helen beautiful was like calling the sun bright; while technically true, the word failed to encompass the sheer splendor of its subject. Long hair the color of honey skimmed her sharp cheekbones and hung past her elegant neck. I noticed the fine dress she wore and the ceremonial henna that adorned her hands, signs of celebration for her upcoming nuptials. I remembered the stories that the palace guards in Tiryns whispered about Helen's conception, about Zeus himself coming upon her mother in the form of a swan. At the time I found these stories fanciful, but now I wondered if they might hold a grain of truth.

It was only after the initial shock of Helen's beauty faded that I noticed the unhappiness etched into those perfect features. She was so distracted by her private misery that she didn't even turn to acknowledge me. Her slim fingers continued to push the shuttle of her loom back and forth in a desultory fashion. I wondered if she might have a stomachache or some hidden injury. How could one be so sad on such a happy occasion?

Penelope turned back to her weaving. *Sister*, she had said. When I looked hard enough, I supposed that I could see some family resemblance between Penelope and Helen, though it was like comparing a duck to a swan.

I sat down, and for the first time in my life I was confronted with the daunting and unfamiliar prospect of a loom. I knew how to do many things: tell the size of an animal from its prints, move soundlessly toward my quarry in the underbrush, shoot unerringly from foot or horseback. But I did not know how to weave. In retrospect, this seemed like an unfortunate gap in the education of a royal girl.

I glanced at the other women to see what they were doing, but that was little help. Penelope's hands moved as though they had been made for the task, pushing the shuttle back and forth with a satisfying clack, and even the pouting Helen's work was smooth enough. Yet every time I tried to imitate the other women, I was left with nothing but a snarled mass of string. Why did women need to weave all the time, anyway? How much cloth did one household really require?

"You're looping the warp under the weft." A small hand swept up beside mine to untangle the threads. "You want to fold this part under, see?" I looked over, and the sweet, trusting face of Iphigenia smiled up at me.

I returned her grin. "Thank you. I've never done this before."

"You haven't?" A crease appeared on Iphigenia's forehead. "A girl who doesn't know how to weave? That's like a bird who doesn't know how to fly."

I frowned. "So what if I can't weave? I can shoot down a bird on the wing! Atalanta herself taught me."

I was satisfied to see the girl's eyes widen. "You've met Atalanta? And you know how to shoot a bow? Amazing! Will you teach me?"

A flush spread over my cheeks. For so long now, I had spent most of my waking hours with Atalanta, separated from the other children of the palace. I was too rough for the girls and too girlish for the boys, who didn't like to be challenged at their games by a rogue princess. I'd never before had a friend my own age.

"I'd be delighted to teach you," I told her. "But don't Spartan girls already know such things?"

Iphigenia dropped her voice. "I'm not Spartan. I've always wanted to learn archery, but Father says it isn't proper for a girl. But my—"

"Iphigenia," Clytemnestra snapped. "Stop chattering. It isn't proper. 'Silence is a woman's greatest adornment,' never forget that."

I had heard the proverb once or twice before from my nurse Maia, who usually used it as a jest. I had always considered it satire, a bit of mockery, but Clytemnestra seemed deadly serious. Iphigenia fell silent at once. I met my aunt's glare, unwilling to be cowed, until she finally turned back to her task with a disapproving sigh.

A low sob startled me, and I looked up. Helen was weeping, fat tears rolling down her flawless face and onto the cloth of her loom. She hiccupped theatrically, snot dribbling from her nose.

Clytemnestra's lips narrowed disapprovingly, but it was Penelope who spoke up first. "Helen, we have guests," she said, her fingers not straying from the weaving. "Do try to pull yourself together."

"I can't help it," Helen wailed. "I'm being sold like a cow to some man I've never met!"

"He's your husband, Helen, and you *have* met him. You actually got to choose him, if you recall." Penelope's voice held only a hint of scorn, but it was clear that her patience was growing thin.

"I picked him out of a lineup! I don't know anything about him. What if he hits me? Or drinks until he's blind? Or chases the servant girls?"

"You ought to be grateful you had any say at all in who your husband would be," Clytemnestra said sharply. "Most women don't."

Helen sat up straight and glared at Clytemnestra. "No one gave me any choice in the first place! Everyone was pressuring me to choose a husband, and the suitors were going for one another's throats. Sparta needed a successor." Helen sneered, showing her teeth like an animal and yet still managing to look more lovely than other women at their most alluring. "I was made for better things. I wanted to see the world and fall in love, not spend my life chained to some hairy lout."

I glanced at her. I had been so taken with Helen's beauty that I had missed the glint of intelligence in her eyes. I had the feeling this happened to her quite often.

"Helen." Penelope's voice was hard now, all indulgence gone. She paused her weaving, pinning her sister with a glare. "None of us had a choice. You think I wanted to marry Odysseus and go to Ithaka, where sheep outnumber people and rocks outnumber sheep? We are women, and we must follow our duty. At least you get to stay in Sparta."

"I've said it before and I'll say it again: 'Silence is a woman's greatest adornment,'" Clytemnestra pronounced primly. I wanted to throw her loom into a river.

Helen's shoulders sagged. Finally accepting that there was scant sympathy to be found, she turned back to her loom. But she did not bother to stanch the flow of tears that continued down her cheeks.

My mind churned as I added more lumpy rows to my weaving. Helen's predicament troubled me, and the thought only worked itself deeper when I tried to dislodge it. Though the concept of my own marriage had always felt distant and nebulous, I was only a few years younger than Helen. Soon I too would be expected to submit to a union with a man I barely knew. I had always thought about weddings as grand parties full of music and food; I had never given much consideration to what happened to the brides after the festivities.

I had long noticed that the stories of heroes were mainly about men, Atalanta being one of the rare exceptions. Women, when they had roles to play at all, appeared only as mothers or lovers or sometimes monsters.

I had the Oracle's prophecy, but what was a prophecy against the silence of legend?

I realized, with creeping unease, that the gulf separating me from Perseus and Bellerophon was not one of divine parentage after all, but one of sex. The sons of the gods received a hero's training, divine gifts, and everlasting fame. Their daughters, like Helen, were prizes to be won.

Zeus had come upon Helen's mother, Leda, as a swan, people said, but he wasn't acting very much like one now. I had seen swans nesting on the high lakes in the forested mountains; they were dedicated parents, leading their rows of fuzzy children everywhere. The gods, on the other hand, left their mortal children to fend for themselves until they were useful. If the look in Helen's eyes was any indication, marriage was a pit of lost possibility. A chain binding her to a man she did not know, who ruled her body and her future.

If this was the best that the daughter of a god could hope for, then what was there left for me, mortal-born on both sides?

The wedding was a riotous affair. The men were in good spirits, red-faced with drink and shouting songs off-key. There was a tradition in Sparta, Iphigenia had warned me, that the groom would carry away his bride. It was an old custom, meant to preserve the woman's chastity before she was snatched by some bad spirit or a trickster attracted by the festivities; it predated even the worship of the Olympian gods in these lands. At least, that was what Iphigenia told me in between whispered instructions to correct my weaving.

Clytemnestra scoffed when she heard this. "No, it's for the benefit of the men. They're not used to women who aren't screaming."

Still, when my uncle Menelaus tossed his bride, Helen, over his shoulder like a sack of grain and carried her out of the room, I found my hand flexing at my hip, wishing it held a weapon. Helen did not bother to blink back her tears, and I understood that her watery eyes represented a kind of bravery, a refusal to hide her opinion of the proceedings. She would not smile prettily for her captors.

The rest of the men followed after Menelaus. Once their shouting had faded, Penelope gestured for the rest of us to rise and follow her.

My mother waited for us in the feasting hall, cheerful despite the lingering dark circles under her eyes. My father sat on the other side of the room with the men, next to the enormous man I recognized as my uncle Agamemnon. I hadn't seen Alkaios among the men who had taken Helen, and I tried unsuccessfully to assure myself that my father would never participate in such barbarity.

I did not tell my mother about what had come to pass in the women's quarters, though I watched her from the corner of my eye, wondering. Had my fragile mother wept like Helen before her own wedding? Had she been carried away by my father to shouts and boasting? My parents had always seemed like such a natural match, but now I knew what secrets might lie in the dim shadows of the women's quarters.

Menelaus, seated on the newlyweds' dais, was glassy-eyed with wine but wore an expression of beatific happiness. After all, he had won the bride and the kingdom that came with her. Helen, seated next to him, looked like she was presiding over her own funeral.

There were toasts and oaths, of which I understood very little. My mind was elsewhere. I asked at my mother, "Will I get married someday?"

Astydamia smiled indulgently. "You will, my dearest. You shall have the grandest wedding of all."

My mother's attention was pulled away suddenly by Penelope, so she did not notice the expression of dread on my face.

A plate of food was set before me, but I had lost my appetite. There were musicians and acrobats, but I could not focus on their performances. All I could see was the misery in Helen's eyes, a fate that awaited me as well. All I wanted to do was run away from the world of men and women, back into the forest where I could be a wild creature again.

The next morning, I heard a knock on the door.

I lifted my head from the pillow, startled. Rosy-fingered dawn was just beginning to reach in through the windows. My parents slumbered in the great bed nearby, and servants lay scattered around on pallets, still snoring. I crossed the room on silent feet and opened the door.

Iphigenia stood there with a bow, a quiver of arrows, and a mischievous expression. "I got these from my brother, Orestes," she explained. "All I had to do was threaten to tell Mother about that servant girl he goes off with." The bewilderment must have shown on my face, because she added, "You said you would teach me archery."

"So I did!" I whispered. "The bow's a little big for you, but we'll make do. Come on."

I looked back into the room where everyone slept soundly. It seemed unfair to wake my parents to ask their permission. So I took Iphigenia's hand, and together we ran soundlessly through the palace, past the heaps of dozing wedding guests who still lingered in the halls. The morning air was brisk, and I hadn't had time to grab my sandals or a cloak, but I didn't care.

We found an empty courtyard that was large and window-less enough to act as an archery range. I found a sack filled with sand and propped it awkwardly at the rim of a large flowerpot to serve as our target. I showed Iphigenia how to position the arrow and draw back the bowstring. Her arms quivered with the effort, though her mouth was set in a fierce line.

"Good, good," I said. "But drop your elbow. You won't get any power behind your shot otherwise."

The elbow dropped at once. Iphigenia took aim and released; the arrow clattered uselessly against the flagstones. I opened my mouth to offer some encouragement, but my cousin didn't need it. Already she was pulling another arrow from the quiver, frowning.

This one lodged in the rough fabric of the sack. Iphigenia squealed with happiness, clapping like a little child, though she was careful not to drop the bow.

"You're a natural," I said. Though Atalanta might have used this moment to assess her technique, all I could do was grin with unbridled pride.

Iphigenia glanced at me shyly. "I've watched Father's men practice plenty of times. It's not as difficult as it looks."

My curiosity was piqued. "You said you weren't Spartan. Where is your city?"

Iphigenia shrugged her small shoulders. "Here and there. My father fights for whoever will pay him, so we go where he's needed. Some people think it's frightening to live with a war band and travel from place to place all the time, but it's not. Father's men are kind to me, though I rarely have other girls to play with. Well, there's my sister Elektra, but she can't even talk yet."

"I don't have any siblings," I said, wondering what it was like to live with a war band. It sounded exciting. "Sometimes I wish I did."

"Then I'll be your sister," Iphigenia said in a rush. She slung the bow over her shoulder, leaving her hands free. Her fingers twined with mine, softer and smaller but no less strong. "Sworn sisters. We'll take an oath, like Father's men do, and practice archery in secret forever." She beamed at me, and I couldn't stop myself from grinning in response. Whenever Iphigenia smiled at you, it was as though the warmth of a summer afternoon settled upon your soul.

"And so we will," I said, squeezing her hand tighter.

Iphigenia tilted her head like a bird, thoughtful. "You said your teacher was the great Atalanta, didn't you? She's a favorite of the goddess Artemis, and I think Artemis must have brought us together." My cousin dropped her voice to a whisper. "I dream of the day I'll be able to dedicate myself to the goddess. Father says I'll marry a king and bear his sons, but I don't want that. I want to become a priestess of Artemis."

My heart swelled. We were sisters indeed, bound not only by the blood we shared, but by the things we loved. "I will too," I told her with fierce conviction. "I'll become her priestess and then I'll be a wandering hero like Atalanta."

Iphigenia crinkled her nose playfully. "You can't be both, Psyche. You'll have to pick one. But whichever you choose, I promise I'll be with you."

I was robbed of my response by a thundering voice that cut the silence of the early morning air. At the door stood my uncle Agamemnon. His eyes were bloodshot from the festivities of the night before, and a tremendous stink rose from him, the scent of unwashed flesh and alcohol.

Iphigenia drew back as he stalked toward us. "Father, I'm sorry. I—"

Crack. Iphigenia staggered back, the force of her father's slap nearly knocking her from her feet. I was aghast; my own father would never have struck me like that, not for any infraction under the sun. Instinctively, I found myself moving to stand between Agamemnon and his daughter, the shaft of an arrow clutched in my hand. Its tip was as sharp as any knife.

Agamemnon's reddened gaze turned toward me, flicking down to take in the arrow. A rumble emerged from the depths of his chest, and it took me a moment to recognize it as a low chuckle. "And what exactly are you planning to do with *that*?" Then he paused, squinting, getting a good look at my face for the first time. "Oh, I see—you're Alkaios's girl."

"I am," I replied, quivering like a bowstring pulled taut as I looked up to meet his eyes. He loomed above me, a mountain of flesh and muscle. Each of his hands was larger than my head, and a blow would send me flying.

I thought of the great bears that roamed the woods outside of Mycenae. I hadn't killed one yet, but Atalanta had promised to teach me one day. If I could learn to face a beast like that, then surely I could face my uncle, who had no fangs or claws.

Agamemnon considered me for a long moment, his gaze inscrutable. Finally, he turned his attention back to Iphigenia, who was still holding her reddened cheek. "What have I told you about playing with weapons, fool girl? You'll break something valuable. And as for you," he barked, bloodshot eyes turning to me, "my brother can raise you any way he likes, but you will leave my daughter out of it."

He grabbed Iphigenia's arm and dragged her away from me like an errant pup. I heard her murmur some vague apology, which Agamemnon ignored. As they disappeared through the door, she caught my eye and raised her free hand in a forlorn, brief farewell.

It is no surprise to me now, looking back on this incident, that a man like Agamemnon would be covetous of the little authority he possessed. His eldest brother Alkaios had inherited the state of Mycenae from their father, and his younger brother Menelaus possessed not only Sparta but Helen, the greatest beauty in the world. And what did Agamemnon have? A wife like a bitter lemon, one child who did not trust him and one too small to know any better, and an assortment of mercenaries for oath men. He didn't even have a palace of his own in which to quarter them. A sad man, when all is said and done, sad and angry, though that does not excuse what he did or what he would go on to do.

4

EROS

The moon set and the sun rose, and day followed night as surely as Zeus chased after nymphs and lesser goddesses. My boredom grew unbearable. I was sure I had seen everything worth seeing, every marvel this world had to offer.

Then came humanity.

Prometheus shaped the first humans from clay and used his own divine breath to infuse them with life. They were frail things, their appearance an imitation of our own godly forms, but far less durable. The slightest illness or injury or simple lack of maintenance could do them in, sending their souls fluttering down to Hades's realm like cold smoke. Their stories were written on a mayfly timescale, too brief for me to follow.

Despite myself, I felt a flicker of curiosity. For so long I had hidden away from the other gods, fearing how they might demand use of my gift. But perhaps love was never meant to be bestowed on gods; after all, immortality meant living forever with the consequences of one's actions. Perhaps what had been a curse among the gods might turn into a blessing among mortals. A shorter life might mean keener joys. Hadn't Ouranos and Gaia been happy for a little while?

So I tried my arrows on mortals and waited to see the results. I watched as love exalted the lowly and rendered the dull incomparably beautiful, making fragile lives sublime. But my hope soon faded. Just as it had been with gods, love also had the power to destroy in the same swift stroke. It turned the humans jealous and mournful and violent. In the end, I had only given them a new kind of madness.

But soon I realized that in humanity's hands, desire spread like wildfire. Love sprung up, persistent as a weed, in places I had never sown my arrows, in the hearts of mortals I had never even seen.

I was shaken. I had unleashed something into this world that I could not control. Had I truly thought myself to be so powerful? Was I a wielder of love, or merely one of its subjects? If I was not careful, I might fall prey to it as well, a scorpion poisoned by its own venom.

In my quest to understand, I asked Zephyrus about the nature of his own power.

Zephyrus looked at me as though I'd asked him how to breathe. "The winds are simple," he replied. "I will it, and they blow."

"But you can't possibly rule every wind that blows across the world," I replied.

"I only rule the west winds."

I scowled. "That's not what I mean."

"Then what is it you're asking?"

I shook my head, unable to explain the thought that vexed me: whether it really was I who ruled this force we called desire, or if it merely moved through me like the wind that rustled a forest of trees.

Sometimes a peculiar thing happened: The initial frenzy of desire sparked by my arrows deepened into something else, something infinitely richer and slower.

I watched as an old man and woman lay down next to each other in the same bed they had shared for decades, her back pressed into his chest, his arms holding her tight. They drifted off to sleep with a simple, calm contentment inscribed in their features. This was not the pulsing heat or urgent wanting that my arrows instilled, and yet I sensed it had somehow been the source. The emotion these two people shared held as little resemblance to desire as a sheet of papyrus does to a reed, but I understood nonetheless that desire was its foundation.

It disturbed me to think that my power might not be preeminent, that humanity had uncovered a love far stronger than the one I could give them. Even more, I loathed that these creatures enjoyed something I could not, a fruit that I would never taste.

One afternoon, Prometheus came to my doorstep. He did not cajole or threaten or demand favors, as the gods who sought me out so often did, so I invited him inside and poured him a glass of ambrosia. His name meant *foresight*, and though he was a Titan, he was well regarded even among the Olympians. He gave good advice and had an easy, endearing friendliness. It was he who had breathed life into the first humans when they were no more than clay.

Prometheus swirled the contents of his glass distractedly as I waited for him to explain why he had come.

Finally, he said, "I have gifted humanity with divine fire."

I nearly dropped my own glass. To give away what belonged only to the gods was an unspeakable act. "Zeus will not forgive this," I said gravely. "He may love you for serving him in the past, but he won't show mercy to someone who breaks his laws so blatantly."

"I know," Prometheus replied, and though we were discussing his ruin, he remained eerily serene. "My freedom was forfeit the moment I handed the humans that little flame. I am sure Zeus will find a way to make me wish for death, unobtainable as it is."

I could not understand how he spoke so calmly, as if his own eternity did not hang in the balance. "Why would you do this for them, the humans?"

Prometheus managed a weary smile. "I made them. We are responsible for what we create." He looked down toward his hands, turning the palms up and flexing his fingers, as if he could not quite believe what they had accomplished.

"Do you know what the average human life span is, Eros?" he continued, the faintest trace of a smile on his face. "Only thirty-five years. They were made—*I* made them—in the image of the gods, and yet they are nothing more than ants compared to us. If they can now go to sleep with bellies full of cooked meat instead of raw, or warm their aching bones in the winter's chill, what difference should that make to gods such as you and I?"

"You've gone mad," I told him. "Gifts to mortals can unleash consequences we never intend."

"It may be as you say," Prometheus said as he poured more ambrosia into his glass. It was likely to be the last he'd enjoy for a very long time. "But I suggest that you reassess your opinion of humanity. They are very much like us. They may even achieve godhood themselves if given the chance. I am content to have helped them along the way."

The thought of kinship with these mayflies, driven so strongly by their passions, made me flinch. *Surely we are better than them*, I wanted to say. *We are eternal, we are gods.*

Silence stretched between us, broken only by the calling of the gulls and the low thunder of the ocean waves against the shale. "Why did you come to me, then?" I asked finally.

Prometheus's eyes were a dark green that shaded toward blue. The same color as the sea that churned below us, and just as deep. "I wanted you to hear this story from my own lips, so that you might realize the value of humanity. You wield a great and terrible power, my friend, one that can change the direction of a mortal's life. You can either be their ruin or their salvation."

I almost laughed. "That's what you've come to tell me in the last hours of your freedom? To be nicer to the humans?"

Prometheus shrugged. "You may view it that way. Or you may look at it as my way of helping you prepare for your destiny."

Foresight, his name meant, and I shivered at what he might have seen. I quickly changed the subject. "Well, Zeus seems quite fond of humanity—did you hear about his new half-mortal son Dionysus? Perhaps the Thunderer will spare you."

"Perhaps," Prometheus replied with a sad smile. In it was the foreknowledge of what would come: a rocky crag and a hungry eagle and a torn-out liver, day after day without end.

Once Prometheus's sentence was carried out, I thought long on his words and turned my attention back to humanity. I wanted to know what Prometheus had seen in these strange creatures that persuaded him to accept such horrific torture on their behalf. Besides, I had little else to occupy my time.

I drifted lazily into one of their cities—Tiryns, they called it. It was little more than a large village at the time, just a cluster of houses around a central palace encircled by a low wall. The humans gathered here to trade the things that they had learned to make after receiving Prometheus's gift of sacred fire: beautiful woven cloth, rich wines, ornate jewelry of silver and gold.

A procession caught my eye, one with a gilded palanquin at its center. Inside was a young woman at that brief age when mortals seem almost as beautiful as the gods. She was dressed in exquisite finery, but her fingers tangled at the edges of her dress, worrying the fine threads of embroidery. I felt a wave of sympathy and wondered why a creature so lovely looked so sad.

I watched as the palanquin was borne to the palace, where the girl was bequeathed to a gray-bearded man. He wore a golden circlet atop his head and barked stern orders to those around him. Various actions and utterances were performed—oh, how mortals loved their rituals. I perched on the rafters, allowing my divinity to obscure me. I learned that the girl was called Anteia and the man Proetus, king of this city. When the rituals were done and the feasting finished, Proetus led Anteia to his bedchambers. He lay his old, heavy body on top of hers and heaved inexpertly until he shuddered with release, then rolled over and fell asleep. Anteia did not move, staring wide-eyed at the ceiling.

My lip curled in disgust. Desire was my realm, and this was a perversion of it. Both humans and immortals found endless ways to turn my gift into something despicable, it seemed. But perhaps there was still something to be done.

You can either be their ruin or their salvation, Prometheus said. He had wanted me to help these creatures. And I was certain such a lovely girl should know more of love than this.

And so, I sought out a more appealing candidate for Anteia's affections. I found one in Bellerophon—the son of the sea god Poseidon, born of a human woman. There were many such children born in those days, mortal like their mothers but possessed of divine gifts. He was strong, handsome, and only a few years Anteia's senior. A much better match.

As Bellerophon came to the throne room to kneel at Proetus's feet and swear his loyalty to the king, I fitted an arrow into my golden bow. I aimed it at Anteia, who was seated beside her husband.

My arrows never miss. I saw how Anteia shivered when the invisible arrow hit its mark, her veil ruffling in front of her face as she exhaled sharply. She leaned forward as Bellerophon rose. Though the veil obscured her eyes, I felt her gaze linger on Bellerophon's form as he stood and walked away. I thought she might run after him, but instead she remained seated, motionless as a statue. Once her duties were discharged, I watched as she fled back to her quarters and lay in bed as though she had a fever.

I waited for my gift to take effect, but Anteia began to avoid the feasting hall altogether, forsaking her husband's side whenever Bellerophon had news to report. She refused food and drink, growing thin and pale. I was puzzled. Had my arrows caused some kind of illness? I had never seen this happen before, but mortals were odd, and love was odder still.

One evening, to my delight, Anteia snuck away from her chambers. She wandered the corridors of the palace until she found Bellerophon in an empty hallway. She stood still, watching him, her breathing rapid. Then she stepped toward him and snaked her slender arms around his body, tilting her face up to his for a kiss.

Bellerophon pushed her away so violently she nearly fell. With an expression of utter disgust, he snarled a condemnation about her disloyalty to Proetus and stalked away.

My heart sank when I realized the extent of my miscalculation. I had assumed that a virile young man like Bellerophon would need no assistance desiring such a beautiful young woman. But I knew nothing of mortal customs and even less of the constraints of marriage.

I watched as Anteia fled to her husband Proetus's chambers. She knelt at his feet and offered a garbled version of the unfortunate encounter, one in which Bellerophon had accosted *her* in the shadowed hall. I was baffled; why should Anteia feel shame at her decisive action?

Proetus's wrinkled face flushed red with rage, and he pledged that Bellerophon would be sent to face the dreaded Chimera, a monster whose breath was white-hot flame. Surely no hero could survive such an encounter.

From a high tower in the palace, Anteia watched Bellerophon depart on his quest. Once he was out of sight, she found a long rope and affixed it to a beam in the ceiling. I watched with curiosity as she tied a loop into the rope, then dragged a chair beneath it and stood upon it. Anteia settled the rope over her collarbone like a necklace and kicked the chair away.

Horror seized me. I cast aside my concealment and rushed forward, my fingers fumbling to untie the knot. By the time I succeeded, it was too late. I held Anteia's stiffening body in my arms as her soul departed her body and flew like a stray dove down to the Underworld. I had wanted to offer her the gift of love, and instead I had doomed her to die.

Anteia's death was like a stone tossed into a still pond, leaving no ripples behind. Within a fortnight, Proetus took another wife, a princess from Ethiopia. Not long after, I watched Bellerophon ride back into the city to cheers and celebration after his victory over the Chimera, and I despised him with an intensity that made me tremble.

I was certain of one thing. Prometheus had designed humanity in the gods' image, but he had only succeeded in wrapping all our worst traits in their flimsy mortal shells. They were scheming and avaricious and cruel. My gift was wasted on them, and, furthermore, they did not deserve to be saved.

I told the story of Anteia to Gaia, whom I visited from time to time. I was the only one who ever did; the other gods had forgotten her, caught up in their own petty misadventures. But I remembered the one who had been my friend when the world was young. Even if she lay catatonic beneath the empty sky where Ouranos had once held sway, I knew she would listen.

"And then after Bellerophon left, she hung herself from the rafters," I finished. "What a waste! I do not understand it in the least."

Silence yawned. I knew better than to expect an answer, but silence yawned nonetheless. Normally I enjoyed the chance to speak freely without interruption, but today Gaia's silence perturbed me. I desperately wished that she would say something, anything, that could illuminate where I had failed. Whether Gaia missed Ouranos or hated him, I would never know. She only stared into the sky, unmoving, unfeeling, as close as a god could come to death.

Then I realized: Death was a mercy.

Death was the one thing that truly set humanity apart from the gods. Death shaped their lives and gave them purpose. Knowledge of death enabled Bellerophon to rise to unimaginable fame, for what immortal had the ambition to become a hero? And now I understood that death had freed Anteia from her suffering. There was no joy or pain in the Underworld, and the waters of the river Lethe washed away all memory.

Death brought about change, birthing untold possibilities. A human being in its lifetime might be a child, a warrior, a parent, a healer, a sage, and finally a corpse. A god could only be a god, unchanging, fulfilling its allotted functions as surely as a planet circles the sun. Death, I was certain, had been responsible in some way for the unbreakable bond between the old man and woman I had seen so long ago. They were dust now, but their peace haunted me still.

Perhaps it was my natural greed that led me to covet the one thing forbidden to me. Or perhaps it was my lingering confusion around the death of Anteia, or a compulsion to taste what she had experienced. Regardless, I was seized by a single-minded fix-ation: I wanted to know death.

I opened my veins with slivers of obsidian, though my skin knitted itself together again at once. I cast myself down from great heights, only to feel my bones crack back into place and my torn flesh heal. I drank deadly poisons, but woke from a dream-less sleep to a pounding ache in my head.

The pain was a counterbalance to pleasure, which had ruled my life up to that point until it lost all meaning. My days melted into one another, and I learned nothing from them. They were punctuated by mindless amusements: an order from Aphrodite, a visit from Zephyrus, petty backstabbing among minor gods. I pared my life down to its bare bones, to the sky and the sea and the rock. One year stretched into another, and still there was nothing that stirred my soul.

Repetition was my life back then. The dull procession of years made no impression on me, like footprints in the sand washed away by a rising tide.

5

PSYCHE

After I returned from the wedding in Sparta, two things happened.

The first was that my nurse Maia died. One day she was upright and bustling about the palace, the next she collapsed suddenly and died before sunset. Some of the servants whispered that a god had struck her down, but my mother, who was as learned as any healer after consulting so many for her own ill health, insisted that Maia's heart had always been weak. One day it had simply given up.

Whatever the cause, I went from Helen's wedding to Maia's funeral, watching the pyre devour the great soft body that I had once held so dear. Perhaps this is why love and death became so intertwined for me.

That was the first thing that happened. The second was that I became beautiful.

It happened nearly overnight. When I woke and glanced at the dim mirror in my bedroom, I was shocked at the woman's face I saw in the reflection. A narrow chin rising to full cheeks, dark eyes, and a riot of curls. I had been a skinny feral thing, but now my breasts pushed against the front of my tunic and my hips began to spread, which hindered my sense of balance and made archery practice a challenge. I began to bleed with the dark of the moon, which I found a terrible nuisance.

I was not the only one to notice these changes. Dexios would trip over himself as he took my filly's reins now, sneaking glances at me when he thought I wasn't looking. My father's oath men, never solicitous, gave me an even wider berth.

Worst of all, I received my first marriage proposal.

I wasn't told of this directly; that would have been improper. Instead, I overheard my mother and father whispering about it one evening in the garden. I had come to ask my father for fletching for new arrows, but instead I found myself frozen behind a pillar, holding my breath as I listened to their exchange.

"You must admit, it isn't a bad arrangement," my father said.

"Yes, but Psyche is so young!" my mother protested. "Don't we have a few more years with her at least?"

I was only thirteen, but many girls became betrothed by that age. My heart began to pound in my ears, and my hands gripped the pillar like claws. I crept back the way I had come, the question dead on my lips.

After that, I threw myself into my training with a renewed fervor. Gone were the days when I complained about hill sprints or sword drills; no longer was I a malingerer when the heat of the day grew too fierce. Now I completed every exercise Atalanta gave me and asked for more besides.

Atalanta noticed this. Atalanta noticed everything. She could tell an animal's temperament from the faint traces of its prints, and she could read the traceries of discontent in the human heart. She confronted me in her laconic way one night when we were camped in the woods around Tiryns.

"I will tell you a story," Atalanta said, words that never failed to command my attention, "about the hunt for the Calydonian boar."

I looked up sharply from the embers of the fire, which I had been prodding with a short stick. Around us the night lay like velvet on the earth, the dark outlines of trees arcing up against a cloudless sky scattered with stars. The air was cold, but the licking flames warmed us.

I looked expectantly at my teacher. Atalanta had been holding this particular story in reserve for years, and I was hungry for it.

"As you know," Atalanta began, "the Calydonian boar was sent by Artemis to punish the people of Aetolia. The king of that country was Meleager, and he summoned the finest hunters to take down the beast. I was one of them." A brief smile of remembered pride crossed Atalanta's face, though it soon faded. "There were those who disagreed with his choice, who claimed that the presence of a woman was unlucky. But Meleager insisted that I was an honored member of the hunting party, and this choice served him well. When the boar charged, I was the only one who didn't break and run."

I stared at my teacher, nearly forgetting to breathe. I could almost taste the pungent musk of the beast, see its bulk unfolding like a mountain come to life.

Atalanta went on. "I scaled a tree to get better aim. I hit the boar in the eye, and while it raged and blundered, Meleager cut its throat. Once I was down from the tree, I stabbed it in the heart as well. You can never be too careful with boar.

"Since it was impossible to decide who had delivered the killing blow, Meleager declared that I had drawn first blood and would receive the pelt. The other men did not like this. I had gone from being an unlucky omen to the most fortunate of them all, and they hated me for it. When I declared I would offer the pelt as a sacrifice to Artemis Far-Shooter, I thought this would settle the matter. Who can fault piety to the gods?

"But then one of the men tried to rip the pelt down." Even years later, this sacrilege still drew a sneer from my teacher. "I was on him at once. He pulled out his sword, but before he had a chance to use it, Meleager ran him through. I learned later that this man was Meleager's own cousin."

Atalanta looked at me across the fire, head tilted. Her gaze flicked over me like I was a fishing net she was trying to untangle. After a long moment, she said, "When you choose a husband—and I think the time is coming for you to do so—do not choose a man who is merely handsome or rich or powerful. Choose a man like Meleager."

I looked away, back toward the darkness, my heart sinking. This wasn't how I was expecting the story to end, and this wasn't the moral I wanted to hear. "I don't want to get married. I want to be a hero and a priestess of Artemis like my cousin Iphigenia."

Atalanta blinked in wild confusion. I think she was prepared for the confession of a childish crush or fear about leaving home; she did not expect outright refusal. "Psyche, you are the princess of Mycenae," she said. "The man you marry will become the next king of your country, and your son will inherit the throne. You have a duty to your people."

I thought of Helen, whose wedding marked the grave of all her ambitions. "My duty is to become a hero like you," I said.

"I was married once too, Psyche," Atalanta said, direct as a spear. "When things are right, love is not an obstacle to becoming a hero. It's the very reason heroes rise."

Though I knew Atalanta had a son, I'd never thought of her as a wife. I toyed with a twig as I considered this, twisting it in my fingers until it snapped. "Was Meleager your husband?"

My teacher turned her face toward the depths of the forest, the firelight casting sharp lines along her cheeks. "No," she said softly. "Meleager died soon after the hunt for the Calydonian boar. The story of how I met my husband is a tale for another day, and my mouth is already dry from talking. Rest assured that he was no less brave or virtuous than Meleager."

"It's not like it matters," I replied. "Women don't get to choose their husbands."

Atalanta scoffed. "Who told you that? Some girls get traded off, it's true, but you're the daughter of the Mycenaean king. You'll have your pick of suitors."

I sighed and hugged my knees. I thought of my mother and father, leaning toward each other in the garden like two matched trees. Perhaps marriage wouldn't be so bad when I was ready for it, but that was still many years away. "Fine. But I want to finish my training first," I declared.

"It would be a waste for us both if you didn't," Atalanta replied tartly, coaxing a small smile onto my face.

The next step, Atalanta decided, was for me to prove myself as an athlete at one of the regional competitions. These were held for young women to show off their abilities to both the gods and prospective husbands, and the greatest of them was the Heraean Games, held in honor of the goddess Hera, queen of heaven and goddess of union. There, I would compete for the winner's laurels.

I could not hide my awe when we disembarked from the ship. I had never seen so many human beings in one place, not even during Helen's wedding. There were people from Sparta, Argos, Thebes, faraway Crete, even little Athens, all of us baking together under the unyielding sun. Atalanta, who despised crowds, took refuge in her tent like a surly cat as soon as the servants set it up. I, on the other hand, scanned the assembly for a familiar face. Soon I found it.

Iphigenia waved at me from a cluster of priestesses who had come to officiate the sacred rites for the event. I ran to her, nearly knocking her from her feet with the force of my embrace. We had planned this reunion through the letters we exchanged frequently, but to see her again was a joy like no other.

"Look at you, a priestess of Artemis!" I said once we released each other, tugging playfully at her robes of office and the fillets in her hair.

"Not a full one, I'm still only in my novitiate," she corrected laughingly. "I still can't believe I got Father to agree. And look at you, an athlete and a hero!"

I was about to tell Iphigenia to save her praise for after I won, but I was distracted by the looming presence of a senior priestess behind Iphigenia's shoulder. She was broad as a hill, taller than Atalanta, probably even taller than my father. Her stern face could have been carved from granite, and she crossed her arms as she considered us.

"Iphigenia, you neglect your chores," the elder priestess chided. Behind her, I could see the others setting up tents and kindling cookfires. "Who is this?" she added, gesturing at me.

"Psyche of Mycenae, my cousin," Iphigenia replied sweetly. "And I'm so sorry about the chores, Callisto. Once Psyche leaves, I'll join at once."

That fierce glance turned toward me. "Psyche," the priestess called Callisto repeated, sounding out the syllables of my name slowly. "You are Atalanta's student, are you not?"

I nodded, not trusting myself to speak. I had thought my teacher was the most frightening woman I'd ever met, but Callisto outdid her.

The priestess nodded. "I know Atalanta by reputation. If you are her student, then you will be competing in the games today. May victory be yours. Iphigenia, join us once your conversation is finished." With a whirl, she turned back to rejoin the group.

Iphigenia grabbed my hands, giddy with delight. "From Callisto, that's as good as shore leave! Come on, let's go have some fun."

There were a few hours yet before my race; events were held in the morning and late afternoon, with a break when the sun was at its zenith and the whole world felt like a hot bath. In that moment, nothing sounded more appealing than an adventure with my cousin.

But I soon found out, to my dismay, that Iphigenia's idea of fun was sneaking conversation with a pair of boys from some backwater city in Thessaly. Their names were Achilles and Patroclus, and they were a year or two older than us. Iphigenia looked as though she might leave her position as priestess of Artemis to worship at the altar of Achilles, her wide eyes fixed on him. I never thought my clever cousin would be one of those girls who prayed to Aphrodite and her son Eros for love, but now, with a sickly feeling in my stomach, I saw things might be otherwise. I hoped Iphigenia wouldn't actually leave the order of priestesses to pursue this oaf.

I disliked Achilles at once. He had the beauty of a god and the arrogance of a prince, a distasteful combination. Besides, I hated to see my cousin act like a dog begging at the knee for scraps.

"People always say I'm intimidating," Achilles began in a lazy drawl. "But Patroclus is the one who's actually killed somebody. Just another boy, but a kill nonetheless." Achilles nudged his friend. Both were perched on the same stool, their bodies touching with easy familiarity.

Patroclus smiled good-naturedly, though there was a shadow in it. He was all salt and earth, taller than Achilles but somehow an afterthought, the last person in the room that drew your attention. "It's true. An accident during a game of dice, but it happened. Psyche, Iphigenia tells me that you'll be competing in a few hours."

Being in the company of a murderer unsettled me, but I was pleased by the change of topic. "Yes, in the footrace. But I'm not worried about winning, since I've had the best of teachers."

Achilles took notice of me for the first time, his eyes wandering down my body. "And who would that be? You certainly look like you've been trained well."

"The hero Atalanta," I replied proudly, ignoring the way my skin prickled under his stare.

Achilles stifled a laugh. "She's a second-rate hero at best. *I* was trained by Chiron himself, son of Kronos and mentor to heroes for generations. What's Atalanta done? Gone on a sailing trip and killed a pig. She never fought in a war or triumphed over the champion of an opposing army. And you know why that is," he continued smoothly, denying me an opening. "It's because she's only a mortal. All the greatest heroes have a god for a parent. It gives them an edge."

I was on my feet at once. "Not true!"

Achilles was unmoved. "There's me, for example," he continued. "My mother is the sea nymph Thetis, and you can see it in my speed. I move like sunlight on water. As for you, you look like you've got *some* immortal blood in you, but it's not recent." He eyed me skeptically.

"My father is the grandson of Zeus himself," I snapped. "Tell that to your little sea nymph mother. And I'll win today, no matter what you say." With that, I stomped out of the tent, leaving Iphigenia calling after me in dismay.

Later, when the air had cooled and the shadows were growing long, I found myself poised at the starting line beside the other runners. We did not look at one another, and certainly not at the stadium seats filled with spectators. Instead, we kept our eyes focused on the white mark in the dust—the finish line. My tendons quivered like bowstrings, and Achilles's words still rankled in my heart.

From somewhere in the crowd, I could feel Atalanta's eyes on me. She had given me only one piece of advice before the race: "*Don't lose.*"

The race began and we were off. The ground was hot as a cooking stone on my bare feet, but I moved so quickly that it didn't matter. Every time my feet struck the hard-packed earth, I imagined they were landing on that idiot Achilles's head. Another racer was gaining on me, a tall girl with hair like a raven's wing, but my native stubbornness took hold. I put one last burst of energy into my stride, and the world telescoped to nothing but the ground and my breath.

A cry went up from the crowd. I looked back and saw the white mark of the finish line far behind me.

I panted in the burning sunlight and searched the crowd until my eyes fell upon Achilles. His disappointed frown was far sweeter to me than the victor's crown of laurels.

When I was seventeen, Atalanta decreed that the time had come for the final test. I might be destined to kill a monster feared by the gods, but the beast hadn't been quick to present itself. The great monsters of ancient times, prey of earlier heroes, had all but disappeared from the world. Even prides of griffins grew rarer year after year. So when Atalanta heard of a drakonis only a few miles to the south, she declared I would meet it.

A drakonis was an enormous snake, coils upon coils of fanged menace. Atalanta and I discussed strategies to face it, though some things could only be decided in the moment. We set out in the early morning through the Lion's Gate. When I looked behind us, I saw to my surprise that a motley crew of Mycenaeans followed. They maintained a respectful distance, but their course mirrored ours unmistakably.

Atalanta did not discourage them. "They want to see what will become of their unusual princess. This is good; we'll need people to tell your story. Encouraging gossip is cheaper than commissioning poetry."

Fear flitted in my belly. If I did not succeed, they would also bring reports of my shameful failure far and wide.

My teacher and I made camp not far from the glade where the creature had been reported. By then it was late afternoon, and there was no point in going after the beast now. The hangers-on settled down some distance from Atalanta and I, close enough for us to smell their cookfires and hear their banter.

My teacher and I did not say much to each other. There was nothing to discuss; we had already made all the preparations, and now I would succeed or fail. I lay down on my bedroll as the sun slipped below the horizon. I slept poorly, my dreams haunted by images of sharp fangs and broken bones, and I woke at dawn. A pair of eyes met mine from across the tent—Atalanta was awake as well.

I knew from Atalanta that the drakonis was cold-blooded and would be sluggish in the morning. This would be my best chance to strike, when the day was still new and unformed.

My teacher helped me don my armor, a set of boiled leather. "Isn't this too flimsy?" I asked.

Atalanta was focused on tightening the lacings. "If the drakonis catches you," she said, "it won't matter what kind of armor you're wearing."

When she was finished, she took me by the shoulders. "I won't tell you not to be afraid," she said fiercely. "You won't have time for it. That creature will be on you before you can blink, and you'd better not disgrace us both by forgetting everything I taught you. May Artemis Far-Shooter bless you." With that, she sent me out of the tent.

I went alone to the monster's glade. The softness of the morning light was a gentle lie over the menace of this place and the ugliness of the task that lay ahead of me. My boots brushed through grass still wet with dew, and I knew I had arrived at the right place when I heard the singing of the birds lapse into silence. As Atalanta had taught me, this was the first sign of danger.

I climbed up the low hill and saw the drakonis sunning itself lazily in the first rays of morning. Gods, it was enormous! Why hadn't anyone told me how big it was? Indeed, it looked like an ordinary snake, but each of its fat coils was as wide as the walls of Mycenae, and its wide mouth could swallow me as easily as a man eats an olive. I could see the muscles rippling under its scales and knew with sick certainty that the drakonis could move with all the lightning speed of its smaller cousins. The creature shifted its head to drink in the sunlight and revealed a set of fangs the length of my arm. Those teeth, I knew, excreted a poison that melted stone and caused death with excruciating slowness.

Dread chilled my bones. I wondered if my legend would end before it had the chance to begin, but I quickly pushed this idea from my mind.

I scaled a nearby tree. Gripping the trunk with my legs, I pulled an arrow from my quiver and took aim at one of the drakonis's eyes, which blinked in leisurely stupefaction. I let fly, and there was a terrible scream that rattled the hills and shattered the serenity of the glade. An arrow protruding from its eye, the drakonis thrashed about in agony and cracked fragile saplings with its tail.

I took aim and fired again, registering another scream as my arrow took out the beast's remaining eye. I scrambled down the tree and pulled my sword free from its sheath, ready to finish what I had started. But I made a grave miscalculation: Like a snake, a drakonis doesn't rely on sight alone to hunt.

The beast's tongue flicked through the air and its head swung toward me, blocking the weak sunlight from the little grove. I saw those liquid muscles tense, and that was my only warning. I rolled out of the way just as the drakonis's fangs struck the place I had been standing only moments before.

I remembered my training and was on my feet in a heartbeat. I knew from Atalanta's lessons that when a snake strikes, it commits all it has to the blow. With no arms or legs, it must take a few moments to gather itself up. I had a few heartbeats, perhaps less, in which to make my move.

I swung my sword, cutting a gash in the soft flesh just behind the drakonis's head. I felt the blade skim across bone before I pulled free, and the resistance made me stagger.

A gout of blood drenched me, warm as bathwater. When I leaped free, I dashed it out of my eyes with the back of my hand, ignoring the tang of copper on my tongue. Pedaling backward, I watched the creature thrash in the dirt for a few more minutes, but slowly its movements stilled, and its eyes grew dull as old bronze. Perhaps I should have felt elated, but instead I only marveled. It had all happened so quickly.

I returned to camp with the dripping head of the drakonis, dragging it through the dirt with both hands. By then more people in the camp of hangers-on were awake, drowsily tending cooking fires. A cheer rose from them when I appeared. People I had never met before slapped me on the back and handed me cloths to wipe the blood from my face and arms. Someone pulled out a skin of unwatered wine, heedless of the early hour, and I took a swig so large that I had a headache for the rest of the day. We danced and drank and feasted on the drakonis's meat, which tasted somewhat like fish.

Atalanta came to me during the celebration. Her face, normally hard and expressionless, had broken into the most radiant expression of joy I had ever seen. She pulled me into a fierce embrace.

"You were the first student I ever took on, and you will be the last," she told me. "I will return to my forests, for I have nothing left to teach you. And don't cry!"

Her image shattered into a thousand fragments as tears filled my eyes.

The people of the camp escorted me in triumph back to the city of Tiryns, bearing the head and hide of the drakonis. Another celebration awaited me there in the gentle glow of my parents' radiant pride. When I walked through the Lion's Gate in my armor, a victor at the height of my triumph, I could hear people comparing me to manifold goddesses: Artemis for my skill, Athena for my cunning, Aphrodite for my beauty.

Of all these, it was only Aphrodite who took issue with the comparison. She never could tolerate competition.

6

EROS

One day in an endless string of days, a letter arrived at my seaside house, bearing the stink of hidden places. The cold of a lightless realm crept up my arms as I unfolded it. I knew who had sent it, and I knew at once that I would agree to her terms no matter what they were.

The request came from Persephone, queen of the dead. She wanted me to bring her the love of some mortal, a hapless hunter named Adonis who had recently been a favorite of Aphrodite herself. The two had a long-standing rivalry over some forgotten insult, and Persephone never missed the chance to slight the goddess of love.

I read the terms with interest. Though I rarely granted any favors to the gods, Persephone had the ability to fulfill my fervent wish to taste death.

I knew the rumors about her. The Underworld was barred to all the gods save Hades and his bride—and Hermes when he deigned to do his duty as psychopomp, guiding the souls of the dead—but rumors circulated nonetheless. Persephone had arrived in the Underworld shivering and alone in the back of her uncle Hades's chariot, kidnapped while picking flowers in a meadow. But even lost and terrified, she was canny. Within a week, Persephone had all the servants of Hades's palace answering to her; within a month, she had the fealty of its magistrates. In a seamless coup, Persephone took command of the bureaucracy of hell as her ineffectual husband watched. It was said that even the three-headed dog Cerberus, guardian of the Underworld, rolled belly-up at the rustle of her skirts. Hades was relegated to the shadows of his own castle.

When her mother, Demeter, demanded her return, Persephone sat at the table with her downcast husband as the messenger delivered the news. Unruffled, the goddess pulled a pomegranate from the bowl on the table and ripped it open with her bare hands, juice dribbling like blood over her fingers. In defiance of the messenger, she ate six of the jewel-like seeds that had never seen the light of the sun, binding herself to the Underworld forever. Eventually, Persephone went back to her mother, bringing a reluctant springtime in her steps. But every autumn when she returned to the kingdom of the dead, she did so with a smile.

A favor from her would be priceless beyond compare.

And so I found myself in an Anatolian forest suffused with the light of early spring, following a man named Adonis as he stalked through the underbrush. Adonis was good-looking enough for a mortal, and I could see why he had drawn the attention of not one but two goddesses. He did not look like a particularly complex man, but then again, Aphrodite did not seek complexity in her lovers. She'd adored oafish Ares, who didn't have two thoughts in his head to rub together. I knew less about Persephone's preferences, but I was sure that she preferred to keep her men securely under her heel. A dimwitted man was easier to rule than an intelligent one.

I unslung my bow and nocked an arrow, aiming carefully at the distant back. Then a sudden gust of wind nearly dislodged me from my perch, sending my arrow careening off into the treetops.

It was Zephyrus, his sky-blue eyes made luminous by tears.

"Eros! At last, I've found you. He's dead, my dear sweet Hyacinthos is dead, and I need your help."

By the time I looked back, Adonis had disappeared in the underbrush. I was forced to hop to another branch to catch sight of him again. Luckily, the mortal man's attention was entirely focused on something along the forest floor—tracks of some kind, it seemed.

Zephyrus followed me, persistent as a flea. "Didn't you hear me? Hyacinthos is dead!" he wailed again, raking his nails over the tender skin of his face and neck, leaving long red welts that soon vanished. No god bore wounds of the flesh for very long, but injuries of the heart were another matter.

"That bastard Apollo killed him," Zephyrus continued, tears carving twin tracks down his cheeks. "He was obsessed with Hyacinthos, and he couldn't stand the fact that Hyacinthos chose me. 'If I can't have him, no one can, certainly not Zephyrus.' That's what Apollo said, one of his own nymphs told me so! He shone the sun in my sweet Hyacinthos's eyes in the middle of a game, and the lad missed a throw. The discus cracked his skull like an egg." This was followed by a fresh gale of weeping.

I recognized Hyacinthos as the name of Zephyrus's most recent lover, a handsome mortal youth. Zephyrus never stopped chattering about him during visits to my seaside house. "I'm sorry to hear it," I told my friend. "But you must have known what you were getting yourself into when you fell in love with a mortal. I don't know what you expect me to do about your situation."

"You're the only one who can fix it!" he cried. "Now that my beautiful boy is dead, all the love I had for him is nothing but a burden. I beg you to undo your work. Pull your arrow from my heart," Zephyrus finished, pulling aside his tunic to bare his hairless chest.

"I never shot you," I said flatly. "You know that."

Zephyrus's love was one of those that had occurred without my active intervention. There had been more and more such cases: love springing up where I had planted no seeds, aimed no arrows. There were now so many mortals and gods in the world that I could not possibly strike them all myself, and yet they continued to fall headfirst into desire. It unnerved me, that even as I retreated from the world, my curse had taken root and continued to flourish. Despite this, of course, mortals and gods alike continued to blame me for their ill-favored love affairs.

Zephyrus gazed at me helplessly, his lower lip trembling.

"There's nothing I can do to help you," I said. "What gave you the impression, over our many years of friendship, that I have the ability to heal hearts?"

"You *must* be able to do something. You're the god of desire."

"And what I desire right now is for you *to be quiet*." I turned back to follow Adonis's progress through the undergrowth. Fortunately, something else continued to draw his attention away from the caterwauling in the treetops.

I fitted another arrow into my bow and took aim. At least I could still concentrate my will when it suited me, aiming arrows that would have a sure result. I saw that the mortal hunter had taken his own weapon in hand—a stout spear with a long cross-guard—and his attention was focused on something in the brush. A boar! I could see its beady black eyes through the leaves. It let out a squeal of alarm when it noticed its pursuer and shifted its bulk, pawing the ground.

Now was my chance. I let fly, my arrow piercing Adonis's back and dissolving at once into the ether. A strange, wistful expression crossed his face, as though he had drunk too much wine. He must have been thinking of Persephone—how beautiful she was, how much he longed for her, although he had never seen her face.

The boar chose that moment to charge.

I tried to call out a warning, but it was too late. I winced; there was a lot of blood. It seemed that Persephone would be welcoming her new lover sooner than anticipated.

When I returned to my seaside house that night, Aphrodite was waiting. She sat in one of my plush armchairs, raising a glass of ambrosia to her red lips. One of my cats was nestled on her lap. The beast had the audacity to turn its sleepy half-lidded gaze toward me as it purred under my adoptive mother's delicate hand.

I readied my excuses. I hadn't meant to kill poor Adonis, but mortals had an unfortunate tendency to die without warning, and those with dangerous hobbies like hunting wild beasts died even sooner. Aphrodite could pin nothing on me.

"I need a favor," Aphrodite said in dulcet tones. "As you have begun to ignore my letters, I thought I'd pay you a visit. I need you to use your skills on a particular girl from Mycenae."

Nothing about Adonis. She must not yet know. Well, I was happy to play along.

"A potential lover?" I asked, my tone easy and innocent. "I did not think you cared for women, Mother. Especially ones who rival you in beauty."

I watched with gratification as the false sweetness melted from Aphrodite's face like the wax of a long-burnt candle. "It's not that, you insolent fool. She's an arrogant little creature who thinks she's better than the gods, and she needs to be put in her rightful place." Aphrodite's hands tensed into claws, making the gray cat shift uneasily in her lap. "She hasn't even offered any sacrifices at my shrines, and *all* mortal girls her age do *that*."

"This hardly seems like a major crime," I noted.

Aphrodite's eyes, rimmed by thick lashes, narrowed. "We can't let the mortals get out of line, or everything will truly be lost. *Apotheosis* might even turn those sniveling meat bags into one of us. Have you not heard of Zeus's new cupbearer, Ganymede? That old lech took a fancy to some mortal youth, and now this Ganymede waits on Zeus in Olympus, eternal as any of us." Aphrodite's full lips peeled back from her teeth in a sneer, as though she would rather share divinity with a slug.

I thought again of what Prometheus had told me. *They may even achieve godhood themselves if given the chance.* My heart ached at the thought of a mortal giving up the gift of death in favor of this wasteland of eternity.

I heaved an exaggerated sigh. "How very like you to use my arrows as a punishment rather than a blessing. And if I agree, what do I get out of it?"

A tense silence followed. I waited as Aphrodite appraised the situation, calculating how far she could push me before I balked. I was her vassal, and she could order me to enact her will without recompense, but that was not in keeping with the balance of power that had developed between us. She had chosen to call me her son, not her slave.

"A favor," she finally replied, leaning back in the chair. "Perform this task for me, and the goddess of love herself will owe you a favor. Within reason," she added hastily.

It was useful to have a goddess in your debt. I already had one boon from Persephone, but I would happily accept another from Aphrodite. "I accept your terms," I said.

"Excellent!" Aphrodite cried, her good humor returning. "Now give me one of your arrows." She held out her palm, waiting.

I pulled one from the quiver at my waist and offered it to her. She rolled the wooden stem between her fingers, then lowered her face to whisper to the fletching. A haze of darkness surrounded the arrow, and I felt the chill of magic in the air. All our kind know how to perform magic as easily as breathing. But I had not seen such a powerful display since Gaia carved my home from the bones of her earth, and I had not seen one so ugly since Eris worked her first cruel intrigues.

"There!" Aphrodite said, handing the arrow back to me in a flourish. Its surface had blackened, and I felt a sense of unease when I touched it. I hurried to place it back among its fellows in my quiver.

Aphrodite smiled, pleased with her work. "Now it carries a powerful curse of my own creation. When the girl is struck, she will fall helplessly in love with the first person she sees. And, even better, when she finally approaches her beloved and they look upon each other's faces, they will be separated forever. The curse will split them apart like a flame drives away shadow. Imagine it—to forever crave what you can never have!" She picked up the glass of ambrosia and took a satisfied sip.

I nodded, unimpressed. Tormenting mortals did not appeal to me as a pastime, but a deal was a deal. "How will I find this unfortunate girl?" I asked. "What is her name?"

"She is called Psyche, the princess of Mycenae."

"Psyche," I said, tasting the name. It was an unusual one.

Aphrodite cocked her head. "Do you not think my curse is very clever? Now she will never have a chance at happiness."

"Hmm. It seems I was right after all," I replied dryly. "This girl must be very beautiful indeed to earn your ire, even more beautiful than you."

The glass soared through the air and shattered against the rock wall mere inches from my head. Aphrodite stood, causing the cat to bolt from her lap and hide beneath the table. I stayed still as she stomped past me to the thrown-open window overlooking the sea.

"See that it is done," she warned, voice as black as the arrow that lay in my quiver.

Aphrodite hurled herself into the air in the shape of a dove and did not look back.

I sidestepped the broken pieces of glass, unbothered. They would tidy themselves in a moment through the magic of the house.

I wasn't worried about the cat either. That little traitor could use a lesson in loyalty.

In the quiet hours before dawn, I settled onto the branch of a tree outside the Mycenaean palace. I had spotted the sleeping mortal Psyche through the window of her bedroom. She was pretty enough, I supposed, though the effect was somewhat ruined by the fact that her mouth hung open as she snored, and drool stained her pillow.

The memory of Anteia intruded into my consciousness. This was the same city where she had once lived, though it was almost unrecognizable after so many years. Psyche was nearly the same age Anteia had been when she ended her own life, a fact that made me heave a deep sigh. All mortals were the same in the end, indistinguishable from one another. All would pass into the realm of death soon enough. It was unfortunate that Psyche had become the subject of Aphrodite's rage, but there was no reason to bemoan her fate. I unslung my bow and reached for the cursed arrow in my quiver.

In all the millennia I'd lived, I had never fumbled with an arrow—not once, then or since. Never had an arrow's point so much as grazed my skin. But on that day, I felt a prick of pain. I looked down, not understanding how my hand had missed the blackened shaft and instead closed around the sharp tip. When I pulled back, I saw that the arrowhead had made a thin cut along the pad of my finger.

A single drop of golden ichor wept from my skin and fell upon a leaf. The cursed arrow, its purpose fulfilled, vanished as though it had never been.

My wound healed in an instant, but the damage was already done. I looked up, and my gaze fell upon the sleeping form of Psyche. Had I thought her merely pretty? No, she was the most radiant creature I had ever seen, god or mortal. Her tangled hair fanned out like the rays of the sun, and even the pool of saliva on her pillow was sweeter to me than the rarest honey—

"Oh," I whispered. "Fuck."

I fled at once from the Mycenaean palace, though I could not escape the horror that consumed me. I knew the symptoms, having caused them so often in others. Obsessive thoughts, racing heart, general malaise. All the elements of lovesickness. But I'd never experienced them *myself* before, and it was worse than I had ever imagined.

It felt like starvation, though I had never known hunger. It was like an itch I could not reach, like longing for a place I had never been. Every moment drove needles of the wickedest kind into my soul. My self-imposed solitude had been its own kind of oblivion, and that fragile peace was now destroyed. With the intensity of a lightning strike, the curse had destroyed the protective cocoon of isolation I'd built around myself for centuries. Now I wandered through the blasted wasteland, utterly exposed.

I hoped, as the days and weeks passed, that the feeling would fade. Sometimes desire did that, evaporating like dew on leaves. But the days went on, and the gnawing curse inside me only continued to grow.

My predicament was a dangerous one. There was no chance

my affection would be requited, since the curse would separate Psyche and I should we ever come face-to-face. Lovesickness was a horrible fate, especially for a god who might go on yearning for all eternity without any hope of relief. I might end up like Narcissus, who fell in love with himself so completely that he had to be turned into a flower to be worth anything at all.

When ignoring the curse did not work, I tried to drown it. I charmed the oceanids in the seas beyond my cliffs and the dryads in the forests, and led them to my bed with giggles and coy smiles. They were flattered to receive the attentions of a primordial god—they would brag about it to their sisters, no doubt, showing off the golden bracelets I gave them as gifts. Such minor goddesses were always jockeying for position and would quickly seize any advantage they were offered. But I found myself cold in their embraces. The perfection of their immortal beauty did not arouse me, and our coupling was mechanical and uninspiring. I closed my eyes for much of it, dreaming up Psyche's face instead.

It was like contenting myself with water when all I wanted was the rich taste of ambrosia, though even that fine vintage felt dead on my tongue. The pale imitation brought only a sharper sense of what I lacked. Eventually I resigned myself and ceased to summon any more companions to my seaside house. Without any release, desire wrapped like a noose around my throat and pulled tight.

I began to spend most of my time in sleep, which was the only reprieve I could find from this vortex of longing. I even removed the windows from my bedchambers so that the sun would not wake me. Only through the emptiness of sleep could I forget the all-consuming curse.

But then dreams of Psyche began to haunt me—her dark hair, the curve of her hips, the flash of her eyes—and I was pulled back into the waking world once more.

Psyche's presence drew me like a lodestone. I found myself

drifting back to Mycenae and its environs, hoping to catch sight of her. I glimpsed her at archery practice, all her attention focused on the target. Muscles moved like water under her skin as she drew back the string, her lovely eyes narrowing as she took aim. Her feet were planted firmly on the earth, sandals lacing up her delicate ankles.

When my eyes fell upon her, the howling of the curse eased into blessed silence for just a moment, though it came thundering back with even crueler intensity. Stolen glances weren't enough; I wanted to know Psyche, to hold those delicate ankles in my hands, to hear the melody of her voice speaking my name. But I did not dare to push further. It was a mercy that the curse was only half-active, and to unleash its full power did not bear thinking about. If Psyche looked into my eyes, I would never see her again.

Months passed and my torture went on. I wondered if I should call in my favor from Persephone, who owed me for Adonis, but the thought of dying had lost its luster. Death might have brought relief for Anteia, but it would do nothing for me. All I craved was Psyche, and I would go on craving her even in the lightless Underworld. Such was the nature of Aphrodite's curse.

There was someone who might offer me assistance, who helped those beyond all other help. Hekate, goddess of witchcraft and sorcery. Older than the sun and moon, mistress of the crossroads. She lived beyond life and death, dwelling deep within the forest in a hut that rested on chicken feet. Hekate would know how to remove the curse. She must. But I thought of what she might ask for in return and shuddered.

Another idea lit upon me. Aphrodite had forged this curse, and as far as she knew, the blighted arrow had been delivered to its intended target. She owed me a favor, did she not? Perhaps she could offer a cure.

I visited Aphrodite's abode on the slopes of Olympus, where

the spires of towers lost themselves in a low wreath of silver clouds. I worried that she would smell the lovesickness on me at once, but I had no other options.

The goddess received me in her bath, where she lay resplendent among the foam. I was relegated to standing awkwardly at the edge of the pool while attendant nymphs combed out her hair and kneaded the tension from her shoulders, all while sneaking glances at me from under their lashes and snickering to one another.

Aphrodite clapped her hands with glee when I relayed the news of my success. "Oh, tell me more! Who did the Mycenaean princess fall for? An elderly porter? A shit-caked stable boy? It must have been some months ago now, but I want to hear all about it."

"I did not stay to find out," I lied smoothly, trying to summon the bland disinterest she was used to seeing from me. "You told me to shoot the girl, not eulogize her. I've done what you asked. Now I want to claim the favor you owe me."

She moved closer to the edge of the bath where I stood and propped her elbows on the lip of the tub. Her hair was slicked back, all the better to accentuate the sharpness of her cheekbones. She looked up at me with dark eyes, the curves of her breasts rising above the foam like twin images of the full moon over the hills. I thought of Psyche, and knew that if Aphrodite guessed what had truly transpired, the girl's life was forfeit.

"And what favor would you have me grant?" Aphrodite asked.

I kept my voice steady. "I need an antidote for lovesickness."

Aphrodite raised one perfect eyebrow, eyes slitted with suspicion. "An antidote?" she replied with an uncertain laugh. "Why would you want that?"

My mind raced. "For Zephyrus," I replied. "He is still in love with a mortal who died."

A flicker passed over Aphrodite's face, but it was soon gone. "That's a pity. But you understand, don't you, that I can't simply give away antidotes to lovesickness? The agony of love is what makes our power so strong. What use would our magic be if any fool could cure their broken heart?" One corner of her mouth curled, as wicked as a fishhook.

"You promised me a favor," I replied. "I upheld my end of our bargain. Would you break your word?"

Aphrodite drifted back to the other side of the pool, studying me through narrowed eyes. I felt as though all my secrets were scrawled across my skin. At any moment, I was sure, she would know what I had done. The death of Adonis, the markedly *un*-cursed state of Psyche, the feverish dreams that would not abate. Somehow Aphrodite would know of my deceptions and punish me for them.

But instead, Aphrodite raised a graceful arm above the water, revealing a small crystal bottle in her hand. Without warning, she threw it toward me, and I watched the only object that could save me arc through the perfumed air. I scrambled to catch it before it shattered against the stone floor, sagging with relief when it landed in my outstretched palm.

Heart pounding, I bowed in thanks and made my exit. I knew I should wait until I was safely within my own home, but the temptation of relief was too strong. I made it to the relative seclusion of a hallway outside Aphrodite's chambers and stared down at the object in my hands. The glittering vial was no larger than my thumb, filled with a liquid as clear as water and corked with a jeweled stopper. In it lay the remedy to the torment that had dogged me for months, a balm to break my fever. I pulled the stopper from the bottle with trembling fingers and swallowed its contents in a single gulp. It was sweet, with a finish that fizzed on my tongue. Tension unspooling from my shoulders, I leaned against the wall, and—

Felt no change in the warmth that bloomed in my chest whenever I thought of her. Psyche.

I threw the bottle against the stone wall, watching dully as it fragmented into a thousand shards. I should have known that the antidote would be useless. It might have worked on the pain of ordinary heartbreak, but not a curse from Aphrodite's own hand. My misery had no cure.

Aphrodite may not have noticed the change in me, but my old friend Zephyrus did.

Zephyrus had welcomed himself into my house with the western breeze, and we sat together on the wide terrace that overlooked the ocean, beneath a sunset that painted the sky in wild shades of red and gold. Zephyrus, though, was not looking at the sunset; he was looking at me. He crouched on the chair next to mine, forearms resting on his knees, staring at me with the same intensity as the cats when I was about to offer them food.

"What's wrong with you?" he demanded. "You've been acting odd for some time now, but I've never seen you like this. All wilty, like a dying flower." He grimaced. "Are you ill? Sometimes Hyacinthos acted like this when he was ill, but I never imagined it could happen to a god. I can't catch it, can I?"

I glared at him dully. "No. It's just . . ." I waved a hand. The curse was like a poison draught in my limbs, thwarted longing weighing me down like a millstone.

The intensity of my suffering was too much to bear in silence any longer. I had to tell someone what had happened. I would go mad if I didn't. I had known Zephyrus since the beginning of the world. Surely I could trust him.

"I'm in love," I told Zephyrus.

He screeched like an owl and nearly fell off his chair.

I relayed the series of events that began with Aphrodite's

request for a favor and ended with the destruction of the useless vial. When I was finished, Zephyrus pinned me with an expression better suited to his brother Boreas, god of the frigid north winds.

"So you *did* have an antidote to lovesickness," he said very slowly, chilling the air between us. "And instead of giving it to me, your dearest friend, in my hour of terrible need while I mourn my beloved Hyacinthos, you drank it yourself. Knowing that you were cursed by the goddess of love herself and there was no help for you."

"Didn't you hear anything I said?" I implored. "I am in misery. I cannot sleep, or taste anything that touches my tongue, or feel joy at any touch that isn't hers. And I will never have her, because the curse will only force us apart."

"Ah, yes," Zephyrus replied, crossing his arms. "How horrible to never see your beloved again."

I glared at him, enraged at his dismissal of my suffering. "Stop being so selfish. You might have lost your mortal pet, but this one still lives. Help me!"

I was familiar with Zephyrus's many moods—his pranks, his pettiness. If I hadn't been so thoroughly consumed with my own anguish, I would have known the provenance of that mischievous glint in his eyes. But on that day, I was distracted by thoughts of Psyche. I did not notice the wicked smile that crossed his face as he replied in a silken tone, "Fear not, I know just what to do."

7

PSYCHE

A year had passed since the slaying of the drakonis, and I had very little to show for it. Now and then a nest of griffins needed to be cleaned out or a deer hunt held to fill the palace tables, but such things did not make a hero. I rose every day to move mindlessly through the exercises Atalanta had taught me and waited for the day my destiny would come.

One day, my parents summoned me to their chambers for a private dinner, and we sat at a small table set just for the three of us. I watched them over the rim of my goblet as I drank my wine. Both my mother and father were sneaking quick glances at each other and hiding smiles behind their hands, seeming more like excitable children than august rulers. I puzzled at the reason for this behavior. Had a monster been sighted? Had the day to fulfill my prophecy come at last?

"Dearest daughter," my father said, beaming. "It is my pleasure to announce that we have found a husband for you."

The wine nearly slipped from my grip. "What?"

"A royal husband," my mother echoed, the smile enlivening her pallid face. "Nestor, King of Pylos. You have known him since you were young."

My mouth hung open and cold panic rang in my ears. "*Nestor*? But he's *old*."

My mother winced but did not disagree. Nestor was in his

fifties, while I was only eighteen. I had seen him at several dinners of state throughout the years, and even when I was a child his hair and beard had been gray. While Nestor might have been a virile man in his youth—and he was renowned for droning on at length about his past exploits—those glorious days were long behind him.

"Besides, does Nestor not already have a wife?" I asked. "He has a dozen children."

My parents glanced at each other. Clearly, they had anticipated a more enthusiastic response. "Nestor's wife passed into the realm of Persephone last year," my mother finally said. "But he seeks to marry again, to ease his loneliness."

I remembered Helen and her bitter tears as she was carried away to her husband's bed. My flesh curdled at the thought of Nestor's wrinkled fingers touching me in such a way.

"I'm not going to be a sop to some old man's loneliness," I snarled.

My father's face fell. "Psyche, mind your manners! Nestor is renowned for his gentleness and wise counsel. He has promised to permit you to continue your training after marriage, provided it does not interfere with your duties as a wife. And he already has an heir from his prior marriage, so your sons would be able to ascend the throne of Mycenae unfettered. You could even stay here in Tiryns for part of the year. Isn't that wonderful?"

I stared at my father as I contemplated the dissolution of my world. *Is this all I am to you?* I wanted to scream. *A link in the chain of succession? You held me when I was fresh from my mother's womb, you called me after your own soul and set me on the saddle before you during the hunt. Are you really going to force me into an old man's bed?*

My hands balled into fists. "I will not marry Nestor," I declared.

My mother gave a little cry of dismay, and my father placed his goblet down hard, sloshing the wine. He opened his mouth to speak but my mother held a hand up to stop him.

"Psyche, my dear daughter," she began. "You are young and know little of the world, but Nestor is an excellent match. You will not find a better one. He knows of the prophecy and has promised that you will enjoy a level of freedom in marriage that few women do. Besides, all of Mycenae will benefit from the alliance with Pylos."

"Ah, now I see the true reason you made this match," I replied sardonically.

My father brought his hand down on the table, making the plates jump. "That is enough!" he declared. "The contract is as good as signed. You will do your duty." I knew I must have pushed him very far indeed to provoke this rare display of anger, but I did not care. I pushed back my chair and stormed to my personal chambers.

Later that night, I sat by my window. Beyond the palace was the city of Tiryns, and past that was the road that led to Pylos. I tried to imagine departing down that road for the last time as an unmarried woman, never again able to remake the journey without the explicit permission of the man who called me wife, and I gritted my teeth at the thought.

Eventually, I heard the door creak open, followed by footsteps that came to a halt behind my shoulder.

"I know you are upset," my mother said. "But you must understand that your father and I have your best interests at heart."

I did not reply. Anger stuck in my throat like a chicken bone, though I did not doubt that my parents loved me.

"I was afraid before my marriage too," she continued. "Terrified, even. Who wouldn't be afraid, to leave her home and everyone she has ever known? But my match suited me well, and I only wish for you to have the same."

I understood. Seeing my parents together, his head bent toward hers, you would think they had been made for each other. Even Atalanta had once been married to a man she respected. There were things about marriage that anyone would want—a companion to keep you warm at night, someone to share joys and sorrows—but there were other things in life I wanted far more. Could I only have one and not the other?

Longing twisted my guts like a rag, an undertow that pulled me toward some fathomless desire.

"Just don't let it be Nestor," I said at last.

My mother laid a warm palm on my shoulder and smiled conspiratorially. "I have some other candidates in mind. All shall be well, my dear daughter."

After she left, I continued to stare out the window as night laid its cloak upon the city, where a hundred cookfires sparkled like stars fallen to earth. I imagined fleeing from the palace and disappearing into the wilderness. Perhaps I would find Atalanta again. Perhaps Iphigenia and I could run away together, as we had dreamed as children.

But destiny has its ways of finding us, one way or another. The next morning, mine came for me.

The survivors claimed that the monster came on a gust of wind the likes of which no one had seen before, destroying one of the small villages on the outskirts of Mycenae. Houses were uprooted and thrown into the air like children's toys. Families were scattered as they ran in terror. And yet, as the survivors staggered through the gates into the capital of Tiryns, no one could explain what the creature looked like. It was as if the beast were made of air.

A letter arrived by messenger hawk at the palace, purportedly written by this very monster. An outlandish claim that might have provoked incredulity, were it not for the undeniable fact of the leveled houses, the ruined fields. My father locked himself behind heavy wooden doors with the letter, but I managed to discover its contents by bribing one of the palace slaves. I knew the price the letter laid out for freedom from future attacks: that the princess Psyche should meet the monster alone on a peak outside of Tiryns.

I strode to the room where my father met with his counselors and threw open the door, which thudded against the stone wall. Alkaios and one of his advisors sat up like two boys startled at a game of dice. The advisor looked at me as though I had interrupted him in the privy, shock warring with indignation on his features. My father, on the other hand, seemed stricken. We had not spoken since our discussion about my engagement the evening before.

"Let me face the monster, Father," I said.

Alkaios blanched.

The advisor looked thoughtful, hazarding a glance at my father. "It would be best not to stretch our troops too thin," he pointed out. "In the event of Dorian raiders. If we can eliminate this threat without losing warriors, that would be to the benefit of all."

"We don't know who or what is responsible for this threat," my father began. He frowned, deepening lines etched into his face by a lifetime of care and worry. "It could be a trap or worse. We cannot offer up a member of the royal family like a lamb upon an altar, especially so soon after her betrothal. Besides, what kind of monster writes a letter?"

"Some sphinxes are remarkably literate. And, Father," I said, trying to keep my tone even, "remember the Oracle's prophecy."

My heart beat like a drum of war. Here at last was the monster whose death would secure my fame—here at last was my destiny. I knew it as surely as I knew my own name.

Understanding dawned on my father's face, though there was no joy in it. Exultation sung in my veins, and I already could hear the songs the blind poet would weave about me. But my father looked at me with desperate sorrow, as though he feared he would never see me alive again.

I decided to don the same armor I'd worn against the drakonis. It had served me well then, and it would be a fine choice for this new enemy—even if I was not yet sure what it might be. Securing the straps without Atalanta's help was a challenge, but I managed. I slipped my sword into the belt at my waist and headed to the grand doors of the palace.

My mother and father were waiting for me. Despite my lingering anger at their plans for my betrothal, they seemed so tender and precious that I wanted to weep. When had my parents, always so strong and solid in my mind, become old? My mother bent against my father's arm, frail as an autumn leaf. My father anxiously stroked his beard, where white hairs had begun to outnumber black.

Before I had a chance to speak, they embraced me. I closed my eyes and breathed them in deeply—my father always smelled of woodsmoke and leather, my mother of medicinal herbs. When they released me, Alkaios laid a hand of blessing upon my head.

"May victory be yours, daughter," he said.

I could only nod, not trusting myself to speak.

To my surprise, a crowd was waiting for me on the palace steps. There were men young and old, curious children, and even a few women veiled modestly against the eyes of the crowd. As I stepped out into the courtyard, their eyes turned on me expectantly. I raised my hand in greeting and they erupted into cheers.

The crowd followed me as I journeyed on, through the gates of the city and across the empty plains of Tiryns. At last, I came to the place where the hills rose out of the flat earth, giving way to forested hills. I drew closer to a single ragged peak that pierced the sky like the bones of Gaia splitting the earth. I had passed by this place during my travels with Atalanta, but she had always made a point to avoid it, saying there was no game to be found near such a barren place. Palace gossip told even darker legends: It was said that old women sacrificed puppies to the goddess Hekate there on the nights of the new moon, and lovesick maidens occasionally threw themselves from its peak. This was where the monster would meet me, where I would make my final stand.

Well, I was neither a puppy nor a lovesick maiden. I strode forward to meet my destiny.

The path was narrow and rocky, and I skidded backward on pebbles more than once as I made the ascent. The heat of the sun rested on me like a blanket of molten gold. The wind rattled the arrows in my quiver and whipped my hair around my face. Most of the townsfolk who had followed me this far faltered back, I was disappointed to see. When I finally reached the cliff's edge, I braced myself for the first sight of my enemy. Would it be a gorgon with writhing snakes for hair, or a great sphinx with a lion's body?

Instead, I was greeted only by emptiness. Wind blew up from the drop below, whisking across my face. There was no sign of a monster.

I looked back toward the scattered observers who waited behind me, suddenly feeling self-conscious. What story would they tell of this day, when the princess Psyche was spurned by a monster?

I unsheathed my sword and sent my voice ringing. "I am Psyche of Mycenae, and I have come in answer to your challenge!"

Distant echoes of my voice were the only response. I lowered my sword, feeling the heat rise to my cheeks.

A gust of wind ruffled my clothing, then became a gale. It whipped my hair and tugged at my garments, then grew fiercer still. It tore the sword from my hand, flinging it end over end. A sudden weightlessness seized me as I felt my feet rise from the earth. The wind tumbled me through the air like a stone in the surf. When I righted myself, I saw the shocked faces of the onlookers shrinking to pinpoints as the earth fell away below me.

A scream rose in my throat, but I bit it back; screaming wouldn't do me any good. I struggled to assess my situation. No talons gripped my flesh, no teeth pierced my armor. I was simply floating, as if through water. No monster that I knew of could cause such a thing, but I concentrated on fishing my knife out of my boot just in case.

"Stop wriggling around. It makes it much harder to carry you."

The voice seemed to come from everywhere and nowhere all at once. It was male, lilting, but filled with irritation. I whipped my head around, desperately seeking its source.

"Who are you?" I demanded. "Who sent you?"

There was no response, only empty air and silence. All I could do was marvel as the coastline sped past beneath me. Above, plush clouds dappled the blue horizon like a herd of sheep in a meadow. Gooseflesh prickled across my skin from the stinging cold, but my exhilaration warmed me. I watched as entire villages flashed by below my feet, tiny as the civilizations of insects. To my left, sunlight glittered like stars across an endless sheet of water. Awe filled me; even if these were to be my last moments, at least I would die seeing things no mortal eye ever had.

After what felt like hours but was only a few minutes, I found myself sinking toward the earth. My heart pounded, and I braced myself for a painful fall, but to my surprise my feet were placed upon the ground gently. I was standing on a shale-covered beach, tumbled by the sea.

Then the bodiless voice spoke once more. "Go to the one who awaits you," it said. "He will arrive at nightfall."

I had no idea where I was, save that it was very far from Mycenae. I looked up toward the cliffs and saw a dwelling above me. The curved terraces seemed almost like natural formations protruding from the stone, but their perfection suggested they had been made by a conscious intelligence rather than natural forces. Soaring verandas overlooking the sea melted into the cliff's edge, and perfectly square windows were cut directly into the pale rock. It was as if the house had been carved directly from the cliffside, just as seawater chisels caves and inlets along the shore.

Where had I found myself? What sort of hands made such a place? I shivered and reached for my sword before I remembered it was gone.

A stairway led up to the distant abode, the steps cut into rock worn smooth by long ages.

Go to the one who awaits you, the mysterious voice had said. I didn't have much of a choice; there was nowhere else to go. Not knowing whether to expect a monster or a miracle, I began my ascent.

The climb was steep and long, and the midday sun bore down until rivulets of sweat dripped into my eyes. I flicked them away with the back of my hand. This journey was interminable, I groused to myself. Whoever lived here must have wings.

When I reached the top, I passed through a courtyard lined with potted plants in full flower, and a trill at my elbow made me jump. I turned to see a beautiful blue-green peacock staring at me before turning to peck at seeds on the ground. A long, magnificent tail dragged behind the bird, each of the patterned eyes glinting in the sun. More peacocks wandered the courtyard, and I wondered if they were a clue to the identity of the owner of this strange house. Peacocks were sacred to the goddess Hera, but as far as I knew she dwelled on Mount Olympus with her inconstant husband, not here on a desolate beach.

At last, I reached the entrance to this grand, mysterious house—a heavy oak door reinforced with iron and set into the rock. I tested the door, but it remained firmly locked. The noonday sun was relentless, burning my skin and drying my parched throat. I needed shelter, there was no way around it. I knocked in the door with a firm kick, splintering the portion that anchored the lock. This was a breach of *xenia*, the sacred laws of guest-friendship, but I hoped the inhabitants of this peculiar house would understand.

Once my eyes adjusted to the dimness, I peered into the depths of the house and was greeted by the sight of a tabby cat lounging in a plush chair. He mewed in inquiry at the sight of me, leaping from his perch to twine around my legs, purring like a hive of happy bees. I reached down to scratch his head, feeling oddly reassured. A cat so friendly must be accustomed to peace and safety. Perhaps this was the home of some kindly hermit or a cloistered mystic.

I continued my exploration, marveling at the beauty of the place. The whitewashed walls rose up around me, curving into a domed ceiling like the belly of some enormous creature. As I passed through an arched doorway, I let my hand skim across the frame; the stone was smooth as a child's cheek, unblemished by a single mark from a carver's tools. I could see other rooms spread out through the interior of the cliffside like a rhizome. To my right were wide windows cut into the stone, open to catch the breezes. Higher up were squares of colored glass set high into the rock, lighting up the interior of the cave-house with magnificent spills of blue and red and yellow.

One might imagine that a house carved into a sea cliff would be damp and musty, but this one was bright and cozy, smelling of fresh salt air and the faint scent of roses on the terraces outside. My feet whispered across carpets of stunning quality, woven with vibrant patterns I had never seen before. Not a single snarl or stain marred their perfection.

I saw no sign of the resident of this place. No clothing had been hung out to dry, no discarded plates waited to be washed. I passed a room with a long wooden table, the chairs drawn neatly around it, set before a large window overlooking the cerulean water. In another room, darker with no windows, I found a large bed made up with fresh linen sheets. In the next room I found a freshly drawn bath; steam wafted from its surface, where newly-plucked rose petals floated.

It was a poet's imagining of a house, a place that could only exist in the wildest of dreams. I could not find a single flaw—not a speck of mold or crack in the ceiling. Who lived here? Who commanded such wealth?

When I passed by the room with the great table again, I gasped. Only moments before the table had been empty. Now a feast had been laid out: a glistening roast lamb, wrapped grape leaves, three different kinds of bread, and brightly colored roasted vegetables. Such a spread could only have been prepared by a large staff working in a noisy kitchen and carried in by bustling servants, but the yawning silence of the seaside house remained undisturbed.

I had not eaten since that morning. My stomach sent up a growl like the cry of a wolf, and I glanced around. Well, if there was no one to claim this untended feast, then I would. I fell on it at once, tearing the bread with my hands and using it to scoop up the rest. I drank from the ewer of clear sweet water until it dripped down my chin.

When I'd had my fill, I sat up and contemplated my situation. Could this be Nestor's doing? What if my opposition to the marriage resulted in my kidnapping? But this was certainly not Pylos, and no royal abode would be empty of guards or attendants.

I wandered back the way I'd come, planning to inspect the perimeter of the property once more. With a shock, I realized that the door I had broken down upon my arrival was back on its hinges, the wood unsplintered and whole. The hair on the back of my neck prickled as I ran my hands over the fine-grained wood in disbelief. A repair like this would have taken days, if it could be accomplished at all.

I should have been terrified, though this place was too tranquil to inspire fear. Yet I could not forget that it had been a monster's threat that lured me here. I could not let my guard down; I had to remain alert.

I sat by the window and watched as the sun sank down to the distant horizon. Shadows lengthened and vibrant colors drained to muted tones. I resigned myself to the increasingly clear reality that I would spend the night in this strange place. Better here than in the wilderness, although who knew what the dark would bring.

I began to formulate a plan. I'd seen a small firepit on the terrace with a poker nearby. I padded through the shadowed halls and snatched the rod up, then brought it into the windowless bedroom with me. At least here there was only one point of entry.

I closed the door and shoved a low trunk in front of it. If

someone tried to come in, the door would catch on the trunk. Then I would make my move.

I sat on the bed, my shoulders drawn together in wary watchfulness. I pulled out the knife I'd stowed in my boot and gripped it in one clenched fist, the poker in the other, my nerves thrilling at the inevitability of conflict. When the master of this peculiar place returned, I would be ready.

EROS

Zephyrus was waiting for me when I arrived that evening. He leaned over the balustrade of the terrace, the last light of evening playing along his face, highlighting the smug, self-satisfied grin he wore.

"There's a surprise waiting for you inside," he said in a singsong voice.

I frowned. "Depositing strange nymphs or satyrs in my bed will not mitigate the effects of the curse."

Zephyrus laid a hand to his breast in exaggerated outrage. "As if I would ever be so gauche. No, no, my friend. I've brought you the princess herself."

I froze, a white-hot knife of panic sliding into my ribs. "Psyche?"

"None other!" My friend beamed.

I could only stare at him in stunned silence—the kind that comes between a flash of lighting and a roar of thunder.

"Zephyrus," I said, and though I managed to keep my tone light, it carried a chill. "Are your wits as wandering as your winds?"

"I thought this was what you wanted," he said with hollow sweetness.

"If you found an ugly weed, would you plant its seeds in my terrace garden?" I forced out through gritted teeth. "If there was a food that made me ill, would you serve it to me for lunch? Why then, I ask, would you think that *this* was a good idea?"

"Oh, come now, old friend," Zephyrus said. "Don't I deserve a word of thanks? She's yours now." A wicked smile crept over his face, and I knew that this had been no mistake. He had not forgiven me for the antidote that should have been his.

I ran a hand through my hair in exasperation. "We are doomed if we look upon each other's faces. And now she is in *my house*."

Zephyrus waggled a finger. "It's only a problem if you actually *see* each other, correct? Visit her by night and the problem is solved! I even took the liberty of removing all the lamps from your house."

My mouth fell open and I stared at him. "And why on earth would Psyche invite the company of a shadow? She doesn't know who I am."

"Worry not," Zephyrus crowed. "Mortal women are easy enough to appease, and I've already thought of a solution. Simply tell her that you are her new husband, then she won't mind."

Most mortal women would, in fact, mind this quite a bit. But Zephyrus knew little about the proclivities of human women, and I knew even less. The specificities of marriage varied widely between human societies, and I could never keep track of the differences. Marriage was Hera's realm; it was desire that belonged to me, and desire was the same everywhere.

Zephyrus was looking at me expectantly. His trap had been set; now I had no choice but to step into its snare.

But perhaps not all was lost. I thought of Psyche, her graceful neck and dark hair and slim ankles, always beyond my reach. To have her here was a gift I had never expected, a possibility I had never dared entertain. And though I knew this could not end well, a peculiar feeling rose in me. It took me a moment to recognize it as hope.

"Zephyrus," I said slowly, closing my eyes and pinching my nose. "This is the stupidest idea I have ever heard. If your foolish stratagem backfires, I will make you fall in love with a hedgehog."

I pushed past him and made my way into the house.

PSYCHE

Despite myself, the lingering heat and my full belly tempted me toward slumber. More than once, I found my head nodding down to my chest and the knife nearly slipping from my hands.

Then I heard the rhythmic tap of footsteps moving through the hall. I sat up straight, clutching the knife and the fire-poker in each hand. At this hour, the room was so dark that I could not even see them in front of me. But lack of sight heightened my other senses.

Listen, my teacher had told me long ago during our first lesson in the Mycenaean forest, and that was what I did now.

I could make out the distinct sound of bare feet moving across the stone floor—not claws or hooves or the slither of a snake, but simply human feet. A man's, judging from the heavy tread. The footsteps moved slowly, stopping now and again as if searching for something. Then they started down the hall, approaching my door. I held my breath and waited.

The door creaked open and collided with the trunk I'd placed in front of it, prompting a low mutter from the stranger. I gauged his height from the sound, then swung the poker where I suspected his head would be. It connected with something solid.

I heard a distinctly male yelp of pain, and then a thud as his body crumpled to the floor at my feet. I reached down until my fingers wrapped around a tuft of his hair, then pulled his head up so I could place the cool blade of the knife to his throat.

"I am Psyche, Princess of Mycenae," I declared. "Who are you?"

The stranger did not reply. I heard a gulp as he swallowed and felt his throat bob against the metal of the knife. I pressed it closer to his skin in warning.

"Your husband," he answered at last.

8

PSYCHE

The knife nearly fell out of my hands.

"Husband?" I echoed, my mind racing. This wasn't Nestor, of that I was certain; the voice was too young and unfamiliar. The events of the last few days rose up and rearranged themselves in my mind. My strange flight to this place took on a new meaning—the sudden departure of a wife from her natal home.

I remembered my mother's words the night I told her I would not marry the old king. *I have some other candidates in mind. All shall be well.*

Had my mother, in defiance of my father's will, arranged a better husband for me? The lack of a ceremony did not overly concern me, but why had she not told me of her plan? Then again, I mused, I had not been the most grateful recipient of her original choice.

"Yes, your husband," the voice said. "Now, I'd greatly appreciate it if you removed the knife from my throat and helped me to my feet."

I pulled the knife back and relinquished my grip on his hair, offering my hand to help him stand. I knew relatively little about the intricacies of marriage, but I was certain they did not include concussing the bridegroom. The hand I grasped was undeniably human, and though the total darkness of the room prevented me from making out more than a silhouette, I sensed the shape of him as he padded across the room to sit down on the bed. I joined him in sitting on the bed, though I kept my distance.

"Who are you?" I demanded, racking my memories for all the eligible youths my mother might have approached. "What is your name? Your father's name? What city are you from? Where are we now?"

"I have no city, and my father is irrelevant." The voice was liquid and musical, but I was stunned by his words. A man might not know his father, but among the Greeks, to have no city was like lacking a head.

"At least tell me your name," I demanded.

"My name?" the voice replied, and I heard a curious hitch, as if he had not expected me to press.

"Yes!" I barked, spurred on by my racing heart.

A long pause. "My name is Cupid," the unseen figure answered at last. "I am a god, a small one, of the sea and cliffs."

I was glad I had put down the knife, because surely it would have fallen through my nerveless fingers. I felt as though I was in a dream. A god! Even if only a minor one, a deity was not to be toyed with. And I had just held a blade to his throat!

But he had called himself my husband. My mind whirled. How could my mother have arranged such a union? What dowry does one offer to the divine?

"Cupid, I must be truthful," I began slowly. "I do not know what sort of wife I will make you. I have never cooked, save for meat at a campfire. I am a hopeless weaver. I know nothing of managing a household."

"That matters not to me," Cupid replied. "This house cares for itself, as I'm sure you have already seen."

My racing heart was threatening to burst from my chest. His voice was even, his intentions indiscernible. I wished I could read his expression to understand what he wanted. "I can't see a thing in here," I lamented, waving a hand in front of my face. I could not see a hint of movement. "Light a lamp at once."

"No!" I felt him flinch in genuine alarm. "There are no lamps permitted in this house."

I was baffled. "Why?"

"You would be burned at the sight of my face," my new husband replied, and the sudden intensity of his tone chilled me. "Just as Zeus turned Semele to ash by showing her a glimpse of his true self, so you would be destroyed if you looked upon me. I wish it were not so, but this is the only way. You must believe me."

I knew the story he spoke of. Semele, mortal mother of the god Dionysus, had demanded to see the true form of her mysterious lover Zeus. When the king of heaven finally obliged, Semele was burnt to a cinder by his radiance, and her unborn son had to be sewn into Zeus's thigh to survive.

But Cupid was not mighty Zeus, bearer of thunder; he was only a minor deity of the earth. Besides, the gods always found ways of revealing themselves to mortals when they wished.

"So you have taken me as your wife and brought me into your home," I began slowly. "Knowing that I would be destroyed if I saw your face. That seems like a poor foundation for a marriage."

EROS

Psyche had a point, I had to admit. Who would take a spouse they could not even see? A poor start indeed.

And yet, I could not bring myself to tell Psyche the truth, just as I could not bear to tell her my real name. To have her here with me now, to speak with her, soothed the open wound of my longing like a healing balm. If she learned the true reason she had been brought to me, surely she would leave. My heart cringed away from the thought. No, I could not lose her now.

"This is the safest place for you," I told her. That, at least, was not false. Aphrodite would not let us go unpunished if she discovered Psyche uncursed. One lie could be permitted if it protected her from a greater threat. "A monster pursues you, a terrible one."

I had thought my somber words would mollify Psyche, but I was quickly proven wrong. I heard a thump as she jumped off the bed, then the swish of her frenetic pacing across the dark room, as if her body could not contain her excitement. There was a clang and a hiss—she must have stubbed her toe. Then the bed dipped beside me as she leaped onto it and grabbed my hands.

"You must tell me where to find this beast," she ordered, voice wild. "It must be the same one that destroyed the Mycenaean village. I am trained to fight such monsters. I am a child of prophecy, destined to destroy a monster that terrifies even the gods."

To emphasize her point, she squeezed my hands tighter. I was startled to discover their roughness. I was unused to calluses, and Psyche's small hands were roughened by her training. But the curse thrilled at her touch and flooded me with heat—an ecstasy I had not felt in centuries, though I knew how perilous my hold on it was. I had no idea how to keep Psyche here with me if she refused. Perhaps I could turn her into a tree for just a little while, only to ensure sure she didn't do anything rash . . .

"Well?" Psyche's voice cut through the darkness between us, and her hands vanished from mine. The warmth drained from my body at the absence of her touch, the curse once more taking up its mournful howl within my soul. "You will bring me to this monster, won't you?"

"Stay with me." The words escaped unbidden, and I was horrified to note the begging tone in my voice. Gods do not beg, generally speaking, but recently my days had been filled with all sorts of unpleasant novelties. "We can discuss this more tomorrow. Stay for a while," I repeated. "This is our wedding night, after all."

PSYCHE

"Our wedding night," I repeated, my mouth suddenly dry. "And I'm sure you're here to fulfill your . . . husbandly duties."

I'd heard stories of what gods did to the mortal girls they favored. It was said that Helen herself had been the product of such an encounter. I realized I might be in the presence of something far more dangerous than a mere monster.

But I thought as well of the servant girls who giggled about their lovers in stolen whispers. I thought of my mother and father, arms linked as they walked through the palace gardens in the evening. Cupid demonstrated no cruelty, and fear warred with curiosity in my belly.

"I confess that it did cross my mind," my unseen husband replied. "Though now that you've knocked me about the head, I'd rather get some sleep." I felt him lower himself onto his side, the blankets shifting as he made his way beneath them.

My shoulders relaxed, and I breathed a sigh of relief.

After a moment, Cupid asked, "Are you going to sit up all night, or will you get some sleep? If you want sleeping clothes, the house will provide them for you."

I glanced down at myself. Though the darkness obscured my vision, I knew I still wore the battered leather armor I had donned that morning. The idea of changing clothes in front of this stranger, even if he was my so-called husband, made my cheeks flame with embarrassment.

"I have no need of such things," I replied. Gingerly, I lay down on top of the blankets, and was astonished to note that their quality was even finer than my parents' linens back in Mycenae.

"I have one more request," I said, staring up at the ceiling. "I want to write a letter to my mother and father, to let them know that I am safe."

"Then I will give you writing materials and swift messenger hawks. I will be gone when the sun rises, but this house will provide you with anything you need. I'll come to you again when night falls." With that, Cupid rolled onto his side and said no more.

I had never felt further from sleep in my life. My body hummed with excitement. I did not know what to make of the god who called himself my husband, but such a change in station only brought me closer to my heroic destiny. I had found the trail of the monster that would ensure my legend. Cupid claimed to know of this beast, and so I would make him lead me to it.

But Cupid also had his own reasons for bringing me here, and I had the sense of events taking shape beyond my understanding.

I looked toward the place where I heard his quiet breaths. "I know nothing at all about you," I said. "What do you enjoy? What do you dislike?"

I felt the sheets rustle beside me. "Well," he murmured. "I am skilled at archery. I like cats and birds, but not dogs . . ."

I lifted my head from the pillow, my interest piqued. "I like archery as well."

"Then perhaps we can practice together sometime," he murmured, his words melting together. After some time, faint snoring rose from his side of the bed. I had not known that gods snored.

As he slept, I occupied myself with thoughts of strategy. Tomorrow I would resume my hunt for the monster that had destroyed the Mycenaean village. Though my sword had been lost, perhaps I could find a lance or bow. I would seek out this creature and kill it, and then everything would make sense.

Though I had been certain that I would never sleep again, my exhaustion along with the softness of the bed and the evenness of Cupid's breathing eventually soothed me. My eyes finally closed, and I fell into a dreamless sleep.

EROS

What does it say about the difference between gods and mortals, that you might mistake one for the other in the dark? I have often wondered about this. Sight reveals the gods' true nature, as our beauty is too piercing to be anything other than divine, but in the darkness all things are equal.

I woke before dawn and realized with a sense of marvel that I had slept the whole night through. I waited for the crushing longing of the curse to sink its talons into me, but it did not come. Instead, there was only the sweetness that came from a craving indulged. I sat up and looked to my side; Psyche was still with me.

The door was cracked open from our confrontation last night, and dull yellow sunlight illuminated the hallway. Psyche was sprawled awkwardly on the bed above the covers, arms and legs akimbo, still wearing that ridiculous dirty armor and taking up far more space than seemed possible for one woman. Yet all I could think of was her loveliness—better still, when she slept, I could enjoy the heady pleasure of the curse fulfilled without trying to manage all her questions. I propped my chin on a hand and gazed at her.

I loved Psyche, but I wasn't sure what to make of the girl

herself. She was loud, restless, and more than a little spoiled. She was relentless when something caught her attention, seizing it the way a terrier grabs a rat. Her interest in weapons was peculiar. But Psyche was here with me, safe from Aphrodite's wrath, and the curse purred like a kitten in her presence. That was enough for now.

Misgivings gnawed at the corners of my mind. Why had I lied to her? *Cupid*, I said my name was. There was a place along the Etruscan coast, a small village set in the middle of seven hills, where the people spoke a tongue as even and regular as cut marble. It was my name in this, the Latin language, that I had given to Psyche.

If I had been forthright with Psyche that night, what would she have said? A love god cursed to suffer his own gift—would she have accepted me as her husband? Of course not. Psyche would have fled, a risk I could not allow, since I was certain that Aphrodite would find her.

I was shaken from my thoughts as Psyche stirred and rolled over in her sleep. It was dangerous to linger in the light like this. Hurriedly, I left the room.

Zephyrus was waiting for me outside. He leaned against the cool stone of the cliffs in the faint light of morning, right where I had left him the evening prior. I wondered if he had stayed there all night.

"How did you enjoy my little gift?" the wind god said, grinning wickedly. "You are cured of your lovesickness—how wonderful! You haven't thanked me yet."

Zephyrus could be as irritating as a gadfly, but even I had to admit that his jest had resulted in the first night of peaceful sleep I'd enjoyed since the curse had taken hold. I shrugged noncommittally.

"Now, tell me all about your wedding night." Zephyrus placed his hands on his cheeks in anticipation.

"She hit me with a fire-poker," I replied flatly.

Zephyrus laughed. "Mortals certainly are full of surprises, aren't they? But I'm more interested in what happened afterward." His eyes glittered with prurient curiosity, and his eyebrows waggled.

"Nothing," I replied. "We went to sleep."

"Sleep?" Zephyrus was incredulous. "No consummation of desire, no passionate lovemaking after you finally managed to get her alone? What's gotten into you? Perhaps you should use one of your arrows, if you want to be sure she reciprocates."

I reared back at the suggestion, revolted. The memory of Anteia rose in my consciousness, her delicate fingers tying the noose around her neck. "Never," I hissed.

Zephyrus tilted his head. "Why not?"

Because I don't want to hurt her, I wanted to say. *Because I will not compel what should be chosen freely.* But this was only the curse sinking its claws into me once more.

"Stop, Zephyrus," I said instead, beginning to lose patience. "Psyche was confused and far from home. She didn't want to do anything."

Zephyrus looked at me as though I was an oceanid from the deepest trenches of the sea or a satyr from the trackless forest, not a friend he'd known since the beginning of the world. "When has that ever mattered before?" he asked.

He had a point. When had gods ever cared about the thoughts or feelings of a mortal, even one they loved? Adonis's desires hadn't mattered to Persephone when she'd asked me for the favor of my arrow. Nor had Apollo had Hyacinthos's best interests at heart when he'd killed the youth in a fit of jealous rage.

Perhaps Prometheus truly cared about the mortals, but

Prometheus was a criminal and had been punished dearly for his crimes.

What god had ever set aside his or her own needs for those of a mortal? I had, it seemed. The thought left me uneasy.

The gods have only one word for love, but perhaps they can learn more.

9

PSYCHE

When I woke, the bed beside me was empty, and light streamed through the open door. There was no sign of my mysterious husband, and I didn't know whether to be relieved or disappointed.

I was still wearing the armor I'd donned the day before, but a clean chiton was folded neatly on a low table nearby. It was just my size, and my favorite color as well—a shade of blue that was almost violet. In another room I found a hot bath ready, laden with flower petals and perfumes that wafted like steam from its surface.

Once I had cleaned myself and dressed, I sat down on the lip of the tub and stared at my reflection in the water, feeling as though I had been the one hit in the head by a fire-poker. A whirlwind had deposited me here in a house of fantasy. A god had claimed to be my husband. The monster who would seal my destiny stalked me. In the daylight, these claims strained credulity. Yet the evidence was undeniable, as tangible as the cloth that draped my body.

There had been no wedding ceremony, but perhaps gods did not observe the same customs as humans. Maybe when we returned to Mycenae, Cupid and I could be married according to my people's traditions. I still didn't understand how my mother had arranged such a match, but at least I had not been given to ugly old Nestor.

I shook myself out of my reverie and padded through the halls. When I approached the great oak table, I saw that Cupid had kept his word. A collection of writing materials—papyrus, ink, a stylus—were arranged neatly next to my breakfast of bread and honey. Outside, I heard messenger hawks calling to one another in their cages.

After I ate my fill, I dashed off a letter to my mother and father under the watchful eye of a white cat who was intensely curious about the process. *I am well and unharmed,* I wrote, *and safely ensconced in the house of my new divine husband.* After a moment's consideration, I penned a letter to Iphigenia as well. Though a vast distance separated me from Iphigenia, throughout the years we confided all our secrets in our letters. I gave sparse details about my new husband, however, since I barely knew what to make of him myself.

Out on the terrace, I tied these messages to the feet of the birds. Then I released their tethers and watched them disappear into the cloudless sky.

What to do now? I sat, resting my chin in my hand. I found myself at loose ends, a feeling I had rarely experienced before. I desperately wanted to find the trail of the monster, but there was no point until I could get more information from Cupid, who would not be back until nightfall. I turned away from the edge of the balcony, then jumped back in alarm.

A stranger stood at the entrance to the house, watching me intently.

His eyes were a washed-out pale blue, and they rested lightly upon me. He was angular, all muscle and sinew over bone, dancing forward on the balls of his feet to investigate me in a manner that echoed the movements of the peacocks along the length of the terrace. I knew that this was not my husband; the newcomer was slighter than the form that had met me in the dark, and I was not engulfed in flames at the sight of him. But I was certain that this stranger was a god.

I can't say exactly how I knew this. Certainly he was beautiful, features shaped with a precision that was almost uncanny, but some mortals rival the gods for beauty. Perhaps human beings carry the recognition of divinity in their blood—a legacy from Prometheus, who made us. Or perhaps it is the same instinct that prompts a rabbit to recognize the shadow of a hawk.

But I was no rabbit. I was the mistress of this house, and I stood firm. "Who are you?" I asked.

"Ah, Psyche," the stranger said, inclining his head. "I was wondering when you'd wake. You certainly like to sleep in, don't you? I'm so glad to meet you properly! I am Zephyrus," he concluded with a flourish and a bow.

Unlike Cupid, this name was familiar to me. Ruler of the west wind, subject of odes by venerable old priests in the temples of Mycenae. But my awe was overshadowed by outraged recognition. "I know your voice! You were the one who brought me here!"

Zephyrus nodded. "Just so. I wanted to see for myself how you were settling in."

Rage flared in me. "Were you the one who destroyed the village in Mycenae?" I demanded. I remembered the hollow eyes of the refugees pouring into the capital city of Tiryns.

"Ah, yes. Quite an effort, blowing all the houses around to get your attention, but I see it worked." He flashed me a wide grin that only heightened my anger.

"The village is destroyed, and the planting season is approaching," I snarled. "People lost their homes!" I fought the urge to hurl one of the flowerpots at him. I couldn't kill a god, but I could certainly make one hurt.

"Did they?" He arched one brow lazily.

"You will make reparations to assist with the rebuilding of the village." The venerable priests of Mycenae would tell me I should not make such bold demands of the divine, but after all he had done, Zephyrus owed me this. "You are a god. Don't tell me you lack the means."

Zephyrus stared at me blankly. Then he threw back his head in raucous laughter and slapped me on the back like an old friend. "You're bold for a mortal, aren't you? Well, I suppose I owe you a wedding present. I have no small wealth, and I will put it toward this cause that you ask."

"Good," I replied, my wrath easing.

His gaze slid away from mine, looking out to the sea. "Besides, I take no joy in the misery of mortals," he added, speaking more to the water and sky than to me, his angular face softening slightly. "I loved one of them once. His name was Hyacinthos."

Was, he said. A chill crept along my skin. "What happened to him?" I asked.

"Apollo killed him." Zephyrus's voice was flat and bleak.

"Oh," I replied, feeling a peculiar hollowness in the pit of my stomach. Why did this unsettle me so? I had always known that mortals who became entangled with the gods often lived truncated lives.

But now I was one of them.

Zephyrus shook off his melancholy and turned to me. "Tell me, what do you think of your new husband?" he asked, his initial brightness returning. "Do you find him handsome? Appealing? Are you in love with him?"

I felt the heat of a blush rise to my cheeks. "I've only just met him. But he's . . . kind, certainly," I said, unsure. "Though I can't say if he's handsome because he won't let me see his face. He comes to me only in darkness and refuses all lamps." The words tumbled from my mouth before I had a chance to assess the wisdom of saying them.

Zephyrus nodded gravely. "Ah, yes," he said. "The curse. I'm pleased to hear he's managing that well."

"What curse?" I asked, frowning. Cupid made no mention of such a thing, but perhaps it explained the peculiarities of the night before.

"Oh, you know." Zephyrus waved dismissively. "That rule against seeing each other's faces. You understand, surely."

I didn't understand in the slightest, but I wasn't going to plead to this strange god for answers. I trusted him even less than Cupid. "I hardly think confining me to darkness counts as managing things well," I remarked. "Who on earth would marry someone they cannot even look upon?"

"Someone driven to distraction by love," Zephyrus replied.

I blinked in shock. My husband had said nothing about love, though I had sensed some affection in his voice. Perhaps it was love that had driven him to risk the wrath of a curse—though I was the one who would suffer if we saw each other face-to-face.

I looked again at Zephyrus. Lounging against the terrace railing in a posture of calculated ease, he vibrated with unsaid words like a nest of bees.

"Zephyrus," I said suddenly. "Who is my husband? Who is he really?"

He grinned. "I was hoping you would ask." He produced a vial of liquid in one of his long-fingered hands, seemingly from nowhere, and held it out to me for inspection. "This potion will allow you to perceive the true nature of things. One who drinks it can see even in the darkest of nights. I think it will satisfy your curiosity well enough." He bestowed a broad grin upon me, eyes flashing with delight.

I took the vial from him and examined it, tilting it up and down to watch the contents move sluggishly within. I frowned, eyeing Zephyrus warily.

With a roll of his eyes and a heavy exhale, the wind god snatched the vial back from me and uncapped it. He looked at me pointedly as he tossed down a measure of its contents and swallowed. Then he handed it back to me with a flourish.

"There," Zephyrus said. "See? Not poisoned."

I crossed my arms and raised my chin. "You are immortal, and I am not," I replied.

Zephyrus eyed me. "If I wanted you dead, I would have dropped you from that cliff instead of bringing you here. Believe me, your husband would never let me hear the end of it if you died, and an immortal can hold a grudge for a very long time."

I looked down at the vial again, still half-full. Curiosity drove its spurs into me as though I was an unruly horse. I had to know who my so-called husband was; the need consumed me.

"Though, if you are a coward," Zephyrus goaded archly, "I'll take the tincture back."

That was enough. Fortune favored the brave, and besides, when had I ever refused a challenge? I threw aside the cap and drank the contents in a single gulp.

All at once, a shudder ran through me. The bottle fell from my hands as the terrace rapidly expanded in size. But even as my bones shrank and rearranged themselves, even as I knew that I had been deceived, I felt no pain or fear. I caught a glimpse of Zephyrus's pale eyes as they crinkled with laughter, but by then my thoughts were reduced to one single-pointed commandment: *Fly*.

I rose from the abandoned chiton, my wings lifting me higher and higher into the morning air.

10

EROS

When I returned to the seaside house with the shadows of evening, I expected to find Psyche there. Perhaps she would be lounging by the table, or perhaps she would already be in bed. The curse thrilled at the thought of her voice, the possibility of her touch.

I did not expect what I found: an array of smashed furniture and broken plates, and at the center of it all, Aphrodite.

Her olive skin had taken on a reddish hue from exertion, and her chest rose and fell dramatically. Her hair was lank around her face, like that of a drowned woman. I had never seen Aphrodite like this in all the centuries I had known her. She looked reduced, almost mortal.

Psyche, where is Psyche? Aphrodite hadn't found her, that much was clear. Otherwise, she would have greeted me with the girl's mangled corpse. Wherever Psyche was, I hoped she had the good sense to stay put until I could evict Aphrodite.

"You killed him," Aphrodite snarled. The words seemed to be wrenched from her by sheer force of grief. Her eyes were red and swollen.

I closed the door behind me and tried not to appear disconcerted by her sudden appearance. "Dear Mother, I have no idea who you could possibly mean."

"Adonis!" Aphrodite wailed. The name brought a fresh

wave of tears down her cheeks, and she pressed the back of her hand to her mouth. It took me a moment to recall the young mortal man, dead these past few months. My gift to Persephone. I hadn't killed him, not exactly—that had been the boar's fault. But I doubted Aphrodite would appreciate the difference.

"My lover," she choked. "I had not seen him for some time. When I went to confront him for his negligence, I found out he was dead. Dead!" She wailed the last words, drawing her nails along her beautiful face. "Adonis is gone forever. I will never touch him again, never feel him next to me. He is nothing but cold mist in the Underworld, and I am alone." Her words trailed into sobs.

I felt a twinge, knowing I would be lost if such a thing happened to Psyche. But I could not reveal my role in Adonis's death, so I feigned carelessness. "Ah, such a shame. It's a pity that mortals don't live very long. Zephyrus lost one recently as well. Perhaps you two could comfort each other."

Aphrodite's eyes narrowed. Her lips pulled back from her teeth and color appeared high on her cheeks. "It was always you, wasn't it, pulling the strings from the shadows?" she spat. "Ares, Hephaestus, and now my dear sweet Adonis. I will tolerate no more betrayals."

"Really, Mother," I replied. "I don't know what you mean."

I should have known better than to lie. Despite my skill for trickery, I have never been very good at outright mistruths. Desire does not lie.

Aphrodite drew herself up to her full height. "I swear to you," she snarled in a voice like the earth shattering. "I will find the thing you love most in the world and destroy it."

Nothing moved in the house, not even the smallest of the cats. Her head high, not looking at me, Aphrodite crossed to a window. White wings sprouted from her back, arching to brush the ceiling. Her body telescoped to assume the shape of a dove,

and she fluttered out through the open window, though not before she defecated pointedly on my floor.

Once she was gone, I jolted into action. *Psyche.* I had to find
Psyche. I ran from room to room, frantic with terror, wondering
if I would find Psyche dangling from the rafters or dismembered
on my marble floors, a parting gift from Aphrodite. But instead
I found nothing at all, which was even worse.

A breeze burst through one of the open windows. It coalesced
into the shape of Zephyrus, who held a tiny form cupped in his
hands. A butterfly.

"Gently, gently," he said to me. The butterfly's wings beat
weakly. "She's exhausted herself. Fetch a glass."

I did so. Zephyrus performed the complicated maneuver of
transferring the contents of his hands to the upturned glass.
Once he had accomplished this, both of us leaned down to peer
at the tiny black-and-gold creature fluttering inside.

"Zephyrus," I began. "I don't suppose that's my wife, is it?"

Zephyrus gave a sunny grin. "You are correct, my dear Eros.
She tried a bit of the moly tincture I got from Circe, and, as you
can see, it seems that the shape of her soul is a butterfly. It's rather
funny, don't you think? A fierce thing like her, nothing but—"

"Zephyrus." I was losing my patience. "Turn her back immediately!"

I carried the jar into the darkened bedroom, mindful of the
love curse. Once we were enclosed in darkness, I felt rather than
saw Zephyrus make a gesture in the air.

And then Psyche was in my arms, gasping for breath against
my chest. She clutched at me, trying to steady herself, and I held
her desperately. For all her fierceness she was impossibly delicate,
her limbs like sapling trees that might be snapped in a strong
wind. The curse sang in my blood, fear turning to elation. Psyche,
alive and unharmed, restored to me at last.

Dimly, I heard the glass roll away to some distant corner of the room.

"Th-that . . ." The words sounded thick and heavy on Psyche's tongue as she struggled to adjust to her human body once more. I stroked her back, hoping to calm her. What an ordeal she must have experienced! Of course she would be frightened and confused.

"That . . . was amazing!" she finally managed. "Incredible! Can I do it again?"

I was certain I had misheard her, but Psyche tried to sit up and swayed with the effort. I eased her back down again.

"I wouldn't recommend it," I said darkly, noting that Psyche was even odder than I initially realized. "Transformation is taxing for a mortal. You might forget you were ever anything other than a butterfly, drifting in the wind. You need to sleep. I'll stay with you until you do."

Psyche's excitement faded as physical exhaustion won out. I eased her onto the bed and carefully settled the blankets around her, stroking her hair. It was not long before her breathing slowed.

"Perhaps I should leave?" Zephyrus piped up from a darkened corner of the room.

I was irritated at his carelessness, but I understood how differently this evening might have gone if Aphrodite had found Psyche alone. Cold terror sluiced through me like seawater.

"Not yet," I told Zephyrus. "Your trick with the moly, unacceptable as it was, has opened new possibilities. It seems that Psyche and I can indeed look upon each other, so long as one of us wears a face that isn't our own."

"New possibilities, and new limitations as well," Zephyrus remarked. "Such a waste that your new bride cannot look upon your handsome face. The only blessing is that she does not know, or her sadness would be unrelenting."

I grimaced. "I think it is indeed time for you to leave," I said.

Zephyrus departed in a swirl of air that left the door swinging back and forth. I held my head in my hands and considered the situation. Psyche would never really know me, never look upon the face that so many worshipped, and I found myself strangely relieved by that fact.

But how did I make her stay? Something must give, something must change. We could not skirt the edge of this curse forever.

I loved Psyche, a fact over which I had no choice, but I did not *understand* her. Already she had proved unwieldy, willing to take unknown potions from questionable strangers. And her wild enthusiasm for monster hunting struck me as tiresome at best and bizarre at worst. Was this what all mortals were like? I knew so little of them. I needed to speak with someone who understood mortals, who could show me how to keep Psyche safe.

An idea struck me like a bolt of Zeus's lightning. There was one god who understood mortals better than any other, who once drank ambrosia on my terrace before his long imprisonment.

Prometheus would know what to do.

11

PSYCHE

I was naked when I woke. This startled me at first, before I recalled the events of the previous day: a mysterious stranger who called himself Zephyrus, a flight through the air. Colors shifting around me, the air filled with cacophonous sounds. My world plunged into darkness, and my wings beating futilely at walls of glass. Then finding myself gasping on the floor of the windowless bedroom, my unseen husband's arms around me and his voice whispering gentle comfort in my ears.

I shook myself free from these wisps of thought. I rose and went to the great oak table, which was once again heavy with food. The house itself provided for me, it seemed, a miracle of the gods. One of the cats called out a greeting, but no other sound echoed from the stone walls. I was alone in a way I had rarely been throughout my short life. There had always been my parents or the palace servants, and later, Atalanta. But now I was truly alone, at least until the evening when Cupid returned.

I looked out at the sun glittering invitingly on the waters like hammered metal. The day promised to be dry and hot, and I knew at once how I wanted to spend it. The house seemed to agree with my idea; I noticed a folded cloth neatly draped over the chair nearby. I was certain it had not been there the moment before.

I frowned at it, running the textured fabric through my fingers. I found myself watching narrow-eyed for the moment when objects in the house appeared or mended themselves, as if I might see invisible hands at work. But no, things simply winked in or out of existence, as if they had always been this way.

A swim would be good for me, I decided.

The steps winding down the cliffs were a trial, but when I arrived at the beach, I forgot my aching muscles from the beauty of it all. Seagulls snatched clams from tidal pools and flew upward, dropping them on the rocks below to expose the tender meat. It was a clever trick, one the birds must have taught themselves.

Shell fragments littered the ground, and I had to be careful lest the sharp edges slice my tender feet as I made my way across the rocky shale. I walked to the place where the waves lapped at the shore and let them tumble over my feet. The sea belonged to the god Poseidon, but it belonged to itself as well and had moods that were separate from his. Sometimes the sea was stormy and contemptuous, at others merry and coquettish. This was one of its happier times. The sun shone through the clear waters to the sandy sea floor, and manta rays swept through the blue like the shadows of great birds.

I braided my hair and tied it tightly back. Glancing around, I was assured that no one else was watching, so I slipped out of my chiton and into the waves.

The water shocked me with its coldness, but my blood quickly warmed. I shifted smoothly into the long, reaching stroke that Atalanta taught me, losing myself in the fierce joy of pushing my muscles like a charioteer's horses. The swim was a welcome respite from the roiling mire of thoughts that filled my mind: the shock at my abrupt change in station, lingering puzzlement over my divine husband's true identity.

It seemed that I lost track of my progress, or else the current took me farther out than I intended. When I looked up, the shore-line was only a distant sliver on the horizon.

Panic rose in me, but I quickly quashed it. I could swim back and sleep off the exhaustion over the long afternoon. Surely I would be able to make it.

A sound caught my attention, and I turned. A face with a bulbous head and a long snout peered at me from the water, and I recognized it as belonging to a dolphin. I had never seen one in person before, but I knew what they looked like from paintings on the pottery imported from Crete. The dolphin was sacred to a number of gods, said to rescue sailors lost at sea.

"Hello there," I said to the smiling creature.

"Hello, Psyche," it replied.

Later, I wasn't sure whether I swam, flew, or simply walked on water, but when I paused to catch my breath, the dolphin's head was much farther away than it had been before.

The dark form glided toward me, resurfacing. "Psyche!" it called again. "It's me!"

I recognized the voice. "Cupid?!"

The dolphin rolled on its side and peered at me with one onyx eye. "The very same. I saw you heading into deeper waters and came to help you back to shore."

His tenderness was endearing in its way, but I would not be treated like a child by my own husband. Anger flared in me. "Why would you think I need your help? Are you my nursemaid? I am no infant. I was trained to hunt and fight monsters. An undertow is nothing to me."

"You are halfway out to sea," Cupid remarked. "Forgive me for thinking you are not immune to drowning."

I opened my mouth to respond but was struck by the peculiarity of arguing with a speaking dolphin. "Is this what you actually look like?" I interrupted. "I thought I would be turned to ash if I looked you in the face." I treaded water with long legs that were distinctly not cinders.

He clicked disapprovingly. "No, but your incident with the moly gave me the idea. It seems that if one of us wears a face that isn't our own, the curse no longer binds us."

I recalled soaring higher into the sun-soaked sky on wings as delicate as papyrus, and the distorted shapes of faces beyond the glass that contained me. Zephyrus had told me of a curse, but Cupid hadn't mentioned it himself until now. What kind of curse could rule a god? The uncanny sense of a mistruth lodged in my mind like a splinter.

I pushed it aside. "How have you accomplished this?" I asked, gesturing at his shape. "Have you possessed the dolphin?"

"All gods are shape-shifters, and I am no exception." His tail slapped the water, throwing droplets into the air like shimmering stars.

Then why not appear to me with the face of a man? I wondered. I remembered the broad-shouldered form in the darkness. I would rather meet that shape, or something like it, instead of a dolphin.

"Now, if you will get on my back," he said, "I will take you back to shore in time for the noon meal."

I scowled at him. "I told you, I don't need your help."

"Oh, I have no doubt you can accomplish it yourself," he replied. "I merely thought it would save time. Besides, how many mortals can say they've ridden a dolphin?"

I reconsidered, mollified by his response. Besides, my belly was rumbling with hunger. "Well, I suppose it would be rude to refuse after you've come so far."

The dolphin's skin was smooth, and I could feel his muscles contract and release beneath me. Cupid picked up speed, turning the world into a kaleidoscope of sea-foam and sunlight. I got a mouthful of seawater more than once, but I didn't care. A laugh of sheer joy tore from me as I skipped like a stone upon the waves, and I heard an echoing cry of delight from the dolphin.

Cupid slowed when we drew closer to the shore, and I released him once my own feet could touch the sea bottom. We considered each other for a moment, rocked by the low swells of the waves.

I remembered then that I was naked, and I ducked my shoulders below the water in a sudden paroxysm of modesty. He might be my husband, but it still brought heat to my face to think of him viewing me, especially when he wore another form.

Mercifully, Cupid turned away and rolled on his back, gazing at the sky. "I will see you after dusk. Be well, Psyche."

"And you," I replied.

He turned and dove into the surf. Through the jewel-like waters, I could see the dark wedge of his body speeding toward the horizon. Only when I was certain that he was gone did I step from the waves and hastily don my chiton.

EROS

The memory of Psyche's touch stayed with me for the remainder of my daylight hours. I had not fully appreciated how the curse might be turned into a blessing at the simple feeling of her skin, how the howling of my longings could shift to music. Yet even this fulfillment only led to more wanting, more cravings: the desire to feel her body against me when I could reciprocate more fully.

When darkness fell, I found Psyche waiting in the lightless bedroom, sitting up on the bed. "Ah, so you're wearing the shape of a man again," she said. "I wasn't sure if you would come to me as a fish."

I thought about reminding her that I wasn't a man, and that

dolphins weren't fish, but decided against it. Psyche had been wrenched from her home and subject to all manner of peculiarity. I wanted to offer her something real.

"I cannot let you see what I look like," I replied, kneeling on the bed. "But I can let you feel."

I found her hands in the darkness and moved them to my face. The calluses were rough as stone but more familiar to me now. Her fingers moved over my eyelids and nose, feeling the ridge of my jawline. I could hear Psyche's breath hitch, absorbed in fascination, and she shifted closer to get a better reach. I basked in the feeling of her hands as they skimmed over my face like summer rain. I wondered what it would be like to take those hands in my own, to lean in where I knew Psyche's face must be and to kiss her.

I flinched back abruptly, my heart slamming shut like a startled clam. It was only the curse digging its claws into me; the faster we broke it, the better it would be for the both of us.

Psyche's hands paused at my movement.

"Satisfied yet?" I asked.

The hands left my face. "Yes," she replied. "Thank you."

I remembered my plan. "I have a favor to ask of you, Psyche. I would like you to accompany me on a journey. There is someone I want to speak to, someone I would like you to meet."

I told Psyche that I sought Prometheus, and she yelped with excitement. "Of course, I will join you! And the monster, will we find the trail of that beast as well?"

"We might," I said darkly, thinking of Aphrodite and her threat to destroy what I treasured most. "But I know that you were trained to fight monsters."

"Good," she said, laughing. "It seems you're finally beginning to understand me."

There was a rustling of sheets as Psyche slipped under the blankets, readying herself for sleep. I did the same.

"Are you truly not afraid?" I asked.

"Not at all," she replied, voice muffled by the pillow. "After all, I travel in the company of an immortal god. What do I have to fear?"

A great deal, I thought grimly, Aphrodite's tear-stained threat rising in my thoughts. But I said nothing of this to Psyche, and soon she was asleep.

As I lay back, I realized that my face ached slightly. At first, I thought it might be a remnant of Psyche's touch, but then I realized that I was smiling.

That morning, I dithered over what form to wear. I could take on the shape of a handsome mortal youth, but I didn't want to add another lie to the stack that already weighed down our relationship, and I disliked the idea of Psyche gazing affectionately at a face that wasn't mine.

I finally decided on the shape of a magnificent rooster, the gold feathers around my proud neck contrasting sharply with my blue-green wings. The comb atop my head brought to mind the plumed helm of Ares. I paced the terrace with my three-clawed feet, ruffling my magnificent plumage. Even the peacocks drew back from me in awe.

When Psyche emerged, I saw she had put on the light armor I'd left out for her, far finer than the cumbersome set of boiled leather she'd arrived wearing: a front breastplate and back of worked bronze, along with matching greaves.

Psyche also wore a skeptical expression. A chuckle escaped her when she caught sight of me. "Are you a chicken now?"

I ruffled my feathers in consternation. "I am a *rooster*, I'll have you know. This shape covers more ground than a dolphin,"

I muttered. Apparently the magnificence of the form—golden feathers shading to fire-red, my regal bearing and fierce strut—was lost on my mortal wife.

Psyche glanced around. "Where are our supplies?" she asked.

I indicated a satchel propped against the stone wall of the cliff. She shot me a look of alarm. "That can't be everything. That bag couldn't hold more than a wineskin."

"Haven't each of your needs been taken care of since you arrived here?" I said. "Why do you think it would be any different on the road? You travel with a god. All will be well."

Psyche rolled her eyes at this, but she picked up the satchel and we set off, making our way down the long, winding staircase that led from the house to the beach. I led her to a path that ran through the dry, dusty hills, walking until we could no longer hear the sea crashing against the rocks.

It was not long before we were ambushed by a group of bandits, emerging from the craggy landscape like malevolent spirits. They were men with no city who made their living preying on unwary travelers, and I suppose we seemed like easy pickings: a lone woman traveling with an elegant pet.

Two bandits emerged from the scrub brush in front of us. When I whirled around, I saw two more on the road behind us. They all bore blades pitted with rust and unrelenting expressions.

I was no warrior; my arrows were not made for battle. Besides, I was unprepared to see mortals act like this. I was a god, accustomed to being worshipped. I was used to humans being obsequious or oblivious, not threatening.

I pondered my next course of action, but Psyche was faster.

She pulled an arrow from her quiver and shot the man closest to me in the throat. He fell clutching the shaft, wearing an expression of absolute bewilderment. A moment later an arrow lodged itself in the chest of his companion, who gave a brief shocked cry.

Psyche whirled in the opposite direction. One of the bandits behind us charged, his mouth open in a battle snarl as he swung an axe. He was enormous, shoulders as wide as an ox, and for a second Psyche was frozen by the animal shock that comes with facing something much larger than yourself.

Psyche scrabbled backward, away from the man's charge, and nearly stumbled into the dust. A scream rose in my throat, but she quickly recovered herself. She ducked into the opening left by his wide stance, pulling her knife from its sheath and dragging it along the outside of the man's thigh. The bandit howled with agony and swung wildly at her, but she had already jumped out of reach.

The last of the bandits, a lanky man in the most ragged clothing I had ever seen, didn't even bother to challenge her. Instead, he grabbed the man she had just stabbed and dragged him into the maze of low rock and brush around the path. A trail of spattered blood on the dry earth was the only sign of their passage.

I had seen Ares and Athena, the gods of war, fight in the skirmishes that cropped up among divinities, but Psyche moved differently. Less perfect and slower, though with a beauty that drew the eye. Athena and Ares would never have stumbled or nearly fallen when facing an enemy, and never would have recovered themselves so well either. It was like comparing the cold unyielding beauty of the stars to the bloom of a flower, something impermanent and imperfect but all the more lovely for it. Psyche wasn't fighting because she was born to it; she was fighting because she loved it.

Psyche was breathing hard, bloodied knife in her hands.

"Now I understand what you meant when you said you were trained to fight monsters," I said. "Where did you learn to move like that?"

Psyche glanced at me and grinned, becoming once again a young mortal girl instead of a fighter of shocking skill. "I was taught by a hero, Atalanta," she replied, "to fulfill the prophecy from the Oracle of Delphi, that I would conquer a monster feared by the gods. But I've never killed a person before. I've never needed to." Psyche reached up to smooth back her hair, and now I saw that her hands were shaking, that her smile wavered at the corners.

"They would have killed you without a second thought if you hadn't done it first," I assured her.

Psyche's gaze swung toward me. "You know," she said wryly, "most men would be ashamed that they could not protect their wife from bandits."

I spread my wings in mock surrender. "Then it is good that I am not a man. And why should I be ashamed to have a wife who can fight like you? You move like a whirlwind. I've never seen the like."

Psyche flushed, pink showing through her brown skin, and glanced away from me. "I should leave coins in their mouths, to pay their passage across the Styx," she said, considering the forms of the two arrow-struck men. "But I have none."

Dust still drifted through the air, kicked up by swift-moving feet. I began to groom my feathers to ensure no dirt dulled their brightness. "Check the satchel," I told Psyche.

She looked at me in confusion, which only increased when she dipped one hand into the satchel and pulled out a pair of small objects that glinted in the sun. Two coins, enough to set the souls of the bandits at rest.

We continued on our way. Sweat beaded on Psyche's brow as she stared vacantly ahead. I could tell something weighed on her mind. "I always thought I would become a hero one day," she said at last, "instead of merely an executioner of bandits. I thought I would be like Bellerophon or—"

My feathers ruffled in agitation as I remembered the so-called hero who had rejected Anteia so cruelly. "You're better off as you are. Bellerophon was a great fool." *And not nearly as beautiful as you*, I did not add.

"Bellerophon was brilliant!" she shot back.

"He was a fool," I repeated. I had never forgotten the sneer on Bellerophon's face he pushed Anteia away.

"If you know so much about Bellerophon," Psyche snapped, "then by all means, enlighten me."

I did.

I painted her a picture of an arrogant man, drunk on myths about his own importance. Someone who thought everything in the world belonged to him. A bully and a blowhard, too stupid to conceal his naked ambition, destroyed by his own endless grasping when he tried to ride winged Pegasus to the peaks of Mount Olympus.

"And he was cruel to the woman who loved him," I finished.

"I see," Psyche replied, frowning.

We continued walking in silence. The road led through desolate country, far from any walled cities or even minor villages. The landscape was unchanging, low hills marked with rocky outcroppings and small stands of gnarled trees. Psyche's sandals kicked up small clouds of dust from the dry earth, and my clawed feet left only the slightest indentations.

A thought drifted to the forefront of my mind and lodged there. "Why did she kill herself?"

Psyche turned her head to peer at me, eyes creasing with confusion. It took me a moment to realize I had said the words aloud. "Anteia," I clarified. "After Bellerophon spurned her. I've never understood it. Mortal lives are so fragile. Why deliberately end your own?"

Psyche considered the question, tilting her head in an almost birdlike gesture. "I think she was heartbroken. The man she loved felt nothing for her, and she betrayed him. Besides, her husband wouldn't have let her live after disgracing him like that."

I glanced at Psyche in alarm but saw only solemnity in her face. I did not understand why old Proetus would feel disgraced, but the finer points of mortal marital customs continued to elude me.

We said nothing more until the sun began to sink down in the west. "It's time for camp," Psyche said, and I saw exhaustion clinging to her like the dirt of the road. "Although I don't know how we're going to do that, as we have no supplies," she added with a sidelong glance at me.

"Check the satchel," I said.

Psyche stared at me as though I had suggested pulling a tent post from her own nose but did as I instructed. She unslung the bag from her shoulder and reached inside, then let out a yelp of surprise as pulled out a long wooden beam ten times longer than the satchel itself. She watched in awe as the planks unfolded themselves from the tiny scrap of fabric. Long lengths of canvas ballooned like a ship's sails, and in a few moments a tent stood before us, arch-domed and fit for an emperor.

"I suppose I shouldn't have expected a god to sleep on the cold earth," Psyche remarked, peering up to admire the structure.

"I would never endure such a thing." I shuddered at the thought. "And I would never ask you to do so either."

That night, I stared at the vaulted canvas ceiling of the tent and thought about Anteia. It had been many years since I had reason to recall the wan, sad princess, but my conversation with Psyche brought me back to the halls of that old palace. An uncomfortable idea had taken up residence in my mind: Had Anteia felt the same way I did after the slip with Aphrodite's arrow? Had she ached for Bellerophon the way I ached for Psyche now? She too had been the victim of a love curse, but I had been its cause.

I thought about what I would feel if Psyche rejected me as Bellerophon had Anteia, and my soul balked. I could not imagine the pain. Yet even that had been a clean break, before they had the chance to become rooted in each other's lives. I had taken Psyche into my home, conversed with her, shared sleep with her. Even now she lay next to me, and I touched her leg with a toe just to assure myself she was real. To lose her now would be like tearing off a limb.

The thought robbed me of sleep, and I tossed and turned throughout the long hours of the night. Tomorrow I would speak with an old friend of mine, the god whose knowledge of humanity exceeded all others.

12

PSYCHE

When I woke that morning, it was to an effervescent lightness in my heart. It took me a moment to place its source. Then I remembered Cupid's praise after my fight with the bandits, the awe and delight in his voice. I had always longed to be respected for my training, exalted even, but I had never expected to be *liked* for it.

Another voice rose in my memory. *Choose a man like Meleager*, Atalanta once said. Someone who didn't tolerate who I was, like Nestor would have, but cherished it instead. Though I had not found my husband in the usual manner, it seemed that in some roundabout way I had arrived at the right place.

I shook away the last tatters of my dream and pushed aside the tent flap. I saw a white horse waiting for me, perfect as a creature from legend. The new sun glowed on his flanks like the full moon.

"It is time," Cupid said, flicking his tail. "We have almost reached him. Get on my back."

Behind me, the miraculous tent folded itself up again into the satchel, and I took it as I climbed onto the horse's back.

I was used to riding bareback from Atalanta's lessons, holding with my legs as the mount picked up speed, but this was different. The world itself seemed to wheel around us, and I squeezed my eyes shut as the wind whipped tears from them.

All at once, Cupid slowed to a trot. The air smelled different, and I knew we were a long way from the place we had made camp that night. I was about to chide my husband for concealing this form of fast travel when I opened my eyes and forgot all speech. We were among the craggy fastness of mountain peaks, reaching up toward the sky. The air was thin here, and cold. I saw a sole figure chained there, bare-chested and hauntingly beautiful.

The breath left my lungs. I dismounted and approached the stranger, feeling as though I was dreaming. Cupid had told me of the purpose of our quest, but I didn't truly understand until I saw *him*.

"Prometheus," I whispered.

I knew who Cupid and I had come to meet, but it was one thing to know a plan and something very different to see a god in person.

Prometheus's bare feet scarcely touched the earth, and he was nude except for a single loincloth and the harsh silver links of the chains that cut into the soft swells of his arms. His face possessed the same sharp symmetry I had seen on Zephyrus, though there were hollows under Prometheus's eyes and a beard that furred his chin. Curls of unkempt black hair fell over his face, and a healing wound marred his side, scabbed over with dull gold ichor.

"Greetings, my old friend," Cupid said, stepping forward and shaking his mane. "I wanted to introduce you to my wife."

Prometheus's brows lifted. "Your wife! Did she marry you like that?" With a flick of his chin, he indicated the horse's shape.

I reddened, but Cupid snapped, "Don't be absurd. My current shape is an unfortunate necessity."

Prometheus's face turned to me, though I could see him flinch a little as the movement tugged the healing wound at his side. I thought I could see stars in the depths of his eyes, but perhaps it was just a reflection of the sun. "Forgive me, lady," he said, sounding sincere. "I did not mean to question your virtue. Tell me, what is your name?"

"Psyche," I replied. "And I'm sorry, I should have brought a gift, a tribute." Though what one could offer to the creator of humanity, I had no idea.

"Ah, 'soul,'" Prometheus remarked. "And my name means *forethought*. What a pair we are, Forethought and the Soul. And as for tribute, don't trouble yourself with that. The company of a beautiful woman is more than enough of a gift."

Heat crept up my face. Cupid pawed the ground with a hoof. "I came to ask you a question, not to let you flirt with my wife."

"There's plenty of time for questions," Prometheus replied smoothly, as though he was in one of the receiving rooms on Mount Olympus and not bound in chains on a mountainside. "I'm merely enjoying the rare pleasure of conversation." He turned back to me. "Should you desire a less surly companion, my dear, you are always welcome here."

Cupid snorted and wheeled away.

I turned to Prometheus. "Stop it!" I ordered, my shy pleasure at his flattery turning to annoyance. "My husband is your guest, and we have traveled a long way to speak with you. He does not deserve your mockery, even if his manners leave something to be desired." Perhaps it was not wise to scold a god, but the laws of hospitality came from Zeus himself.

Prometheus gave a low chuckle. "Perhaps my friend has learned something after all, if he has won himself such a wife."

Cupid cropped at the grass several paces away, lifting his head to shoot us a bitter look.

I turned back to Prometheus, but his mirth dissolved into

discomfort as he looked down at his wound. The scab had opened with his movements, fresh ichor beading to the surface. His eyes closed, and his breath hissed through clenched teeth.

I knew the reason this god was tortured so. A question nibbled at the corner of my mind like an insistent mouse, one that I had wondered from the first moment I heard the blind poet's rendition of Prometheus's story.

"Why did you do it?" I asked breathlessly, words falling over one another. "Why did you give fire to humanity? We're grateful for it, but you must have known what Zeus would do to you."

Prometheus's shoulders rose and fell, making his chains rattle. "I suppose I did it for the same reason any immortal does anything: I wanted to see what would happen." He paused a moment as though weighing a secret, then added, "And because I have found that a life spent protecting what one loves is the greatest satisfaction of all."

Do you love humanity? I wanted to ask. Gods did not love human beings, generally speaking, but an artisan might be fond of what he created. But before I had a chance to ask, Prometheus's eyes lifted to the sky. I followed his gaze and saw that a black speck had appeared in the endless expanse of blue.

Prometheus sighed with a weariness as old as the earth itself. "It's the same eagle every time, you know," he said. "You notice these details as the years go by. Sometimes I wonder what the poor bird's crime was, and if it dreams of eating something other than liver every day."

"It will eat nothing today," I said fiercely, pulling an arrow from my quiver. *A monster feared by the gods*—perhaps I had found it at last. This eagle was feared by one god, at least.

"Stop!" Prometheus's refusal was like a hand on my shoulder, and I nearly dropped my bow in shock. "Don't kill the eagle. Zeus will only punish you for your actions before finding another bird to take its place. You are young, and I would not have you bring such a fate upon yourself."

My fingers tightened around the bowstring. "I am destined to become a great hero. The Oracle of Delphi said so herself."

Prometheus stared at me. It was as if his gaze was boring straight through me, as if his eyes could see secrets that I did not even know I was carrying.

"You will not be remembered as a great hero, but a great lover," he finished.

A chill ran through me. I heard the resonance of prophecy in his speech. But what an inane thing to prophesize, especially after the glory of the Oracle's promise! A great lover? I would rather have a hero's altar and a legend told around the fire.

Concern creased Prometheus's forehead when he saw my expression. "You don't know who your husband is, do you?" he finally asked. "Who he really is."

The hair on the back of my neck prickled. Some distance away, the white horse lifted his head to track the eagle's progress across the sky.

"I know him well enough," I replied hotly. "And I know something else too. If I can't free you from your torment, I can at least give your wound a chance to heal cleanly."

When the eagle dove for Prometheus's liver, I was there to meet it. It took three arrows to drive the beast away, fired in rapid succession. The last veered so close it tore a tuft of plumage from the eagle's back, but at last the bird gave a cry of supreme frustration and soared back up toward the sun, circling above us before going back the way it had come.

Prometheus's mouth twisted, his dry lips cracking, and I realized that he was smiling. I could not help thinking he seemed rather unpracticed at it. "My thanks," he said. "You do me a great service, girl, though you deprive the eagle of a meal. I believe your husband wishes to speak to me, so I must graciously ask for your leave. Forethought thanks the Soul, and bids her farewell."

I had been dismissed, but with such kindness and grace that I could not protest. On weightless feet, I wandered away. But Prometheus's voice continued to echo in my mind, the words filled with sad understanding: *You don't know who your husband is, do you?*

EROS

After Psyche left to sit on a boulder and stare at the ground, I approached my old friend.

"Does love cause them pain?" I asked feverishly, not bothering with preamble. "The humans, I mean." The question had chafed my mind ever since I recalled the incident with Anteia. I had to know if she once felt the same pain I did now.

"Has falling in love with one of them caused you to realize their value?" Prometheus's eyes glittered with amusement. "You know, a marriage isn't exactly what I had in mind when I asked you to care for humanity."

"Don't be foolish. My love for Psyche is the result of a curse."

"You could have done worse as far as love curses go," he commented wryly. "But to answer your question: Yes, the mortal girl you love is like a thousand other mortal girls, all of whom feel pain and happiness. Sometimes love causes one, and sometimes the other—much as it is among the gods. I'm more concerned about the fact that you're lying to Psyche." It should not have been possible for someone bound and shackled to look stern, but Prometheus managed it.

I glanced at my wife, who was resting her chin on a hand and gazing unfocusedly into the distance. I had never seen her look so thoughtful. "It's safer for her this way," I said.

"Is that what you've told yourself? All these vain attempts to keep her in the dark will not ensure she stays at your side. Lies always catch up to you."

His words carried a bitter truth—one that I had known from the start but tried to ignore. The longer this went on, the more it would hurt both Psyche and I later.

I was growing frantic. "But what do I do about it? Nothing can break the curse. An antidote from Aphrodite's own hand failed to ease the torment. *What do I do?*"

I thought that Prometheus, lover of mortals, would know the direction I must take, but he remained maddeningly calm. "I suppose you simply love her as best you can and for as long as you can, until her mortal soul goes down into the Underworld."

The words hung in the air between us. I had always known that Psyche was mortal and therefore death threatened to part us, but to hear it said aloud was intolerable.

I shook my head. "Even death is no guarantee that the curse would end."

"For you, this is true," Prometheus said. "But Psyche, at least, would be free. The waters of the river Lethe wash away all memories."

I flicked my tail back and forth uneasily. It was unfathomable, the thought of living on forever as Psyche's unknowing soul wandered beyond my reach.

"I wish you happiness nonetheless," Prometheus declared. "Enjoy the time you have together, however brief it may be. All my hopes for you have come to fruition."

I eyed him. "And what were those hopes?"

"That you would be able to call yourself beloved, to feel yourself beloved upon the earth."

Strange words, as though he was quoting a poem that had not yet been written. But then again, Prometheus had always been a little mad.

It didn't matter. As I said farewell and went to collect my wife, the seed of an idea took root in my mind and began to sprout.

As Psyche and I continued our journey over rocky mountain paths, my new plan took shape.

Prometheus had spoken of Lethe, one of the winding rivers of the Underworld. If a taste of those waters was enough to wipe away the memories of a mortal life, what could they do to an immortal? All this time I had been seeking ways to *remove* the curse when I should have been trying to *forget* it.

The plan was not without its flaws, I knew. There was no guarantee that the Lethe water would remove the curse without scrubbing away all my other memories. But that was a small price to pay to blot out the curse, to free me from this weight that hung like an anchor around my neck. I could not live through the numberless days of my immortal existence with a love-poisoned spirit.

How to get the Lethe water? Gods were not permitted into the Underworld, save for Hades and his bride, Persephone, and sometimes Hermes. But Hermes would never help me as long as Aphrodite held her grudge; he'd been infatuated with her for centuries and would do nothing that might displease her. I could call in the favor that Persephone owed me, but I did not want to trade so valuable a boon for something so small as a cup of water. Then another idea occurred to me.

Psyche.

She, like all mortals, could travel into the Underworld. If she did so while she was still alive, surely she could return just as easily. She could bring me the water of Lethe and break the curse once and for all. I would ask her tonight, I resolved. I knew that she would not flinch from the journey. She had shown unwavering courage during the time I had known her.

And what would happen to her afterward? Perhaps I would ask Psyche to drink from the waters too and forget she had ever known me. We would part, and she could go back to her life in Mycenae. Aphrodite would not recognize Psyche if she didn't recognize herself. Psyche could go on to live an ordinary life among her fellow human beings. It would be for the best.

If I tried, I could almost bring myself to believe this. The curse howled within me, but I pushed it back down firmly. I had to free myself, to bring an end to this madness that consumed me.

PSYCHE

You don't know who your husband is, do you?

The question haunted me through the long hours of the journey, as we wound through mountain paths rough with tumbled stones. I scrambled over piles of rocks, and in much the same way, I sifted through my thoughts. I was determined to know Cupid better.

That night, when Cupid's broad-shouldered man's form joined me in the tent, I was ready.

"Let us play a game," I said, clapping my hands. "You said you were a skilled archer, did you not?"

"I am," he said slowly. "But what on earth are you up to, Psyche?"

I reached down, fumbling with my bow and arrows in the darkness. "Let us match our skills," I said. "Whoever can hit the tent post wins!"

I did not wait for his puzzled grunt of assent. I fumbled my way through the darkness to ascertain the position of the wooden post holding up our tent. I tapped it with my foot, then traced my way back.

"This isn't exactly fair," Cupid told me. "Your senses are not as sharp as mine. You are at a disadvantage."

I didn't answer. Instead, I nocked an arrow to my bow, trusting in the knowledge of my body and the precision of my tools. I lined up the arrow over my foot, pointed at the post. I released and was rewarded with a satisfactory *thunk* as the arrow hit the wood.

I yelped in delight, and even Cupid murmured impressed acknowledgment. I felt the bow and quiver leave my hands as he took them, and then the creak of the bowstring as he lined up his shot. A moment later came a similar *thunk*, along with the sound of wood splintering. I shuffled through the darkness to the tent pole and ran my hands over it, feeling the curve of wood like the unfurling of a flower. I realized his arrow had split mine down the middle.

"Well, I suppose that's to be expected of a god," I replied airily, a bit miffed at his precision. Even Atalanta could not accomplish such a feat as this. "But don't you think I did well?"

"You did," he replied, as if to a child. He guided me back inside the tent. I heard him settle into the wide bed at the center of the room.

I joined him beneath the sheets. "Next we'll try our hands at shooting down birds on the wing," I said. "It might be difficult to do so at night, but not impossible."

"No," came the reply. "I am . . . loath to use my arrows on living things. The outcome does not please me."

"Oh," I said, wilting with disappointment. I'd hoped to go

hunting with him, as Atalanta had with Meleager. "I suppose it would be too difficult, anyway. Since we can't see each other's faces."

"I've been thinking about that, Psyche," he said. I heard him shift and thought he might have propped his chin on his hand. "There might be a way to break the curse. But I will need your help, and the quest will be long and dangerous."

"How?" I demanded, intrigued at the possibility. "Where?"

The thought of seeing Cupid in the daylight made my nerves sing with excitement. I wanted to rest my eyes on the planes of the face my fingers had danced across in darkness. I wanted to know him, all of him.

"The cure lies in the Underworld," came his reply. "Gods cannot enter, but mortals can. You must bring back water from the river Lethe. That should be enough to break the curse."

A tendril of fear curled through me, but I dismissed it. Mortals who went down into the Underworld were not supposed to return to the land of the living, but Cupid was a god and possessed strange magic. He must have found a way to ensure I would be able to travel to the Underworld and return with the waters of Lethe. "Of course I will go!" I exclaimed.

Cupid laughed uncertainly at my eager response. "Have you no questions? Is 'the Underworld' the name of a pleasant hot spring or lovely valley among your people? This is the land of the dead I speak of, Psyche."

"No, you were quite clear," I replied. "But a journey like this is the stuff of legend. And if the curse is broken, we'll finally be able to see each other." At last, I would know who he really was.

"Naturally," he said after a pause. "I am pleased to hear it. I knew I could trust you. Goodnight, Psyche."

I heard him roll over, so his back faced me. I frowned into the darkness, puzzled that he wasn't more enthusiastic about the thought of not needing to hide, but warmed by his words. Cupid trusted me.

Hungry for something I could not name, I lifted a hand and stroked the warm skin of his shoulder. When I felt his body ease and turn back toward me, I wrapped my arms around him and laid my head on his chest. The darkness lent itself to intimacies that were unthinkable in the daylight hours.

Cupid tensed for a moment, then relaxed. An arm lifted to embrace me. It occurred to me that he was not used to being touched; gods were solitary creatures, it seemed, like tigers or bears. I could feel his body against mine—cheek to chest, thigh upon thigh, his arm encircling me. Lean, strong, so much like a man's that I might believe him mortal if I didn't know the truth. How well we fit together, how pleasingly he moved against me. A longing woke in me, a hope for more.

I wanted to ask what Prometheus had said to him, or to tell him what Prometheus had told me. Especially the part about being a great lover instead of a great hero. I wanted to ask for something I had never known, never felt except in fleeting moments between twilight and dawn when I lay tangled in my bedsheets, alone until now.

But the words slipped away from me like shadows swallowed by the night. I didn't want to ruin what we had. I didn't want to feel Cupid draw away from this warm moment like a turtle into its shell.

Wrapped in his arms, I fell asleep.

The next day dawned hot and bright, and I was thinking about sex.

I knew what sex was, vaguely. I'd seen horses and sheep in the act, and I'd heard the servants in the Mycenaean palace whispering about their various dalliances. I understood the basic mechanics, even though a well-bred girl was not supposed to know such things until her wedding night. But my own wedding night had come and gone, and I knew nothing more than I did before.

I glanced at my husband, who had taken the shape of a lion today, ambling along the path. He was quiet, perhaps focused on the task ahead.

Abruptly, he halted. We had arrived at a low cavern set in the earth, its yawning mouth disappearing into darkness. It looked much like any of the other small caves that dotted this mountainous landscape, but something about this one gave me pause. The shadows beyond its low entrance were pitch-black, swallowing all light. I had the sense that if I tossed a pebble into the cave, it would make no sound.

Such places existed on the fringes of the world, in the oceans far beyond sight of land and in remote stony regions like this one. I knew where we were. My flesh itself knew; I found myself drawn inexorably to the mouth of the cave, the ultimate destination of all mortals.

"We're here," Cupid said, leonine tail flicking back and forth. "We've come to the cave of Taenarum. This is the gateway to the Underworld."

EROS

I made Psyche tie a rope around her ankle before her descent, which caused her to laugh and wrinkle her nose at me. "Am I a Phoenician pearl diver, leaping into the Mediterranean?" she asked playfully. "Will you drag me out by your teeth if I run into trouble?"

"I will if I must," I replied, my tail lashing from side to side. There was an electric thrum in the air, a frisson of anxiety. Psyche was going where I could not follow. *But mortals go into the Underworld and return all the time*, I told myself; there had been the hero Heracles, and the singer Orpheus, and even the wandering prince Theseus. Mortals knew all sorts of tricks for such things, and Psyche's enthusiasm suggested she had matters well in hand. And if she did not, I would pull her out myself. Yet I could not shake the thought that I was forgetting something.

"You worry too much for a god," Psyche remarked.

"I worry exactly as much as I need to. Here, take this with you," I added, pawing a bowl free from the satchel. It was white and smooth and fit perfectly into the palm of Psyche's hand. "Use it to collect the water. Go as quickly as you can, and do not be alarmed if it is night when you return. Time moves differently in the land of the dead."

Psyche took the bowl and paused, studying me expectantly

with her deep brown eyes. She chewed her lip as she turned the bowl in her hands, as though waiting for me to say something. But what does one say before watching one's spouse descend into the Underworld? What is the proper etiquette for such a situation?

"Swift journeys," I said awkwardly.

Psyche nodded. "I'll see you again before long."

PSYCHE

I began my descent, clambering down over a scrabble of rocks until I reached the proper path leading into the darkness. Here at the edge of the Underworld I felt a chill, but I quickly dismissed it. I was a god's wife and made this descent under divine protection; I had nothing to fear.

I entered the cave. The dirt was remarkably smooth under my feet, and the light from the living world soon vanished. But I was used to darkness and unafraid. The rope whispered behind me in the dust.

It was not long before I saw another light, duller and weaker than that of the living world. When I reached it, I marveled at a place that shocked me with its strangeness. The Underworld.

I stood on a slight incline that sloped down to an empty road of hard-packed earth lined with cypresses—dry, desiccated things reaching up to a colorless sky. Beyond that was the arch of a small bridge, and then a vast forest of naked wintertime trees devoid of all leaves. The scene before me was painted all in black and gray, as though color had been leeched out of the world.

A heavy mist lay over the landscape. Neither the light of sun nor that of the moon could pierce its veil to reach to this infernal place. There was only an arching darkness that must be the underbelly of the earth or the ribcage of Tartarus, the Titan slain to make this hollow dwelling place for the dead.

Far beyond the forest, I saw a palace of white marble adorned with turrets, rising like needles to pierce the hollow sky. There was something defiant about that royal structure, springing up so abruptly from the dull landscape. It was a snub to the muted sensibilities of the mortal dead, who would never again be able to grasp anything as solid as those walls. This must be the dwelling place of the queen of the dead, Persephone, and her husband, Hades.

The low swells of other hills rose behind the palace. I knew some of their names—the Fields of Asphodel and the Isles of the Blessed, where the souls of heroes went. But many more were the nameless places where the pale shadows of the dead loitered for all eternity, the brief dreams that had been their lives growing ever more distant.

A thick black band encircled the palace. This must be the River Styx, across which the ferryman Charon delivered the newly dead. Other rivers meandered across the landscape like inky black veins. One of them must be Lethe, my goal.

I began to walk in that direction, but abruptly stopped short. It was as if I were a dog snapped to the end of its tether. I took a breath and steeled myself, pushing forward again, but some great weight blocked my path. I pressed harder until I felt a wrenching pop of release. I stumbled, feeling suddenly weightless.

I realized why when I looked back and saw my own body crumpled on the path, limbs askew. The fine white bowl Cupid had given me lay shattered on the ground.

PSYCHE

Cupid and I, each assuming the other had a plan, overlooked one important fact: Mortals who attempt the *katabasis*, the Underworld descent, must bring an offering. Heracles gave his own blood, while Orpheus paid for his passage with a song. But I had come empty-handed, save for a bowl to take what had never been given, and now I paid the price.

My ghostly form could no longer feel the adrenaline rush that comes with shock, since I no longer had adrenal glands or a heart. All the same, shock is the best term for what I felt, staring at the discarded shell of my mortal body.

"There's no use in gawking," a harsh female voice said. "There's no help for it now."

I whirled. A woman—or what I took at first to be a woman—waited nearby. She was peculiar-looking, too striking to be truly beautiful. Her cheekbones flared outward like the face of a cat, with narrow almond-shaped eyes that gazed mistrustfully at me over a wide, flat nose. Her hair was a rich mane of black tendrils—braids, or so I thought at first, until the hair moved and tasted the air with forked tongues.

A jolt of recognition. I remembered Perseus's shield in the hero's room at the Mycenaean palace, and the face depicted on it. Medusa.

"I am aware that I am a strange choice for your escort into

the land of the dead," Medusa continued. "Normally Hermes would serve as your psychopomp and escort you into the Underworld, but it seems you've offended his dear Aphrodite. So the queen sent me instead." She looked at me with her lip slightly curled, as though I was a latrine she had been ordered to empty. "I cannot say why Persephone tasked *me* with fetching my murderer's granddaughter, but here we are."

"Perseus wasn't a murderer," I replied hotly. Even with my own corpse at my feet, I would not let such an insult stand. "He was a hero."

Medusa was unimpressed. "Then why did he kill me when I was alone and pregnant in my own home?"

I was too startled to reply. This was not the story that my father had told me in the hero's room so long ago. "You were a monster," I said, which seemed a strange thing to point out to the monster herself.

Medusa scoffed. "I was a nymph by birth, I'll have you know. I was only transformed into a gorgon as punishment for someone else's crime. Monstrous things have been done to me. Was it any surprise that I became a monster myself?"

I stared at her undulating mane. "I don't understand," I said.

She sighed heavily. "When I was young, I used to bring offerings to Athena's temple every morning at sunrise. One day Poseidon found me there alone and raped me."

Medusa's eyes were cold. She looked out over the mist-decked road of cypresses. The pain of this story had faded for her, leaving only bitterness, but for me it came as a shock.

"Athena came upon me later that morning," she continued. "I had long been her worshiper and had asked her for many things, but on that day I had only one request, whispered through cracked lips. 'Let this never happen again.'

"Athena nodded. We both knew that Poseidon wasn't done

with me yet. He liked to toy with his conquests, and I was too minor a goddess to oppose him. So Athena gave me a gift: the ability to turn mortals and gods to stone with a look. Poseidon left me alone after that. Though I soon discovered I was pregnant, I was safe. At least until mortal men seeking fame began to hunt me. Legends of a gorgon stirred would-be heroes into action. Perseus was only the last in an endless procession."

I blinked in confusion. My grandfather Perseus was heralded as a protector, a guardian of the people. The portrait Medusa painted did not align with the stories my father or the blind poet had told me. "But heroes protect their people—" I began.

"What were those men protecting their people from? A tired old goddess who only wanted to raise her sons in peace? I would have left these so-called heroes alone if they had granted me the same privilege." Medusa added, voice dripping contempt, "And if heroes look to protect their people, why don't they feed the hungry or warm the shivering? Hunger and cold are more common than gorgons, and far more deadly. No, 'hero' is a title granted to the one with the most impressive kills to his name. I don't see how a hero differs from a pig farmer. Both are butchers."

I had no rebuttal. I loved my grandfather Perseus—or what I thought I had known of him—but I could not shy away from the truth I heard in Medusa's words.

Finally, I said, "The Oracle of Delphi prophesied that I would become a hero. But when I met the Titan Prometheus, he told me that I would not be remembered as a great hero but a great lover."

"Good," Medusa replied. She looked at me appraisingly, as though I might actually be worthy of her attention after all. Her hair writhed and flicked the air with its tongues. "Maybe there is something worthwhile in Perseus's line after all. Better to be a lover than a dealer of death. Now come, you've wasted enough of my time already."

The gorgon began to stride down the long road lined with cypresses. I trailed after her, even as I glanced over my shoulder at the forlorn shape of my mortal body. Understanding washed over me: I was dead, truly dead.

"But now I'll never be anything," I whispered, shifting my eyes down to my ghostly feet. I could see the packed earth of the road through them, an unnerving sight. "Lover or hero or even just a living woman. Do you know, I only got married a few days ago. It was an odd match, and the circumstances were odder still, but I think we might have come to truly care about each other. We never even got to consummate the marriage." Medusa's honesty had quickened my own, and sometimes my mouth gets ahead of my mind.

The gorgon halted and stared at me in naked astonishment. "Here I stand at the boundaries of the Underworld with my murderer's granddaughter," she said, "and she talks about *consummating her marriage*?"

Laughter bubbled up from Medusa, and she threw back her head in a wild cackle. Once she had calmed herself, she added, "You're bold, granddaughter of Perseus, and frank as well. If what you say is true, then you have my condolences. Lying with someone you love is one of life's great delights."

Now it was my turn to be astonished.

"Don't forget that I was a nymph before I was a gorgon," Medusa said, and I was startled to see her wink.

Before I could formulate a reply, a tremor passed through my body and the landscape rippled like a reflection in a troubled pool. Far away, the dark shapes of the hills and the towers of the white palace vanished into nothingness. As I watched, the long road and its cypresses began to roll up like a scroll, trees disappearing into the folds.

Medusa clicked her tongue. "It seems as though your soul isn't ready to be separated from your body. I'd imagine that husband of yours has something to do with it, now that he's realized his mistake sending you here empty-handed. No matter. Eventually you'll come back here, and when you do, I will be waiting for the answer to my question." She met my eyes and for the first time I noticed their color—brown like my father's, brown like my own.

"What is it that makes a true hero?" Medusa finished.

The Underworld vanished, collapsing in on itself until nothing remained. The last things I saw were the glowing eyes of Medusa, like torches in the dark.

EROS

I paced uneasily across the rocky ground as the sun slid through the sky, still in my lion's shape. Next to me, the rope uncoiled with the smoothness of water as it tracked Psyche's pace in the Underworld.

I had been restless since the moment she made her descent, turning over my makeshift plan for gaps and flaws. Lethe water as a solution to the curse wasn't foolproof, but it was the best of my limited options. And Psyche—

I froze, one paw suspended above the earth. I had been dogged by a sense of something forgotten ever since we departed the seaside house, nibbling mouselike at the back of my mind. Now I remembered: a gift for the dead, a token for the Underworld to ensure her safe passage back.

Suddenly the sinuously uncoiling rope went still. The fur on the nape of my neck lifted. Nothing could stop Psyche once she set her mind to a task.

It was not too late. It could not be too late. I seized the rope in my jaws and began to pull but met with heavy resistance on the other end. I pulled as hard as I could, trying not to think too deeply about what might have happened to Psyche, or the scrape of sand on mortal flesh.

Turning back to my true shape, I raced to the entrance to the Underworld and felt the limits of space and time tugging at my divine form. Gods cannot enter the land of the dead, but in my desperation, I refused to be moved. I began to haul the rope hand over hand into the light.

As I did, my mind raced. Desperate to be free from my suffering, I had brought upon both of us the very fate I feared. I had sent Psyche thoughtlessly into living death, assuming that her self-assurance signified actual preparation.

Time moves differently in the Underworld, I had said to Psyche. From her perspective, no more than a few minutes had passed, but by the time I dragged her body into sight, stars were beginning to dapple the blue of the western sky.

I ran to her side, shaking. She was limp and cold, eyes unseeing. Her flesh was clammy, reminding me unpleasantly of the clay from which Prometheus had shaped her kind.

For a few seconds, I did not move. The curse rose within me like a cruel wind, spiraling out through my marrow. Psyche was dead, and I had lost her through my own foolishness. I understood why Gaia had taken refuge in the cold darkness of the earth after the loss of her husband, Ouranos. Nothing could preserve me from the grief that threatened to pull me down like an undertow. I had loved Psyche from the moment the arrow gashed my skin, an unpleasant fact over which I had no control. But recently, I had begun to *like* her.

I shook her corpse helplessly, a cry of desperation tearing itself from my throat. I tried to breathe what life I could into Psyche's corpse, to startle her heart back into motion. I had no idea if any of this would work, no idea how fragile the mortal form truly was. But I was the god of desire, and I desired her to live. Psyche had only been gone for a few moments as the living world reckons time. Perhaps I could still bring her back. Perhaps.

15

PSYCHE

I drew a long shuddering breath as my soul fell back into my body. The night air was the most wonderful thing I had ever tasted, clear and sweet. I didn't know where I was, only that it was dark, and I was not alone. Hands tangled in my hair, lifting my face.

A familiar voice whispered, "You're alive! Oh Psyche, I was a fool . . ."

My husband, Cupid. His hands moved over me, checking my limbs for scrapes. There were more than a few, not that I cared. His anxious tone almost made me laugh—since when did my proud husband speak like that?—but at this moment I didn't want laughter or recriminations, or even speech. I wanted something else, wilder and more primal, something connected to the pulse of life itself. I thought about what Medusa had told me about life's greatest joys. I wanted a torch to drive away the last remnants of the darkness.

I wound my fingers in Cupid's hair and pulled him in for a kiss. I was rewarded with a startled cry reminiscent of the peacocks on the terraces back at the seaside house, but soon he was kissing me back with fierce intensity. He was like a dam that had spilled its banks, a drowning man seeking air.

I pulled away, hungry for more. I grabbed his tunic and attempted to pull it over his head. This succeeded only in smothering him, though he quickly caught on to what I was trying to do. In a flash, his clothing was gone. He began to work on mine next, pulling my chiton over my head. I lifted my arms to let him.

He kissed me again with such skill and softness that I marveled. I could feel the excitement thrumming under his skin, and it endeared him to me. He maneuvered me to the ground, trying to position us over the pile of fallen clothing, but by that time I didn't care. I had been kept from sex all my life, shielded from it with propriety, and now I was ready to see what all the fuss was about.

The night air prickled my bare skin, and I was reminded that we were only a stone's throw from the edge of the Underworld. Then Cupid's chest was pressed against mine, hot as a furnace. He kissed me again, more softly this time, then left my lips bereft to move lower. I felt his hair tickle my breasts, moving over the planes of my belly, stopping near my pelvis. I caught at his hair, trying to drag his lips back to mine, but he evaded my grip. He must be confused; perhaps he was trying to check for wounds, though this wasn't the time. I was certain he had gone mad when he wrapped his hands around my thighs, bringing his head between my legs.

Oh.

Oh.

He worked on me with lips and tongue until I was nearly incoherent, feverish with desire. Then he positioned himself above me. I was afraid it would hurt, but Cupid knew how to kindle my body like a fire, so that the pain was brief and quickly washed away by delight. Having him was sweeter than honey, more exhilarating than riding a wild horse. I locked my legs around him to pull him deeper, digging my nails into his back, savoring his ragged breath in my ears. The fire of the stars had poured into my veins, and at his touch it exploded into light.

Afterward, we didn't bother with blankets. Instead, we pressed ourselves to each other, our body heat just enough to offset the chill of the night. Chest to chest, forehead to forehead, so that each of Cupid's exhalations tickled my eyelashes. Never before had I felt so laid bare in front of another living being, though the feeling wasn't entirely unpleasant. Rather, it was like sharing a secret I had carried all my life, confiding it in a trusted friend at last. I knew Cupid more deeply than I had known any other living creature, even though I had never seen his face.

I sought to fill the silence. "I wasn't able to retrieve the water of Lethe," I said.

"I noticed," he replied, amused.

I paused for a moment, feeling his eyelashes move against my skin like the wings of butterflies. "I wish I could say that I was sorry. But if this is the result, I'm not very sorry at all."

I felt rather than saw his smile. "Neither am I."

16

PSYCHE

When I was young, my father sometimes took me to see the glassblowers in the artisans' quarter of Tiryns. Alkaios liked to walk among his people so that he would know them and therefore see how to rule them best, and the artisans inclined their heads in respect at his passing. I marveled at the spindly designs the glassblowers wove from sand and fire and breath, molten glass expanding like a bubble.

The first days after my return from the Underworld were like that: beautiful but impossibly delicate, of a sweetness that I knew could not possibly last.

We took our time on the journey back. Though the trip to Taenarum had taken us only three days, our return lasted over a month. We had been husband and wife in name since I came to live at the seaside house, but this marked the beginning of something new.

Cupid did not speak again of the curse, and I made no mention of the beast I was fated to slay. He did not speak of our failed venture to retrieve the waters from Lethe, and I did not ask about his true form. Instead, we talked of other things.

I told him about my glimpse of the Underworld, that place of dead forests and mist and winding rivers. As a god, he could never go there, and he was curious about it. I told him about meeting Medusa and what she had said to me about heroes.

He remarked that she had a point, and only laughed when I scowled at him.

Our nights were spent doing other things.

Cupid seemed to know a seemingly endless variety of ways that two bodies could come together in pleasure, and I was all too pleased to learn. There were times when I felt as I had when I had been a butterfly: thoughtless, warm, floating in bliss.

One night as we lay beneath the covers in the darkness, Cupid told me haltingly of something he had seen long ago. "A mortal man and woman," he began. "Of the wrinkly kind."

I bit back a laugh. "Elderly, you mean?"

"I think so, but that's not the point. They were so gentle with each other, such tenderness flowed between them. I had seen them once when I was younger, but this was different. What did it mean?"

"It's nothing very mysterious," I told him. "I think they were just in love."

Love. I had never had much use for the concept, had never gone to the altars of Aphrodite or her sweet-cheeked son Eros begging for some pretty youth to notice me. Even now I didn't think of love, not in the abstract—I only thought of Cupid, and waited with bated breath for night to fall so that I could take him in my arms again.

Eventually we returned to the seaside house, where I found several letters of increasing concern from my parents waiting for me. They rejoiced that I was well but were alarmed at the husband I mentioned. They knew nothing of Cupid.

My hands clenched the edge of the table, white-knuckled. My mother had not arranged the match after all. I tried to tell myself that it didn't matter, that everything had worked out for the best, but I could not ignore the unease that settled into my heart like a nest of fruit flies in a rubbish heap.

Happy though I was during those weeks after I returned from the Underworld, I felt a certain listlessness. Sometimes Medusa's words would echo in my head, or I would wonder about the human world I had left behind. The monster that supposedly hunted me had never materialized; I knew it could not be the monster that had destroyed the village, since that had been Zephyrus. The wind god had paid his promised share of the repairs for the village, I learned from my parents' letter, in the form of ancient gold coinage mysteriously dropped from the sky over Tiryns.

After a tirade at Zephyrus for his trick with the moly, I accepted his sincere apology. Since then, he had begun to visit regularly, and I found that his company made the time go faster during the long daylit hours when my husband was away.

"Are things supposed to be this easy? Being with him, I mean," I asked Zephyrus one day as we sipped wine on the terrace overlooking the ocean.

"They *should* always be so easy," Zephyrus replied. "Not every marriage has to be a travesty like that of Zeus and Hera. Things were easy for Hyacinthos and me too before he died." There was a trace of wistfulness in the curve of his mouth, but it soon vanished.

Even during these golden times, doubt crouched in wait. The fact remained that I was mortal and Cupid was a god. He would be my entire life, and I would only be a brief passerby in his.

There was also the fact that he still would not let me see his face. I began to wonder if I truly would immolate under his regard, or if there was something else he was hiding from me. It was too convenient that he could steal the face of an animal during the daylight hours, only to come to me in the shape of a man at night.

During the nights of the new moon, we went outside to lie on the flagstones of the terraces, looking up at the undimmed stars. We would point out the constellations that the gods placed in the sky and tell each other stories about them. I knew the versions passed among mortals, but my husband told the old tales as though he had actually been there; indeed, in some cases, he had. We bickered over whose version was better.

I snuck glances at him in the starlight, but I could never quite make out his features. I tried to persuade him outside on the nights of the full moon, when I was sure to catch at least a glimpse of his face, but he always refused.

EROS

I began to notice things that I had not truly seen in a thousand years. I saw how the cats played and the peacocks set themselves on display. I became aware of the intricate beauty of the flowers that grew along the terrace, tended by the magic of the seaside house. Before, my days had been numberless and weightless, but now everything was thrown into sharp relief. The curse, now declawed, sang within me. With Psyche, my life was limned in gold.

I found that I liked having someone to talk to in the evenings. If I saw some particularly arresting sight or amusing occurrence during the day, I would think *I cannot wait to tell Psyche about this later*. I would imagine the sound of her laugh and feel as though I was soaring high above the earth even when my feet were solidly planted on the ground.

I was wise enough to know that my happiness was balanced on the edge of a knife. By loving Psyche, I was setting myself up for tragedy. Even if I somehow managed to keep her safe from Aphrodite and to circumvent the curse, the fact remained she was mortal and I was not, a gulf that yawned between us.

"If I could go back," Zephyrus said, "I would have ensured that I gave Hyacinthos his apotheosis. Just so I could have him with me, if nothing else. You still have time with Psyche." He shot me a glance. "Don't waste it."

I leaned back. We were in my favorite forest grove, sunlight falling through the trees like colored glass, dappling the brush in the shaded colors of a tiger's fur. I came here during the day when Psyche roamed around the seaside house, to ensure that she did not catch sight of my face and set off the curse in its completeness. Sometimes Zephyrus joined me.

"Not every mortal can achieve apotheosis," I replied, speaking of the process that transformed mortals into gods. "Only those who have distinguished themselves. Also, the majority of gods must approve, and when have they ever all agreed on one thing? Aphrodite would forbid it, certainly." I'd thought about this more than once, my mind going around in wheels within wheels, and I had found no resolution to the problem. My love for Psyche had to remain a secret.

Zephyrus was drifting through the air like a swimmer upon a river, reclining on his back with one knee up, his hands laced behind his head. "Well, don't blame me if her mortality proves more fragile than you thought."

Despite this, I still thought that all might turn out well. At least until the day I found an intruder picking my roses.

The roses grew on my terrace in abundant bloom. There was not a season that those velvet petals did not grace this arid place, a piece of magic I delighted in. But now someone was tangling with them, rustling the leaves, and breaking off the lovely blossoms. Golden hair flowed down her back.

The figure turned, and I recognized my sister Eris. She had not aged, of course, but the passage of time had sharpened her features, making them crueler and leaner. More herself, in other words.

"Ah, dearest brother," she said with a smile that did not reach her eyes. "I was wondering when you'd come to greet me." Her falsity put me in mind of Aphrodite; gods are always polite when they despise one another. We prefer vengeance by proxy.

"What are you doing here?" My question cleaved the air. The shorn roses raised mournful shoots above the soil, and the peacocks raised their heads at the sudden sound of my voice.

"Isn't visiting my brother reason enough? Oh, I simply must tell you about a recent jest I concocted. I stole one of the apples of the Hesperides and wrote upon it 'To the fairest.' Then I rolled it among the Olympians gathered at some wedding, and do you know what? Hera, Athena, and Aphrodite fell upon one another. Each thought it was addressed to her! 'To the fairest'!" She giggled, immensely proud. "The Olympians can't stand it when one of them possesses something the others lack, but your foster mother won, of course. She ingratiated herself to the poor little mortal they found to judge their contest, a wretch named Paris from a place called Troy."

"Don't toy with Aphrodite," I warned my sister. "No good will come of it."

Eris tilted her head, a dainty hand covering her mouth. "I'm not seeking your advice, sweet brother. I'm merely warning you. Aphrodite promised Paris the hand of the most beautiful woman in the world, and I wouldn't want it to be that human girl you're keeping as a pet. Psyche, I think her name is? Watch her closely, dear brother."

My body tensed, and my eyes darted toward the house. Before I could respond, black wings snapped open over Eris's shoulders and she launched herself into the abyss of the sky, still holding the bundle of stolen roses in her arms.

17

PSYCHE

One night a few months after our return from Taenarum, Cupid asked, "Psyche, why do you have two heartbeats?"

It was not long after sunset, and we were cuddled together in the wide bed. My head rested on his chest, and his fingers ran idly through my hair. I pulled away at this question, turning my face toward him though I could see nothing in the dark. "What on earth are you talking about?" I asked.

"You have two heartbeats," he replied. "Normally you have only one, but now I can hear another, though it is much fainter. Is this a common condition among mortals?"

Slowly I realized the provenance of his words. My blood had not come with the new moon, but I had thought this was due to the strain of travel. Then it dawned on me that Cupid had never met a pregnant woman before.

Haltingly, I told him what this meant. I felt the blankets shift as he sat up, and for a moment I feared he might flee. Then I heard a bark of delighted laughter and felt his arms twine around me.

"I have never had a child before," he said. "Never in all my centuries."

His kissed me and laughed, his lips as sweet as wine. I relaxed into his arms and let exhilaration fill me. A child, *our* child. Mortal or demigod, it would be loved.

"We must make a visit to Mycenae," I said excitedly. "I must tell my mother and father about their grandchild, and when my time comes, I want to give birth in my home city."

I'd learned to read the subtle shifts of my husband's body and voice as easily as others could read the emotions on a face, and I felt the warmth ebb from Cupid. He shied away from my touch. "We cannot," he said. "It's far too dangerous."

I felt as though the stone floor had fallen away beneath my feet. "Going to Taenarum and descending into the Underworld was far more dangerous!" I said, outraged. "This is my home we're speaking of."

"*This* is your home now."

Anger rose in me. I would not be a sow, whelping my husband's children in darkness. "I did not grow up here in these halls where no mortal voice breaks the silence. Come with me back to Mycenae. Meet my mother and father before the baby comes." I reached for his hand, but he squirmed from my touch.

"It's not that I don't see the appeal of such a plan," he said, choosing his words slowly. "But it is not worth the risk. Danger trails you like a lamb running after its mother. After Taenarum, I will not see you place yourself in danger needlessly."

I was shaking with rage. I had been told that pregnant women swing from one emotion to the other like a pendulum, but it was my husband's obstinacy that fueled my fury now.

"What am I to you?" I asked sharply. "A wife, or another one of your pets that you keep locked away in this lonely place?"

My accusations were met with stunned silence. I could tell that Cupid had not expected such anger.

"What happens when the baby comes?" I demanded, words rushing out of me like arterial blood. "Am I supposed to give birth here, alone, with only a shadow for an attendant? Will Zephyrus be my midwife? And the baby, will he be god or mortal?"

My heart was galloping in my chest, and my fingers were clutching the bedsheets the way a drowning sailor holds a rope. Other fears loomed in my mind, too pertinent to ignore. "Cupid," I began, a quaver in my voice. "What will happen when I grow old? When you remain young, and my face is creased by wrinkles?"

He did not reply at first, only sighed heavily and turned away. I listened to the rustling of the sheets as he settled himself in. When he did speak, his voice was rancid vinegar. "If you only listen to me about staying in the dark, I will never notice the wrinkles."

Outrage flared in me. I turned my back on him and rolled into a ball, staring into the merciless night until sleep took me.

EROS

I could not explain to Psyche that a goddess had made threats against her life. Psyche would only insist on charging into battle against this enemy, despite all my attempts to talk sense into her. Aphrodite would crush her without the slightest hesitation. I could not risk Psyche's life or the child's on such foolishness. Nor could I risk bringing the full weight of the curse upon us.

I came to Psyche the next night with the beginnings of a compromise. "We cannot go to Mycenae, but you may receive a visitor here."

I expected gratitude, but instead she snorted. "How generous, to allow me a visitor in my own home." Psyche was vicious when she was angry, like a cornered polecat.

I recoiled. I had come with an olive branch and received a blow from a switch.

"And how are my mother and father to get here?" she continued. "They rule a kingdom. They are not free to travel whenever they like. And furthermore, what will I tell them about a husband who refuses to make an appearance?"

I was quickly losing patience. "Then invite someone else," I replied, desperation fraying the edges of my words. "Perhaps that cousin you talk so much about, the priestess."

Psyche laughed bitterly and did not reply. "And what will I say to her? That my husband is a dolphin, a bird, a horse?"

I was finished and wanted only to sleep. "Tell her as much or as little as you like," I said, settling into my side of the bed. "You complain when I tell you what to do, so I leave it to your discretion."

I lay down, but Psyche remained upright, a pillar of seething resentment in the darkness.

"Can't you understand?" she said after some time. The haughty tone was gone from her voice, replaced by a plaintive note that speared my heart. "I don't even know whether you have a mother or father or siblings. You've never told me anything about that. There's so much I don't know about you, so much you won't share with me. But won't you let me share this with you, at least? Won't you come and see my childhood home, the place where I grew up?"

"I wish I could," I said to placate Psyche. "But let us see how your cousin's visit goes first."

This was met by an expectant silence from Psyche's side of the bed. I did not elaborate, and after some time, Psyche gave a huff of impatience and threw the blankets over her head.

18

PSYCHE

My first thought when I saw Iphigenia was that she had changed.

She was taller, for one thing, her coltish adolescent frame softened by the curves of adulthood. Her features were sharper, more solid. I noticed that she wore an ordinary woman's chiton instead of the robes of a priestess of Artemis, a fact I resolved to bring up later.

From the moment I saw her father's ship dock in the cove below, I paced the halls of the seaside house like an enthusiastic puppy. When Iphigenia made her way up the winding staircase to the front terrace, red-faced and out of breath, I threw my arms around her. My oldest, dearest friend, returned to me at last.

She laughed and extricated herself from my embrace, gazing at me with amazement. "I am so glad to see that you are well, Psyche," she said. "The accounts of your disappearance were . . . concerning."

"I wrote you letters. And as you can see, I am as well as I have ever been," I replied cheerily, then sobered as a thought occurred to me. "King Nestor, is he angry?"

Iphigenia shook her head. "No, only puzzled. He has moved on; when it became clear you would not return, he took a princess from Corinth as wife."

My shoulders softened in relief. "That is a mercy," I replied. I directed Iphigenia into the house, toward the fine oak table laden with food.

"What a beautiful home," Iphigenia breathed, admiring the colored glass that let in bright sheaves of sunlight. "Tell me more of your husband!" she said.

Panic gripped me. I had told Iphigenia as little as possible in my letters. How could I explain that a god had taken me as his wife and came to me only in darkness? She would think I had gone mad, or else she would be wild with fear.

"He's a noble prince who has elected to live a solitary existence here by the ocean," I said, though the lie pained me. I had never kept secrets from Iphigenia before. "Unfortunately, he cannot join us today, but he is handsome and wealthy and very kind. He . . ."

I trailed off. I couldn't simply tack one vague description onto another. I had to think of something more convincing. "He loves hunting and archery, so we have a great deal in common," I finished awkwardly.

Iphigenia looked at me expectantly, waiting for more. I made a grand flourish that nearly knocked over the ewer of wine and asked her to tell me more about events at home.

She had been waiting for this. A sly grin crossed my cousin's face, and she leaned forward conspiratorially. "There's news from Sparta."

Helen had vanished, an event that coincided with the departure of a Trojan trade delegation. Menelaus organized a panicked search before a letter in the queen's own hand arrived some days later, explaining that she had gone to live with the prince Paris in the city of Troy.

I thought of the beautiful, miserable woman I had met so many years ago. *I want more than this,* Helen had said on her wedding night. *I wanted to fall in love and see the world.* I thought of her in faraway Troy, hanging on the arm of a foreign prince. It seemed that Helen found a way to get what she wanted after all.

I said as much to Iphigenia, and her eyes flashed with grim excitement. "But there's still the oath to contend with," she said. "Don't you remember the oath that Helen's former suitors made at the wedding?"

I didn't. My memory of the event was obscured by ambient misery. Fortunately, Iphigenia was happy to elaborate.

"They swore that any man who absconded with Helen would face all the rest in battle," she reminded me. "Some of the men were still bitter that they hadn't been chosen, and the oath was necessary to keep the peace. But who thought that Helen would be kidnapped by a foreigner, and a guest at that?" Iphigenia shook her head at the sacrilege of it.

"I don't know if Helen needed much convincing," I replied, picking at a piece of lamb wrapped in soft bread. "The woman I remember would have commandeered a fishing boat to get away."

"But don't you see, Psyche?" Iphigenia continued, clearly delighted by these conspiracies. "The former suitors are honor-bound to assist her husband Menelaus in getting her back, and so are Sparta's allies. Even men like Father, who were never competitors for Helen's hand in the first place, have been dragged into the war with Troy. Uncle Menelaus doesn't have nearly the military experience that Father does, so he's tapped Father to head the forces. Oh Psyche, what an army it's going to be! Men from all over Greece are gathering, you've never seen anything like it. Not even the Argonauts were as grand as this. Soldiers from cities that have been at one another's throats for years are playing dice together in the camps. The poets will sing about it for centuries to come."

"They'll need all the men they can get if they want to pry

Helen from the arms of her handsome prince," I quipped. I thought of my own happiness with Cupid and wondered if Helen felt a fraction of the same joy with this Paris. I wondered if she even wanted to be found.

"Troy has never fallen," Iphigenia told me, her eyes bright. "But it's never faced Father with a full army at his back either. Oh Psyche! I haven't even told you about the most exciting thing yet—I'm going to be married! To Achilles!" Iphigenia said with a little squeal of glee. "He and his men have joined the army bound for Troy. Father said it will strengthen ties with the army if their champion is wedded to the commander's daughter. The ceremony will happen within the month."

I recalled the irritatingly handsome prince I had met so long ago at the Heraean Games. I was glad to see Iphigenia excited, but I couldn't imagine that Achilles would make a decent husband.

"I thought you were going to be a priestess of Artemis," I said before I could stop myself. "You were going to become a priestess and never marry."

Iphigenia's face darkened. Her eyebrows rushed together like storm clouds, and her mouth took on a hardness I remembered from her mother Clytemnestra. "And I thought you were going to become a hero," she shot back.

I jerked back as though I had been slapped. For the first time, I saw the shadow of Agamemnon in his daughter.

It quickly passed. Iphigenia's hands flew to her lips, her natural sweetness returned. "I'm sorry, Psyche. It isn't my place to say such things. It's just that everything has changed so suddenly that I can scarcely find my footing. Father ordered me to leave the college of priestesses behind for this marriage, and how could I refuse him? We need this alliance. And I like Achilles, so it's not all that bad."

"Of course," I replied unsteadily. I wondered where Iphigenia had learned to speak so coldly. From her mother or father, perhaps, or from the priestesses of Artemis whose words are as sharp as arrows.

"But enough about me," Iphigenia said with a wave. "You've hardly told me anything at all about your new life."

"Um," I began, frantically casting about for a cover. "My husband is older, so he's confined to his bed . . ."

Iphigenia tilted her head. "I thought you said he was a young man, and you enjoyed hunting and archery together?"

I cursed myself for being a fool. Not wanting to worry Iphigenia, I had only succeeded in arousing her suspicion. "He's a man of middle years," I added awkwardly. "You know, not quite young or old."

Iphigenia gazed at me, placid amber eyes filled with curiosity. "What's his name? Where are his people from? How did he contract the marriage with you?"

Her questions felt like stones hurled from a sling, and I hurried to dodge them. "His name is Cupid," I replied. That much I could be truthful about. "And his people have lived in these hills for many years. As for how he proposed marriage, well . . . it was a rather sudden affair." I shoved a piece of bread in my mouth and shrugged.

My cousin's forehead was cleft with concern. "Psyche," Iphigenia said, dropping her voice so that no one else would hear. "Is your husband one of the Dorian tribesmen?"

The Dorians were a barbarian people, unwashed horse riders from the plains whose incursions upon the Greek city-states grew bolder year by year. Already some of the smaller, more remote towns had fallen under their sway. Agamemnon had spent much of his career fighting the Dorians, and even my father went forth to do battle with them when they ventured too near Mycenae. More than once the Dorians had stolen women from the cities of the Greeks to take into their hills.

"Of course not!" I snapped.

Iphigenia raised her hands in surrender, though uncertainty lingered in her eyes. "You were taken so suddenly, you will forgive me if I worry about such things. Especially with everything that's happened with Helen.

"But if your husband *was* a Dorian, for argument's sake," she continued seamlessly. "It could have serious consequences. The man you marry is next in line for the throne of Mycenae, and your children are after him in the line of succession. If an enemy of our people has taken you for a wife . . . You understand what that would mean."

I did. It would give our most dire enemy a strong claim to one of the great houses of Greece.

"Then it's a good thing my husband is not Dorian," I replied fiercely. I pushed my chair back with a screech and stood. "Since when have you learned to act like such a politician?"

"Since I dedicated myself to serving my family rather than my own interests," Iphigenia replied coolly. She had not risen from her seat, staring at me unruffled as I fumed above her. "You might consider doing likewise," she finished.

When I did not reply, Iphigenia rose from her chair with fluid grace. "Perhaps I should take my leave," she said, face unreadable. "My father's men have been pulled away from the war effort to escort me here, and I should not waste their time unnecessarily. I will bring word to your mother and father that you are well."

As I watched Iphigenia descend the long staircase to the beach, I thought about calling her back and explaining everything, but I quailed at the thought. Some things could not be explained, not without raising even more questions.

I watched the ship launch into the wine-dark sea and wondered what had happened to the bright-eyed cousin I'd known, and the brave young woman I had once been.

Doubt is a seed, and once planted it is sure to sprout.

It was no one's fault. Iphigenia scented a lie, and her counsel held true based on her knowledge of the situation. I was certain that my husband was no Dorian, but I knew very little else about him.

And try as I might, I could not forget Prometheus's words. *You don't know who your husband is, do you?*

I didn't, not really. And now I carried his child.

After Iphigenia's departure, I settled myself in one of the chairs and looked at the ocean through the wide window, lost in thought. Shadows wheeled across the interior of the seaside house, marking the transition into late afternoon. Still, I did not move. One of the cats brushed against me in greeting, and I scratched his ears absentmindedly but did not look away from the water.

I wondered what Iphigenia would say if she knew that I had never seen my husband's face.

Doubt blossomed as the shadows stretched into dusk. I did not really believe I would immolate like Semele before Zeus if I saw my husband's face. We had spent so much time together without any harm befalling me.

And my children were next in line for the throne of Mycenae, as my cousin had so ungracefully reminded me. A thought seized me the way an owl catches a mouse, thrusting its talons through my heart: If the child was male, he would grow up to become the next king of the city-state of Mycenae. He would take the seat my own father held and lead the nation in times of peace and war.

That settled it. I had to know who my child's father was, for the good of my people.

As the sun dipped down toward the horizon, painting the landscape bloodred, I went to an alcove near the bedroom and began my preparations.

19

PSYCHE

When Cupid joined me in bed that night, I played the part of the delighted, loving wife. I gave an abbreviated version of Iphigenia's visit, then rested my head on his shoulder and asked a nonsense question to set him at ease. "Do the cats have names?"

"Of course," Cupid replied, laughing uncertainly. "But it would be impossible for you to pronounce them. Your mouth couldn't make all the necessary sounds. Even I can only understand them when I'm in cat shape myself."

"Well, I have some ideas," I began, settling my head into the hollowing of his shoulder and skimming my fingertips over his chest. "The fat tabby with the gray eyes is Glaukos. I think that suits him, don't you agree? The tortoiseshell female who eats everyone else's food is Scylla. You know she'd devour a whole ship full of sailors if she had the chance . . ."

I continued in that vein for a while, light and playful, while Cupid's hands stroked my hair. When at last his movements slowed and his breathing evened out to the steady rhythm that signaled sleep, I rose quietly and made my way through the darkened house.

The objects were in a row where I had left them in the alcove. My fingers danced over the concavity of a bowl filled with oil and pierced by the twist of a cloth fiber, then the hard edges of a flint and bronze. My hands were shaking so badly that it took several tries to make a spark. Once I did, the flare was quickly taken up by the wick in its bowl, and the light of the makeshift lamp nearly blinded me before my eyes had the chance to adjust. I took the little bowl in my hands, careful not to spill the burning oil. Shadows careened as I walked back to the bedroom, rendering the familiar halls alien. I had never seen the house by candlelight before.

My heart beat in my ears like a butterfly's wings. This was a betrayal, and I knew it. It was the one thing Cupid had asked of me, the one thing I promised. I might be dooming myself by daring the curse, consigning myself to a fiery death, though I no longer really believed that story. I needed to know who my husband was, and that need drove out all else.

I opened the door.

I did not burst into flame when I saw my husband lying there, sprawled out on the bed. His hair was curled gold that shone in the lamplight, and one arm was thrown carelessly across the pillow in the languor of sleep. His bare chest rose and fell with the peaceful breath of dreamers. Cupid was no monster or barbarian. He was beautiful in a way unknown to mortals.

I leaned forward to get a closer look at him, unconscious of my movements. I jostled the bowl of burning oil, and some of it slopped over the side onto his chest.

With a cry of pain, Cupid opened his eyes.

They were green, the color of the leaves during the summer days I had spent with Atalanta in the forest. Green as meadows, so rare in rocky Greece. Green wells I could fall into, losing myself. They widened in horror at the sight of the lamp, and I knew with sick certainty what I had done. I felt no panic, only a dull shame. Like Anteia, I'd betrayed the man who loved me.

Except he wasn't a man. No mortal man could have endured

the curse that gripped him now. His spine snapped like a sail in strong wind. He cried out, but the sound was strangled and wordless. I reached out to him, desperate to help and horrified at my betrayal, but his fingers slipped through mine. Time and space bent to let him through. He was pulled from our bed like a thread through the eye of a needle, and I found myself staring at the empty space where he had just been.

My pulse beat in my ears. A curse, he had spoken of a curse, and now I understood what was coming.

Rumbling started deep in the earth. I screamed as dust fell from a fissure in the ceiling where the stone cracked in two. Severed from its divine master, the house began to come apart.

Another crack split the floor like a bolt of errant lightning, and the door swung open wildly. The single lamp cast wild, fractured shadows over the scene. I snatched a sheet from the bed before racing from the house; I was wearing nothing more than sleeping clothes.

The lamp was still in my hand as I fled to the terrace and down the long stairs. Hot oil seared my skin, but I did not let it slow me down. Cats darted around my feet, and the raucous cries of peacocks split the air as they floated to safety on wide wings.

As last, I reached the safety of the rocky beach below. By the wan light of the sickle moon, I watched my home fall into the sea, crashing into the water as though it was made of nothing more substantial than sand.

20

PSYCHE

The first night alone was the hardest. I had grown used to sleeping in a soft bed with my husband's warm presence beside me. Now I was utterly alone, tossing as I attempted to find a comfortable position on the night-chilled rocks. Even when I had slept on the rough ground in the wilderness in my youth, Atalanta had been there with me. Now I didn't even have a knife or the tools to make a fire, only the clothes on my back and the bedsheet I'd been quick-witted enough to snatch. I'd lost the lamp somewhere along the way.

The sea lapped at the shore as the moon made its way through the sky, and feelings churned within me as deep as the ocean. It was impossible to describe what I felt. Shock was a large part of it, but grief and rage made appearances as well. I suppose it would be most accurate to say that I felt *robbed*.

Robbed of my husband, of the life we had begun to build together. Of his strong arms that circled my waist, his soft voice against my ear, his fingers weaving through mine. Then I remembered the way the curse gripped him with such unrelenting horror, and I buried my face in my hands.

The knowledge that I had brought this misfortune upon myself was no comfort; I burned with shame and anger. I had broken Cupid's trust, but he had lied to me. Lied in ways I was still trying to comprehend. The inveracity tickled my unconscious mind, making me invasive in my curiosity. He had told me of a curse, but never in my wildest imaginings had I guessed that *this* would happen.

Tears made their way down my cheeks, cold in the night air. I shook with sobs, venting my grief into the silent indifference of the darkness.

After a long time, my breathing slowed, and I took command of myself again. I wiped my face on the sheet wrapped around me and told myself sternly that survival was my goal now, and there was no point in dwelling on what had occurred. As the stars wheeled through the sky, I buried the shards of my broken heart and tried to sleep.

A goddess came to me in the depths of the night, when nothing stirred and no wind blew. Looking back, I was never sure whether I was awake or dreaming when I met her.

I lifted my head from the ground to see a figure perched delicately on a nearby outcropping of stone. Her skin glowed slightly in the darkness like a drawn-down version of the moon, illuminated by its own inner radiance. Hair spilled like ink over her shoulders.

"So this is where he's been keeping you," she said, looking at me like a tigress considering her next meal. "I swore I'd destroy whatever he loved most after what he did to Adonis, but it seems you've already accomplished that yourself." She glanced up at the ruins of the seaside house, sniffing in distaste.

I sat up slowly, meeting the stranger's gaze. I did not dare make any sudden movements. I had met wildcats and bears in the wilderness and knew not to show fear. I recalled Cupid's warnings about the monster that hunted me and wondered if it was the same as the figure who stood before me now.

"Are you speaking of Cupid?" I asked.

The stranger scoffed. "Is that the name he gave you? How like my adopted son to lie about such a vital point. No, his real name is Eros."

Eros, god of desire. I'd heard the hymns in praise of him: winged, golden-haired, dispensing love to mortals and gods alike. I recalled the glimpse of him I'd seen by lamplight and knew with horrible certainty that she spoke the truth.

I stared at the figure before me. If Eros was her adopted son, then this stranger was none other than Aphrodite.

"Where is he?" I demanded.

Aphrodite crossed her smooth arms. "Why would I tell you such a thing? Only be sure that he never wants to see you again."

Her words cut me. In the light of the crescent moon, Aphrodite's beauty had the deadly perfection of a naked blade. Why would such a sublime creature choose to torment a mortal like me?

Aphrodite inclined her head condescendingly, looking at me as though I was very stupid. "He didn't tell you the truth about the curse, did he? It seems my son has wreathed himself in lies."

She laughed at my confused expression, a bell-like sound. *Laughter-loving*, the poets called Aphrodite, but they never considered who or what she might be laughing at.

"A love curse," she said. "One intended for you, but it seems he took the weight of it upon himself. An accident, I'm sure. Dear girl, do you really think Eros would have noticed you otherwise? He is a god. You are nothing but a little mortal with skinned knees."

I could not speak. A lump filled my throat, but I would not weep in front of my enemy.

She rested her chin on her hand. "Truly, this is all for the best.

You two could not have continued forever, creeping around in darkness. Even if you'd both kept to the terms of the curse—and the fact you're here is proof that you didn't—what future would you have? You would have grown old and withered while he remained young. Imagine that: a god visiting a brittle-boned hag in the dead of the night. Who ever heard of such a thing? Better that he left you now."

"Why are you here?" I asked. "I have no home, no husband. Will you take my life as well?"

"Oh, heavens no," she exclaimed. "We are family now. You carry his child within you."

My hand flew to my belly.

"I will not be accused of killing my own grandchild," Aphrodite continued. "Swear yourself to me as a loyal servant, and I will look after you until the child is born. Perhaps I might even offer you one more glimpse of Eros."

Hope flickered and died within me. I noticed Aphrodite made no mention of what would happen after the birth, whether I would be allowed to raise the baby or even be permitted to live. No, I was done making deals with gods.

Besides, if Eros did not want me, then I did not want him either.

"Forgive me, lady," I said bitterly. "But I must decline your offer. I was born into the world of mortals, and I will find a place for myself there once more."

Aphrodite tucked a lock of hair behind her ear. "Very well. But I do not think you will find a better bargain. Call for me if you change your mind. I will find you wherever you are."

A promise and a threat. The goddess stood with a rustle of skirts and vanished into the night.

I lay back down on the hard earth, wrapped in the tattered bedsheet, falling into an uneasy sleep. When I woke, the sky was the pale blue that signaled dawn was near, and I saw a small shape move beside me.

I leaped up. It was Scylla, the plump tortoiseshell cat, sitting primly on a rock. My breath caught in my throat at the sight of her. At least a few of the animals had escaped; something of the world I had built with Eros survived.

I reached out to the cat, fingers shaking. Scylla sniffed me, hissed, and ran into the undergrowth.

In the morning, I slipped over shale until my feet found solid earth once more, following the ruins of the staircase up the rock. When it terminated in the jagged debris of the seaside house, I climbed hand over foot to reach the plateau beyond, the same that Cupid—no, Eros—and I had taken on our way to Taenarum. The memory, once so sweet, now felt as bitter as hemlock.

I moved quickly and made little noise. I soon took grateful refuge in a forest, far safer than the unsheltered plain, and prayed that I did not run across any bandits.

It was afternoon when a breeze stirred over my skin, a welcome relief from the day-ripened heat. A pair of ghostly fingers skated over my arm, materializing in a wiry form beside me. Zephyrus.

"Psyche! What happened to the house? Where is Eros? And you, are you hurt?" There was a panicked note to his voice that I had never heard before.

Once when I was practicing sword fighting with Atalanta, she hit me so hard by accident that I could not draw breath for several seconds. Seeing Zephyrus again felt like that—a reminder of a world lost, a pain so sharp it froze my heart.

I wasn't physically hurt, save for a few scrapes and burns. But inside me was a ragged wound, salted by my encounter with

Aphrodite the night before. And anger, endless anger at both myself and Eros. All this rage spilled out of me now, venting itself upon Zephyrus.

I swept Zephyrus's hand from my shoulder and stepped back. "You knew about it, didn't you?" I accused. My nails dug into my palms hard enough to leave red half-moons. "You knew. And you never told me."

Zephyrus wrinkled his nose, perplexed as a puppy. "What?"

"The curse," I snarled. "You knew that Eros—who you let me believe was some fake god named Cupid—was cursed to love me. And to disappear before my eyes if we ever saw each other face-to-face. Oh, you must have delighted in such a jest." I was trembling now, as though my bones might leap out of my skin to claw at him.

Zephyrus was staring at me as though he did not know who I was.

"The curse," I continued. "It was the only reason Eros cared for me, wasn't it? And why we could only meet in darkness. I should have known. Eros never loved me, he only wanted me as a . . . a pet, a distraction. Like your little Hyacinthos," I added, spitting the words.

Zephyrus looked at me with the expression of a man run through with a spear. "Hyacinthos was never a distraction," was all he managed.

"You are a monster," I thundered on. "I should have known when you destroyed the Mycenaean village just to draw me out. Not a god to be worshipped, just a monster. I imagine Hyacinthos saw that too."

That was enough. Zephyrus's shoulders rose and a wrathful wind stirred his hair. "Then run away!" he shouted as the trees began to bend and sway around us. "Whatever you've done, whatever evil you've brought down on him and yourself, I will leave you to it. As for me, I will go looking for Eros."

I was blinded by a gust the same way I had been that fateful day on the plateau near Mycenae. I threw up my hands to protect my face as the wind whipped my flimsy garment.

A moment later, I was alone in the grove. Sunlight shone through the branches and birdsong echoed in the air, as though no god had ever been here at all.

21

EROS

A lightning flare of pain startled me from sleep. I looked up into brown eyes rich as the earth itself, a face framed by hair that was a lion's mane of perfect curls in the lamplight. Psyche.

A lamp. A light.

I felt a flare of anger—she had broken her promise, she had betrayed me—but by then it was too late for anything but resignation.

The curse struck with the force of a tidal wave and dragged me down. Agony drove its knives through my immortal body, and I tried to scream, but the sound was torn from my throat as I was wrenched from my familiar bed. I fell through ice and fire, through rock and whirling veils of nothingness. I should have known that Aphrodite would make the process of separation as painful as possible. She had left barbs in the curse, sufficient to cripple a mortal. It was not enough to destroy me, but it did leave me drained. I could not die, but I could fade until I was nothing more than a spark of attraction leaping between two sets of eyes. I could become like Nereus, a wash of foam who had forgotten he was ever a god.

Then I was back in my body again, and I sagged forward. Rings of fire burned at my wrists, forming manacles that held my body upright. But crueler still was the pain from the burn on my chest, caused by the hot lamp oil Psyche had spilled on me. I remembered her face, her wide eyes and the awed circle of her mouth, illuminated by the lamp I had forbidden her to light. The knowledge of her betrayal was more bitter than the burn.

I thought she understood. I thought she wanted to stay.

I opened my eyes, scarcely noticing the difference. The darkness in the room was oppressive, relieved only by a dim rectangle of light shining around the outline of a door. But I could tell I wasn't alone.

"I should have known something had gone wrong," a familiar voice said, "when that mortal wench vanished so suddenly, and I saw no evidence of her humiliation. I told myself it was only baseless worry and that all was well. I should have known better than to trust you."

"Aphrodite," I replied. "Alas, I can only give you a poor greeting in my current state. Now, where is Psyche?"

"Last I saw, she was near the ruins of your little house, weeping her eyes out. Really, my dear boy, I don't understand what you ever saw in her."

Aphrodite had been sitting in a corner, a dim form in the darkness. She rose now. I could hear her footsteps approaching, and she stopped when her face was only a few inches from mine, close enough to feel her breath on my cheek. It was a horrible reversal of my nights with Psyche—which was probably exactly what Aphrodite intended.

I couldn't see the ugly twist of Aphrodite's face, but I could imagine it all too clearly. I knew how she liked to gloat over her conquests, romantic and otherwise. I tugged the cuffs, jangling the chains.

"Don't bother trying to break out of those," Aphrodite commented. "Their only twin binds Prometheus. Hephaestus made them for me himself, though you'll be glad to know I didn't tell him who they were intended for."

"How kind of you," I replied, trying to see how far I could lower my arm. "It would certainly put a damper on my friendship with your husband if he knew he forged the chains of my imprisonment."

"You are in no position to be making jokes," Aphrodite said darkly. "You know, this whole affair reminds me of something that happened to my mortal friend Paris, prince of Troy. His parents tried to abandon him in the wilderness, but instead he was taken in and raised by a herdsman. I suppose it's not an exact parallel to your situation, though—when you took the princess into your home, you decided to fuck her instead."

My heart was pounding in my ears. "What have you done to Psyche?" I demanded.

"Nothing at all. I've decided to leave that little vixen to her own devices for now, though I might still send her into the Underworld as payback for Adonis," Aphrodite said, her breath spraying over my face. "But you are my focus now, and I intend to hold you accountable for all of your numerous crimes."

I heard Aphrodite's steps move around me in a circle like a vulture around a carcass as she named all these slights. I pictured her tallying them on her long, elegant fingers. "Lying about the completion of your task, allying yourself with one of my enemies and hiding her for months, and demanding a favor in return for something you never did. That love antidote would never have worked, you know," she added. "Mothers must keep their children in line, and I have been too lenient with you."

"What do you want from me?" I asked, sagging against the cuffs.

"Oh, nothing but your suffering," Aphrodite said sweetly. "Compensation for all the times you've wronged me. I've got you in a storeroom below Mount Olympus, a place where no one goes. I have all the time in the world for your punishment."

"Aphrodite," I said, growing somewhat shaken. "This is ridiculous. Let us go before Zeus and have him arbitrate."

She chuckled, long and low. "Oh, my dear son, I have already spoken to Zeus. He was the one who offered me the use of this room. He's as weary of your mischief as I am."

Wasn't the curse enough? I thought. *Binding me to someone only to forbid me from seeing her—wasn't that enough?*

"What do you have planned?" I asked, managing a certain insouciance. "Will a wolf eat my heart day after day? Will you fill this cell with water and watch me drown over and over again?"

"No. That's too good for you—it gives you something to do, a method for tracking your days," Aphrodite said, her words dripping wicked pleasure. "No, I shall simply leave you here, with nothing to do and no food to eat and no one to talk to, until the end of time."

With that, she left, enclosing me in fathomless darkness.

22

PSYCHE

A few days later, I came into sight of a remote mountain village. It was scarcely more than a cluster of little houses wreathed with smoke from cookfires, but to me it was as grand as a palace. Here I could find rest and a bit of nourishment before I headed on to Tiryns.

I was beyond exhausted. Thorns tattered my clothing, and the soles of my feet were gashed and scraped. Atalanta had forced me to train barefoot, but even she had not prepared me for days on end alone in the wilderness without even the most meager of supplies.

I walked past the fields and into the little dirt lane that served as the main road of this place. The people of this village lived much as their ancestors had after Prometheus shaped them from clay, scratching a paltry living from the dirt and pasturing their herds of lean goats in the high meadows. It was a life of grinding difficulty, and they were a suspicious lot.

I strode toward the first person I spotted, a young man feeding chickens in the shadow of a rickety house. I called on the ancient law of xenia, the hospitality ordained by the gods. The young man stared at me open-mouthed, grains falling through his open fingers like sand in an hourglass. I could imagine what he saw: a woman like a ghost come from the forest. The color of my skin marked me as a stranger to these arid lands, and I wore only sleeping clothes without so much as a veil for propriety.

The young man took me to the chieftain, whose hut was only slightly bigger than the others. He was a granite-faced man as unyielding as the mountains themselves, and his eyes crawled over my body.

"Where is your father, lady? Your husband?" he asked.

"I was separated from my husband during a raid on our caravan," I lied. "I must get back to my family in Mycenae. In the name of xenia, I ask your assistance—"

The old chieftain waved a hand, cutting me off. "You shall have it. We are no strangers to the laws of Zeus." But even when an older woman arrived to lead me away, his eyes still lingered on my backside.

A tin tub filled with lukewarm water and a hard lump of lye soap were all the woman offered. I had known there were people who lived like this, but I had never experienced such poverty myself. It was a far cry from the luxurious baths at the seaside house, but I made do. I wouldn't be here long.

The woman was a decade or so older than me, stout as a mule, with fish-belly-pale skin and a hard face. I decided she must be the chieftain's wife.

The woman took a seat at the head of the tub as I lowered myself and began to scrub. "It is said," she began, "that the husband is the head of the household. The wife serves him, but there is happiness in that service if you do it well. Even if he is heavy with his hands or short with his tongue, a closed mouth and a lowered gaze are your best responses. It's simply the way of things. Marriage may be hard, but life is easier with two people." The set of her mouth was firm. "You will understand when you have children yourself."

A knife of panic pierced my belly, and I drew my limbs together

189

protectively. It had been less than a fortnight since Eros's remark about my two heartbeats, but perhaps this woman could read the subtle changes of my body that signaled pregnancy, see the floating spark in my womb.

She was watching me closely, and I realized what she was truly implying. "You think I ran away from my husband?"

The woman shrugged. "Many girls your age struggle to adjust to the demands of married life. I know the signs." The woman paused for a moment, then added, "Unless you are a slave or concubine, but I doubt that. You speak as though you are used to people listening to you. Perhaps that is why your marriage was not successful."

"You know nothing of my marriage," I interrupted sharply. "And your advice is not welcome."

For a moment there was no sound in the little room. I was naked in the bath and the chieftain's wife loomed above me. It occurred to me that she could push my head beneath the waters and hold it there until I stopped struggling, and no one would ever be the wiser. No one would bother to avenge the death of a strange woman who appeared like a phantom.

I met the woman's gaze unflinchingly. She looked away first.

She left and returned with clothing. It was shapeless and threadbare from a thousand washes, the sort of simple tunic worn by both men and women in this remote place, but at least it fit well. I was led to a table occupied by three small boys, quiet and well-behaved, tiny versions of their expressionless father. The chieftain and his wife ignored each other, and they ignored me as well. Family meals with my parents had always been happy affairs, filled with conversation and laughter, but this was as dismal as a funeral. I thought of Eros, and briefly wondered what it might have been like to raise our children in the marvel of the seaside house. The thought stung like ocean water in a raw wound, so I pushed it away.

That night, for the first time since I was driven from the seaside house, I lay down on a mattress, though it was straw-stuffed and itchy. But I still found that I could not sleep. The heavy breathing of the rest of the family, punctuated by snores and farts, kept me awake. If some shadowy figure was to creep up on me, I would not hear until it was too late.

I finally fell asleep before dawn, dreaming uneasily of walking through a field of long grass speckled with wildflowers and never reaching my goal. I was startled into wakefulness hours later by a particularly vociferous rooster. I sprung up, certain it was Eros, but it was only an ordinary chicken.

That morning, the chieftain greeted me at breakfast alone, a porridge-filled bowl in front of him and another waiting for me on the other side of the table. He did not say where his wife or the children were, but a pair of young men loitered by the door—stout men, bulky with muscle from years of dragging plows through the rocky dirt.

"We have given you clothing and accommodations above the demands of xenia," the chieftain said, his gaze lingering on my chest. "It is time to discuss payment."

I frowned, and my palms began to sweat. The law of xenia quite clearly demanded hospitality without any exchange of payment, but I had planned for this eventuality.

"I saw claw marks on the backs of your sheep when I passed through the fields," I said. "You are plagued by a griffin infestation, are you not?"

The chieftain's jaw quivered. "Yes. We have dealt with the vermin for quite some time." He looked puzzled at this apparent change in topic.

I nodded. "If you give me a bow and arrows, along with a knife and sturdy shoes, I will rid you of this problem. Would that be sufficient payment?"

The chieftain stared at me. I think he would have laughed had his shock not been so great. "*You* will kill the griffins?"

I met his gaze coolly. "If I fail, what have you lost? A knife, a few arrows, a pair of shoes. A small price to be free from a dangerous nuisance."

That convinced him. He accepted my bargain.

I went up into the mountains with a rare lightness in my heart. The weight of a quiver and bow felt good at my side, and my limbs hummed with joy. With the warmth of the sun and the cool of the forest's shade, I could almost forget everything I had lost.

I found the griffin aerie on an outcropping of rock a bit taller than the walls of Tiryns, on the side of a narrow stone canyon. I made my way toward it stealthily, keeping to the dry undergrowth that grew in sparse patches. I spotted one of the griffins lounging in the nest, splintering a bone with its sharp beak. Abruptly, it raised its head and gave a cry of greeting.

A shadow passed over the nest and another griffin landed, carrying a dead rabbit, and the two tore into the carcass together. The newly arrived griffin was larger, a female. I realized I must be looking at a mated pair. Even from a distance, I could see the gray fur threading through the female's back, and I noticed that the male favored his left side, compensating for some old injury. No wonder they had resorted to stealing goats and sheep; more challenging prey was likely beyond them.

A mated pair. The memory of Eros's pained expression as the darkness tore him away flashed behind my eyes, and I bit back my grief. I had to complete this task. I would not return empty-handed.

Once the griffins settled down, I made my move. I burst from the undergrowth and drew my bow in the same fluid motion. A second later, the male griffin screamed. An arrow protruded from his eye, and he pawed at it frantically. His mate gave a cry of outrage and snapped open her wings, nearly blocking out the sun. She took to the air, trying to drop upon me from the sky.

I sprang back at the last moment, pivoting to strike her with my bow. The wood was yew, old and flimsy, but hard enough to knock the female griffin off course and send her crashing headlong into the rock. The bones of griffins are hollow like those of birds, and they can be incapacitated by a blow that would only annoy a drakonis or a hydra. The female griffin was dead before she hit the ground.

A cry from above drew my attention. It was the male griffin, rising on unsteady feet. Blood sheeted across his face and body, but he made his way unsteadily down the cliff face. I tensed; though I still had a few arrows left in my quiver, my bow was now a useless ruin. I pulled my knife from its sheath, but to my shock the griffin ignored me entirely and ran to the body of his mate, nudging her and mewling pitifully. He did not even notice my approach until I was close enough to wrench his head back and slit his throat.

I watched the life fade from his eyes and felt his body grow limp beneath my hands, and I felt a wave of sudden disgust at what I had done. I saw the iridescent color of his mate's pinfeathers in the dust and wanted to weep that I had destroyed such beauty. I turned and vomited into the dirt.

As I caught my breath, Medusa's words rung in my mind: *I don't see how a hero differs from a pig farmer. Both are butchers.*

I wondered what exactly it was that made a monster.

I buried the griffins as a last gesture of respect, an honor afforded to a noble enemy, scrabbling at the dirt with my hands, using a sharp stone to dig when my fingernails began to splinter. I took a pinion from each before consigning their bodies to the earth, unmistakable evidence of my victory. The feathers were enormous; balanced on my toes, they reached well over my head. I tied them to the quiver at my side and made my way down the mountainside.

If I had expected celebration upon my return, I was sorely disappointed. Instead, the people of the mountain village peered at me with suspicion from windows and doorways, scurrying away as I passed. They feared me more than they did the griffins. Those creatures were comprehensible at least, part of the natural order of things, but I was something else, and that made me far more terrifying.

I found the village chieftain waiting for me at the rough wooden table in his house, and I saw no trace of his wife. There were a number of men crowded into the room, at least five or six.

I laid the pinions down on the table. "I have fulfilled my word and slain the griffins that plagued your flock. I thank you for your hospitality and will depart shortly," I said.

A man might go a lifetime without ever holding a griffin's feather in his hands, but the chieftain was unimpressed. He looked at me with eyes as flat and cold as the surface of a winter lake. "You did not bring the pelts," he said. "Griffin pelts are valuable, and they were our property."

I flushed with irritation. "You asked me to slay the griffins, and that is what I did. You mentioned nothing about pelts."

The chieftain lifted one of the long feathers and inspected it with an air of disdain. "Then you have robbed us of our property, though you were welcomed as an honored guest. And how do we know you didn't pull this pinion from a corpse that had already died?" he added. "Or maybe you tricked someone else into killing them."

I was truly angry now. I had tolerated this man long enough. "Who could I trick into killing the griffins, when none of you were up to the task?"

A cold silence descended, one filled with malice. The eye of every man in the room was upon me. While I had been speaking with the chieftain, more men had entered the house. How many of them were there now—ten, a dozen? I was outnumbered.

The chieftain made a gesture, and the men surged forward with one will. I knew what they would do to me, and that they would do it in cold blood. I was an aberration in the order of the world, a woman who did not know her place, and I needed to be corrected.

A wild laugh filled the room and echoed from the high ceilings, paralyzing the men. They had been prepared for tears, even screams, but not laughter. It took me a moment to realize that the laughter had come from me.

"You don't know who I am," I snarled, barely recognizing my own voice. I had no time to grab a weapon, but my tone held the men like insects in amber. "You don't know *what* I am. I am the granddaughter of a hero and the daughter of a king. I am the wife of one god, and I carry another in my womb. I came here to test your grasp of xenia, and you have failed—all of you have failed. And now the judgment of the Thunderer shall be upon you."

My voice rose as I spoke. By the time I was done, it shook the walls. I had the presence of mind to marvel at myself. Where had I learned to speak like this? When had I become bold enough to talk like a god?

Probably during the many nights I spent sleeping beside one, I thought wryly. Eros would have been delighted with me.

The men stared at me like sheep, frozen in a tableau of shock. I summoned an eerie calm as I added, "Do not afflict yourselves further by impeding my journey."

I turned and walked out of the hall. I had no food, though at least I now wore new clothing and carried a knife. I waited for an arrow between my shoulder blades, but it never came. I kept my spine straight until I disappeared into the timberline.

Only when I was out of sight of the village did I pause. My steps slowed, and I squatted down on the earth and leaned my forearms onto my knees. Digging my nails into my scalp, I gasped for ragged breath as all the fear I had held at bay flooded its banks like a river in spring.

23

PSYCHE

The morning after my escape from the village, I lay in the nest I had made for myself on the forest floor, nothing more than a few boughs cut from a low tree. I woke to sunlight and stretched indulgently. Then I caught sight of a small bird perched on a nearby branch. Illuminated by the morning sun, at first it appeared to be made from gold.

For a moment, my heart soared. My husband was here, he'd found me, the nightmare of our separation had come to an end—

Then the little bird took flight, winging its way through the trees, and I realized that it was not Eros but only an ordinary bee-eater.

The realization knocked the breath from my lungs and brought all my grief to the fore. Before, my pain had been a persistent yearning, paling beside the agony of the physical starvation that chewed at my entrails. I had not let myself truly mourn until this moment, so focused had I been on simple survival. Now my loss was laid bare in the quiet morning air.

I had lost my companion in the darkness, my lover, my child's father, the god I had not known was mine until it was too late. Or had he ever been mine at all? Aphrodite said Eros would never have paid me any mind without the curse. I had no doubts about my charms, but in the end, I was only a mortal girl. What had I been to him—a pipe for the opium addict, lotus for the lotus-eater? Had he loved me for myself, or only for what I gave him?

And did *I* love him, despite all his lies?

When I was young, Atalanta had shown me bear tracks in the woods. A series of clawed prints, larger than my hand, leading away into the brush. The creature who had made them was long gone and could only be defined by the impressions it had left. Love was like that, noticeable only by its absence.

Tears burned my eyes, and I did not bother to brush them away. The pain was so sharp that my hands brushed over my body of their own accord to check for wounds, but of course there were none.

I mourned the loss of Eros, and I mourned the cats and peacocks lost during the destruction of the seaside house, innocent victims of a betrayal in which they played no part. I cursed myself for not trying to take one of those creatures under my arm, for not trying to hold on to something of that peculiar, beautiful life.

There was no reason I should still want Eros. Certainly he did not want me anymore, if Aphrodite was to be believed, and the fact he had not come looking for me after the destruction of the seaside house seemed to prove this. The wisest and most practical thing would be to move on and forget him; there was no other way to ensure my survival and that of the child I carried in my womb. And yet I could not forget the memory of Eros's voice in my ear or his body moving against mine. I could not set aside the wild hope that he might be looking for me.

I thought of Aphrodite's offer, pledging myself in servitude for a glimpse at Eros again. My stomach churned.

I could not bring myself to keep moving, and I lay back down. Once, Circe's tincture had turned me into a butterfly, but now I was more like a chrysalis-bound caterpillar, entombed in living death.

When I woke again it was evening. The sun had sunk near to the horizon, and a nearly full moon floated through the sky. I stirred and found a little stream where I drank my fill, then a berry bush laden with the fruits of late summer. I ate a few, then sat back on my heels as the ache in my stomach eased.

All around me, the creatures of night were awakening. A fox prowled through the undergrowth and an owl took wing overhead, while mice and voles skittered through the grass. The evening wind sighed through the trees. There was a whole world around me, one that took no notice of my grief.

I looked at the fledgling moon and thought of the goddess Artemis. She was the one to whom Atalanta had sworn herself, Iphigenia's beloved patroness. In addition to being goddess of the wilderness, Artemis was said to be the protectress of young girls and pregnant women. She was a huntress of unparalleled skill, which was why Atalanta loved her. I myself had offered sacrifices to Artemis now and then, though it felt like sending gifts to a distant relative who never came to visit. I had no sacrifice to offer now, nothing but my heart and my voice.

I did not love the goddess. I wasn't required to. To the gods, love and hate were irrelevant so long as the proper sacrifices were made, or so I had been taught.

Yet hadn't Prometheus acted out of love when he gave the gift of fire to humanity?

Didn't Eros love me, even if he had lied?

Empty-handed beneath the moon, I made an incoherent cry to Artemis. There were no words in it, only a desperate call for help. Nothing stirred except the leaves in the evening wind, but I felt better afterward.

Whether Artemis heard, I cannot say. But a day later, as I was making my way through the scrub, I heard the rustling of human feet in the undergrowth. I tensed, wondering if the men from the village had found me, or if a pack of bandits had picked up my trail. I was no match for them in my current state; I was unarmed save for my knife and a few arrows, not to mention bone-tired and half-starved.

I snatched my knife, ready to make my stand. But to my amazement, the figure that emerged from the undergrowth was none other than Atalanta.

24

PSYCHE

I sat across the campfire looking at my teacher and felt as though I had fallen through time.

Atalanta was older; it had been nearly two years since I had seen her last. There was more white than gray in her thick hair, and she moved with a stiffness that betrayed her age, but I felt the same sense of reassurance in her presence that I always had. Her camp may have been a ramshackle affair with only a small lean-to for protection against the elements, but it was *hers*. Atalanta's bay mare, looking as gray as her mistress, gave a snort of greeting when she saw me.

"Where have you been? I heard you disappeared during a hunt," Atalanta said, breaking the silence. She had embraced me with unrestrained joy when we found each other, but now her ornery nature reasserted itself. Her eyes were bright in her gaunt face as she looked at me across the fire.

I realized how I must look. I wore secondhand clothes from the mountain village and had clearly been sleeping on the ground for several days. My hair had become tangled beyond all recognition, so I had used my knife to cut it all off. Now my head looked like a field around harvest time, with short and long patches.

"What happened?" Atalanta asked. "I taught you better than that."

"You did," I replied. I sipped the rich venison stew flavored with mountain carrots to buy myself time. "But one thing led to another and before I knew it, I found myself married."

Atalanta stared at me. "Married?" she repeated, sounding like a magistrate trying to withhold judgment in a particularly clear-cut case. "Who was he? Did you . . . consent to the match?"

I told Atalanta what I had told Iphigenia: that my husband was a wealthy and mysterious man who showed me nothing but kindness, and from whom I had been separated by a chance event. Part of me wanted to tell Atalanta everything, to lay my story at her feet, but fear held me back. I was tangled up in the affairs of the gods, and I could not risk dragging Atalanta down with me.

My halting explanation did nothing to allay Atalanta's suspicions. "If he's so wonderful, how did you end up here?" the old hero demanded.

"After our villa was attacked by Dorian raiders, he told me to seek safety in Mycenae," I lied. "He said he would meet me there once all was well."

"I see," Atalanta replied. Squinting at me, she demanded, "Was he good to you?"

I recalled my teacher's long-ago advice: *Marry a man like Meleager*. I thought about my conversations with Eros under the stars, our archery contests. I thought about the awe in his voice after seeing my battle against the bandits.

"Yes," I said simply.

Atalanta nodded. She knew truth when she heard it, and my contentment was all she cared about.

I suddenly felt very weary. We spread out our bedrolls next to each other under the night sky, and I lay down at once. But Atalanta sat up, gazing at the fire, hunched over the bony knobs of her knees. She looked ancient and wild.

"Did I ever tell you about my husband?" she said at last.

My heart leaped. From the way she asked the question, I recognized it as a preamble to one of her hero tales. "No, you only spoke of Meleager," I replied. I snuggled into my blanket and felt the familiar thrill of old happiness.

"His name was Melanion," Atalanta began, the mere utterance of the name prompting a faint smile. "He could scarcely be called a prince, since his father was only the headman of some small village. He was not very strong, but he was clever. And he could make anyone laugh.

"I told you of the hunt for the Calydonian boar, but I have not told you of what came before it or after. When I was born, my parents did not desire a daughter and left me on a barren hilltop, which is not unusual. But I did not die. Instead, I was raised by a pair of hunters who lived in the forest, who said they found me in an old bear den with drops of milk on my lips. The bear is sacred to Artemis, and so I have always honored the goddess for her gifts. I honored the bear as well, and I think she appreciated it more."

I shivered as I thought of my own wild prayer to Artemis in the dark woods and Atalanta's appearance shortly afterward. It seemed that the gods—at least one of them—still listened to me.

The fire crackled and sparks flew up to join the stars. "After I won fame as a hero, my father recognized me and summoned me home," Atalanta continued. "He claimed me as his daughter, an honor I could have done without, and declared that I would marry a prince. If I'd had a lick of sense, I would have run back to my forests. But I was young and foolish, and I wanted a father who loved me. So I agreed, on the condition that I would only marry the man who could beat me in a footrace."

Glancing sharply at me, Atalanta added, "I didn't tell you about this when you were younger because I didn't want to give you foolish ideas."

I nodded. That had been wise.

Her gaze returned to the fire, its light making twin moons in her eyes. "Now, I had been chasing down deer since I could walk. Nothing on two feet could outrun me. Still, men came from all over Greece to try. Most viewed me as an oddity or a prize they wished to claim, or as an unfortunate accompaniment to the generous dowry my father offered. But none of them could beat me."

"Then there was Melanion," I prompted.

"Yes." Atalanta nodded. "There was Melanion. He was different. Playful instead of sullen or brutish. He danced lightly over the earth, and I knew he would never seek to claim another human being as his own. He sought me out in my father's hall, though the other men stared at him. 'I look forward to hunting with you,' he said. 'I am a skilled runner but a terrible shot with a bow.' I was caught off my guard and actually laughed at his words.

"Melanion gave me a gift before the race—a single ripe apple, gold as a queen's treasure. They weren't in season, and to this day I have no idea where he could have gotten it. He said he'd heard it was my favorite fruit.

"I was half-charmed, but I kept to my oath. I faced Melanion on the track the next day, and soon I took the lead. Then something shimmered on the path before me, and my concentration wavered. I broke my stride, hurrying over to see what it was. Before me on the road were more ripe, golden apples. While I was distracted by them, that bastard Melanion made his way across the finish line."

Atalanta laughed, and so did I. This was the first time I'd ever heard of my teacher losing.

"He was always full of mischief, but I was happy. We were happy. And so we were wed. Later I had my son," Atalanta finished awkwardly. I waited for her to say more, but instead she looked into the fire with an expression of distant longing.

I imagined my teacher as a young woman, gazing at her husband with affection and delight. I could scarcely picture it, but that didn't mean it wasn't true. I knew what it was like to be surprised by love.

"What happened to Melanion?" I finally asked.

Atalanta seemed to be dreading this question. She sunk in on herself, shoulders rising to her ears. For the first time in all the years I had known her, she truly looked like an old woman. "He died a few years after we were married. My son was still a baby, fostering with my mother's people in far Arcadia, and Melanion and I were on a hunt for a hydra that had been spotted in the area around Thebes. He and I . . . offended the goddess Aphrodite, and she killed him."

Aphrodite. The same goddess who had come to me, offering me a glimpse of my husband if only I became her servant. Now I learned she had been my teacher's enemy first.

"What could you have possibly done to offend Aphrodite?" I inquired, a question I had asked myself more than once.

The old hero squinted at the fire, carefully avoiding my eyes. "Melanion and I . . . were traveling. We sought shelter in a temple of Aphrodite, as travelers do. Night came on, and we . . . made love, and . . ."

The forest tilted and whirled around me. I could not believe what I was hearing. *You had sex with Melanion in a temple?!*" I demanded. How could she have been so foolish?

To my absolute astonishment, Atalanta's ears turned red, and she covered her face with her hands. It seemed that there was no end to the shocks I would endure. My stunned incredulity faded, and I found myself laughing.

"You'd think Aphrodite would have seen it as a thoughtful offering," I remarked.

Atalanta's leathery face still tinged pink. "One might think so. Instead, she killed Melanion. But she permitted me to live, for reasons I cannot understand. After my son was old enough, I decided to be done with love and take to the forests."

I thought of the child that floated in my womb, right now nothing more than the unpleasantness of nausea in the morning and a wicked edge to my appetite. One day it would be a person, standing before me. The thought filled me with both wonder and fear. I hoped I wouldn't get us both killed before then.

"Where is your son now?" I asked Atalanta.

"He is the head of the Arcadian royal guard. It's a good position and keeps him out of trouble. If he tried to join the army that that uncle of yours is amassing at Aulis, I'd have to go there myself to slap sense into him."

"So you've heard about the expedition to Troy?" I asked, picking at a stray thread on my blanket. "Agamemnon won't be dissuaded, it seems. I wonder what my father thinks of it."

Atalanta snorted. "Your father should be smart enough to put a stop to it, but sometimes men are blinded by gold. War is nothing but a waste of time. I'd go to Tiryns myself to speak with Alkaios if I had the strength."

A thought occurred to me. Why wasn't Atalanta in Arcadia with her son instead of here in the wilderness? Atalanta loved her forests, but she was growing old, and pragmatism called for a more comfortable life in civilization. My teacher was nothing if not pragmatic.

Hesitantly, I asked my question. Atalanta did not answer right away. Instead, she rose from her blankets with a grunt and rummaged around in a parcel of goods sheltered by the lean-to. She pulled out a clay pipe, then a small bag of some sour-smelling herb. She resumed her seat, stuffing a pinch of herb into the pipe, and igniting it with a twig from the fire. She paused a moment before exhaling a cloud of smoke so strong it made my eyes water.

For a moment I thought she had not heard me, and I was about to repeat myself. Then she gave me a long slow look, and said, "Why do you think I am here, little fool?"

My mind whirled. Why would Atalanta come here to this hollow in the wilderness, like a wild animal who retreats to a quiet place at the end of its life?

"You're dying," I said.

The idea was unfathomable, unthinkable, but Atalanta confirmed my suspicions with a curt nod. "There is a lump, here." She indicated her left breast. "It grows, and my strength wanes. It is a common complaint, but when the disease is so far advanced the only outcome is death. And I will not die like a dog in the filth of the city streets," she added fiercely.

"Atalanta—" I began, before the lump in my throat rendered me incapable of speech. I did not want to start weeping now. I was not sure I would ever stop.

"Oh, save your tears. I've had a full life." She poked the fire with a long stick, sending up sparks.

"Let me find you a healer, someone who knows how to treat your illness," I begged.

Atalanta snorted. "I won't let those butchers touch me. With Artemis Far-Shooter as my witness, it will end poorly for them if they try. Let me live out my days under the sky, among the trees. 'Call no one happy until she is dead,' the proverb says. Well, death comes to all, and I am not afraid to meet him."

"Let me stay with you," I implored. "I will look after you in your last days."

"No!" Atalanta spat. "You belong with your family. Leave an old woman in peace. Besides, it is time that you returned to your parents in Mycenae. Unless I miss my guess, you are pregnant." Her gray eyes flicked toward my belly.

"How did you know?" I asked.

Atalanta looked back at the fire, a self-satisfied grin splitting her face. "I didn't know for certain until you confirmed it just now. But you've gotten up half a dozen times this evening to piss, and you ate your own body weight in stew. Add to that the fact that you're a newlywed, and the conclusion is obvious."

"I am not going to leave you here alone," I said.

Atalanta's expression softened. "Go home, dear girl," she said in a gentle voice I had never heard before. She must have used it with her son when he was small, suffering from scraped knees or bruised feelings. "Whatever your husband does, your parents will welcome the child. If it's a boy, he will be the new crown prince of Mycenae," she continued. "You are full of life, and you seek life. This is a place of death. Soon you will need more help than I can provide."

"I'm afraid," I admitted, my voice trembling. "I'm so afraid. What if it goes badly?" *What if the baby dies in childbirth? Or if I die, and the baby is left without either parent?*

Atalanta nodded sagely. "That is always a danger," she said to me. "Hunting monsters is not nearly as terrifying as becoming a mother. I will not fill your head with useless platitudes."

She pulled out the pipe once more and puffed its foul-smelling smoke; she claimed that the herb, a plant from Scythia, eased the pain of the disease that gnawed at her bones.

"What can I do?" I asked.

"Nothing." Atalanta deposited the ashes on the bare earth, tapping the pipe a few times to clear it completely. "The fear never goes away. But in time, love makes it bearable."

I insisted on staying with her for three days. I built up stores of food and firewood for Atalanta, setting numerous snares for small game to contribute to the smokehouse, and stacked wood outside her lean-to. A deer or two would have done nicely, but I did not have the time for an extended hunt. Atalanta clucked her tongue at me all the while, but I think she was secretly glad for my company.

Before I left, Atalanta insisted on giving me an extra blanket, a knife, and a bundle of dried meat. "Tiryns is not far, but I will not have you suffer hunger or cold on the journey."

"You are dying!" I shot back. "I will not take your supplies."

"That's exactly why you should take them!" Atalanta replied. "You will need them longer than I will."

In the end, I accepted her judgment.

On the morning that I departed for Tiryns, Atalanta held my shoulders and gazed at me for a long time, memorizing every line of my face. At last, the old hero said, "You are not like a daughter to me. I would never rest easy if I had a daughter; the world is too cruel. But you have been like my little sister. I have watched you grow into the fullness of your strength, and it has been one of the great joys of my life. I am glad I had the chance to see you once more before I die."

I left before Atalanta could see the tears on my cheeks and did not look back.

25

EROS

Aphrodite had not been idle in her threat to imprison me in this lightless place. At first, I told myself it was nothing. I had chosen solitude before when I made my home in the lonely cliffside above the sea, and this was no different.

I was wrong. Days passed, morning and night, and no one came to loosen my chains. I found that I could not stretch my legs or arms, which caused my joints to lock and spasm. A mortal might have been crippled, and though my divinity sustained me, it did little to ease the pain.

I could not die, but I could experience endless deprivation. My tongue dried to the consistency of leather, and eventually even my tears ran dry. Hunger scraped me hollow. I tested the chains with all my divine strength, but they would not be moved. I tried grinding them against the rock, but they were god-forged, and it would take centuries to make the slightest indentation.

Worse than any of this was the thought of Psyche. I imagined her wandering alone in the wilderness, skin scraped raw by thorns and brambles, certain that I had discarded her. Even if I managed to escape this place, I would never be able to find her; if we set eyes on each other, the curse would only pry us apart again.

I slept as much as I could, trying to find a moment of peace through oblivion. Soon Aphrodite found a way to take this from me too.

More than once I was startled awake by the snarl of Aphrodite's voice in my ear. I had no idea how she managed to come and go so easily from this windowless room, but she would do this often in the days to come, shaking me from peaceful sleep into the cold truth of my circumstances.

On this occasion, she chose to rebuke me about the incident with Typhon, a hideous monster I had cursed to love her. "He hunted me for a month," she hissed, the silver bell sound of her voice ragged with fury. "The ugliest creature I've ever seen, as tall as a mountain with scales like a flounder, and he wouldn't stop hounding me. He had me holed up in a cave in the hills while his feet shook the earth. 'Aphrodite, where are you, my beloved?' I don't know what I would have done if he had grabbed me with those crusty claws of his. I had to turn myself into a fish to escape. Such humiliation, all for your silly little jest."

When Aphrodite was gone, my flayed nerves waited in agony for her return. I could not relax into sleep knowing that I might be so rudely startled out of it. Worse, I found myself desperate for the sound of another living voice. Even Aphrodite's presence was better than the nothingness of being alone. Even the steady drip of her bile was better than silence.

Or at least, that was what I thought, until the day she told me about Psyche.

It may have been morning, or it may have been the darkest night. Time did not exist in this little room lit only by the glowing rectangle of the door's outline. My head was lolling to my chest when a sharp voice like a poison-coated spear shocked me awake.

"Do you miss your human wife?" Aphrodite asked. "That little

Psyche. I went looking for her after the curse split you apart, you know. I thought I might make her an offer, to take her as my hand-maiden until she delivers my grandchild."

"No," was all I could manage, in a frog-like croak. I wanted to spit in Aphrodite's face, but my tongue was a dry leaf in my mouth. She knew how to plunge the knife in and twist, torturing me with what I could not change.

"At first all I saw was devastation," Aphrodite continued, her voice lapping at the shell of my ear. "That rock house of yours crumbled to ruins when the curse took you, and now nothing remains. I saw your little wife weeping, and then I saw her take matters into her own hands."

Satisfaction twisted Aphrodite's voice, and I knew that she was smiling. "She hung herself from the cliffs, a sheet tied around her neck. I suppose your deceit was too much to bear, the poor girl. Psyche is dead."

I thought I was familiar with pain. The flaming sear of hot oil, the dull agony of joints pulled out of place, the howl of the curse. But this was a supernova of agony that eclipsed them all.

"You lie!" I surged against the chains, and a roar escaped my parched throat. I might not be able to break the forged metal, but perhaps in my rage I could fragment the rock they held me to. I heard the swish of Aphrodite's feet as she backed hastily away from me, not expecting such a reaction.

"Whether I lie or speak the truth, it does not matter," Aphrodite replied, maintaining her composure. "You will never see Psyche again."

All around me was darkness. In my delirium, I embraced it.

I did not know whether I stood or swam or floated, which way was up or which down. I was adrift in inky blackness, velvet as a blanket. Details slid away from my desiccated mind like sand through an hourglass. I fell into the depths of my longing like a luckless laborer into the shafts of a salt mine. My mind had always been so quick to fix itself upon the changing world, but now, without Psyche, there was nothing.

I recalled the madness of Gaia: empty-eyed, staring, void of thought or feeling. How would I know if I went mad, if there was no one around to tell me?

Then again, perhaps madness was preferable to a world where Psyche was dead and our child gone before it had taken its first breath.

Nothingness, endless nothingness as I spun across the void. I withered with pain and hunger like a carcass under the desert sun.

When I could bear it no longer, I closed my eyes so that the nothingness was truly complete. In this darkness there were dreams and memories: flashes of images, appearing and disappearing like lightning on the underbelly of clouds. A stuttering of light and color, before oblivion reigned once more.

I saw a house carved into a cliff, all of a piece with the mountain, its windows open to the sky. I could smell the scent of roses and the salt from the sea. I saw an eagle, silhouetted against the bright disk of the sun, gathering its wings close to its body and dropping like a spear.

I saw the face of a girl, haloed by black curls, staring at me in shock by the light of a lamp.

My heart broke upon itself like a crashing wave, throwing up a glittering swarm of needle-sharp diamonds that embedded themselves in my chest like arrowpoints. The sight of the girl pulled at fishhooks in my soul, and I plunged deeper into the realm of dreams, seeking her once more.

I passed through gardens and castles and the ruins of burned cities, the dreams of a thousand gods and mortals. At last I found the girl, walking in a meadow scattered with wildflowers of blue and gold, cutting like a scythe through the grass. The wind whipped the shapeless garment she wore and blew the curls around her face. She paused to wipe the pearls of sweat from her brow; her delicate jaw was set in a fierce line.

This was not the Psyche of my rose-tinged memories, a mere image too perfect to be real. No, this was a living woman; I was seeing inside her dream. Sometimes minds attuned to each other can touch in sleep. Desire, after all, always finds its target. A mortal may walk in the dreams of a god, and vice versa. I knew this was one of those rare dreams, a gift of Oneiros that showed me the workings of another sleeping mind. This one was Psyche's.

I almost laughed with delight. Psyche was alive! Alive and spending her nights dreaming of her goals. Now I saw Aphrodite's lie for what it was. Of course Psyche would not have taken her own life. She would never admit defeat so easily.

I tried to call out to Psyche, but the dream shivered around me, shattering like a broken mirror. I found myself back in my body, imprisoned in the depths of Olympus.

A laugh began in the pit of my stomach and rang against the walls. I had found a way, however limited and imperfect, to escape Aphrodite's clutches and see through her lies. Psyche was alive, and I held on to the memory of her face like a star. Somehow, I would find her again, if only in the world of dreams.

But my laughter faded as I realized the task before me. Even dreaming took effort now, strength I did not have. I wondered how long it would be until my divine powers went dormant and I entered an eternity of dreamless sleep, staring sightlessly into the dark.

26

PSYCHE

Several days later, the city of Tiryns came into view, and I gasped aloud in relief. The familiar sight soothed my heart. From my vantage among the mountains, the city looked like a fresco painted in miniature. I recognized those proud walls, the rounded roof of the royal palace. Everything else in my life had changed, but the city of Tiryns remained the same. My heart pounding, I began to run.

At last, I was among familiar forests and fields. Here was the clearing where I had sat with Atalanta on that first day of training. There was the high rock where Zephyrus had spirited me away to my new life with Eros. I was home at last, and soon I found myself running down the hills that dipped toward the plain.

The guardsman at the gate did not recognize me at first, and actually laughed when I told him I was the princess Psyche. It was only when another, more familiar face peered down over the wall that he was informed of his mistake.

"Dexios!" I called to the new arrival.

In a moment my childhood friend was down the stairs, staring at me in wonder. We might have embraced, but it did not suit the differences in our social stations. He bowed to me awkwardly instead.

"Welcome back, Psyche," he said. "I'll escort you to the

palace." He did not ask me what had happened or where I had been, and I was too relieved to find this odd.

"First, you must tell me what you're wearing," I said, catching sight of his armor—not boiled leather, but real metal. Where did stable boys come by armor like that?

"Do you like it?" He grinned and glanced down at himself. "It was given to me when I joined the Myrmidons."

We passed below the gaze of the stone felines that adorned the Lion's Gate, though they seemed much smaller than I remembered. "The Myrmidons?" I asked as I followed Dexios into the city. *Myrmidon* meant *ant-man*, which left me with a number of questions.

"Prince Achilles's personal fighting force," Dexios answered. "We are called Myrmidons because we move with the coordination of a colony of ants. Achilles takes any man who shows skill, not only those born to warrior families. Soon we'll set sail for Troy. No more shoveling out horse stalls for me!"

The triumph in his voice made me smile, but I was soon distracted by the sights and sounds of the city. Tiryns was preparing for war: The fires of various forges laid a thick veil over the streets and houses, and the ringing of blacksmiths' hammers echoed against the walls. Preparations for Agamemnon's troops, I assumed. More than a few soldiers, armored like Dexios, strolled the streets. The few ordinary citizens we passed seemed harried and downcast. None of them recognized me, and I wondered about this. Were they focused on their own concerns, or had I truly changed so much that my own people didn't know me?

"We leave within the week to join the fleet at Aulis," Dexios told me.

He led me through a series of winding alleys to one of the smaller doors of the palace, a servant's passage. From there, I found myself in a small courtyard garden. It was a favorite of my mother's, well shaded and filled with flowers. Astydamia tended this garden herself when she felt well enough, singing softly as she pruned browned leaves from the plants. But I noticed several dead leaves today; perhaps preparation for the war had kept her away.

Behind me, I heard Dexios say, "I will send word to the lady of the house."

I turned to ask why he had smuggled me in through the servants' passage like a bundle of contraband rather than bringing me through the front door for a proper welcome, but he was already gone.

I sat on the familiar stone bench and examined the mosaic that ran along the edges of the garden. It depicted dryads who darted around trees and flowers, pursuing one another playfully. It had the same flaw that I remembered—a tile had fallen out of one nymph's cheek, leaving her half-headless. That small detail convinced me that this homecoming was real and not some fragile dream, and relief loosened my limbs like sweet wine.

At last, I was home, and could set down the fears and uncertainty I had carried for so long. Within the walls of the palace, all my problems shrank to pinpoints, and the pain of grief receded like a low tide. Within moments my parents would sweep me into their protective arms, and I wondered how I could describe all that had happened. Should tell them of my pregnancy now, or wait until after I had explained the rest?

"*Psyche?*" The voice was Iphigenia's, and I whirled to see her standing in the doorway, wearing a dress of stunningly fine fabric. Her hands flew to her mouth, but she did not rush to embrace me.

"What are you doing here?" I gaped. I would have been less surprised by the sudden appearance of Medusa. "Where are my father and mother?"

Iphigenia's mouth opened, then closed. "No one told you?" she finally managed. "We tried to send word, but the messenger hawk returned with the letter unopened."

I looked for Dexios, but he was nowhere to be found.

The lady of the house, I thought wildly. *Dexios said he would find the lady of the house. He didn't say that he would find my mother.*

"Psyche," Iphigenia said, choosing her words with the care of a child leaping from one slick river rock to another. "In the absence of a direct male heir, the throne goes to the princess's husband, or her son if she has one. If that man cannot be found, it goes to the king's closest male relative . . ." She trailed off again, gazing at me with horrible pity.

"What are you trying to say?" I demanded.

Clytemnestra appeared like a shadow behind her daughter. Unlike my gentle cousin, Clytemnestra did not attempt to soften the blow. "Psyche, your parents are dead."

27

PSYCHE

I stood before my parents' mausoleum and felt grief twine like a serpent around my heart.

The tomb was a beautiful structure of soaring columns and white marble, though it bore the marks of hasty completion. Most rulers, if they had any authority at all, began work on their tombs when they were still relatively young. My mother and father had been no exception. The builders must have thought they had many years to finish it, but the mausoleum was serving its intended purpose sooner than anyone expected.

Alkaios and Astydamia had been carried off by illness. Iphigenia had told me this the day before, as I lay weeping on the tiles of my mother's garden. Astydamia had gone first, burning with a fever, which was no surprise given her frailty. My father's decline had been more unexpected, but at the news of his wife's death, he seemed to give up his hold on life.

It isn't surprising to anyone who really knew them, I thought, swallowing my grief. *He wouldn't want to live without her, is all*.

I should have been there, even if all I could do was wipe the fevered sweat from their brows. If only I had left the seaside house sooner. If only I had not pursued the monster that fateful day, the last time I saw my parents alive.

I wondered briefly if this was Aphrodite's doing, but quickly dismissed the idea. The goddess of love would not have opted for so clean a death as fever.

Following custom, the mausoleum served as a shrine to the deceased rulers. I could see the evidence of offerings—half a burning stick of incense, a few copper coins. Sometimes the grave of a ruler would become a permanent place of worship, but I knew this would not be the case for my parents. They had served their people faithfully for many years, but they would be footnotes in chroniclers' dusty tomes, if they appeared at all. The looming war with Troy overshadowed everything.

A gentle hand fell on my shoulder. "Psyche," Iphigenia said. "It's time to go. Odd wants to see you."

I wiped away my tears. I knew one thing for certain: My father would never have wanted the first fruits of Mycenae to be sacrificed for a foolish war.

Odd, it turned out, was Odysseus, the king of Ithaka and Agamemnon's most trusted advisor. I could not guess where Iphigenia had conceived this nickname, but she had managed to endear herself to all her father's generals in one way or another.

I walked through the palace without truly seeing it. After the deaths of my parents, this was not a home. It was only a roof set over stone walls, which I moved through like a ghost.

Odd had taken over a small room in the administrative wing of the palace as his private office. He stood as I opened the door. He was not a large man, and in fact he stood a few finger-widths shorter than me. He walked with a slight stiffness, the relic of an old hunting injury, and that was how I knew he was truly dangerous. Agamemnon would never keep a limping man around if he was not a killer.

Odd greeted me as though we were old acquaintances, asking me to sit and make myself comfortable. And would I like some watered wine? I knew such politeness was as hollow as a rotted log, but I accepted it smoothly. Over the next hour, Odd peppered me with a seemingly endless barrage of questions, each a subtly different variation of *Who is your husband?* and *Where is he now?*

Once I realized what he was doing, I laughed. "You are trying to figure out how likely it is that my husband will walk through those gates and stake his claim to the city."

Odd was too practiced an interrogator to respond directly to my claim, but the tension in his jaw showed me that I was correct. "Agamemnon is about to fight a war," he told me. "He doesn't need to worry about issues of succession in his kingdom. Your husband—"

"Is a very private individual. He would have no interest in ruling," I replied. My heart thundered in my chest; now was the time to make my move. I laid my hands on the table, spreading my fingers to root myself in place. "Give the crown to me and I will rule in his stead. I am of the royal line, and I was raised here. I know this land."

Odd's eyebrows shot up to his hairline, but I squared my shoulders. This was my birthright. I was the sole scion of the former king of Mycenae, and I had grown up in this palace. I could hold the throne until my child came of age and find my place in the mortal world once more.

An incredulous bark of a laugh escaped Odd's bearded mouth. "You? Impossible," he chuckled. "The law is quite clear. Perhaps a woman could rule some barbarian place like Egypt, but not here. Agamemnon sits on the throne of the kingdom of Mycenae now, at least until that husband of yours—how did you put it?— walks through these gates."

Rage nearly blinded me. I considered telling Odysseus that my husband would do no such thing, that such a paltry title as king was beneath a god, but then thought better of it. Agamemnon held the throne now by right of succession. The ground shifted and swirled beneath me, and I understood that despite my lineage I was only a daughter of the former ruler, tolerated at will. The knowledge felt like a snare, stealing the breath from my lungs.

Odd appeared to soften as he said, "Do you understand what is at stake in this war? Why Agamemnon is marching on Troy?"

The sudden change in tone disarmed me. "Because of Helen," I answered, "and the vows her former suitors swore."

He bestowed a condescending smile upon me, one meant for a precocious child who still did not know the ways of the world. "No, no, dear girl, that's only pretext. Here's the truth: Troy is the waypoint for every caravan crossing Asia, Africa, and Europe. It's no secret that King Priam, the father of Helen's abductor, sits on a pile of gold and picks his teeth with jeweled combs. Go along with what your uncle wants, and you'll be a wealthy woman. We will all be rich by the end of this campaign." The light of that gold glittered in Odd's eyes, and I realized he had already decided how to spend his share of the loot. I knew his like: I saw that same restless hunger in the eyes of the jackals that prowled at the edges of the firelight after Atalanta and I took down a kill. Hungry but cunning, willing to bide their time.

"Agamemnon is the rightful heir to the throne, and his son Orestes will serve as regent in his absence," he continued. "Unless your husband reappears, which seems unlikely. You say he disappeared fighting the Dorians, and we both know that those savage people do not take prisoners. Your husband is gone, and you are here."

I opened my mouth to reply, but Odd was quicker. His sternness faded and was replaced by a conspiratorial look, as though we were sneaking pastries from the kitchen. "I think only of your well-being," he insisted, softening his voice so that I had to lean in to hear him. "I can tell you are god-chosen just as I am—the gray-eyed lady has favored me since I was young. We mortals who are loved by them must help one another, for the love of the gods is beautiful but terrible."

I was unsurprised by Odd's claim to belong to Athena—as soon as I met him, I felt a presence redolent of old papyrus and naked bronze—but I was disconcerted by his statement that the gods were both beautiful and terrible. My husband was beautiful, certainly, but he had never been terrible. Even if he had lied to me and left me in the end.

"In light of our divine connection, I offer you some advice: Don't fight this," Odd continued. "The law of Mycenae is on your uncle's side, and so is popular opinion. Cooperate and you will find yourself accorded all the respect due to your station as a childless widow and daughter of the former king."

I noticed he made no mention of what would happen if I did not cooperate.

But I wasn't a childless widow, and that was the problem. I fought the urge to touch my belly, then noticed Odd watching me very closely. He had been testing me for this very sign, for some indication that I carried a future prince of Mycenae in my womb, a snag in the orderly line of succession. I kept my hands carefully folded on my lap.

Finally, Odysseus stood, an indication that I should rise as well. "I thank you for your time, lady Psyche. I will not keep you longer from the women's quarters—I'm sure you are still weary from your journey."

A dismissal, one I was powerless to fight. Bile rising in my throat, I went back into the shadows.

I had spent very little time in the women's quarters during my youth; I'd passed most of my days in the company of my father or Atalanta, out in the fields and forests. The section of the palace designated for the women of the household was organized around a long hallway, and turning down it, I could hear the echo of Iphigenia's voice.

"Are you blind? Does this look like purple to you? At the very best it's a dull crimson . . ."

I sighed and pushed open the door. I saw that my cousin, her cheeks flushed with anger, was berating a terrified young servant and an older matron who had the competent look of a seamstress. Both women looked as though they wanted to disappear into the stone floor.

I considered the fabric, tilting my head. "I think it is a rather attractive shade."

The seamstress and her assistant took my arrival as an opportunity to flee, pushing past me with deferential murmurs.

Iphigenia gave a ragged sigh. "I'm sorry, Psyche," she said, collapsing on the bed and throwing an arm over her face. "It's not really about the clothes. The wedding is in two days. Two days! I know I'm lucky to be marrying Achilles. At least I like him. Elektra will probably be married off to a Trojan prince for a peace treaty, and I get our army's champion. But gods help me, I miss being a priestess, Psyche. I miss it so much." She drew in a choked breath, and I thought she might cry.

I wrapped my arms around my cousin, drinking in the once-familiar scent of her curly hair. She leaned into me, her arms snaking around my torso.

"It was one thing to become a priestess when Father was a simple mercenary," Iphigenia continued. "Now he's a king and the commander of the greatest army Greece has ever seen. But I'm afraid, Psyche. What kind of husband will Achilles be? What will the wedding night be like?" She hesitated, then asked, "What was yours like, Psyche?"

I smiled at the memory. "He snuck up on me in the darkness and I hit him with a fire-poker."

Iphigenia gasped, pulling away so that she could look at me. When she realized I was serious, she dissolved into laughter as pure as spring snowmelt. I joined in, unable to help myself. For a moment we were children again, sneaking into an abandoned courtyard to practice archery.

"Did you love him, your husband?" my cousin asked when we recovered.

The question startled me, and I pulled away from Iphigenia. I frowned at the floor, considering her question. I thought about the nights Eros and I had spent under the new moon, the stories we had whispered to each other. The archery contests in darkened rooms, his steady presence by my side in the shape of various animals during our journeying. Was this love I felt, this sparkling happiness? With sudden shock, I knew the truth.

"Yes, I love him," I replied. "I still do. That isn't in the past."

"Of course," Iphigenia said, her glance sliding away from my face. She, like everyone else in Mycenae, thought that my husband was dead.

Eros was not dead, could not die, but that didn't matter. Whatever the truth of my own feelings, his had been nothing but an accident and a curse. He had further proven his indifference through his absence during my wanderings in the wilderness. I pushed the memory of Eros from my mind, painful though it was, and turned back to Iphigenia.

"Psyche," Iphigenia began, her brown eyes liquid and lambent. "Will you come to my wedding at Aulis?"

I took her hand. "Of course," I replied.

Iphigenia let out the breath she had been holding and clutched my hand so tightly it threatened to go numb. "Thank you," she whispered.

I squeezed her hand in return and tried not to give any sign of the idea that sparked to life in my mind: that perhaps once Agamemnon sailed away to his foolish war, I could take the throne of Mycenae myself, even if unofficially. Even if it set a wedge between Iphigenia and I forever.

"I'm so glad you'll be there," Iphigenia continued. "It will be a relief to have you with me. Otherwise it would just be me and Elektra and Mother, and you know how Mother can be."

I did. It was as though Clytemnestra feared she would cease to exist if she was not complaining about something.

"Don't worry," I assured my cousin. "Your mother can't keep up her nagging all the way to Aulis."

28

PSYCHE

I was appalled to discover that Clytemnestra could, in fact, keep up her nagging all the way to Aulis.

She nagged Iphigenia for slouching, yawning, speaking too much, and then for speaking too little. We were packed tightly into the carriage as it bumped haphazardly over the road, and I could feel the spray of Clytemnestra's breath as she continued her unyielding invective.

It was Elektra who finally spoke up. An infant when I had seen her last, Iphigenia's sister was now about six years old. She was small and solemn, a miniature version of her disapproving mother, one of those children who seem to have been born middle-aged.

"Mother," Elektra interrupted, "Iphigenia knows how to sit and speak. She's going to be a married woman soon with a house of her own. Let her be."

For a moment I thought that Clytemnestra would strike the girl, but instead she huffed and turned away to face the dusty curtains. "I just want to make sure she's well-prepared, that's all," Clytemnestra spat. "This is a very difficult day for me."

Iphigenia looked exhausted, as if she had been drained of some vital essence. She reached out a hand and laid it on her mother's, linking fingers, and Clytemnestra's harsh expression faded. Elektra sighed heavily and turned her attention to the floor, but to my relief no one spoke again until we arrived at Aulis.

When our carriage finally shuddered to a stop, I lifted one of the curtains and peered out at the Greek camp. I saw hundreds of ships docked at the harbor—longships and triremes, with eyes painted on the hulls so that each craft could see its way.

There were men everywhere. They picked fights with one another or oiled their shields as the sun bronzed their naked backs. Maleness floated like a ground mist over the camp. Clytemnestra reached over and yanked the curtains shut.

Stale, blisteringly hot air filled the enclosed space, and sweat began to trickle down my back. I wanted to disembark, but Clytemnestra refused.

"We will wait for my husband to greet us," she stated primly, hands in her lap. "That is the proper way." Sweat beaded her upper lip and dripped down her temples.

When at last someone arrived, it was not Agamemnon but Odysseus. "It seems I shall serve as your host!" Odd chuckled, all laughter and merriment now that it served his purpose. "Your husband sends his regrets, queen Clytemnestra, but he has been pulled away by his war councils."

I wondered if "war councils" was not a polite way of saying "carousing and drinking." I wondered further at a man who would not come to greet his own wife and daughters on the eve of the eldest's wedding. But all of us were eager to leave the cramped interior of the carriage, and I did not waste our time by asking any questions.

Ithakan soldiers formed a periphery around us, and we were led to a large tent in the middle of the camp. It stood near an even more magnificent tent that I was certain must belong to my uncle Agamemnon, though I saw no trace of the man. I noticed more soldiers peering at us, eyes bright with curiosity and perhaps other desires as well, but then my line of vision was abruptly cut off by the fall of the tent flap.

On the night before her wedding, it was traditional for a bride's kinswomen to bathe her in rosewater, braid her hair, beautify her hands and feet with henna, and fill her ears with all the information a new wife needed to know. This was what the women had done for Helen's wedding so long ago, although my mother and I had arrived too late to join in the ritual, and this was what we did for Iphigenia now.

The festivities were muted. Clytemnestra looked ashen, like a woman forced to sell her only child for bread. The rest of the women followed her lead and remained subdued. I told myself that this was because the bridal party was so small, and the tent was so stuffy. With the war, there was simply no time to summon all of Iphigenia's relatives for a more elaborate ceremony. The only ones in attendance were Clytemnestra, little Elektra, and me, along with a pair of Messenian slaves whose names I never learned.

As I traced intricate patterns of henna paste onto Iphigenia's hands, it occurred to me that I had never experienced these rituals myself. My own marriage to Eros—if it could be called that—was swift and unexpected. I hadn't even had a proper wedding ceremony, let alone anyone to paint my hands and feet so beautifully. Though it would have made no difference in the way things turned out.

Grief speared my heart. I had lost Eros, Atalanta, and my mother and father as well. And I knew that however much I despised Agamemnon, however much I longed to claim the throne of Mycenae as my birthright, I could never do something that would sever me from Iphigenia. She was the only real family I had left, save for the baby growing in my belly.

I assumed that Clytemnestra would take the opportunity to

expound upon the behavior expected of a young bride or at least share conversation with her daughter. Instead, to my surprise, Iphigenia's mother took to her bed after supper.

"Weddings exhaust me, you know that," she snapped before settling down underneath her blankets.

The tent was not large. If one person wanted to sleep, it made no sense for the rest to stay up. Reeling with the abruptness of it, we extinguished our lamps and lay down as well.

I chose a spot next to Iphigenia, so close that I could smell the lingering scent of rosewater on her skin. After some time had passed, I heard a whisper.

"I want your opinion," Iphigenia said. She spoke softly to ensure that no one else would hear, though snores already rose from Clytemnestra's bedroll. I felt my cousin's words as much as I heard them, the vibration reminding me of those sightless nights with Eros.

"I've been thinking about what can go *wrong* with Achilles, and not what I must do to ensure that things go *right*," she whispered. "After the wedding, he'll be gone for a year or so on the Trojan campaign. I've been assuming I'll stay in Mycenae, but—what if I go with him? If the wedding night goes well, that is," she added hastily. "If he's a brute, it's back to Tiryns for me."

"An interesting idea," I remarked. Brides didn't usually go to war with their husbands, but these were not usual times.

"My question," Iphigenia continued, her voice thrumming with excitement, "is this: Would you come with me, Psyche? All the way to Troy?"

Noticing my stunned silence, Iphigenia added hurriedly, "If I go as his new bride and you come as my companion, even Father won't be able to prohibit it. I'll have to ask Achilles what he thinks, but I'm sure he won't mind. What man wouldn't want his new wife with him? Besides, I'm a trained priestess of Artemis, and the soldiers will want me there to perform the sacred rites. And you'll get to fight in the war if you want to. It'll be wonderful! I'll be the priestess I've always wanted to become, and you'll be the hero you were meant to be."

I pondered this. My plan to seize the throne of Mycenae now seemed like nothing more than a naïve scheme; no one could stop the forward momentum of the war. But perhaps I could modulate it. I would have some sway with Agamemnon if I distinguished myself in the army. My fighting skills were adaptable, as I had learned on the road with the bandits. The other soldiers might balk at a woman's presence at first, but they would come around. And Iphigenia was right that warriors far from home would appreciate the comforting presence of a priestess.

Another thought occurred to me. In my brief idyll at the seaside house and during the long brutal journey after, I had nearly forgotten the prophecy that the Oracle of Delphi spoke over my birth. Perhaps my own destiny lay at the other end of the sea at Troy. Perhaps it was there that I would become a true hero.

Even though it meant leaving behind any hope of seeing Eros again.

"Well?" Iphigenia's breath was hot on my cheek, her tone hopeful.

I smiled. "Give me the night to think about it, Iphigenia. I have just come home, and I do not know if I am ready to leave again so soon."

Iphigenia heaved a dramatic sigh and rolled over. Soon her breathing slipped into the easy rhythm that signaled sleep.

I lay awake, staring up at the darkness. Even as the sounds of revelry began to die away outside, I continued to gaze at the arch of the tent. Some instinct would not let me rest. At last I stood up, threw on a cloak, and, after a moment's thought, strapped a long hunting knife to my belt. I needed air and the open sky.

I padded on silent feet to the entrance of the tent, careful not to wake the other women. This effort was spoiled when I pushed back the tent flap and nearly collided with an armored figure. I should have known we would be under guard. This was a military camp, after all.

"Lady Psyche, what brings you out at this late hour?" one of the guards demanded.

It took me a moment to place the voice, not to mention the face that stared at me from beneath the plumed helmet. "Patroclus?" I asked wonderingly.

He nodded, pulling off his helmet. Patroclus had grown since that day at the Heraean Games, which now seemed like a lifetime ago, but his face had the same simplicity.

"Where are you headed this evening?" he asked. "I would be happy to escort you."

"Nowhere. I only wanted to see the stars and listen to the ocean."

Patroclus nodded. "It is unseemly for a lady of your standing to go walking alone among so many men. I will go with you. Remain at your posts," he ordered into the darkness. I realized that two other warriors stood before the tent, each wearing the same armor as Patroclus. More of the Myrmidons, Achilles's men.

Patroclus began to walk, and I followed him. An idea dawned: Perhaps I could establish an alliance with this man, and together we could form some coalition to face Agamemnon. I noticed the camp was oddly calm, and though I could hear laughter and voices from the tents, we encountered few soldiers. I remarked upon this strange fact as we wound our way around the tents and fires to the fringes of the camp.

"We've had to institute a curfew," Patroclus replied. "Fighting was a major problem in the first few weeks. There are fewer injuries if everyone is in their tents by dark. Of course, there are always rule breakers, but we've found that if I take first watch, I can talk most of them down. Agamemnon sends out his own patrols later at night, and they are less gentle."

I noticed how he said the word *we*, how it rolled off his tongue with practiced ease. "You and Achilles are organizing patrols? Isn't that the duty of the commander?"

We crested a dune at the outskirts of the camp and paused. Free from the noise and stink of human habitation, I felt as though I could finally breathe again. I watched the black waters tumble onto a shore gilded silver by the stars.

Patroclus shrugged. "It is. Agamemnon can issue all the orders he likes; it doesn't mean anyone will listen to them. In the beginning, he tried to calm the tension with proclamations. They weren't worth the papyrus they were written on."

"What of Menelaus?" I asked. "Wasn't it his wife Helen's abduction that led to all of this? Why doesn't he take a more active role in leadership?"

Patroclus shot me a withering glance. "Menelaus isn't fit to command a hunting party, and we both know it. The Spartans, his own people, dislike him so much that they offered up only a symbolic number of men."

I didn't bother to defend my uncle, who was a stranger to me. This kind of talk bordered on treason, but there was no one to hear us except the sand and the night wind.

"Patroclus," I began, feeling once more the unease that had sent me out of the tent. "You said that the army has been here for weeks. Why haven't you already left?"

Patroclus frowned, the moonlight casting strange shadows on his face. The rest of his body seemed encased in darkness, armor blending in with the black night. "It's the weather that's the problem. Specifically, the wind. The strong trade winds you normally get at this time of year are absent, and a fleet like this can't sail to Troy on mere breezes. So we wait. The men grow restless, and Agamemnon tries in vain to keep them in check."

"Agamemnon will be Achilles's father-in-law soon," I observed. "Family ties create harmony, or so it is said."

"Yes," Patroclus acknowledged hesitantly. "Which is something I don't understand. This marriage places Achilles in the line of succession for kingship of Mycenae, and I can't imagine Agamemnon wants to risk ceding his throne to Achilles. They despise each other."

"I gathered," I replied dryly. "What I want to know is where Iphigenia fits into all of this. Will Achilles be good to her?"

"Of course," Patroclus replied. "Achilles is good at everything he does; marriage will be no exception. Besides, Iphigenia is a sweet girl with a remarkable head for strategy, and it's clear that she adores him. Achilles likes to be adored." On the lips of someone else, this might have been an insult, but from Patroclus it was only an observation of preference. It seemed to me that Patroclus spent a great deal of time observing Achilles's preferences.

"Do you love him?" I asked suddenly.

Patroclus stared at me. He continued to stare unblinking for several seconds, and even in the dim light of the stars his expression might have withered the hardy beach grass on the dunes. I felt as though I had stumbled upon a bedroom tryst, sheets tossed aside and limbs all akimbo. I reddened and averted my gaze. Patroclus hid his feelings behind defenses as impenetrable as the phalanxes he led. He would reveal nothing that could leave Achilles vulnerable.

"Everyone loves Achilles," Patroclus replied lightly, turning away from me. "Myself included. Everyone except Agamemnon, which is why I don't understand this marriage. There are rumors that the lack of wind is divine punishment, sent by Artemis in return for Agamemnon killing a sacred stag. But if he offended

Artemis, why try to appease the goddess of virginity by marrying off one of her sworn virgin priestesses? And why to Achilles, of all people?" He glanced sidelong at me. "If you have more information, I would be eager to hear it."

I understood now why Patroclus had brought me to this remote place, far out of earshot of the camp. The hair along the nape of my neck prickled, and I realized I was in the presence of a man who was as dangerous as Achilles in his own way. I recalled the mention of a boy killed in a game of dice and wondered if it had been a mere accident after all.

I knew nothing about Agamemnon's motivations and said as much to Patroclus, who absorbed the information with equanimity and looked away, the light of interest fading from his eyes. I had nothing more to give him, and so he graciously but firmly escorted me back to the women's tent. But Patroclus's question gnawed at me: What *was* Agamemnon thinking when he contracted this marriage? What was I missing?

I crawled back to my bedroll next to the softly snoring Iphigenia and fell into an uneasy sleep.

29

PSYCHE

It was the morning of her wedding, and Iphigenia looked beautiful.

She was dressed in a long-sleeved gown of saffron. It proclaimed her the daughter of a powerful man, since only a woman who never did any housework would wear such a garment. One of the Messenian slaves managed to find flowers, a rarity in a military camp, and Elektra used them to fashion a crown for her sister. Under the flowers, Iphigenia's curly dark hair had been combed back and braided into two parts. She looked like springtime itself, like the goddess Persephone come to earth.

I watched as the crowd parted for my cousin. The army was in full regalia, sweating and muttering, but they fell silent as Iphigenia passed.

I caught my first glimpse of Agamemnon on the dais, wider and grayer but otherwise unchanged since Helen's wedding all those years ago. Clytemnestra stood with me and the other women in the crowd. Neither she nor her husband acknowledged each other.

Achilles was waiting on the dais as well, taller and even more infuriatingly handsome than he had been at the Heraean Games. I noticed that he stood as far from Agamemnon as convention allowed. I was not surprised that they disliked each other. Agamemnon might be the commander, but Achilles was the beloved hero.

As Iphigenia approached the dais, a hand tugged at my skirt. "Can you lift me up? I can't see." It was Elektra, lost amidst the excitement.

I lifted the child onto my hip and smiled as Elektra marveled at the crowd. The girl was hardly heavier than a few sacks of grain, though her arms around my neck offered reassuring weight. I wondered if it would feel like this when I held my own child.

When she spotted Iphigenia, Elektra whispered into my ear, "Her braids are uneven. The left is much bigger than the right."

A few of the soldiers around us chuckled, and I felt my cheeks turn red. "Hush," I told the child.

Iphigenia ascended the steps with an air of absolute dignity, one at a time. When she reached the top, she turned and bestowed a dazzling smile upon the assembly. Where had she developed this instinct for commanding a crowd? Certainly I had never possessed it.

When Iphigenia reached the men, Agamemnon embraced her. Then he took a dagger from his belt, and in one swift motion, slit her throat.

A moment of utter silence followed. Not a single person in the crowd of thousands moved. Crimson appeared in wild patterns, stark against the yellow of Iphigenia's dress. Her hands fluttered to her throat, unable to stop the red river that poured from it. The whites of her eyes showed in panic.

Those are flowers, not blood, I thought, my mind careening desperately. *This is a wedding.*

Iphigenia fell to her knees, and blood spattered the wood. She collapsed onto the wooden planks of the dais, her skull bouncing disconcertingly.

Someone screamed. I was never sure who it was.

The crowd exploded. The bloody death had whipped them into a frenzy. They were an army with no war to fight, trapped on a lonely coast while their enemy gloated behind his walls on a distant shore. A woman had been taken by the Trojans and a woman had been sacrificed here, and that was how it should be. She was merely the appetizer before the feast.

I watched in numb silence as Achilles ran toward Iphigenia's limp form, his mouth open in a wordless cry. He had scarcely made it halfway before one of his personal guard, probably Patroclus, dragged him to safety. Agamemnon watched him go with utter indifference, his daughter's corpse at his feet.

I should have acted. I should have grabbed a sword and vaulted up to the platform, cutting down Agamemnon where he stood. But vengeance would not breathe life back into Iphigenia's still body, and shock had left me numb. The world careened around me, unreal as a dream.

A howl rose from the army, a thousand mouths giving vent to one voice, a vicious song punctuated by the crashing of shields. The men had come here for a formal occasion. They hadn't expected such a show.

Agamemnon was addressing the crowd, but I could not hear what he was saying. I could not tell if he felt any regret or shame for murdering his own daughter. I could not see anything beyond the spatters of blood on his face and hands. Iphigenia's blood. No wonder he had not bothered to visit before the wedding. But what could he stand to gain by killing his daughter?

I struggled for breath and realized that Elektra's arms were locked tightly around my neck. I could feel the child trembling, and knew with horrified clarity that she had seen everything. I had not even thought to cover her eyes.

Talons dug into the meat of my arm, and a voice hissed in my ear. "Don't run, but move quickly."

It was Clytemnestra. I glanced back toward the dais where Iphigenia's limp form lay, but my aunt's nails dug more deeply into my arm. "There is no help for her," Clytemnestra said, dragging me away.

Elektra clung to me like a burr as I made my way across the sand. Around us I noticed the soldiers from Ithaka, wide-eyed with drawn swords. They were not unaffected by the madness sweeping the assembled troops, but they stuck to their duty to protect us. I was dimly aware that they were forced to draw blood more than once during our retreat, which passed in a distant blur.

I looked back once we reached the entrance to the women's tent and was stunned to see that a celebratory atmosphere had come over the camp. I could not make sense of it. Some of the men had dispersed for a round of rotgut or a game of dice, but others were loading ships, fighting, and shouting at one another. Still others were practicing that terrible sport my people call *pankration*, anything-goes wrestling.

I could see the dais, empty except for a single limp form. Iphigenia.

A wind began to blow through the camp, cooling the sweat on my brow and shaking the cloth of the tent. The pervasive miasma lifted. The sails of the Greek ships billowed out, causing them to tug at their anchors like eager ponies. The wind had returned, a fair wind to blow the fleet to Troy.

Later, some would insist that Iphigenia was a sacrifice to Artemis, offered by her father to replace the sacred stag. I disagree. By killing the goddess's own priestess on her wedding day, I think that Agamemnon intended to send a threat. He wished to show his troops that he did not fear gods or men, that the walls of Troy were nothing to him. The warriors who already adored Agamemnon loved him even more for this, and those who disliked him began to fear him. Despots of every age know that fear is better than love.

Why Artemis permitted the winds to blow is less clear to me. Perhaps she simply dropped their reins in shock when she saw what Agamemnon had done.

Iphigenia's corpse, when it was finally returned to us, was far smaller than she had ever seemed in life. I found that the task of preparing the body for burial was easier if I pretended it was a clay doll with Iphigenia's face, if I tried not to think too much about the cold hands that still bore my imperfect henna designs from the night before.

Clytemnestra and I rinsed off the blood as best we could, though the knife wound gaped like a second mouth at her throat. Clytemnestra sewed it up with unsteady fingers, but there was only so much she could do. The Messenian slaves brought buckets of cold seawater to assist with the washing, though I do not know how they managed to make their way through the crowd.

The camp outside was in disarray. I could hear the sounds of men and horses beyond the tent, almost as though we stood on a battlefield. Agamemnon must have taken advantage of his men's enthusiasm, ordering them to ready the ships.

There wasn't enough wood for a pyre on this desolate beach, and besides, I could not stand the thought of flames consuming my beloved cousin. Let the soft earth welcome her instead. Someone helped us dig a grave just outside our tent, but I cannot remember who it was. Odysseus appeared at one point, and I vaguely recall him saying something as his hands gripped my shoulders, but I could not hear his words. Then he was gone too.

By the time we were ready for Iphigenia's burial, the Greek

army had dissipated. Not a man remained on that windswept beach, only piles of strewn debris and the blackened ruins of fire-pits. A small band of attendants was there, including the Messenian slaves who had been tasked with seeing us women back to Mycenae.

The distant white of the sails were visible on the horizon. Agamemnon did not have the time to see to anything so paltry as the funeral of a daughter.

Clytemnestra and I wrapped Iphigenia in the cleanest linen we could find and laid her in the earth, placing a coin on her tongue to pay the ferryman in the Underworld. I said the words that would guide her soul down into the realm of Persephone and Hades, since by that time Clytemnestra was no longer capable of speech and Elektra was too young to know the verses.

We covered Iphigenia with round stones smoothed by centuries of ocean currents so that the crows and wild dogs would not devour her. A carved inscription would have been the next step, but there was no time for that. Perhaps we could have painted Iphigenia's name on one of the rocks so that anyone who passed by would know who lay here, but that would not last beyond the next rain.

After we buried Iphigenia, Clytemnestra turned toward the sea. She picked her way through the silent ruins of the camp, striding numbly into the water until her gown was soaked to the knees. She clutched her skirts and let loose a howl of pure anguish.

The sheer cliffs beyond the beach echoed with the sound. I stiffened, prepared to spring up if Clytemnestra tried to drown herself, but my aunt merely swayed knee-deep in the surf.

"I think Mother is doing well, all things considered," a voice said. Elektra sat down next to me, folding her legs neatly.

I remembered Clytemnestra's unhappiness the night before

the wedding and felt ill. "Did she know?" I demanded. "Did Agamemnon tell her what he was planning?"

Elektra scrunched up her face. "Of course not. Mother would never have brought Iphigenia here if she thought Father would do something like that." She drew her knees to her chest and rested her chin on them, staring out at the sea. "Father isn't Mother's first husband, you know."

A chill wind danced over my skin. This child was wise beyond her years. "Then who was her first husband?"

"I don't know his name, but he was the king of Pisa. I heard Iphigenia and Mother talking about it once when they thought I was asleep. Father was hired to fight against Pisa, and he won. Mother was his war captive, and Father decided to make her his wife. I think she had a baby when Father took her, but I'm not sure. Anyway, Father would have killed it."

I shuddered. For years, I'd wondered why Clytemnestra treated her husband like a rabid dog. Now I understood.

I thought about what it must be like to lie down every night with the man who had killed your child. I wondered if Clytemnestra had loved her first husband, this nameless king of Pisa, but it didn't really matter. That world was lost forever. I had a better understanding now of the woman's obsession with respectability. Clytemnestra had been a slave in her husband's household, however briefly, and she had not forgotten the indignity of it. For Clytemnestra, the world was nothing more than an ornate cage, and her only hope was making sure it was at least orderly.

The Messenian slaves watched us, wide-eyed and alert. I wondered where they had come from, if Agamemnon had won them in a long-ago campaign as he had Clytemnestra. I thought about all the women and girls of Troy and shuddered at what would happen to them if their city fell.

Clytemnestra let out another scream, one that had blood in it.

Elektra did not run to her mother, neither to ask comfort nor to give it. Instead, she simply watched her with weary, bruised eyes that seemed to belong to someone much older. "I don't know when Father will return from Troy," Elektra said. "But when he does, Mother will kill him."

She said this without dread or judgment, as though discussing when the tide would go out or the sun would rise. "And when Mother kills Father, then my brother Orestes will kill her. He's always been Father's favorite. And when that happens . . . I don't know what I'll do." A sigh shook Elektra's slight form.

A strange feeling came over me. I lifted my gaze to look at the disappearing sails on the horizon and knew with complete certainty that not one in ten of the young men who sailed with my uncle that day would return alive. Agamemnon sailed with the largest army that Greece had ever seen, but it was nothing compared to the size of the armies that the eastern kingdoms could call to muster when they drew on their allies among the Hittites and Assyrians.

The soldiers would die in a thousand ways: thrown from their ships by storms, gutted by Trojan soldiers under unforgiving skies, burning with the fevers that tore through crowded military encampments, raving from wounds gone septic. The few who did come back would be shells of men with eyes that forever reflected the campfires of distant shores. I wondered how the poets would craft something beautiful from the carnage.

Elektra's voice broke in, drawing me back to the windswept beach. "I think I will help Orestes kill Mother, if I have to choose," she said thoughtfully. "Orestes is young and strong. He'll be king after Father."

I stared at her in horror. "Don't say such things. That's

matricide—the Furies would torment you for eternity." Even a child would know about those dread goddesses, bat-winged and eagle-clawed, who pursued murderers to the ends of the earth.

Elektra glanced up at the clear sky, then back at me, her eyes burning like a banked fire. "My father just killed my sister, and there are no Furies here."

She was right. Iphigenia lay beneath the earth as her father sailed off to war. No one would avenge her. Not even me.

Elektra brushed off the sand and wandered back to the tent, murmuring about getting something to eat. I watched her go, but food was the furthest thing from my mind.

Something within me snapped. I was on my feet before I realized what I was doing, and I began to run. I had fled from the ruins of the seaside house, and now I fled from this. This horror, this tragedy, the death of Iphigenia whom I could not save, the atrocity of the Trojan war. To remain was intolerable, like standing in the middle of a fire. So I ran.

Atalanta had been ruthless in her training, and I could keep up a low loping run for miles. It was only when I paused for breath that I realized how far I had come. The women's tent was only a dark speck far down the beach.

30

PSYCHE

I would not go back to Aulis. Clytemnestra and Elektra had attendants to escort them back to Tiryns, but there was nothing for me there now. My parents were dead, Atalanta was dying, and Agamemnon's heirs held sway in Mycenae. And Iphigenia . . .

I did not want to live in a world where a daughter was worth less than a fair wind to Troy. I did not want to raise my own child in such a place.

I made my way up the rocky hills that surrounded the beach until I found a small plateau high above the ocean. Only the hardiest grasses grew here, constantly buffeted by the sea winds, and the cries of gulls were my only company. I sat on a low rock and thought of Iphigenia, and for the first time since her murder I allowed myself to weep.

If Iphigenia had lived, she could have soothed tensions between her father, Agamemnon, and her husband, Achilles, and cooled heads that could be put to work cracking Troy's walls. She could have become a queen of immortal fame. Instead, her bones would lie forever beneath that lonely beach, and the son of Thetis would ride to war under the command of the man who had killed his wife on their wedding day.

Tears poured down my face, tears I could not have shed

when I worked alongside Clytemnestra to put her daughter's body to rest. My beautiful Iphigenia, now nothing more than dust.

What hubris to think that I could pull Mycenae from the war or influence its course. The city itself was bent on conquest, heaving itself into the war effort. There was gold to be found in the east, and the glory of lands and fields that could be ours. I could never have stopped the wheel. I would only have been crushed beneath it.

I realized I would never achieve my hero's dream, not because I was too small for it but because the dream itself was too ugly. *Heroes are butchers*, Medusa had said, and now I saw the truth of that statement. I thought of the griffins, dead in the dust. I thought of Iphigenia, sprawled in the center of the dais at Aulis.

I thought of my naivete upon hearing the tales of the blind poet all those years ago, when I thought a glorious kill was what made a hero. I saw now that the legends were drenched in blood, the blood of women.

After all, Agamemnon would be commemorated as a hero for his achievements.

When the sun set the western sky aflame, I stood. I dashed the tears from my eyes and made my way down the cliffs as the shadows began to grow long.

I knocked on the door of a temple of the goddess Hera located on the outskirts of a small town. The priestess who answered was a woman past middle years, heavyset with neatly braided hair.

"I am a traveler seeking sanctuary," I said. "I am strong of body and can perform work for you in exchange for food and a dry place to sleep."

"I . . . see," the priestess replied. She looked alarmed at my appearance, though she was too well-mannered to say anything about it. I couldn't blame her. I was wearing the same tattered dress I had donned that morning for Iphigenia's wedding, now stained with dirt and spattered with blood along the sleeves.

As it turned out, the temple had recently lost its chamberlain and welcomed my assistance. The priestess, whose name was Kharis, offered me bread and cheese along with a garment more practical for work. She introduced me to the other priestesses, who nodded politely before rushing off to their duties. I chopped wood and carried water for the priestesses as they performed their offerings and hymns in the sanctuary.

In the evening, I joined the priestesses in their dormitory. There was room in the temple for travelers, but these were mostly men, so by unspoken agreement the priestesses decided that it would be best for me to stay with them instead. I watched the priestesses unwind from a day of work, braiding one another's hair and chatting with their friends. I thought of Iphigenia, and was hit by a wave of grief so strong I had to turn my face to the wall.

I became aware that a bubble of silence surrounded me. The chatter of the priestesses had fallen away, and they were all looking at me. I felt the prickle of their eyes upon me, but the sensation was not unpleasant. They were merely curious about this newcomer in their midst.

Finally, a young woman with a narrow nose asked, "Where do you come from, stranger? How did you arrive here?"

I drew in a long breath. I could not tell them about the death of Iphigenia; I could not bear to speak about it. But the rest, I could share.

"I was raised as a princess in my father's house," I began. "Until I was swept away by the west wind to a house full of magic . . ."

I told them my strange story and felt as though I was setting down a heavy burden at the end of a long day. I told them of the beautiful house that overlooked the sea until it fell into ruin in a single night, and the surprising gentleness of my mysterious, divine husband. When I told them his true name, there were gasps of awe.

Somewhere along the way, they ceased to hear my voice telling the story and imagined their own. They saw themselves in it, their own longings for love mortal or divine. A seed was planted that day, the core of a story that would be retold over and over again until eventually it became lodged in a novel by a Latin philosopher. But I did not know this then.

When I lapsed into silence, the priestesses sat still and looked at me. They were wearing the same expression that I myself had worn as a child at the feet of the old blind poet.

"What happened next?" Kharis asked, nearly breathless with anticipation.

"I don't know," I said, laughing hollowly. "I am trying to find that out myself."

The priestesses were satisfied with this answer, though a bit crestfallen to hear the tale end.

Together we prepared for sleep. That night, for the first time since my earliest childhood, I was soothed to sleep by the sound of women's voices.

Perhaps sharing my story with the priestesses of Hera opened my heart in some way, because that night I dreamed of Eros.

In my dream, I was back in the seaside house, which had been miraculously restored to wholeness. I could feel the fur of Scylla as she rubbed against my ankles and hear the peacocks call to one another on the terrace outside. The taste of the air was the same, mingled salt and roses, distant waves flinging up a mist that clung delicately to my cheeks.

Someone was sitting at the great oak table, back toward me. I knew who it was even before he turned to me with those beautiful green eyes, so familiar though I had only seen them once before. Eros.

A thousand words crowded together on my tongue. *You lied to me, you left me alone, you never really loved me.*

But there was no anger in him. Instead, he bore the look of a man at sea who has just seen the coast of his homeland come into view.

"Psyche," he whispered.

My rage pulled up short, like a mounted warrior before the high walls of a city. I had expected excuses or more lies, perhaps a mirror of my own rage. I had not expected him to miss me.

His gaze was a medley of hope and longing, and he took a tentative step toward me. "Finally, I have found you," he began. "I come with a message of warning. Aphrodite holds me prisoner, and she will come for you as well. Psyche, you must—"

I started to run to him, but the dream shivered around me and crumbled. I woke in the priestesses' dormitory, surrounded by the sounds of the temple starting its day.

31

PSYCHE

I stepped outside, watching the sunrise while wrapped in the folds of my thick blanket. I thought about my dream of Eros, and my excuses for missing him fell away like shed snakeskin.

I saw now that what truly mattered was those who loved you. I had lost my parents, my teacher, and my dearest friend, though in a few months I would gain a son or daughter. I had lost my husband as well, the father of my child. But perhaps there was still hope.

He never wants to see you again, Aphrodite claimed, and foolishly I took her at her word. But perhaps matters were more complicated than that.

It had only been a dream, but what if the dream-Eros had spoken truth? Was he searching for me after all? Wherever Eros was, I decided, I would find him again. Even if it was only to grab him by the shoulders and reprimand him for his betrayal.

The next day when my work around the temple precinct was finished, I knelt by the statue of Hera, goddess of marriage. She was five times my height and wore a stern expression, gazing down at me as though I was a mere insect. I bent my head and whispered my fervent prayer.

"Bring him back to me. Bring my Eros back to me."

I repeated these words from the noon hour, when the sweat beaded on my skin and the air was as thick as soup, until the cool relief of evening. Kharis, understanding what I sought to do, gave me some incense and shooed the younger priestesses away from my vigil. My knees ached from the cold marble floor but still I remained, until the priestesses called to summon me to the sleeping quarters. Only then, when the sun had set over the western horizon and the light had drained from the temple, did I stand and shake sensation back into my limbs.

As I lay on my cot in the dormitory, the snores of the priestesses around me, I wondered how mortals could make the gods listen. Flattery was not enough, nor were gifts. Virtuous behavior rarely caught divine notice.

Perhaps, I thought, *the key is to make such a nuisance of yourself that even a god cannot ignore you.*

I knelt on the marble tiles before the goddess the next day, and the next, all while repeating my prayer. I watched as other pilgrims came to ask for a suitable husband for a daughter, or to offer thanks for the birth of a healthy baby. But I asked for only one thing: the chance to find Eros again.

After several days of this, I dreamed a strange dream. I was in an intricately manicured garden, bursting with a dazzle of roses, lilies, and other spectacular blooms I could not name. A garden like this could only belong to a great lady, but when I turned to the figure seated next to me, I knew at once that this woman was not human at all.

She was not young, but the fullness of her beauty made youth seem garish. She wore the veil of a proper wife, and her hands were folded neatly on her lap. She did not look anything like the statue that reigned over the sanctuary, although her face bore the same look of stern disapproval, evoking the faint memory of Clytemnestra. I was in the presence of Hera, queen of the gods.

"What is it that you ask?" Hera inquired dispassionately, like a bureaucrat faced with yet another tedious task.

She had answered! Relief washed over my body like rain after a drought. "I need your help finding my husband," I said in a rush.

"A case of marital separation," Hera said, nodding. "Quite standard, but I must know more if I am to help you. Was he lured away by someone else, or did he leave of his own accord?"

"Neither. A curse pulled us apart."

The expression of polite neutrality on Hera's face disappeared. Her lips thinned and her nose turned up. "You must be Eros's wife," she sneered, as though I was some crawling thing that had emerged from beneath a rock. "Aphrodite spoke of a mortal woman who was living with her son. I fear I can do nothing for you. I will not offend the goddess of love on your account."

"But you're the patroness of marriage," I protested, my hope fading. "You *have* to help me."

"I do not *have* to do anything. I am a goddess," Hera snapped. "And why should I help you? Your husband has made a mess of my own marriage with his arrows. He has been nothing but a thorn in my husband's side and my own. Besides, according to Aphrodite, you can hardly be said to be married, since the proper rites were not observed. Since I am the goddess of marriage, not mistresses, I am further unable to assist you."

I stared at Hera and wondered if she had ever known even a fraction of the happiness I had enjoyed with Eros. Hera and Zeus were yoked like two unhappy oxen, plodding down the road to eternity. I realized I possessed something even the queen of heaven lacked—a husband whose company I enjoyed.

"Whatever crimes Eros committed are in the past," I pointed out. "And I am here now, humbly asking your assistance." I spread my arms wide, palms up, embodying humility as best I could.

"I am not the one who can fix this," Hera said coldly. "If you have any courage at all, you will face the one responsible for the curse. You have been running long enough."

With a shock, I woke in the priestesses' dormitory, blinking into the dawn. But I had glimpsed something in the far reaches of her garden before waking: green eyes behind green leaves, a familiar presence that made my heart snap to attention.

32

PSYCHE

I slipped from the blankets and gathered my meager possessions. I left before the priestesses awoke, though it grieved
me not to have the chance to bid these kind women farewell as
I departed from the temple of Hera.

I had been buffeted about between one desire and the
other like a fallen leaf in a strong current, between my hero's
dreams and my memories of Eros. But only a hero could survive the challenges that lay before me, even if they were of a
different sort than I once imagined. Even if no poets would
ever sing my tale.

You will be a great lover, not a great hero, Prometheus told
me once.

He was wrong. I would be both.

My heart thundered with the audacity of what I was about
to do. I would put myself under the power of my worst enemy
in the vain hope she might keep an offhand promise. I had no
idea what she might demand of me, if she would accept my
wager or kill me where I stood.

I found a cliff overlooking the sea. The wind whipped the
edges of the simple chiton I still wore, provided by the priestesses.

I will come if you call, Aphrodite once said.

So I called.

The goddess obliged, arriving in the shape of a dove before transmuting into the form of a tall woman. She looked around the windswept desolation with an expression of distaste.

"It's early," Aphrodite commented with a sneer. "I don't like to be woken up so early."

I gazed at her, wondering exactly what it was that made a god. She looked almost human, in the same way that a horse shaped from gold might look like a horse formed from clay; the general outlines were the same, but the substance was different. The light of another world seemed to shine on Aphrodite's flawless features.

The sea roared around the rocks, echoing the thunder of the blood in my ears. "I accept your offer," I declared. "I will serve as your handmaiden, but there must be limits and a clear reward. I want more than a glimpse of Eros if I perform a set number of tasks for you. I want your promise we will be reunited."

A curved smile bent Aphrodite's red lips. "And what makes you think Eros wants to see you again?"

I flinched. Like an adder, Aphrodite knew exactly how to strike.

"Whether he does or not," I replied. "That is for him and me to decide. You will not stand in the way."

"Very well," Aphrodite said lightly. "Three services will you perform for me: Fetch my wool, sort my grain, and bring me a bit of beauty cream. If you complete each of these tasks, I will give you back your wayward Eros."

I felt the power of the oath settle on me like a yoke upon an ox. Or perhaps it was only the weight of the choice I had made. Either way, it was heavier than I expected.

Aphrodite's mouth twisted. A spider who has trapped a fly in its web might envy the expression. "Oh, I almost forgot to mention," she added with vicious delight. "The wool is from the Sheep of the Sun in Colchis. The grain is in a pile that reaches to the ceiling of the temple of Demeter. The beauty cream belongs to Persephone, so you'll have to persuade her to give you a sample, if she lets you into her domain at all."

I stared at her, the enormity of the labors rendering me mute. I was only mortal, and these were tasks that the gods themselves might struggle to fulfill. Aphrodite might as well have told me to pull the moon from the sky and use it to make cheese.

"What happens if I fail?" I whispered.

"Breaking a deal with a god is punishable by death," Aphrodite replied, laughing. "A pity about my grandchild, but I'm certain Eros will give me another soon enough, one untainted by mortal blood. I should also mention, you have one week to complete all these tasks. Best of luck!"

Then I was by myself on the high cliff, alone with the crash of the ocean and my own stuttering heart. I wondered if I had jumped from the frying pan into the fire. I took one breath and then another, trying to quell the rising panic I felt at the thought of exactly what I stood to lose. It wasn't my own death I truly feared, but that of the son or daughter I carried. My palm settled over my belly, that small life I held inside of me.

I heard a whisper upon the wind. A voice seemed to emerge from the rocks themselves, from the grass and earth and everything around me. *Go forward, brave soul*, it said. *The earth and everything upon it will be moved to help you.*

Perhaps it was nothing more than my imagination, but the voice brought me back to myself. I was not entirely alone. I still had one friend who might answer me, if he could find it within his heart to forgive me.

I brought my finger to my lips and gave a whistle, one I had learned back at the seaside house when I sought company. In answer, the breeze stirred. The wind took shape into a familiar figure who let out a yelp of delight at the sight of me. "Psyche!"

"Zephyrus." I took a deep breath, steeling myself for recriminations or a renewal of our conflict.

"I am sorry for what I said," I told him. "You are not a monster. I know what Hyacinthos truly was to you. I was hurting, and in my grief, I hurt you too."

I bit my lip. I was not very good at apologies, but I saw nothing in Zephyrus's bright eyes except happiness to see me.

"I have been called far worse," he said, waving away the memory of those bitter words like dust on the wind. "But tell me, have you found Eros yet?"

"No," I whispered. "I hoped you might help me in this matter."

Zephyrus's angular features creased with consternation. "I've looked everywhere under the sun, but I can't find a single trace of him."

I nodded. "I have a plan," I said. "I've made a deal with Aphrodite, and if I complete three tasks for her, she will restore him to me. They will not be easy, but with your help I may have a chance."

I waited with bated breath to hear what Zephyrus would say. I wondered if the wind god would abandon me here, flighty and inconstant as he was.

"Anything," Zephyrus said in a rush. "You will have my assistance with anything you need."

33

PSYCHE

As a child, I had listened eagerly to the blind poet's stories of how Jason and his Argonauts had gone to the rich kingdom of Colchis seeking the Golden Fleece. Atalanta told me her own versions of the stories that were less pretty, but none of them prepared me for the dazzling green of the land across the sea. Mountains reared up from the east and the ocean glittered to the west, and between was a rich land of rolling hills and winding rivers: Colchis. The valley where I stood was far from any city or farmstead, a worthy place for the sun god Helios to pasture his sheep.

I arrived at the valley when it was still morning, borne by Zephyrus's winds. When I saw that the Sheep of the Sun had no shepherd, I assumed my task would be straightforward. I would not kill the creatures; they belonged to Helios, and I did not want to risk inviting the animosity of yet another deity. But I was certain that gathering some wool from a flock of sheep would give me no trouble at all, considering I had run down deer and slain griffins in the past.

I began to walk toward one of the sheep that was grazing on the outskirts of its flock. The sheep stared at me placidly as it chewed. Its wool glowed a burnished gold, as though lit faintly from within. I drew closer and closer, scarcely daring to draw breath for fear of startling the creature, but it only lowered its head to crop another mouthful of grass.

When I was close enough to see the filigreed wings of the flies crawling along the sheep's back, I froze. A single bounding leap and I could grab the beast, locking my arms around its head and pulling out a few tufts of its wool to satisfy Aphrodite.

Before I could make my move, a shudder ran through the animal, and it gave vent to a bleat of alarm. The sheep sprang away from me as though it weighed no more than thistledown, moving more swiftly than my eye could track. It bounded across the turf, coming to a rest some distance away, then lowering its head to continue grazing. Its bleat set the other sheep wheeling away from me like a flock of birds in the wake of a hawk. Well, that was no bother. I would try again.

By midafternoon, I must have tried a dozen times to snatch one of the creatures. I was breathless and sweat-drenched, and no closer to my goal than I had been that morning. Whenever I approached the herd, it scattered out of my reach like a clutch of milkweed seeds on the wind. As hard to grasp as happiness, I suppose. I wanted to tear at the grass in frustration.

I tried wriggling along the ground to sneak up on the sheep, but they detected me and bounded away. I tried to ambush them as they grazed among an outcropping of boulders, but they eluded me effortlessly. Eventually I succeeded in snatching a few wisps of golden wool from one of the slower sheep before it darted out of my grasp, but I knew this would never be enough to satisfy Aphrodite. I stared in dismay at the tiny tuft of wool in my hand, staggered by my helplessness.

If I had the tools, I would have built pit traps or set snares, but I had nothing save the clothes on my back. I was hungry, savagely so, but there was nothing here in this wilderness for me to eat.

Tilting my head, I glared up at the sky. "I don't suppose you could do something about this?" I said to Zephyrus, gesturing at the serenely grazing sheep.

From the breeze that encircled the sky, I felt something like a shrug. "Even the wind couldn't catch one of those dirty animals. Besides, if I help you directly with the task, Aphrodite will claim you did not abide her terms."

I dug my nails into my scalp. Hunger and desperation gnawed at me. I had thought that traveling all the way to Colchis from mainland Greece would be the most challenging aspect of this task, but it seemed that the sun god's sheep were well-protected even without his active intervention. No wonder Jason and his heroes sought the pelt owned by the king of Colchis—stealing the Golden Fleece, even if it was guarded by a sleepless dragon, was far easier than trying to make your own.

I watched the sun move toward the horizon, lengthening the shadows of the grazing sheep, and I felt my stomach sink into my belly. A week. That was all I had to complete three impossible tasks. And the journey into the Underworld alone might take a fortnight if I could even manage it. And if I failed . . .

There is no use moping, I told myself sternly. I made my way to a small river that ran through the center of the valley, the sheep shying away from my path. I cupped my hands and drank from the clear mountain water, slaking my burning thirst.

I lay down flat on my back in the grass, too tired to do anything else. Early autumn was different in Colchis. Back in Greece, the days were still warm, whereas here in the mountains I felt a persistent chill, growing stronger as the daylight faded.

Summer was dying. Time was ticking away.

Above me, a reed nodded in the breeze. I wondered what it had seen, and what it might tell me if it had a mouth to speak. Here among the sheep, I assumed, one day was probably very much like another. As if in agreement, the reed bowed forward in the wind, angling its long shadow under the glow of the setting sun.

I turned my head and realized that the field was made of gold.

I rose onto one elbow, not quite believing what I saw. Small tufts of wool glowed like flame in the light of the setting sun. Over there was a tangle of wool caught among some rocks, here another like a tumbleweed. Tiny amounts insignificant by themselves, but together they might be enough.

I had not noticed because I had not thought to look, so intent was I on my hunt for the sheep. But now the setting sun sparked those threads of gold into flame. I raced to gather them up into a small cloud bunched between my hands, laughing a little with delighted disbelief.

I had won. I had completed the first task.

Aphrodite arrived as the sun disappeared behind the mountain's peaks, sauntering across the wide green meadow with the ease of a shepherdess. Forgoing any pleasantries, she inspected my offering of the golden wool. She snatched the ball of fluff from my hands and teased out a strand, holding it in the fading light while squinting like an old trader. Finally, she tucked it away, seeming almost disappointed. Perhaps she'd hoped I would kill myself running after the sheep, or that Helios would smite me for the insult. A smug satisfaction warmed me.

"Make your way to the temple of Demeter at Eleusis," the goddess ordered. "You will sort the grain that has been tithed to me. And as for *you*." Aphrodite whirled on Zephyrus, who had joined me to witness the goddess's reaction. "You are not to assist her further. If you fly her to Eleusis, I will declare her contract void."

Zephyrus looked startled but bowed his head in acknowledgment. My heart dropped. Eleusis was many days' journey across the sea. I had six days left.

Aphrodite flew away, leaving Zephyrus and I alone. Night was coming on, and the first stars were beginning to appear. I was voraciously hungry and profoundly exhausted. It took everything within me not to collapse in defeat.

Zephyrus produced a small crystal bottle and placed it on the ground between us. Then he looked away and folded his arms, appearing to be fascinated by the rich colors of the western sky.

"Oh dear, I seem to have misplaced my bottle of Circe's tincture," he said aloud to the sunset. "What a shame if someone drank it."

Despite my exhaustion, I smiled. I remembered the weightlessness of the butterfly's shape, the freedom of it. I could make it to Eleusis by myself if I had wings of my own, however small.

"You're not supposed to help me," I told him.

"I'm not helping anyone," he replied. "I've simply misplaced my possessions like the cloud-brained god that I am."

I was about to pull the stopper from the bottle when Zephyrus spoke. "Your last task will bring you to the Underworld," he remarked. "While you are there, you may cross paths with Hyacinthos. Tell him that Zephyrus loves him still."

I felt a pang of empathy. "I will," I replied.

"Friendly winds will blow tonight," Zephyrus said to the sky and the grass. "I'll be certain that my brother Notus ensures it. He knows nothing of this quest, so Aphrodite cannot protest."

"Thank you," I said breathlessly.

"Don't thank me," Zephyrus scoffed. "I'm only a scatterbrain who forgets where he puts everything and enjoys a good southern breeze."

I pulled the stopper and drained the bottle. In the moments

before the tincture took effect, a question occurred to me. "Zephyrus, why is the butterfly the shape of my soul? A wolf or a lioness would be more suitable. So why the butterfly?"

"I cannot say," he replied. "Perhaps someone wiser knows."

I did not respond. By that point, I was unable to. I made my way into the darkening sky, my delicate wings fluttering fiercely.

34

EROS

Some vital quality had vanished from the world.

The people in Greece noticed it, as did those on more distant shores. Goats and sheep ceased to mate in the fields, and their milk ran dry. Spouses and lovers snapped at one another, caught up in petty arguments. Musicians found that their compositions fell flat, and potters discovered that their work remained mere lumps of clay without the spark that made it true art. The gods too found themselves at loose ends. Zeus could not summon any interest in his favorite pastime, and even Aphrodite was moody and inconsolable.

Desire had disappeared from the world, and it was not long before someone decided to ask why.

"Eros? What are you doing here?"

My head snapped up at the voice. It was female, but not Aphrodite's. I tried to call out for help, but only a strangled whisper emerged from my throat.

"I suppose she hasn't given you anything to eat or drink," the voice sighed. "Here."

A waterskin appeared at my lips, and I sipped hesitantly. I was rewarded by a rush not of mere water, but the ambrosia of the gods, restoration of our divinity and vitality. I drank and felt my strength growing, though unseen hands quickly snatched the waterskin back.

"Now, an answer. What are you doing here?"

I licked my lips, chasing the last drops of ambrosia. What *was* I doing here? The events of the last few weeks came flooding back along with recognition of the speaker.

"Hello, Eris," I said, my voice rasping like bones across a dusty floor. "It's been quite some time. It seems I am being punished by Aphrodite for harboring an enemy and telling lies. My adopted mother is quite stern."

"Apparently. It's dark as a hydra's gullet in here. I can't see anything." I felt the flicker of divine magic and a sudden spark.

A light, a lamp. The face of my sister staring at me in genuine astonishment, the first thing I had seen in more than a fortnight. My eyes were dazzled at the brightness.

"Perhaps I should extinguish the lamp," my sister said, flinching back in revulsion. "You look terrible."

"I can assure you that however poorly I look, I feel worse," I replied. "How did you find me?"

"We are two sides of the same coin, Eros. I always know where you are."

"That's a disconcerting thought. Give me more ambrosia, please." The mouthful I'd taken was scarcely enough to slake my thirst, and talking exhausted me.

Eris tilted her head. "No," she said after a moment.

My heart sank. Of course my sister would hold whatever I wanted just out of reach.

A strange curve tugged at the corners of her lips. "I'll break you out of here instead," she finished.

Eris touched their surface and the chains fell away from my wrists. The bindings may have been unbreakable to anyone else, but the goddess of discord possessed the power to drive things apart, which held as true for objects as for living relationships. I crashed to the cold stone of the floor at once, locked muscles and tendons screaming in agony. I scrabbled for a moment until my godhood healed the minute tears and dislocations.

"Why did you free me?" I gasped. *To see me twitch on the ground like a cockroach?*

"Because I felt like it," Eris replied simply. "My duty is discord, and sometimes that means releasing what should be locked away. Besides, it will make Aphrodite furious," she added with a small, sly smile.

I regained my feet and rubbed my wrists in wonder. My divinity healed the worst of the scrapes from the manacles, though I had been so long in chains that blue-black bruises encircled my wrists like bracelets. Still, I was free.

I looked at Eris. Standing there with the lamp in her hands, her sharp features softened by the gentle light, she almost reminded me of Psyche.

"You know," Eris said softly, startling me back to the present. "You shouldn't be so surprised that I would want to help you." Her face was as knife-sharp as ever, but sweetened by an expression of wistfulness I had never seen on the goddess of discord before. "I've always tried to be kind to you. I only wanted to be your friend. Once I even wanted to marry you. You were the one who kept pulling away."

Prior to this moment, I thought that everything Eris said or did had a hidden meaning, a veiled viciousness, some private joke that she would later relay to the worst possible parties. I thought there was nothing save for slyness and cruelty in her character, but now she looked only like a lost girl who had no mother or father or brother.

Eris continued. "The day is coming when the Olympians will

be nothing but forgotten myths, but you and I will continue, dear brother. We are union and dissolution, day and night. It wouldn't kill you to write me a letter now and then."

Eris raised her hand and the door swung open. Light from the hallway beyond spilled in, and I caught my first glimpse of the twining hallways of Olympus in what felt like ages, a reminder of another world beyond this dark prison. Relief washed over me like daybreak, followed by iron determination at the thought of Psyche.

"Thank you," I said to my sister, not knowing what else to say, and ran into the light.

I skidded down the slopes of Mount Olympus in the shape of a vole, determined to shield myself from the eyes of the messengers who came and went from that high peak. This was not solely out of cunning—my power was at a nadir, withered like a dried flower. If I wasn't careful, I would lose the strength to hold my physical form together entirely, which would make me useless in my quest. I returned to my true shape when I reached the foothills beyond Olympus, leaning on an outcropping of rock and panting for breath.

A gust of wind stirred my hair. "Zephyrus?" I called.

Lanky arms snaked around me, the force of his embrace nearly bearing me into the dust. "There you are, Eros!" he cried. "I've been searching the four directions for you, but there's been no trace! Oh dear, what's happened to you? You look terrible."

"I am well aware," I replied. "But it's good to see you, Zephyrus."

"As it is to see you," my friend replied, with a hand on my shoulder and a warmth that nearly brought tears to my eyes. "Oh! I must tell you—I have news of Psyche."

My heart soared, but was quickly dashed when Zephyrus told me of Psyche's deal with Aphrodite.

"Three impossible tasks," I whispered. "My adopted mother may as well have asked Psyche to pull down the sun from the sky and make a pendant from it."

"Psyche has already accomplished the first," Zephyrus said, grinning. "I helped her a bit, though Aphrodite barred me from doing so again. But what should we do now?"

I pondered this. I could not help Psyche myself. I was weak and without allies, and finding her only meant falling prey to the curse again.

I needed help, but where to get it?

Only one name came to mind: Hekate, the lady of the crossroads. I had considered seeking an audience with her once before, when the curse first took root, but I shied away from the possibility back then. I was none too sure she would readily assist me, or what she would ask in return for this boon. Hekate was not my friend; I was not sure if she considered herself anyone's friend. Still, it was said that she offered aid to those who came to her with open hearts, mortal and immortal alike.

My gaze fell on the forest beyond the foothills of Olympus, and I knew that I would find her there. Hekate Soteira, Hekate the Savior. It was said that if one traveled deep enough into any forest, one would always find her there. I had to try, for Psyche's sake.

"Watch for Aphrodite," I ordered Zephyrus, rising on unsteady legs. "Make sure she does not find my trail."

"Where are you going?" Zephyrus called.

"To find Hekate," I replied. "She will know what to do."

Step by agonizing step, I went to find the one who helps those beyond all other help.

I set off in the shape of a stag but found I could not sustain this for very long. I turned into a lion next, and then a small cat, which did not cover ground as quickly but took less concentration to maintain.

I walked through a seemingly endless vista of trees, far from any human habitation, until I was in the deep forest where only dryads hold sway. I could hear those ancient tree spirits chattering to one another in amusement as I passed, but I laid back my ears and ignored them. The spreading branches laced together far above my head, trapping sunlight so that even during midday the forest floor was chill and dim. My paws sunk into centuries of loam as I walked, the rich soil sending up the scent of earth.

Abruptly, I paused. I smelled something new: smoke from a hearth. I followed it, and soon it led me to the place I sought.

The hut was moss-covered and ancient, and might have been mistaken for any small farmer's house save for the fact that it sat on a pair of chicken feet. A rickety set of stairs led up to the house itself, culminating in a stout wooden door. Outside, pigs snuffled contentedly in a trough, and a cow lowed softly at me. A pair of black dogs, looking like blotches of midnight in canine shape, eyed me warily and began to bark.

The noise summoned her. The door blew open, and Hekate made her way unsteadily down the stairs, gripping the railing for balance. Her skin was nearly translucent, and scraggly hair the color of dishwater poured over hunched shoulders. Why did she do this to herself? She could choose any shape she liked, the prerogative of a goddess, and yet she chose the appearance of a hag. The fur along my spine prickled, my tail going bottlebrush. I knew I was in the presence of ancient divine power, of a sort that unsettled even me.

Hekate made her way to the place where I, still in my cat shape, sat panting for breath on the mossy earth. The dogs wove around her legs, their ears tipped forward. I arched my spine and laid back my ears with a snakelike hiss when they came too close. Either of them could crush me in their jaws, a complication I did not need.

The goddess made a sound of disapproval when she saw me. "Look at you. How have you let yourself come to this?"

I drew myself up as well as I could. "I come to your door to ask for your aid, a supplicant to Hekate Soteira, Hekate the Savior."

Hekate laughed. The dogs continued to pace in circles around us, sniffing the air. "That's my favorite epithet, you know. You've arrived at the right place, son of Chaos," she continued. "Though I never thought I'd see one such as you at my door. Let us get you inside."

Son of Chaos she called me, as though I was some ordinary godling and not one of the primordial beings. I realized that I did not know exactly how old Hekate was. It seemed that she had always been here, dwelling at the margins of the world. Perhaps she stood by and watched when I emerged with the other gods from the abyss of Chaos, her two dogs sitting by her side.

Hekate gathered my cat self up in arms of surprising strength. I mewed in consternation but did not protest further. I was weary to the point of collapse, though I could still summon the strength to show my teeth when one of the dogs came too close.

She brought me into a kitchen that was small and covered in a thin layer of soot. I was appalled; I had never witnessed a divine dwelling that was so *dirty*. The shelves were jammed with left-over objects, amphorae and glass jars and other things harder to place. Herbs of unrecognizable varieties hung from the ceiling in bunches, and the place had an oddly medicinal smell that set my teeth on edge. Gods did not, as a rule, require medicines.

Hekate deposited me onto a chair and set a steaming cup in

front of me. I reverted to my true shape and wrapped my hands around it to soak in the warmth. My skin was desiccated, and my tendons stood out like the roots of a withered tree. I realized I must look like a skeleton wrapped in a thin gauze of flesh.

"Drink that," Hekate said. "I need to talk to you, and you're in no state for conversation."

I wondered if the cup contained poison, or moly tincture, or some other noxious brew. Well, what did it matter? If Hekate wanted to reduce me to a stone, she didn't need to make much of an effort.

I drained the cup. Its contents were strong and sweet and burned pleasantly on the way down. I thought I tasted a hint of ambrosia. I felt more solid when I had finished the drink, my purchase on the physical world strengthened.

Hekate took a seat and folded her hands, fixing me with a gaze that would make Zeus himself shudder. "Now, what is it that you want from me?" she demanded. "I already know about the whole business with Aphrodite, so don't waste time with that."

I did not bother to ask how Hekate knew. The goddess of witchcraft does not need to name her sources.

"If you know about that," I asked, "then why are you helping me?"

"I have not yet decided that I will help you," Hekate replied. "You've caused a great deal of trouble, you know. There are more than a few who would like to see you squeezed in a jar for several thousand years."

She let the words hang in the air for a moment before waving them away. "But as you must have known when you called me by one of my favorite titles, Soteira, I am partial to the underdog. Besides, what does Aphrodite think she can do to *me*?" Hekate cackled, chapped lips peeling back to reveal teeth like shattered stones.

What could *anyone* do to Hekate, goddess of darkness and witchcraft? The whites of her eyes had gone yellow, and the raw flesh that rimmed them looked unpleasantly like ground meat. I could see her scalp through her thinning hair.

"Help me find her," I begged. "Help me find Psyche, and give her apotheosis."

My hands gripped the edge of the table like claws, white-knuckled, and my heart thundered in my ears. I understood the enormity of my demand—to make Psyche a goddess was a choice that could never be undone. But it was the only way forward.

"You know how to craft the brew," I insisted. "I am certain you do. Nothing is beyond your capacities. Give Psyche apotheosis—that is all I ask."

Hekate considered me for a moment, her gnarled face like a vision beyond time. "No," she said finally.

I brought my fists down on the table, making the cup jump. "Why?" I demanded.

"The two of you wouldn't know what to do with apotheosis, and anyway, you have to summon the gods and hold a vote before brewing it. Quite the nuisance from start to finish."

I laughed bleakly. "So you will do nothing?"

"I never said that," Hekate replied sharply. "There are other ways to help the girl besides turning her into a goddess."

One of the black dogs padded over and laid its head on Hekate's lap. She reached down and stroked its head; the beast leaned into her touch and closed its eyes in pleasure. "Do you love her?" Hekate asked suddenly, glancing at me. "This mortal wife of yours. Psyche."

"Of course. I have no choice," I replied. "Aphrodite's curse has done its work."

Hekate snorted. "Oh, you simpleton. The curse fell apart like a poorly made wagon right after Psyche brought that lamp into your bedroom. There's not the faintest scent of it upon you."

35

EROS

The curse was gone.

"Shoddy work," Hekate muttered. "Aphrodite was never very good at magic—she hasn't got the willpower for it. Why do you think she had to keep you in chains?"

I felt as though I had fallen through a sheet of ice into freezing waters. I looked at the place within myself where the curse had taken up residence and found nothing but a smoothed-over scab. The howling in my veins had gone quiet. The terror and guilt and longing I now felt was not the workings of some dark magic. I simply *missed* Psyche, an ordinary and unenviable feeling.

Then I realized. If the curse was gone, there was nothing keeping me from Psyche. I was halfway to the door before Hekate called me back.

"Don't be a fool, son of Chaos," she snapped. "Looking for Psyche would only put her in more danger."

I hovered near the door, remembering what Zephyrus had told me. "Aphrodite has taken Psyche as her handmaiden and given her three impossible tasks, with me as the reward. If there is no curse to prevent me, I must help her."

"You cannot keep someone from the battles they were born to fight," Hekate said, her eyes reflecting the candlelight like a wolf's.

I remembered the prophecy Psyche held so dear. *You will conquer a monster feared by the gods.*

I was unconvinced. "This is no battle. It is something far worse."

"Perhaps. Tell me, what are the tasks?"

I ticked off the two that remained. "To sort the grain in Demeter's temple, and to fetch a bit of Persephone's beauty cream from the Underworld."

"A tidy pairing," Hekate remarked dryly. Demeter was the goddess of the harvest and the mother of Persephone. But a journey into the Underworld would be death for a mortal. I had nearly lost Psyche to that darkness once before.

I began to pace the room, hoping movement would quicken my thoughts. The memory of a forest in Anatolia rose in my mind. "Persephone owes me a favor; I brought her the love of Adonis. I will ask her to give Psyche whatever Aphrodite demands."

The rush of it made me light-headed, though Hekate's next words brought me back down to earth. "You could, if it was possible to send a message to the queen of the dead," she said, chewing her lip with the yellow stub of a broken tooth. "But autumn has arrived, and Persephone has returned to her husband's realm, where even I cannot follow."

"Hermes can carry messages to the Underworld," I pointed out.

"Hermes would pluck out his own eyes before offending Aphrodite. He is utterly besotted," Hekate remarked with a withering look.

I slumped down at the table, head in my hands. Success had nearly been within reach. I had nearly allowed myself to believe that I could save Psyche.

Aloud, I said, "I never chose Psyche, you know. She was foisted upon me by the curse, like . . ." *Like my immortality, my divine power, and all the things that make up the shapeless arc of a god's unchanging life.*

"You've chosen her now, haven't you?" Hekate replied. "You could have gone anywhere once you slipped Aphrodite's chains. And yet you chose to come to me, knowing I was your best chance to help Psyche."

The goddess pushed her chair back from the table. I watched as she began sorting through the jars perched on the rickety shelves, taking a few of them down. She fished a small silver spoon out of a cluttered drawer and measured the ingredients, then started grinding them with a mortar and pestle. The dogs watched her curiously.

"You envied them once, didn't you?" Hekate continued, not looking at me. "The mortals. Many of our kind do. Perhaps you thought you envied their ability to taste death, but in fact I think you envied their *purpose*. Mortality has a way of inflicting purpose on you whether you like it or not. Mortals have too little time to waste!" She chuckled to herself.

My sense of unease increased. I remembered the old man and woman I had seen so long ago, made luminous by the love they shared. Perhaps I *had* envied them, in some distant and uncertain way.

"I suppose loving a mortal has given you purpose as well," Hekate concluded. "By learning to truly love someone else, you learn to love the world. And yourself, which may be even harder."

"I don't think lack of self-love was ever my problem."

Hekate chuckled. "Not in the way I mean. You never felt like you belonged, or that you had a stake in the world. Psyche has given you that."

Her observation felt as intrusive as a knife between the ribs. I thought about the desire I once felt to taste death, now a distant memory after Psyche's presence made the world new again. "I don't know what you're talking about," I lied.

"Oh? You don't?" Hekate set a small cauldron above the

hearth, adding the ingredients to it. With a flick of her hand, she made the fire bloom, then turned to me with her hands on her hips. "Then forget Psyche and use those arrows of yours to find another mortal girl to love you. There's no shortage of them. You could find one that Aphrodite doesn't hate so much."

Revulsion seized me. "No," I hissed. "I will not be soothed by a pale imitation." I would not leave Psyche, or the child she carried—our child—to waste away while I chased the skirts of another mortal.

Hekate nodded. "Good. I'm glad to hear you're not a coward or a cad. I wouldn't help you send a message to Persephone otherwise."

I looked up. "So you *will* help me?" I asked.

"I may," she replied. "If you give me what I ask."

"And what do you ask?" I could already imagine what Hekate might demand: the heart of a young mortal, my firstborn child, an arrow from my quiver.

"Only a pair of your feathers, from those lovely wings you like to keep hidden. Nothing more. Oh, what magics I can work with one of the desire god's feathers! Maybe even get myself a lover. It's been some time since I've had someone to warm my bed." Hekate laughed again, smacking her gums.

I summoned my wings from the folds between worlds, and they unfurled from my back, stretching out in two great arcs. I plucked out two of the feathers; it caused no more than a momentary pinch of pain, and then they were in my palms, white as marble and faintly iridescent. Hekate spirited one of them into the pockets of her robe and threw the other into the cauldron, where it sent up a column of thick smoke.

Answering my unspoken question, Hekate said, "It's an elixir, one that will divide your soul from your body—temporarily, don't fret—and allow you to make your way into the Underworld once your divinity is put aside. I'll send a message to the mother, and you will go speak to the daughter. I'm not about to go to Persephone myself," she added with a sharp look. "But this, I can do."

"Will it work?" I asked.

"Of course it will work," Hekate snapped. She lifted the cauldron from the rack and drained its boiling contents through a sieve. The black liquid hissed and bubbled as it dribbled down. "Now choose a form, something that will travel well. You've got a long journey ahead of you."

I hesitated. Once I had wished for death, and now I would follow those lightless roads that no god could tread. It was true that I would not be a god when I did it, but this fact did not make me feel better.

"Will I survive?" I asked.

"That is entirely up to you, child." Hekate placed a steaming cup before me on the table, steam rising from its contents like whirling spirits. "Now drink."

36

EROS

How can I describe a soul separated from its body, a god without his immortality? The best analogue would be a golden butterfly, flapping its way through the dark roads of the Underworld.

When I emerged from those depths, I beat my wings against the windows of the chicken-footed hut. Hekate was working at her loom to pass the time, her dogs by her feet. Beside her was the shell of my immortal body, lying still on a chaise, appearing for all intents and purposes to be fast asleep. It was uncanny to see myself there, no different than an ordinary mortal at rest.

Hekate rose and opened a window. When the winged brightness of my soul made its way inside, she took me very gently in her hands and placed me back in my body. One of the dogs raised its head to sniff me.

I took a deep, ragged breath, pulling air into lungs starved of it. I opened my eyes and stretched my fingers and toes, laughing softly.

Hekate pressed a cup to my lips. "You've made it back. Well done," she remarked.

I swallowed. It was the same draught she had given me upon my arrival, and the brew restored my spent power. Cold fire traveled down my limbs, binding my soul to my body once again.

"The dread queen keeps her word," I rasped weakly. "Persephone will help Psyche. She will even ask her mother to assist."

Hekate nodded. "Good," she said, turning back to her weaving. I closed my eyes and was beginning to drift into sleep when she spoke again. "Do you understand yet?"

I looked at her, uncomprehending. "Understand what?" I demanded.

"The similarities between gods and mortals," Hekate replied. She did not look up from her weaving. The shuttle clicked against the loom, a steady beat. Why did she do this? I could not fathom why a great goddess felt the need to weave her own cloth.

"Our souls are like their souls," she said, "once our immortality is set aside. That is how it was possible for you to descend into the Underworld once you set your body aside. Perhaps Prometheus added something of his divine nature when he shaped the first humans from clay, I don't know. But that is the truth all the same." She chuckled, long and low.

I closed my eyes. Once I had wished for death, but now all I wanted was Psyche. "Tell me," I whispered through cracked lips. "Will she be victorious?"

"That's up to her," Hekate replied. "For you, it is time to rest. You may be immortal, but you'll become no more sentient than a snail if you continue like this. Even gods must take time to restore their strength."

I was unconscious before she finished speaking, the last of my strength sapped dry. Later I would learn that I slept for five entire days.

PSYCHE

The last rays of the sun were warm, and the breeze was fair, as Zephyrus had promised. The world was a dazzle of color and wind.

Gone was the persistent ache of loss that had haunted me since the destruction of the seaside house; a butterfly's brain does not have the complexity for such matters. My only thought was to fly southwest, and my tiny wings beat ferociously.

Then the rain began. Zephyrus had failed to account for the sudden warmth brought by his brother Notus into the cool autumn air of mainland Greece, and a thunderstorm was the result.

I careened around the fat droplets that began to hurl down from the heavens. Raindrops could tear through my delicate wings like a spearpoint through papyrus. Then I was falling, buffeted by gales of wind.

Darkness and confusion. I could no longer tell the difference between earth and sky, tumbling down tail over antennae. I flapped my small wings desperately, knowing that the muddy earth would trap me like quicksand. But despite my efforts I was falling, falling, spiraling downward . . .

When I opened my eyes, I was looking up at the wooden beams of a roof, a hole cut in the ceiling to permit woodsmoke from a central fire to dissipate. I stretched and looked down at the five fingers of a human hand, which flexed when I moved them. I was warm and dry, back in my human form. I could smell something cooking, and my stomach rumbled.

Panic sunk knives into me. I only had a few more days to fulfill my quest, and I did not know how much time had passed. "How long have I been here?" I asked aloud.

"The night and half a day," a female voice answered.

"I must get to Eleusis," I said. I tried to lever myself upright, though nausea quickly forced me back down.

A woman appeared, tawny hair loose around her face. "Don't be a fool! I found you outside in the mud and rain, and you need rest. Eleusis is only a morning's journey from here by foot, if that. It isn't going to get up and move while you recover. Now here, eat this."

The woman handed me a bowl of porridge thickened with cream and honey. I had no time, but I also had not eaten in over a day and was ravenous. "What is it?" I asked.

"*Galaxia* porridge," she answered. "My daughter is only a little older than you, and this is her favorite. Now eat! A young girl like you needs nourishment."

I nibbled the porridge, taking a closer look at my hostess. She was broad in the way of farmwives and moved with relentless efficiency. For the first time in many years, I thought of my nursemaid, Maia, who had died before my return from the wedding in Sparta. My first loss, though not my last.

The porridge was rich and filling, and once I was finished, I could sit up without swaying. When the woman came to take the bowl, I asked her name.

"Sera," she replied, or something that sounded like that, at least. Before I could ask her to repeat herself, she had already turned away to bustle my bowl back into the cooking area. I heard no other human voices nearby and wondered if Sera was alone here.

When I looked down, I saw I was wearing a pale pink chiton. There was no trace of mud upon my limbs.

Sera stirred a pot over the fire. "That belongs to my daughter," she said, gesturing at the clothing. "I don't think she would mind if you borrowed it."

"My thanks," I replied. I paused for a moment. The hourglass passage of time needled me; I had to get to Eleusis as soon as possible, but this woman was here by herself. The law of xenia prodded a guest to show respect to her hostess. I noticed the spindly pile of firewood by the door. At this time of year, winter nipped at everyone's heels.

I stood. "I offer you my thanks in words, and in deeds as well. Your store of firewood grows scarce, so I will bring you more."

Sera protested that I needed rest, but I slipped through the door before she could stop me. The storm clouds from last night had cleared, and though the earth was still damp with rain, the day was clear and bright. A few hours in the sun with an axe felt good; the air was cool, and the effort of the work distracted me from the task that loomed before me: to sort the grain in Demeter's temple. And after that, the darkness from which no mortal returns . . .

When my work was completed, I observed my surroundings. The farm was small but prosperous, with a respectable flock of sheep and goats, and even a few cows that lowed at me from behind a fence. They had probably been the ones to provide the milk for the galaxia porridge. A modest field of golden stalks marked the source of the wheat. Despite its pastoral beauty, there was something eerie about this place. A steading this size should have half a dozen farmhands, children, and slaves, not to mention a husband and other adult relatives. Yet I saw no one.

By the time I returned, it was afternoon. I was trembling with eagerness to set off for Eleusis, but Sera did not share my haste. She insisted on fitting me out with a cloak and pair of sturdy shoes, going back time and again to a great chest of clothing when she decided the first few options did not suit me. She continued, unhearing, despite my gentle pleas to point the way to Eleusis. Then bread had to be put in the stone oven, and then it was time for another bowl of galaxia porridge. Hungry though I was—I licked the bowl clean—I wanted to tear my hair out for the delay.

On the road, Sera moved unhurriedly despite my growing panic, keeping up an unbroken stream of conversation about Eleusis and its rites. Did I know the history of the festivals that honored the goddess Demeter and her daughter Persephone? Alas, the autumn celebrations were a few weeks past, and it wouldn't be until the springtime that Eleusis would host the mysteries marking Persephone's return. Did I know, Sera continued, that those who underwent the Eleusinian Mysteries were said to lose all fear of death?

I listened to my hostess with equanimity, absorbing nothing. Sera may have been fishing for my reasons for visiting the temple, but I would not divulge them. I refused to allow this gentle woman to become caught up in the web of divine conspiracies that bound me.

I was distracted by a thin black line of ants crossing the road ahead. I paused to look at them. Going about their business with military efficiency, the ants evoked the Myrmidons in their neat rows. I recalled the look of pride on Dexios's face when he told me he was one of them. Watching the little creatures meander past, I realized I must seem like a god to them.

I carried a small hard loaf of bread that Sera had given to me for supper. I broke off a piece and left it in the road next to the orderly procession of ants. A few of the little workers, tiny as letters on papyrus, broke off from the process to investigate the bread. I smiled.

When I looked up, I saw Sera staring at me. I realized how foolish I must seem, hopping over insects and wasting good food, but her expression was not one of derision. It was an appraising look, as though I had turned out to be more than she expected.

"So solicitous." She chuckled. "Do you know those ants personally?"

"No." I reddened. "But I know what it is like to be small and easily stepped on."

"You are a good child," Sera said, patting me on the arm. "First you give me firewood, then you make offerings to the ants. A good child indeed."

Soon we reached the temple of Demeter. To my surprise, Sera kissed the head priestess on both cheeks in greeting, as though they were sisters.

The priestess turned to me and inclined her head. "Lady Psyche. We have been expecting you."

She leaned toward Sera and murmured something that I could not quite catch. Sera nodded in understanding, and then gestured for me to follow.

It was Sera, rather than the priestess, who led me down a long corridor as I scurried to keep up with her. I wondered if my hostess was an initiate of the Eleusinian Mysteries. That would explain how she knew so much about them.

Sera escorted me into a room appended to the main hallway. It was empty save for a massive pile of grain that loomed far above my head, an uneasy pyramid brushing the ceiling itself. The pile was a whorl of several different types of grain—rice, wheat, barley, rye, farrow. My eyes swept up its length, and my heart sank.

I felt a hand settle on my shoulder. It was Sera, smiling warmly. "Do not fret. The task will be done before you know it," she told me. Probably she thought I was some sort of penitent, performing this task as an offering to the goddess Demeter. Her attempt at comfort did nothing to reassure me.

I sat down and began to sort the grains. Light shone through high windows that ran along the ceiling. There were only a few hours of daylight left, and I cursed the time that I had wasted at Sera's house. At first I tried to sweep the little grains into piles of related colors, but I soon realized that this was an imperfect strategy. It did not distinguish the grains properly, and Aphrodite was sure to notice the difference.

Priestesses arrived unobtrusively to light lamps once the sky went dark. I did not raise my head to greet them, unwilling to be pulled away from my task. I toiled until my knees grew numb and my eyes could scarcely distinguish one grain from another. I sorted for hours, but even after all that work each heap was only about the size of my palm. It was mind-numbing, a madwoman's task, like counting the grains of sand on the shore.

Of course, this was exactly why Aphrodite had assigned it to me.

More time passed, and my mind began to wander to dark and ugly places. What had I been thinking, accepting Aphrodite's challenge on that windswept cliff? Had I really thought I would be able to pull one over on the goddess of love herself? Folly. It didn't matter that Sera had kept me from this task with various indulgences, that I had wasted too much time in her little farm-stead. I could not properly sort this amount of grain even if I had a full month. I was going to die. I would never see Eros again, and my child would never be born.

Yet I could not bring myself to give up. Feverishly I plucked one grain after another from the pile. The rhythm itself was a kind of comfort. Rye, farrow, wheat, rice, rye once again. My hands moved until they ached, and my eyes burned from strain, and still I continued.

The next thing I knew, sunlight was streaming through the high windows. I jolted upright, then brushed a hand along my face. Grains of several types fell to the ground. I must have fallen face-first onto one of the piles of grain in my exhaustion. I looked for the tower of grain and saw that it was gone. In its place sat five smaller piles of uniform color, perfectly sorted.

"Did you rest well?" Sera was at the door, smiling.

I gestured at the piles. "How . . . ?"

"The ants you met on the road," explained my hostess. She gestured at a line of living ink marks making their way across the stone floor.

Sera continued. "My daughter asked me to assist you in this task, but at first I wasn't sure how. I couldn't do it directly—Aphrodite would never forgive me. But I could ask others to help you, and these creatures are so humble that she would never notice them." She smiled. "I'll have you know that the ants volunteered to help, by the way. They remembered your kindness on the road."

I looked at the piles of sorted grain, so difficult a task for a human being but nothing at all to a thousand ants working together. Then I looked back at Sera and knew that she was not what she appeared to be.

Her face wavered, like a reflection on the surface of a pond. She continued, "I took you in because my daughter asked me for a favor, but I hadn't expected you to be such a polite girl, chopping firewood for me and indulging all my silly requests. It's been so long since I had someone to talk to. And you remind me so much of my daughter when she was young."

As I watched, Sera's form began to change, shedding the illusion that surrounded her. I had seen something like this before in the mountains with Atalanta, hunting high above the tree line, when we had surprised a yearling stag who froze at the sound of our footsteps. His coat blended in so well with the rugged landscape I could hardly see him at first. It was only when I noticed his eyes that the rest emerged as if by magic—antlers, a nose, long graceful limbs.

The goddess revealed herself in much the same way. Her simple beauty sharpened, her tawny hair taking on the golden warmth of a field of wheat in summer. I felt the chill that heralded the arrival of a god.

"Who are you?" I whispered. "I thought your name was Sera. I thought you were an ordinary farmwife."

The goddess smiled. "Not Sera. Ceres. But that is only one of my names," she replied. "In your tongue, I am known as Demeter."

37

PSYCHE

By now I had fought monsters, witnessed tragedy, and spoken with several different gods. Yet I still could not seem to adjust to the intimate strangeness of sitting with the goddess of the harvest and watching the sun go down over her wheat fields.

The sheep called to one another in their pen while the chickens muttered in their coop. The sky was a marvel of colors, turning the fields burnished gold. But I was blind to the beauty before me. All I could think of was the dark journey that lay ahead, the most onerous of my tasks. There would be no talking reeds or friendly ants to help me in the Underworld.

"How did you come by this farmhouse?" I asked, desperate to break the silence. "I've never known a goddess to live in such a place."

Demeter did not answer right away. There was a heaviness about her that distinguished her from the other immortals I'd met, perhaps because she had known loss in a way that few gods had.

"After my daughter went missing, I searched the earth for her," Demeter explained. "I took up a position as wet nurse to a mortal family who lived here and stayed even after I learned that Hades had taken my daughter. The family is gone now, but I remain. I come here every spring to welcome my Kore as she ascends from the Underworld, and every autumn as she goes back down."

"The Underworld," I whispered, shivering. I felt the chill of that place creeping across my skin. I saw once again my own corpse lying on the road lined with cypresses. I looked at the sky and wondered if this was the last sunset I would ever witness.

"Do not fear. You travel as the guest of my daughter, who is queen there," Demeter chided. "Your husband asked her personally for the favor, you know," she added, glancing at me.

Hope bloomed in me like an impossible flower. "Eros? Eros sent word to Persephone on my behalf?"

Demeter smiled. "He did, though I can't fathom how he managed a journey into the Underworld. He must be very fond of you."

My heart contracted. So the dream had been true after all. Eros had not abandoned me but was being kept away from me. I thought about the agony on Eros's face when I had seen him last by lamplight, bent and broken by the curse before being pulled away into nothingness, and I felt a surge of guilt. I had broken my word by bringing the lamp into the bedroom. We had both hurt each other, Eros and I.

I wondered if I would ever have the chance to see him again and speak my apologies. The road to the Underworld was filled with dangers, and even with Eros's help I might never return.

"This is why I looked after you," Demeter said. "My daughter asked me, and I never could deny her. But Psyche, there are things I must tell you before you enter her realm."

I glanced at my hostess. Demeter was lost in thought, frowning. She looked like any fretful mother—at least if you did not notice the sharpness of her divine beauty or the way her cup refilled itself.

"From the beginning," she said, "it was as though my beloved Kore carried a secret world inside herself, one that I could never touch. She was an odd child. When she was born, there was nothing of her father's stern glory or my own golden majesty in her. My little Kore turned away when I tried to take her on walks through fields of grain, preferring instead to see what grew under rotted logs or in hollows filled with decayed leaves. Silly me, I still call her Kore, *maiden*, the name I gave to her as a child, but now she goes by the name Persephone—*bringer of death*. She liked to collect the disarticulated skeletons of creatures she found in hidden places, polishing them to pearlescent smoothness and laying them along the windowsill. I tried to enlist nymphs to look after her, but they all left within days, muttering about unspeakable cruelties.

"When Kore disappeared—when Hades kidnapped her—I was distraught. She was my only daughter, and I feared for her safety, but in truth I also feared for the well-being of anyone who came across her unprepared. My girl always did have a temper."

Goose bumps rippled across my skin. I told myself that this was simply due to the cool of the evening.

The goddess continued. "Separation cannot kill love, as you know, but it is an agony nonetheless. Oh Psyche! Here is what I ask: Tell my daughter that her mother still loves her."

My throat tightened. I did not say that my own mother was somewhere in the distant reaches of Persephone's own kingdom, along with my father. Nor did I say anything about my own daughter or son, still a half-formed dream floating within me.

I took Demeter's hand. "I will do as you ask," I replied.

Demeter and I sat together in the gloaming, a motherless daughter and a daughterless mother, relishing the fragile tranquility of the moment. We watched as the last of the sun's rays vanished and stars scattered themselves like chicken feed across the sky.

The two of us arrived at the temple of Eleusis the next morning while the birds were still calling to one another. There was a chill in the air; the glowing heat of summer, so all-encompassing, had drained from the world.

Behind the temple itself was an amphitheater, with rows of seats fanning out like a peacock's tail before dipping down to a shallow oval at the bottom. The slanted early morning light struck long shadows along the concentric rings, shadows pooling in the recesses designed for feet. During the mysteries, candidates for initiation across the Greek world came here to prepare themselves for the sacred rites. Demeter had told me all of this as we walked; I thought she seemed rather proud of the rituals mortals made of her story.

Across from the seats was a sheer cliff, and set into it was a hole that seemed to devour all the light around it. Eleusis was so different from the desolate waste of Taenarum in its structure, but the darkness was the same.

The Underworld.

I swallowed hard. I stood with Demeter at the lip of the amphitheater, wearing the satchel she had given me. I carried no weapons, per her instructions.

I had protested this at first. "What kind of hero goes without weapons? How will I defend myself in the Underworld?"

Demeter raised one tawny eyebrow. "Weapons will do you no good there. The hero Orpheus descended for the sake of his beloved Eurydice with only his lyre. He came back, and so will you."

This did little to reassure me. Orpheus had returned, but not with his beloved.

Around us the world was coming to life. I could hear the priestesses going about their duties in the temple and the animals waking in their stables and pens. But my eyes were fixed on the dark hollow of the cave mouth, which seemed to swallow all light.

"Look," Demeter said. I followed her pointing finger to see a butterfly making its unlikely way over the amphitheater. My namesake, *psyche*, in the tongue of the Greeks.

"The butterfly is a symbol of victory over death. A good omen," Demeter added.

A butterfly. I thought of Circe's tincture and my question to Zephyrus. I'd wondered what the shape of my soul meant. Now I knew.

Demeter turned, hazel eyes meeting mine. "Go with my blessing, dear girl," she said. "You haven't long now."

She was right. Time moves differently in the Underworld, and I was running out of it. I had five mortal days, but what would that be once I made this descent?

I took a shuddering breath and raced down the steps two at a time, pausing before I entered the tunnel sloping down into the earth. The cold, musty smell of the world of death washed over me, and my nostrils flared like those of a mare scenting blood. Nausea coiled and uncoiled in my belly, sending bile into my throat.

But I had not come unprepared. I lifted a thatch of wheat no longer than my forearm from the satchel and laid it at the dreadful threshold. This was the token offering to the Underworld gods that Eros and I had forgotten at Taenarum during my first katabasis. Demeter had cut it for me herself with her own sickle.

It was enough—it had to be enough. I would not fall. I would not be turned away.

I stepped forward and let myself be swallowed by the darkness, feeling the same chill I had at Taenarum. The earth beneath my sandals was smooth, packed down by thousands of feet. The mouth of the cave was where the hierophant of Eleusis led the new initiates, allowing them to taste the air of the Underworld itself to show them the truth of the mysteries. The initiates went in groups with lighted torches, though never very far. But I came alone and carried no torch, and soon I found myself walking on earth that had never been touched by a living foot. Soon enough, I saw the circle of light that marked the exit, growing larger and larger as I walked. Then the cold hard beauty of the Underworld was spread out before me, the distant palace rising above the lane of cypresses.

I looked down; my limbs were still my own, still living flesh. I allowed myself a breath of relief. I had passed the first test.

Waiting for me was a familiar face. Medusa.

38

PSYCHE

She was unchanged, as if moments rather than months had passed since we'd last seen each other. Her arms were crossed, and she bore an irritable expression, as though I had interrupted her at a game of dice.

"Well?" she said, not remarking on my sudden arrival. "Do you have an answer for me?" The serpents of her hair writhed and flicked their tongues.

I recalled the question she left me with. *What is it that makes a true hero?*

I stared at her blankly. I had forgotten her challenge in the flurry of everything else. "I . . . well . . . A hero is one who stands between humanity and the gods. Who acts without fear."

I was aware how weak and watery this sounded, even to my own ears. Without hesitation, I turned and began to walk swiftly down the long avenue lined with cypresses, hoping decisive action would make up for my rambling.

Medusa scurried after me. "Not bad. Nothing about killing helpless monsters, I'm pleased to hear, though I'm sure you could do better. And yes, you don't have much time. I'm aware of your plans, the queen informed me. There are things I must explain, so slow down!"

Medusa was shorter than me and struggled to keep up, panting her instructions. Begrudgingly, I relaxed my pace.

"Make your way through the forest, then to the banks of the River Styx," she said. "There you will meet Charon the ferryman. Once you offer payment, he will take you to Persephone's palace. You must not speak to anyone you meet, although they are permitted to speak to you. I shouldn't need to tell you not to talk to strangers, but y—"

"Aren't we talking now?" I pointed out. Ahead, I could see the bridge that separated the line of cypresses from the dead forests that lay beyond.

"Pert, ever pert! I'm your psychopomp, which you should be grateful for. How could you forbid conversation with a psychopomp? My purpose is to guide you. Persephone will be able to speak with you as well, and I advise you to treat her with respect if you value your life. And don't say anything about Adonis. Persephone is very possessive of him; he was Aphrodite's toy before he was the queen's, or that's the rumor at least. Anyway, there is one more thing I must warn you about." Brown eyes flashed toward me, her hair writhing. "The Underworld knows you don't belong here, and it will devise ways to pull you in deeper. Be watchful, and remember not to speak to anyone you might meet."

I breathed the cool air, feeling my muscles work. The last time I had walked this barren road, I had been a ghost. It was easier to navigate the roads of the Underworld with a mortal body.

"Tell me more about Persephone," I pressed.

Medusa laughed, a hollow sound. "She is a just ruler, but ruthless to those who cross her. Once her husband, Hades, tried to take a lover, a nymph named Menthe. Persephone solved the problem by turning her into a shrub. Every now and then, she picks leaves from Menthe to brew into tea." Medusa grinned, as if she relished the idea. "So it goes for anyone who opposes her."

"Then it's good I have her favor. Are we near Cerberus yet?"

Medusa shot me a glance. "No, he is farther ahead. Why, do you have some plan to slay the hound of hell? One last attempt to win renown as a hero?"

"No," I replied. "I like dogs, that's all."

"She likes dogs," Medusa repeated incredulously, then cackled. "Do you think he'll roll over and show his belly to you? You stink of mortality."

"I brought a honey cake to distract him," I told her.

Medusa looked almost impressed. "He does like those," she admitted.

We had reached the end of the cypress road. Ahead was a small path winding through a forest of stick-like, leafless trees, but no birds stirred the silence.

Medusa halted. "I can only lead you this far. You must find the rest of the way yourself."

She was silent for a moment, long enough for me to turn and study her face. She had transformed throughout our conversation, becoming more like the nymph she must have been during the first part of her life. Her features were smooth and even, her eyes ordinary rather than the slit pupils of a cat, though they were still the same familiar shade of brown. Her hair no longer writhed and snapped at the air, but instead fell in a profusion of locks around her shoulders.

"You have changed," the nymph called Medusa said to me. "You are not what you once were. The girl who appeared to me before was brash, headstrong, and more than a little full of herself. There's a certain kindness to you now that can only come from pain."

"Is that so?" I asked.

"Yes. I am familiar with it. Why do you think I was so kind to you when we first met, when I knew you as nothing more than my murderer's granddaughter?"

I stared at her, uncomprehending.

Medusa continued. "At first, I wasn't sure why Persephone sent *me* out of all the souls under her command to fetch you, but now I understand. Your grandfather killed me, and I burned with hatred for him, but our encounter has changed you for the better. Now you can become something more than what you might have been, and I can move on from my terrible grief. Persephone has wisdom. If she was merely ruthless, she would never reign here in the kingdom of the dead."

A wind stirred in the airless Underworld, rattling the bare branches. Medusa tipped her head back and allowed it to take her, sweeping her up into the colorless sky. Her soul dissipated like smoke from a fire, and I was alone.

39

PSYCHE

I made my way into the forest, which was little more than a tangle of naked branches against a bone-white sky. There were no other travelers along the road, and I marveled at how empty the Underworld was. For the destination of all living souls, it was an intensely solitary place. Then again, the living world could be quite lonely as well.

I looked up at the branches and thought of Eros. If Demeter's words were true, he too had passed through these desolate paths, and he had done so to pave the way for me. My heart skipped, and I picked up my pace.

It was not long before I came upon a man on the road. He tugged unsuccessfully at a heavily burdened donkey that shied away from his touch. I could see the sweat on the man's brow and the flick of the donkey's tail, but their appearance seemed oddly out of place. They were as real as anything else here—which is to say, as ephemeral as mist.

I noticed that the man had tied the bundle incorrectly. A few more knots in the correct places and he could distribute the weight more evenly over the animal's back. I opened my mouth to instruct him but recalled Medusa's warning against speaking. He would need to find a way to carry his own burdens.

Then I blinked, and the scene before me shifted. I realized the bundle was not composed of sticks for kindling but instead of every grief that encumbered a human life. Sorrow, injury, guilt, doubt, disease, loss . . .

Another eyeblink, and they were nothing more than ordinary bundles once again. The donkey nearly toppled the man, who swore at the beast and continued to tug.

I skirted around them. I knew perfectly well how one thing might stand in for another, how the wind might be a youthful god, or one's own husband the nexus of all desire. Why couldn't one type of burden be a symbol for another? Either way, there was no use in taking on more than I could carry.

I continued through the silence of the withered forest. The trees were leafless and parched; spring never came to this infernal place. The sky was milky gray and wreathed in mists, neither day nor night. The only sound I could hear was the soft crunch of my feet against the dry dirt of the path.

After some time, the road widened. The stick-like trees fell away, making room for something ahead, a dark mound that I thought was an old ruin or a small hill. Until I saw its ears twitch.

I had been concerned I'd miss Cerberus, the three-headed dog that guarded the Underworld, but now I saw those fears were moot. The massive beast slumbered with its heads on its paws, though it stirred at my approach. One of its noses twitched wetly, drawing up the head with it. Yellow eyes as large as my palm opened. Disturbed from their slumber, the other two heads followed suit and I watched the dark bulk of an impossibly large creature unfurl before me. He was bigger than the drakonis, bigger than any monster I had ever seen before. His pricked ears reached higher than the tops of the trees. When Cerberus took to his feet, it was like watching a mountain unfold.

Six eyes focused on me.

Cold terror sluiced through me. Craven instinct compelled me to flee back to the tree line, but I knew better than to run from such a beast. I pulled one of the biscuits Demeter had given me from my satchel; it was the size and heft of a discus. She had made it herself from barley meal moistened with honey, just what Cerberus liked.

Or so Demeter had said. If Cerberus preferred living flesh over bread, I would soon find out.

I threw the biscuit into the air. Cerberus's ears pricked toward it, and one of his heads—the farthest to the right—snapped it up, sending gouts of drool from its mouth. The other two heads did not pay me mind, whirling on their companion, biting and snarling, a sound like thunder. I took advantage of the confusion and crept past.

I kept walking. Eventually the forest thinned, and a river came into view. It was wide and colorless, black waters lapping soundlessly at the shore. This was Styx, greatest of the rivers of the Underworld. On the far shore I could see that palace of unearthly majesty, all white marble and soaring towers, but my attention was pulled away by the crowd gathered along the riverbank.

This was the first time I had seen humans in the Underworld, and there were thousands of them, blanketing the shore like a colony of ants. They were not solid like living people, but fleeting impressions, like the dragons that seem to dance in the smoke rising from temple incense.

I could make out glimpses of many different peoples: Persians in their wide trousers, flaxen-haired barbarians from the northern wastes, dark-skinned people from Egypt, as well as the more familiar Greeks. I wondered if I would see the bandits I'd killed among them—or worse, Iphigenia. But mercifully, I recognized none of the faces around me.

Some bore the wounds that had caused their deaths, dripping phantom blood onto the cold sands, while others appeared whole. Some of the dead paced the shore and howled, while others crouched in stunned silence. Many of them wailed. I only understood the ones who spoke Greek, but that was enough to fill my ears with a host of litanies.

"I loved my husband, but he thought I slept with the village butcher," one cried. *"He strangled me to death."*

"My son watched me die," the ghost of an old man howled. *"He could have called a healer when the fever took me, but he wanted his inheritance."*

"I died in childbirth," said another. *"The pain was horrible . . ."*

I drew back. These were the ones who had no coin to pay their passage, who had never received proper burial. I fought the urge to do something—anything—to alleviate their bitter distress, but I was helpless before the enormity of their loss. Their grief felt like a millstone around my neck.

In this sea of lost lives, what hope did I have? I wanted to join those lonely shades and howl my own losses—my parents, Iphigenia, Eros himself—until they were like tears washed into the ocean. I might lose myself in half-remembered sorrow until I succumbed to dehydration or starvation, and my shade stepped out of my mortal body the way a living person shrugs off a robe. I would live on only in Eros's memory, a mortal girl he had loved once before their sudden separation and her ignominious death, nothing more than a brief dream he recalled on moonless nights. Aphrodite would win, and my child would never know what it was like to walk upon the green earth.

Anger flared. My essential nature reasserted itself. No, I would not be barred from my goal by foolishness and self-pity. I watched a single small boat make its way across the mirrorlike waters and took note of where the ferryman must be docked. I took off running, shouldering my way through throngs of shocked and staring ghosts, parting them like clouds.

At last I stood before Charon, shaking off the chill residue of other people's souls.

The ferryman considered me. He was as old as darkness and as unknowable as night. He wore a shabby black robe and a hood that obscured his face under a heavy cowl. The hands that emerged from his sleeves were so sinewy and skeletal they might have belonged to a corpse, and I shivered. I wondered how many centuries had passed since those hands first took up the oars they held. I wondered at the face hidden behind that hood, whether it possessed the uncannily perfect symmetry of a god or the ruined grin of a corpse.

I pulled a coin from my satchel and handed it to Charon. His wiry hands reached out to take it from me, and the abyss under the cowl regarded me thoughtfully.

"You are still alive," rasped a voice like the stirring of dry leaves.

I prepared to argue my case before I recalled Medusa's warning against speaking. I crossed my arms and planted my feet on the rickety wood of the dock.

Charon chuckled, or perhaps the sound was simply the gentle lapping of the river on the shoreline. He turned and took up the oars. "Alive or no, you have paid your fare. Come."

I boarded the little boat, glancing back at the shore where the ghosts paced and moaned, gradually becoming smaller as the ferryman pushed his boat into the current. Styx seemed like any other river, save that its waters were ebony black. The boat scarcely disturbed their depths with its passage, leaving behind only a faint chevron of ripples. I stared at the back of Charon's faded robe and wondered what his life was like. If he ever rested, if he had a wife or child of his own.

I did not dare ask any of these questions; instead, I gazed idly at the waters. I noticed a face staring back at me. Though the boat moved rather swiftly, the face seemed to keep pace with it. At first I thought it my own reflection, but as I peered more closely at the strange apparition, I saw that it wore an old-fashioned helmet. I leaned closer, wondering if this was an ancestor of mine, a king of ancient Mycenae or a hero, perhaps Perseus himself . . .

A sharp rapping snapped me out of my reverie, and I realized that I was hanging from the side of the boat with my face nearly in the water. I scrambled back, my feet drumming against the wooden deck, making the boat sway with my movements.

The knocking had come from Charon, tapping his oar against the hull like a tutor correcting an errant pupil. I could not read his face, still shrouded in darkness, but I heard the scold in his thin voice. "Do not lose yourself in visions," he said as he dipped his oar back into the black waters. "Souls end up in this river for a variety of reasons, but all are united in their desire to escape. They would take your living body for their own if they could."

I nodded, chagrined. Medusa had warned that this place would try to pull me in. And here I had almost fallen into the water like a foolish child, reaching for the image of the hero I would never be.

We soon arrived at the far shore, where Charon tied his boat to a humble dock. The castle I had seen from a distance towered above us, looming in its majesty. Beyond it were the Fields of Asphodel, where the souls of the dead spent their eternities, but I had a different goal. I disembarked and nodded to the ferryman.

"I know who you are and why you have come. Such stories reach us even here," Charon said in a voice like the creaking of a tomb door. "If you succeed, I will carry you back. You have my word." Before I could reply, Charon pushed his boat into the current, back toward the far shore.

I watched him go, then turned to walk a dirt road to the looming white walls above me. The path led around the alabaster perfection of the castle, but I could see no doors or windows, not even a servant to ask for directions.

Time passed, and my legs grew weary. I was certain that I had passed this particular withered tree before. I sensed I was being toyed with, like a child reaching for a sweet dangled just out of reach. Frustration filled me, even as my lungs burned with cold air and my muscles began to ache. I hadn't come all this way only to be faced with indifferent walls, running laps around a feature-less edifice until my time expired.

I turned a corner and a cluster of three old women weaving and gossiping came into view. This would have been a common sight in Mycenae or any other place under the eye of the living sun, but here their appearance filled me with unease. The three women were indistinguishable, all ancient, with their hair falling in pale white tufts around wrinkled faces. They watched me with eyes like black beads nested at the center of a spiderweb, though their hands continued to move, never breaking their rhythm.

I realized that they were not actually weaving. Instead, they were cutting thread. One unspooled the thread from its skein, holding it between ancient knuckles gnarled as the roots of a yew tree. The second woman measured this thread, the tremor of her hand not disturbing her accuracy. The third used rust-coated scis-sors to snip it.

My skin prickled. These were no ordinary old women. They were the Moirai, the Fates, those goddesses who measure the length of a mortal's life. Had they come to see my story for themselves?

The Fates whispered among each other as I passed, rheumy eyes crawling over me. I could hear snatches of what they were saying, like words of a song caught on the wind.

". . . such a shame about the war . . ."

"What do you think she'll do when the child . . ."

"... I hope she doesn't ... her husband ..."

I froze. In that moment, I wanted more than anything to turn and beg them to tell me the end of my tale. The Fates knew the future, and they could show me the way forward.

But I could not risk undoing my progress, not even for knowledge of what was to come.

I bowed my heads in deference to the women and continued past. I did not need to hear them weave my future. I was certain to attain my goal for one very simple reason—I refused to fail.

I considered the nature of the obstacles in my path. *Don't let grief burden you. Don't lose yourself in visions. Don't resign yourself to the Fates.*

Suddenly a door appeared in front of me, heavy wood set into the palace walls, the first I had seen. I knew who waited for me on the other side of the door with a certainty as cold as the stones beneath my feet. I turned the handle and heard the old hinges creak, then waited to be escorted to the queen of the Underworld.

40

PSYCHE

Persephone.

Her cheeks were smooth as the petals of flowers, white shading into red along the flawless lines of her face. They were like the perfect halves of a pomegranate, though her eyes were as sharp as flint.

Persephone sat on the throne as though it had been made for her. She loomed above me on the far end of the room, a spiked onyx crown resting on her brow. The more modest seat beside her was empty, and there was no trace of Hades. This was no surprise; even mortals knew who truly ruled here. When Odysseus and his men sought to call the spirits of the dead during their long journey home from Troy, they would pay homage not to Hades, but to Persephone.

At first, I mistook the ivory designs on Persephone's throne for inlay or fine decoration. Then I noticed the length of a femur along the armrests and the rounded dome of a skull under each delicate hand. And flowers, everywhere flowers, even in this lightless place. Real ones blooming from pots lining the walls, false ones gracing the sides of her throne in a profusion of jewels.

Persephone, the goddess of springtime. Death gives rise to life, and rotting corpses fertilize the soil so that crops can grow. In many ways, Persephone was better suited to the domain of death than her husband, who had been assigned to it by edict of Zeus.

She, on the other hand, had been born for it.

At Persephone's feet knelt a naked man, his head pillowed on her lap. A heavy collar encircled his neck, set with the same onyx jewels that adorned Persephone's crown. This must be Adonis. He wore not a scrap of clothing, only the blissful smile of one lost in a happy dream.

Heat crept over my face. "Don't you have a cloak you could throw over him?" I asked.

One of Persephone's perfect eyebrows arched. "A guest in my home, and you presume to lecture me on proper attire? Eros was right. You *are* a handful."

"You spoke to Eros?" I asked, my heart rising.

"I did. I was impressed that he made the journey here, and I am pleased to grant the boon he requested. I have beauty cream enough to spare."

"Thank you," I breathed. At least this part of my quest would go easily.

Persephone leaned forward. "But first, I must know: Do you actually love him?" she asked. "Eros?"

I hesitated. This was a question I had asked myself often during my wanderings. I knew the answer but shied away from speaking it to this dread goddess.

My eyes flickered to Adonis. "Do you love *him*?" I asked, indicating the sleeping man.

Persephone's gaze slid down to rest on the man at her feet. "Does one love a fine cup or a well-made comb? He serves his purpose." Adonis shifted in his sleep, smacking his lips, and settled his head more comfortably on Persephone's thighs. The edges of her mouth quirked upward, not quite a smile, and she laid a gentle hand on his curls.

I stared at them. I once accused Eros of keeping me as a pet, as Persephone kept Adonis. I feared that the great gods had no concept of love, only possession. But then I thought of Zephyrus, his love for Hyacinthos undimmed by death. I thought of the way Eros had marveled at my fight with the bandits and traded stories with me in the dark. He had never sought to make me his object, only his companion.

"I do love Eros," I said simply.

Persephone tilted her head. "Fascinating. I never thought that little pest would win anyone's love," she said. "He never had much interest in it before."

"Dread lady, all I ask is what you promised my husband." I bowed slightly.

"Oh, don't simper," Persephone retorted. "It doesn't suit someone of your character."

She snapped her fingers and a skeleton appeared from the darkness behind her throne. It walked as though it thought it was still human, despite the lack of flesh or muscle covering its long white bones. Balanced on its starburst of phalanges was a small wooden box, which the skeleton handed to me. It took all my strength not to recoil when I felt those cold digits brush mine.

"Here is what you seek," Persephone said. "Do not open it yourself—leave that for Aphrodite. And when you see your husband again, remind him that I always repay those who grant me favors." She stroked Adonis's hair.

I ran my fingers over the fine-grained wood of the box, carved with the sigil of a pomegranate. Persephone's beauty cream.

I recalled Demeter's words. "One last thing," I said. "Your mother wishes me to relay a message. She sends her love."

Persephone reared back on her throne, all goodwill vanished from her face. "This is no message. This is an intrusion."

I was aghast at the cruelty of her response. "She loves you."

Persephone was unmoved. "My mother loves what she believes me to be. If Demeter had her way, I would have spent my eternal existence hanging on her skirts, never realizing what I was capable of. I would be a little flower in the shadow of a wheat field, a minor deity associated with the goddess of harvest. Here, I am queen." She looked away from me into the distance.

"I was terrified when Hades snatched me from that meadow, but I have made sure that things turned out for the best. I thought you would understand," the goddess added, her gaze swinging back to settle on me. "As someone else who stood in for her parents' failed ambitions."

The words were a blow. I thought of Alkaios, son of a hero but possessing no heroic gifts himself. Astydamia, robbed by illness of the martial training that was hers by right. My grief threatened to swallow me, but I steeled myself. "My parents have nothing to do with this."

Persephone's eyebrow arched. "I suppose not," she said. "I did not go from loving parents to a loving husband as you did. There was no safe harbor for me, so I had to become more terrible than what I endured."

The faces of my parents and Iphigenia flashed through my mind. "Can I see them? My family?" I asked.

"No," Persephone replied, straight-backed on her throne. "The ones you loved are content in the Fields of Asphodel, insofar as any shades can be. Their stories are no longer interwoven with yours. Besides, you cannot speak to them if you ever hope to leave this place, and that would not make for a particularly satisfying visit. Let them be."

I felt gutted, like a razed house after a fire. This must have shown on my face, because the dread queen softened. "But there is one whose story I can show you," she told me.

She raised one hand in a sweeping gesture, like brushing a veil from a mirror, and the scene before my eyes changed. No longer was I gazing at the queen and her collared lover. Instead, I floated far above the familiar road of cypresses.

A figure walked that lonely path, and I recognized her with a jolt. Atalanta, her white hair bound back, her proud spine unbent from illness. My voice caught in my throat. I was not sure whether this was past or present, whether I was seeing something that had already happened or was yet to come.

I watched my teacher cross the River Styx in Charon's boat, trading a few words of conversation with the ferryman, then saw her venture into the realms beyond. Atalanta walked through the mists of the Underworld until she came across a gray field where groups of shades lounged.

I think she would have kept walking—that was Atalanta for you, always eager to explore the peripheries of any new place—but she paused midstep, a look of wonder on her face. She recognized someone.

Two shades rose from the mist to greet her. One of them was a slight man with dark hair, with a wry and mischievous face. The other possessed a noble bearing that could only belong to a king. I knew at once that this must be Meleager, who had helped Atalanta slay the Calydonian boar and defended her honor against those who said women had no place in the hunt. That meant the slighter man next to him was Melanion, Atalanta's husband, killed by Aphrodite so long ago.

Atalanta's eyes flicked back and forth between the two men, whispering their names. I had never seen such an expression on my teacher's face, amazement and impossible hope, like she was watching the sun rise after the longest night of the year.

The taller man smiled and nodded, exchanging an ironic glance with Melanion. "Your husband here has been telling me what transpired in my absence. It seems you have won great fame for yourself . . ."

Then I came to myself again, standing in the onyx hall. Tears filled my eyes, but there was a lightness in my heart that had not been there before.

Persephone was looking at me with terrible compassion. I saw that what Medusa said was true: It was not only through ruthlessness that Persephone held power here in the Underworld, beyond the gates of death.

"Now go back to the land of the living," Persephone said softly, inclining her head. "This place is not meant to have you yet. Hurry back."

I was dismissed. A door appeared in the fringes of my vision, and I walked through it without a backward glance.

Charon was waiting for me by the dock, his skeletal hands wrapped around the oar. I fished the remaining coin from the satchel I still wore strapped across my body and held it out to him.

The bottomless darkness of the cowl turned to face me. "I gave my word that I would carry you back," he rasped. "You do not need to pay your fare twice."

I did not lower my hand. *Take it*, I thought, remembering the prohibition against speaking to those I encountered in the Underworld, though I willed him to understand. *Apply it to the bill of one of those shades flitting along the far shore of the River Styx, who died without anyone to lay a coin on their tongue. Let them cross the river and find rest at last.*

Under Charon's hood, I saw the glint of eyes, and thought he understood. A sinewy hand plucked the coin from the air and spirited it into the depths of his robe.

I leaned against the side of the boat, watching the waters part soundlessly. I had never been this tired before, not even when I fled from the ruins of the seaside house or the grave of Iphigenia. My knees and feet ached fiercely, and I found myself envious of the dead, who were no longer burdened by the demands of living flesh.

Eventually we reached the other side of the river. Charon said nothing as I set foot on land, but when I looked back, I saw he had raised one hand in farewell.

I walked through the winding trail that cut through the barren landscape like a scar, my footsteps slow and plodding. I met Cerberus, who seemed smaller now. As soon as I saw the ears prick over the treetops, I tossed the last biscuit into the air. I wondered idly if Cerberus would scent the trick this time and tear me apart, but instead the three heads collided with one another once more, snarling and tearing over the scrap of a treat.

I passed through the clearing where I had seen the spectral man and his donkey; it was empty now. Not long afterward I came to the bridge, feeling almost disappointed when I did not see the familiar form of Medusa waiting for me.

Beyond the bridge was the road of cypresses, and beyond that was the dark tunnel that led to Eleusis and the world of the living.

Hope flared in me. I began to run, cypresses whizzing past me. I bounded past the trees and into the darkness of the tunnel, my feet finding their way along the smooth earth. Before long, I stumbled into the light of the early morning sun in the land of the living.

It was just after dawn, and sunlight had not yet reached the shadows of the cave at the center of the amphitheater. I gulped the sweet air and listened to the birds singing, my heart pounding a victory march. I was alive, and I had won. I clutched the box that Persephone had given me, caressing it like a treasure.

I paused for a moment and looked back at the darkness. I was no Orpheus to lose his Eurydice from this folly. I only wanted to remember the way when I had cause to follow it again. Somewhere in that darkness were my parents, Iphigenia, Atalanta, and Zephyrus's beloved Hyacinthos. I had hoped for a glimpse of them, a chance to say the farewells that death had stolen from us. But Persephone was right—their stories were no longer mine.

There is danger in premature celebration, as Orpheus himself could have reminded me. As I clambered up the smooth stone stairs, box of beauty cream in hand, I slipped and missed a step.

In all the years I'd lived, I had never stumbled—not once. I had never been less than sure-footed, but on that day, I tripped. In the moment of weightless shock as I fell, I grappled with Persephone's box, and the cover slid off.

Persephone had warned me not to open the box myself. Unbeknownst to me, she had reasoned she could kill two birds with one stone, seizing the chance for petty revenge against Aphrodite under the guise of keeping her word to Eros.

The box did not contain beauty cream, but a curse fit for a goddess. And I was only a mortal woman.

41

EROS

When I woke, Hekate was sitting by the side of the bed. I flinched back, wondering how long she had been watching me.

Her expression was grave. "I found her. Your wife, Psyche."

My heart rose. I tried to get up but was forced back down by the surprisingly strong arm of Hekate.

"She is at Eleusis," the goddess continued. Haltingly, she explained the situation. Demeter had found Psyche splayed across the steps of the amphitheater at Eleusis, unconscious. Distraught, Demeter summoned Hekate, who was able to establish two facts very quickly. The first was that a pulse flickered at Psyche's wrists; she was alive. The second was that she would not be alive for long, since nothing the old goddess did could wake her.

"Did Persephone do this?" I snarled. The words were harsh and ugly, torn from my viscera. If Persephone had betrayed me, I would stop at nothing to have my vengeance.

Hekate scoffed. "Get that tone out of your voice. The last thing we need right now is a feud between you and the queen of hell. Persephone kept her word. There was an unfortunate mistake, that's all. Persephone's own mother is crying her eyes out for Psyche at this very moment. Demeter is very fond of the girl, though I think she is always looking for another child to mother."

My hands tangled in the blankets. "What do I do?" I asked. "How do I save her?"

Hekate's eyes glowed in the thin lamplight like those of a wolf. "You understand the full implications of what I said about the souls of gods and mortals, do you not? Once you do, all the rest comes easily. You begged me once already for the solution, and though I did not grant it then, I offer it to you now. We have no other choice."

It took me a moment to comprehend what Hekate was saying. "*Apotheosis*," I whispered. "We must make her a god."

Welcoming a newcomer into the ranks of the gods is no small matter, so it is only by assembly that the exercise of this power is decided. Only one deity has the power to call such an assembly—the same one who had abandoned me to the clutches of Aphrodite and once, long ago, slighted me over a glass of ambrosia.

I infiltrated Zeus's private quarters as a fly upon the breeze. He occupied the upper rooms of the great palace on Olympus, a sweeping set of chambers that showed wide mountain vistas through the windows. I waited in the silence for hours in the shape of a creeping spider. When I heard the door open and close, I reverted to my true shape.

"Once you came to my home asking for assistance," I said behind him. "Now I come to yours asking the same."

Zeus whirled, lips quivering beneath his long white beard, his hooded eyes wide. "Eros?" he said, disbelieving. I saw something new on the granitelike face of the king of the gods—fear.

"You might be wondering how I freed myself from the clutches of Aphrodite," I continued in a low voice, filled with banked rage.

I was gratified to see Zeus shrink back. "That's none of your concern, although I won't readily forget how you sold me out to her. But fear not, I haven't come for vengeance. All I want is a favor. Call an assembly to vote on the apotheosis of my wife, Psyche."

Bafflement, outrage, and finally disapproval chased one another across Zeus's stern features. He chewed his bearded lip for a moment before answering. "That is preposterous. The girl is no one. She has no great deeds to her name, no divine lineage. Apotheosis cannot be granted to one such as this."

I would not be dissuaded. "Don't you ever wonder," I said coldly, "when one of your many bastard sons or daughters will grow up to betray you, just as you betrayed your father? Perhaps one of the mortal girls you've seized will bring up her child to avenge her honor, or maybe Hera will befriend one of your byblows rather than trying to destroy them. It's been centuries since you've forsaken her bed, as I well know."

Zeus's face stiffened with rage. Sparks of lightning danced around his white head, flickering like fireflies. I smelled the ozone scent of impending thunder, but I held firm. I possessed a power he could not comprehend. I could draw together opposites, humiliate even the Thunderer himself. I was the god of desire. More than that, I had broken free of the prison where Aphrodite bound me. What else was I capable of? I could see Zeus's mind working behind his storm-colored eyes.

At last Zeus said, "I will send out the word. The assembly will gather before sundown."

The gods came in groups and singly, riding in chariots or upon flashes of rainbow, or in the shapes of flying creatures. They took their seats in the great hall hollowed out from the heart of Olympus mountain, murmuring to one another about the reason for this summons.

I saw all of this from the dais where I sat with Hekate, Demeter, and Zephyrus. On the other end sat Aphrodite with her husband, Hephaestus, and her lover Hermes. Hephaestus looked as though he wanted to vanish into the stone, but agile Hermes was whispering something into Aphrodite's ear as she nodded gravely.

I cursed under my breath. Of course my adopted mother would insist on having the counsel of the god of eloquence himself.

Once the attending gods settled in, it was time for speeches. Aphrodite went first to the gilded podium, bestowing a winning smile upon the crowd. She made a lovely picture, her long dark hair tumbling around her smooth shoulders, and she knew it very well. Every eye was drawn to her.

"I stand before you this day as the grieving mother of a recalcitrant son," she began, her voice ringing out against the stone of the mountainside. "My Eros threw in his lot with Psyche, a mortal girl, despite the fact that she was a braggart, cowardly, and wished to use him only for his divine gifts. But he desired her, and against my counsel he took her into his house. Now he seeks her apotheosis. She would be one of us—this vain, grasping girl who has no respect for her betters! If we allow every talentless mortal who catches the eye of a god to ascend to divinity, we will soon find ourselves overrun."

There were murmurs of assent in the crowd; the gods knew what it was like to have misbehaving children, and all of them loathed mortals who thought themselves our equals. But I noticed something else—the Titans in the crowd, those older elemental gods who looked askance at the grandeur of new Olympus, were not smiling. Aphrodite was a symbol of the new order, but they had known me since the earth was made.

I allowed myself a small smile. It seemed I was not without allies after all.

"Moreover," Aphrodite continued, "Psyche swore herself as my handmaiden, and she did not complete her tasks in the allotted time. She did not retrieve the beauty cream I requested. She—"

"False!" I cried before I could stop myself. Zephyrus put a hand on my shoulder and Demeter hissed disapprovingly, but I was on my feet in an eyeblink.

The gods were all looking at me now. With a lightness in her voice that did not match the malice of her expression, Aphrodite said, "I will hand the podium to my dear son Eros, since he is so eager to account for his defiance."

She drifted back to her seat. As she stalked past me, she hissed, *"This is for Adonis."*

"So I should lose my mortal lover in compensation for yours?" I shot back, but by then she was seated, crossing her delicate ankles.

I took my place and gazed out at the crowd. A thousand perfect faces stared back at me with mingled expectation and indifference. For a single despairing moment, I thought I might as well have tried to persuade a pack of wolves.

I had never been one for public speaking. My gifts were always better exercised in private, and the weight of so many eyes made me want to crawl into a hole. But I could not save Psyche through my silence, and so I began to speak.

"If I have been known to you at all," I began, "I have been known as a nuisance. Few of you have gone untroubled by my arrows."

The crowd chuckled softly. Gods liked to be acknowledged; it was a good start.

"During the summer months," I went on, "you may recall a time when I did not trouble you unduly. I was happy with my wife, Psyche, whose apotheosis I seek today. I could tell you of her many wonderful qualities or regale you with stories of her skill at arms. I could tell you about her great beauty, or the sweet way she snores very faintly when she falls asleep after a long day. But perhaps the greatest evidence of Psyche's gifts is the fact that I am standing here in front of you now. I do not humiliate myself lightly."

Another ripple of laughter. But I knew I would not win over the gods with flowery words. They only cared about one thing: saving themselves. So I continued, "In her I have found my peace, and if she is taken from me then none of you will ever have peace again. No longer will you find pleasure in the arms of your husbands and wives and lovers. Never again will you feel the joy of your craft sing under your fingers. You will know my grief, because you will endure it yourselves."

I was nearly panting as I finished, the high vaulted ceilings ringing with my voice.

An uneasy silence reigned. At last, someone in the crowd called out, "What domain would this Psyche rule over, if we do grant her apotheosis? A goddess must preside over something."

Hekate stirred from her seat next to Demeter. "The human soul has no ruling deity," she said evenly. "I propose we offer this to the goddess Psyche."

This prompted shocked muttering among the crowd. What a thing to rule over, the soul! But the gods' murmuring was not particularly venomous, since no one felt very territorial about this idea. In the end, the crowd assented to this condition.

With the speeches concluded, voting began. Gods like to decide things by vote: It is clear, public, and involves no maiming or bloodshed, both likely to cause centuries of consternation among immortals. Servant nymphs set up two baskets filled with tiles, one black and one white. The former represented a vote against Psyche's apotheosis, the latter a vote in favor of it. An empty basket sat next to them, where the tally would be gathered.

I was vexed but not surprised when Aphrodite dropped a

black tile in the near-empty basket to match my white one. Hephaestus followed suit with his wife, which pained me. Hermes took a black tile as well, though I had expected that. He was always doing whatever he thought might win him Aphrodite's affections.

Hera dropped in a black tile. "I thought you'd be pleased to see that I've settled down," I remarked to the stately goddess.

"What you've done is a mockery of matrimony," she sniffed disdainfully. "That mortal girl has no manners at all."

Zeus chose a black tile, but at least he had the good graces to seem ashamed about it. "Sorry, dear boy," he said with false cheer. "The wife would give me hell if I didn't."

But there were others—many others—who dropped in white tokens. Myself, Demeter, Hekate, and Zephyrus, of course. There was also a dark messenger, envoy of Persephone and Hades, who deposited two white tiles on behalf of the absentee voters and left without a word. Luminous Apollo approached, shooting a glare at his old enemy Zephyrus before dropping another two white tiles into the basket.

"For myself and my sister Artemis," Apollo said to me. "She will not leave her forests, but she is fond of the girl."

Afterward came an array of minor gods and Titans, deities of rivers and mountains, who cast white tiles on Psyche's behalf. From their darting glances, I think they appreciated the chance to get one over on the Olympians.

But still, black tiles predominated in the basket. My palms began to sweat. For the first time, I began to truly consider what it would mean if we lost.

Distantly, I could see Aphrodite's smarmy grin as she observed me with the nonchalant malice of a housecat watching a songbird. Hekate was muttering, and Demeter wrung her hands. My shoulders felt heavy.

319

A thought occurred to me. I had an ally I had nearly overlooked, a source of help I had almost forgotten. I crouched down and laid my hand on the earth, whispering to it.

The ground beneath us began to tremble.

Smooth floors of marble fragmented as the earth erupted. The gods nearest screamed and leaped back, clutching the hems of their robes. The tidal wave of earth grew, soaring up to the domed ceilings. An arm emerged from the roiling mass, then a leg. The rubble shaped itself like clay, taking on the appearance of a woman—a goddess—taller than any I had ever seen, with generous hips and large breasts, loose hair flowing around her shoulders.

She towered over the assembly. Gaia, mother of our world. My elder sister.

With remarkable delicacy for one so vast, Gaia strode leisurely across the hall, each thunderous footstep making the torches jump in their brackets. The lesser gods clung to one another and gaped.

Gaia flashed a dazzling smile as she passed me, teeth white as the peaks of mountaintops. In a voice that echoed in my skull, she whispered, *"The earth and everything upon it will be moved to help you."*

With my head craned up to look at her, I could only manage the slightest nod of acknowledgment, but my heart was rejoicing. Gaia had heard my call. She remembered our friendship stretching over long eons. Or perhaps she merely thought it time at last to take a midnight walk, to see for herself what her great-great-grandchildren had done with this world.

Gaia walked toward the voting baskets. With an enormous blunt-nailed hand, she reached into one of the baskets, then placed a single white chip into the other.

I would have cheered, but stunned awe stifled the cry in my throat. Gaia turned and walked away, her shadow looming over the assembly like that of a passing cloud, until she returned to the ragged hole in the marble from which she had torn her make-shift body. Gaia tipped back her head and spread her arms, fall-ing back into the earth with a crash that rattled the teeth in my head. The marble closed over her like the surface of the ocean, settling down smooth and undisturbed. There was no sign it had ever been broken.

The denizens of the hall stared after her, then burst into a flurry of whispered hissing. I laid a hand on the earth and thanked my sister for the gift she had given me.

But Gaia had cast only one vote. The contents of the basket looked like the variegated wing of a magpie, partly black and partly white. Athena, goddess of justice, tallied them. Though she had once elected to turn a mortal girl into a spider for having the audacity to be a better weaver than her, Athena was consid-ered the arbiter of disputes among the gods.

Athena's mouth twisted as she finished the tally. "Eros's side is still several votes short," she announced to the gathered throng. "The vote goes against apotheosis." She raised one slender hand and turned the thumb downward, a garroter twisting a noose.

I think I would have fallen if Zephyrus had not been there to hold me up. I had committed everything I had to the cause, and still I had failed. My centuries hung around my neck like an an-chor, my divinity worthless as dogshit. I would watch as Psyche's sleep transitioned to death and her body moldered into dust.

The baskets were packed away. One by one the gods began to drift from the room, drawn by more lively entertainments else-where. Dimly I was aware of Aphrodite's self-satisfied grin, of Demeter's shouts of protest and Hekate's muttered cursing. Zeus patted my shoulder in sympathy as he departed, and even Apollo offered a friendly smile.

In time the hall was as empty as it had been at the beginning, dull and distant as a tomb. I stared at the marble floor and imagined Psyche dissolving into cold smoke in the Underworld. Not even Gaia's miracle could save her.

Eventually only I, Zephyrus, Hekate, and Demeter remained in the cold, empty hall. When it was clear there was nothing more to be done, Hekate stood. "Let us go to Eleusis, Eros. Go to your Psyche, and be with her at the end."

No. Fury blazed through me like a wildfire, and I fell to my knees and clutched Hekate's robes. It was a gamble, but I had nothing else.

"When has a goddess bowed to any authority but her own?" I demanded. "When has Hekate Soteira abandoned a supplicant? Give Psyche the gift of apotheosis, with or without the other gods' permission. You know the recipe well enough."

Zephyrus gave a whoop of delight, and Demeter muttered pensively. But Hekate merely looked at me with eyes that blazed like torches in her withered face.

Please, I thought. *If Psyche dies, I will never be finished mourning her. I may not deserve her, but this world does.*

"Very well," Hekate said, standing and brushing off her skirts. "I didn't yank that little Psyche out of the edges of the Underworld only to be thwarted. We tried it one way, and now we'll try it the other. Let us get to work."

42

EROS

I watched as Hekate prepared the brew of apotheosis, moving with such assurance that she might have prepared it every day. A bit of spiderweb, a touch of dried herbs, a silvery strand that Hekate insisted came from a unicorn's mane. All pounded with a mortar and pestle and added to a low cauldron suspended over a fire. I wondered if Psyche or I would be punished for this transgression, though neither of us could be killed after apotheosis took hold. Zeus and Aphrodite would be furious, but likely the other gods would consider it nothing but a minor curiosity. They cared only about themselves.

As I watched, I realized that Hekate's origins were still a mystery to me. Perhaps she had been born a mortal herself, changed into a goddess by her own sorcery. Certainly that would explain the nature of her magic—half-feral, spilling its bounds, existing along the edges of the world. Usually the gods kept to their allotted domains and disdained sly tricks like witchcraft; only a mortal would be such a generalist. But I knew better than to ask such things.

Hekate handed me the cup, a milky liquid that caught the light with a flash of rainbow. "Bring it to Psyche," she told me. "Have her drink it. I will leave you two to your reunion."

Psyche was in one of the rooms in Eleusis, laid out on a marble slab, unmoving as the stone itself. Lamps were set into the stone, casting a flickering light over the scene that brought to mind the last time I had seen her in the bedroom of the seaside house. The sight of her was like a splinter in my heart, and terror warred with joy within me. When Psyche had loved me before, it had been in darkness. I was none too sure she would want me in the light.

At Psyche's side was Demeter, fierce as a guard dog. When I entered the room, she rose and pulled me aside.

"Your lies nearly destroyed her," Demeter snarled. "And then you left her alone. If Psyche never wants to see you again after this day, that is as much as you deserve."

I stared at her. *Is it not enough that I was cursed,* I wanted to say. *Or kept in chains by Aphrodite, or that I descended into the Underworld to send a message to your daughter? Is it not enough that I have been tormented by guilt for exactly the things you describe, every moment that I was separated from Psyche?*

But none of that mattered now. Demeter was right. My lies had caused all of this, and now I could only try to make amends.

"Perhaps Psyche will hate me. Perhaps she will never want to see my face again," I replied. "I am making a choice for her that cannot be unmade. But many are the choices that will flow from this one, and at least she will *live*."

Demeter left the room. I turned to Psyche, motionless as marble, and sunk to my knees beside her as I thought about Demeter's words. I was none too sure that immortality was a gift. Certainly I hadn't taken easily to mine. But there was no other way to save Psyche.

I tilted the cup to Psyche's lips and massaged her throat until she swallowed. A few drops, then a few more, tilting her head to ensure she didn't choke. As I did so, I watched her face intensely, looking for a flash of light or some other proof of transformation. Already the elixir was traveling through her body and turning it into that of a god, but I could see no outward evidence of this process save for a faint, growing illumination.

Psyche opened her eyes.

Brown eyes, which I had seen all too briefly or through the borrowed lens of animal forms. Elation rushed through me like the springtime wind. *If nothing else comes of this,* I thought, *at least I was able to see her one last time.*

Outside the little room, life went on as usual. The priestesses went about their business in the temple, and the gods bickered and backstabbed. Beyond them, mortals farmed and fought, and sheep grazed in a thousand meadows. The sun and moon wheeled through the sky as they always had. But in that room, at that moment, time stood still.

Psyche's eyes were wide. I hoped, wildly, that the transfixed expression on her face was awe rather than shock or dread. The first words from her lips, in the voice I had longed to hear over so many nights, were "Oh, fuck."

An oath, a statement, a question. She stared at me as though I was an apparition.

Words sought to burst from my tongue like a flowing cataract. *I've finally found you,* I wanted to say. *You're really here. I thought I lost you. I'm so sorry.* Or another set of words, one I had not said aloud before: *I love you.*

Instead, I said, "Psyche, your hair is different."

Those brown eyes blinked. She raised her hand to touch the stubble on her head. "It is."

Psyche's hand fell back to her side. I longed to take it in my own, but I could not move. I was afraid that she would vanish if I touched her, that this hard-won moment would be revealed as nothing more than an illusion. That I would drive Psyche away again and be alone forever.

Psyche looked away, color rising to her cheeks. "I didn't think

I'd see you again so soon," she said. "I—" She looked up for the first time, taking in her surroundings. "Where am I?" she asked.

"We are at Eleusis, in the house of Demeter," I said. "Psyche, you're a goddess now," I added gently. It sounded absurd, as if I had said *Psyche, you're a shoe now*.

Psyche nodded, swallowing hard. "I see," she replied, her voice shaking. She looked down at herself, turning over her hands. Her skin glowed as though she had ingested a star, and her beauty was slightly sharper, but otherwise she was unchanged. And yet a goddess nonetheless.

She looked up at me. "I suppose that's why my feet don't hurt anymore."

A bark of laughter escaped me. A little smile crept across Psyche's face, and I began to allow myself to hope that she didn't despise me after all.

"Did you have a part in this?" Psyche asked.

"I did," I replied, wondering if she would lash out at me for making such a decision on her behalf.

"Will I have to go live on Mount Olympus, now that I am a god?" Psyche asked.

My heart drummed, but I kept my voice calm. "You may live on Olympus if you so desire," I told her. "But in truth . . . I hoped you'd come to live with me again."

I realized I was trembling. An ancient god, shaking like a leaf. It would be comical if it was not so agonizing. Longing threatened to burst from me, but I held it tightly in check.

Psyche's face fell, and my heart dropped with it. "Eros," she said slowly. "The house is a ruin. It fell to dust when you vanished."

"I know," I replied. "Gaia will make another. She seems fond of you, in her own way." I paused, waiting for her to accept my offer or refuse it.

Silence stretched between us. I tried to memorize every line of Psyche's face in case I never saw it again.

"I'm sorry I broke my word," Psyche said suddenly. "Bringing the lamp into the room, seeing you face-to-face. It was faithless and dishonest, but I had to know. When I learned I was pregnant, I had to know who my child's father was. But why did you lie to me about who you really were?" she continued, caught between anger and agony. "Why the falsehood about being some little god of the seaside cliffs? And why not tell me about the true nature of the curse?"

Regret needled me. I asked myself these same questions through the many long days and nights of my captivity. "At first, I thought you wouldn't believe me, and that in your skepticism, you might do something foolish and endanger yourself. Later, I feared that if you knew who I was, you would . . . leave me." This thought still preoccupied me, but I tried to obscure the depths of my turmoil.

"You can see how well that worked out," I added dryly.

A laugh escaped Psyche. I drank in the sight of her, shorn head and luminous brown eyes, her stubborn chin and her swanlike neck. All assured for eternity. For the first time I felt the beauty of immortality, that it might ensure the continued existence of someone I loved.

"I am sorry too," I said. "That I lied, and that I left you alone."

Psyche reached out a hand to touch me, running her fingers lightly over the contours of my face. That was how she had known me in the darkness, and that was how she truly recognized me now. I leaned into her touch, the hands of a princess roughened by a lifetime of fighting.

"It really is you," she whispered, and I heard a joy in her voice that mirrored my own. "But Cupid—Eros . . . Aphrodite spoke of a curse. A love curse," she said, her words tumbling over one another. "Is it true? What if you don't really love me, and it's just the effects of the curse? And if you don't really love me, if it's just the curse making you think you're in love, what does that mean about how I feel? Did I—"

I took her in my arms and stopped her words with a kiss.

I had longed for this more than food or drink or even freedom when I hung in Aphrodite's clutches. Psyche kissed me back fervently, and I sensed I had my answer about where she would come to live. There were more discussions to be had, but at least we had made a start.

"Psyche," I whispered, leaning my forehead against hers. "The curse disintegrated after you brought the lamp into the room. It is gone, and I am still here."

The Greeks have three words for love, and that night we knew them all.

43

PSYCHE

A hero may be immortalized in song for a thousand years, but the greatness of a lover is a quieter thing. The most famous lovers are often unhappy, as Helen and Paris discovered to their grief.

Truly great lovers rarely make their way into the public eye. They are too busy with one another.

In time, our child was born. I was grateful for my divinity then, since it protected me from the worst of the pain and ensured my child's life. Against all tradition Eros insisted on being present for the birth, holding my hand through the worst of it.

I gave birth to a girl. I had never seen any creature as unlikely and precious as my newborn daughter, with her tiny perfect fingers and tiny perfect toes. It seemed we had both made it through our trials. Eros and I looked at each other, awed at the young goddess we had made together.

As I lay in bed the night after my daughter's birth—drowsing infant on my breast, and my husband sleeping at my side—I looked back at my life and found it noteworthy mainly for all the different types of love it contained. There was Eros, of course, and there always would be, but there were also my mother and father, my teacher Atalanta, my cousin Iphigenia, and even the old blind poet who had taught me so much. There were Hekate and Demeter too, fretting over me like a pair of grandmothers—love I had never expected. There was Zephyrus, who had been so thoughtless at first and then so loyal in a crisis. He had declared himself an uncle to our newborn daughter, swearing that the winds themselves would protect her. There were all the others who had helped me along the way, from a group of nameless ants near Eleusis to Charon the ferryman. Even pitiless Persephone had shown me mercy. And now here was my daughter, waiting to show me yet another type of love.

Eros and I decided to name her Hedone, which means *Joy*.

When Joy was a month or so old, the three of us returned from the beach to find Aphrodite lounging on the terrace under the afternoon sun.

"What are you doing here?" Eros demanded, laying a protective hand on my arm. I could feel the tension thrumming through him like an electric current.

Aphrodite looked at me with the casual malice of a cat startled from its nap. "I've come to see my granddaughter, of course," she replied. Joy was asleep in my arms, a small mercy.

The goddess peered at the child, then flinched back in revulsion. "She is so small and wrinkled. What did you do to her?"

"Nothing," I replied. "She's a baby."

Aphrodite snorted. "It's probably her half-mortal blood. I haven't forgotten your deception after the apotheosis vote, Eros," she added with a glare. "Bad breeding always shows."

Eros opened his mouth, but I touched his shoulder to silence him. I placed Joy's sleeping form in his arms and asked him to give me a moment alone with Aphrodite. He gave me a puzzled glance but did as I asked.

"Aphrodite," I began. "We are all gods now. I finished the tasks you gave me. Let us find an end to the grudge between us."

The goddess's face darkened. "I will never love you as all the others seem to," she hissed. "They dote on you, though you've done nothing to deserve it. I won't. It is enough that I permit you to share divinity with me, despite all your betrayals. Don't ask me to celebrate it."

"Why do you hate me so much?" I asked.

"I wouldn't waste hate on you, peasant ingrate."

I laughed. I couldn't help it. I could not imagine being weighed down by such petty grudges at the threshold of eternity. "Peasant is a strange insult—even when I was mortal, I was a princess. So why do you dislike me, then?"

Aphrodite stared balefully up at me, her beautiful face twisted. The question seemed to strain at her, until the force needed to keep the truth in was greater than her fear of speaking it.

"He gets to keep you," she finally spat.

I remembered Adonis, who had been Aphrodite's lover before he was Persephone's. And suddenly I understood. All creatures fell in love through her influence, but Aphrodite herself had never been able to taste love in all its aspects. No one ever stayed for more than a season. She attracted men and gods like moths to a flame, but inevitably they burned to a crisp. Real love meant caring for someone else as much as you did yourself, and Aphrodite always put herself above all others.

Perhaps a god could change, but Aphrodite needed to decide that for herself.

Aphrodite left without another word, taking wing in the shape of a dove. Eros peered out at me from the door of the house, tilting his head inquiringly.

I lifted my hands in a gesture of helplessness. *I did what I could*, I wanted to say. Even in a divine existence, it seemed, not everything was perfect.

Joy grew quickly, far faster than a mortal child. She was clever, possessing both her mother's stubbornness and her father's streak of mischief.

As she grew, Joy led me back to the human world I had long neglected. She would go missing, and Eros or I would find her playing with a group of mortal children or sneaking treats from indulgent human mothers. She seemed to know that she had ties to the mortal world, although I never breathed a word about my past.

When I went to fetch my daughter, I saw how much had changed in a few short years. The cities of the Greeks stood empty and dilapidated, their inhabitants having fled. The great markets that had once been the pride of our people were now sparse, with only a few vegetables or fish for sale. The lack of young men perplexed me at first, until I realized that they must have been conscripted to fight on the plains of Troy. The Late Bronze Age Collapse, future historians would call it.

Things came to pass as I had seen at Aulis. The Greek army remained at war with Troy for ten years, and Agamemnon's army went raiding other cities in the meantime. They put entire towns to the torch, slaughtered the men, and enslaved the women. Then came the fall of Troy and all the atrocities that went with it.

Everywhere, chaos.

What should I do for them? I wondered, gazing at the destruction below.

The answer came to me immediately, drifting up from the depths of my unconscious mind.

Anything you can.

I thought of Medusa, saying that hunger and cold were far worse than any monster. Some of the gods fought on the side of the Trojans, and others on behalf of the Greeks. But none of them paid any attention to the old women and hungry children left at home.

Well, Medusa, I thought, as the wind whipped my hair, *I will find you a better answer this time.*

Day after day, I crafted my response. I was only the goddess of the human soul, and my powers were not all that great, but I did what I could. I trusted in the divine power that moved through me, like the wind through a valley of trees. I eased the bellies of hungry children and the aches of gray-haired elders, and spurred on the storytellers sitting around the fires so that the old stories were not forgotten. I brought a spark to the twining meetings of lovers. I soothed the brows of those with festering wounds dying far from home, Trojan and Greek alike.

I discovered a skill for greeting the soul at the moment of death, when it emerged trembling and uncertain from the body. I learned to welcome and coax it into readiness for the journey ahead, keeping it company until Hermes came to escort it down to Persephone's realm. I listened to the soul of the newly dead as it wept about its griefs and comforted it however I could. I knew what it was like to die—I'd done it twice myself, after all.

In doing this, I suppose, I became the hero I was always meant to be.

No temples were ever built in my honor, and no colleges of priestesses ever sung hymns in my name. That was fine by me. The goddess of the human soul needs no such things. Marble crumbles and temples fall, but the soul is endless.

Besides, I had something better. Happiness, and a story. Of a girl spirited away by a monster, of a god who fell in love with a mortal. Our tale, that of Psyche and Eros, spread to different lands, taking on new details and losing old ones. Eros muttered about inaccuracies and imprecisions, but I didn't mind. Let the mortal poets make my story their own. Let them live inside it when their own became unbearable.

Eros. His is the last face I see before sleep and the first when I wake, and I would have it no other way. We have chosen each other, tied our lives together as tightly as the knots sailors use to ensure that their sails do not blow away.

I suppose this makes our tale the strangest of all—a myth with a happy ending. Well, some girls become goddesses, and some gods become more than they were. Every evening we watch the sun set over the sea, Eros and I, looking out at the world together.

AUTHOR'S NOTE

The story of Psyche and Eros is a strange one. Part fairy tale, part neo-Platonist allegory, part ancient rom-com, it defies easy categorization and fluidly moves between boundaries. In its most complete form, it comes down to us today from the second century CE in the Roman novel *Metamorphoses* by Lucius Apuleius, also called *The Golden Ass*.

In this novel, a young Roman man named Lucius is transformed by a witch into the shape of an ass and undergoes a series of adventures before finally being restored to human form by the goddess Isis. The tale of Psyche and Eros is set into the middle of the novel, a story within a story, appearing after Lucius-the-ass is taken captive by a pack of bandits. They have also captured a young noblewoman named Charite, who weeps with terror because she has been snatched away from her true beloved and fears the bandits will rape her. An elderly woman who serves as the bandits' cook takes pity on the girl and tells her the story of Psyche and Eros to distract her. Spellbound, Lucius pricks up his ears and wishes he had human hands to write down the story.[*]

---

[*] Charite is later rescued from the bandits and reunited with her true beloved, although their story eventually comes to a macabre ending emphasizing Charite's capacity for bloody vengeance. For those interested in reading Apuleius in English, I recommend Sarah Ruden's lively 2013 translation.

The novel you currently hold in your hands is based on the Apuleius telling, though I have diverged from the original in certain details. For example, in *The Golden Ass,* a prophecy claims that Psyche will marry a monster; in my novel, the oracle claims that Psyche will *conquer* a monster. In Apuleius's version, Aphrodite demands that Psyche fetch water from the River Styx as one of her labors; I adapted this to become Eros's ill-planned attempt to wash away the curse.

In the earlier myth, Psyche has two jealous sisters who conspire against her; I chose to render instead the sister-like relationships between Psyche and her companions, Iphigenia and Atalanta. I have always despised the flat, mean-spirited depiction of the sisters in the Apuleius telling. If your sister was whisked into the sky and given to a husband she could never see, wouldn't you be a little concerned?

In *The Golden Ass*, Eros is the impertinent young son of Aphrodite, but I decided to pull from the poet Hesiod to make him one of the primordial deities. I based his character on ideas from both the contemporary scholar Anne Carson and the ancient philosopher Empedocles, the latter of whom saw the universe as organized by the central principles of Love and Strife—that is to say, Eros and his twin sister, Eris.

Although the story of Psyche and Eros might be more accurately called a Roman myth rather than a Greek one, I have decided to set it around 1200 BCE in mainland Greece for a variety of reasons: Apuleius's myth is highly ambiguous about its own settings; the story features figures derived from Greek religions; and I wanted to explore the relevance of the Trojan War for the modern cultural zeitgeist. I also wove a number of other myths into the story, including those of Atalanta, Persephone, Medusa, and Hekate, to name but a few.

Eagle-eyed fans of Greek mythology will notice shifts in my

interpretation of certain details. In terms of secondary characters, I drew on a later tradition from the playwright Euripides in making Clytemnestra a former war captive of Agamemnon. Since this meant she was no longer Helen's sister, I decided to cast Penelope in that role instead. In other instances, I have enjoyed the novelist's prerogative to just make things up. I gave Agamemnon and Menelaus a brother in the character of Alkaios, Psyche's father. I borrowed his name from a son of Perseus and Andromeda; it means "strength," which I think suits him. I also chose to make Alkaios and his brothers the sons of Perseus rather than Atreus for thematic and plot reasons. Sorry Atreides, sorry God.

There is some debate over the precise number of words for love in ancient Greek, with some sources naming up to six or seven, but the three I named are the most commonly agreed upon, and I believe they cut to the heart of the meaning.

These are only a few of the changes I have made, and to detail others is beyond the scope of this author's note. Myths are not written in stone. They are organic, evolving structures constantly being adapted to new circumstances and cultures. This is but one reimagining of the Eros and Psyche myth. I look forward to hearing others.

ACKNOWLEDGMENTS

Behind every book is a village of supporters, and *Psyche and Eros* is no exception. It would be impossible to thank everyone who had a hand in the development and publication of this novel, and I will name but a few who were integral to its creation.

First and foremost, I want to thank my wonderful literary agents, Hattie Grünewald and Clara Foster. Both Hattie and Clara possess a rare mixture of editorial brilliance, personal warmth, and keen business acumen. Thank you for helping this novel—and me!—achieve final form. I would shout your praises from the top of Mount Olympus if I could.

I also wish to thank Catherine Drayton and Maria Whelan at Inkwell Literary Management, who were integral to securing publication for *Psyche and Eros*. Thank you as well to the tireless and brilliant translation rights team at the Blair Partnership: Georgie Mellor, Luke Barnard, and Clare Mercer, who got far more than they bargained for with this one.

Enormous gratitude to my incredible editors, Julia Elliott and Charlotte Mursell, who offered insights as sharp as one of Eros's arrows (though far less cursed) and pushed me tirelessly to make this novel the best it could be. You showed me what I was truly capable of, and I look forward to many long years of editing chats, cute animal photos, and memes with you both.

My thanks to my copyeditor, Amy Vreeland, who tirelessly hunted down my questionable uses of commas and accomplished what none of my grade school teachers ever could: teaching me the difference between "further" and "farther."

I extend my deep gratitude to the publishing teams at Harper-Collins/William Morrow and Orion Books, who made the book you hold in your hands a reality. My thanks as well to Shannon Snow, whose comments pushed me to reshape the manuscript and create a better, stronger story. Perhaps we were like ships passing in the night, but you left a mark with this one.

I am grateful to Ursula DeYoung, who helped me hone my query letter and shed light on the remarkably opaque process of publishing a novel.

I wish to express my enormous appreciation for the many people who read *Psyche and Eros* before it was really ready for public consumption, persevering through a whole lot of clichéd writing and questionable POV shifts to offer me valuable comments. Thank you especially to Connor Grenier, Rachel Lesch, Jessie Wright, Norma Heller, Lynn McEnaney, and Jenn Marcos.

There are many others to whom I wish to raise a glass of wine, or ambrosia, in gratitude:

To Hannah diCicco, whose fierce praise for an early draft of this book kept me going when I wanted to quit.

To Matthew Kirshenblatt, who first gave me the idea to turn this story from a rinky-dink fanfic into an original novel.

To Jessica Atanas and Ian Bogert, who helped me survive the pandemic with grace and humor. A thank-you as well to Larry Bogert, whose technological know-how saved an early version of this manuscript from a computer crash, and my sanity along with it.

To Scott Albertine, who offered warm company and a critical

eye during long hours of editing, as well as a superb pair of headphones that have become an integral part of my writing process.

To Ben "Books" Schwartz, whose years of friendship have enriched my life and who so kindly answered my frantic late-night texts about publishing. And to their parents, Cathleen and Peter Schwartz, for hosting the boat trip that gave me the space to begin writing this manuscript.

To my parents, Mark and Janine, and my brother Nathan, for their stalwart support.

To Earl Fontainelle of the Secret History of Western Esotericism podcast, who kindly sent me a subscriber-only episode about the Eros and Psyche myth for free, marking him as one of the rare students of esotericism who possess both scholarly brilliance and deep kindness.

To Dr. Gerol Petruzella, for being the best Greek teacher anyone could ask for. Thank you for your patience during my constant stumbles over declensions.

To the public libraries of Brookline, Boston, and Cambridge, for providing safe havens for books, knowledge, and wayward writers.

An enormous thank-you to my beta reader Effie L. Schwartz-Craighill, for being an unyielding champion of my writing while also being unafraid to call me out on my bullshit. It is no exaggeration to say that this book would not exist without you.

And last but not least, thank you to all of the inconvenient women of mythology, history, and fiction, both remembered and forgotten. May you be stars to light our way in the darkness as we build a better world.

DRAMATIS PERSONAE

HUMANS

Psyche: Princess of Mycenae and prophesied hero; daughter of Alkaios and Astydamia; cousin of Iphigenia; wife of Eros.

Achilles: Prince of Phthia; son of Thetis; lover of Patroclus.

Adonis: Anatolian hunter; lover of Aphrodite; lover of Persephone.

Agamemnon: Warlord and army leader; uncle of Psyche; brother of Alkaios and Menelaus; father of Iphigenia.

Alkaios: King of Mycenae; husband of Astydamia; father of Psyche.

Astydamia: Queen of Mycenae; wife of Alkaios; mother of Psyche.

Atalanta: A huntress and hero; member of the Argonauts; mentor of Psyche.

Bellerophon: A hero and slayer of monsters.

Clytemnestra: Wife of Agamemnon; mother of Iphigenia.

Dexios: A stableboy of Mycenae.

Helen: Daughter of Zeus; wife of Menelaus; lover of Paris.

Hyacinthos: A mortal youth; lover of Zephyrus.

Iphigenia: A clever and capable young woman; daughter of Agamemnon and Clytemnestra; cousin of Psyche.

Melanion: A prince and trickster; husband of Atalanta.

Meleager: A hero and member of the Argonauts; friend of Atalanta.

Menelaus: Husband of Helen; brother of Alkaios and Agamemnon.

Odysseus: A crafty general of Agamemnon; King of Ithaka; husband of Penelope.

Orestes: Son of Agamemnon and Clytemnestra; brother of Iphigenia.

Paris: A Trojan prince; lover of Helen.

Patroclus: A strategist; lover of Achilles.

Penelope: Queen of Ithaka; wife of Odysseus.

Perseus: A hero and slayer of monsters; killer of Medusa; grandfather of Psyche.

GODS

Eros: Primordial god of desire; twin brother of Eris; adopted son of Aphrodite; friend of Zephyrus; husband of Psyche. Also known as Cupid.

Aphrodite: Goddess of love and beauty; adoptive mother of Eros; wife of Hephaestus; lover of many.

Apollo: God of the sun, prophecy, and music; brother of Artemis.

Ares: God of war; lover of Aphrodite.

Artemis: Goddess of hunting, the moon, and young women; sister of Apollo. Also known as the Far-Shooter.

Charon: Ferryman of the Underworld (not to be confused with Chiron, a centaur and teacher of heroes).

Demeter: Goddess of the harvest and the Eleusinian Mysteries; mother of Persephone. Also known as Ceres.

Eris: Primordial goddess of discord; twin sister of Eros.

Gaia: Primordial goddess of the earth; wife of Ouranos; mother of many.

Hekate: Goddess of witchcraft and crossroads. Also known as the Soteira, or the Savior.

Hephaestus: God of blacksmithing; husband of Aphrodite.

Hera: Supreme goddess of marriage and family; wife of Zeus. Also known as the queen of heaven.

Hermes: God of messengers, persuasion, and communication; lover of Aphrodite.

Kronos: Primordial god of time; son of Gaia and Ouranos.

Medusa: Former nymph, changed to a gorgon by Athena; slain by Perseus.

Ouranos: Primordial god of the sky; husband of Gaia; father of Kronos.

Persephone: Goddess of the Underworld; daughter of Demeter; wife of Hades; lover of Adonis. Also known as Kore, or the Maiden.

Thetis: Sea nymph; mother of the mortal hero Achilles.

Zephyrus: Primordial god of the west wind; friend of Eros.

Zeus: Supreme god of lightning; husband of Hera; king of the Olympian gods. Also known as the Thunderer.